HOUSE OF GOLD

by Bud Macfarlane Jr., author of the
nationwide bestseller *Pierced by a Sword*.

"This is Bud Macfarlane's *magnum opus*—his 'great work,'
and I believe it will be cherished for generations by Christians
who have the courage to explore the timeless mysteries."

David Mercer, Writer

"I never thought I'd ever say this, because *Pierced by a Sword*
was my all-time favorite book—but *House of Gold* blew me
away. Move over, *Pierced*. Guys, if you only read one book in
your life, make it this one. Powerful."

Dan Williams, Executive

"I think *House of Gold* should be required reading for every
adult in America. I am not exaggerating."

Christina Brundage, Nurse

"A gripping, emotional roller coaster ride with a climax so
satisfying that I wanted to run back to the first page to ride it
again. It made me laugh. It made me cry. It made me angry.
It made me rejoice."

Angela Terry, Computer Professional

"Macfarlane did it to me again—he kept me up into the wee
hours of the night. This book was brutal, tender, passionate,
profound, and simple all at the same time. You might call it
fiction, but for me, it was real. Read this book—now."

Dave Targonski, Father & Sales Manager

"I loved it—it drew me in and took me to incredible places.
Don't start this book until you turn off the stove burners—and
set aside time for prayer afterwards."

Carolyn Able, Mother & Writer

HOUSE OF GOLD

Soul and body. Water and blood.

Death and life. Evil and goodness.

A story about courage and suffering.

A novel about our times.

A vision for all time.

IF YOU REALLY
LIKE THIS BOOK

Consider Giving it Away.

Saint Jude Media, the nonprofit publisher of this novel, invites you to send for copies to distribute to your family, friends, and associates. We are making it available in quantities for a nominal donation. We will even send a free copy to individuals who write to us directly. There is no catch. It's a new concept in book distribution that makes it easier for everyone to read great books.

See the back pages of this book for more details, or write to us for more information:

Saint Jude Media
PO Box 26120
Fairview Park, OH 44126

www.catholicity.com

Discover a New World.
Change Your Life Forever.

Published by Saint Jude Media
PO Box 26120, Fairview Park, OH 44126
www.catholicity.com

ISBN 0-9646316-3-6
Library of Congress Catalog Card Number: 99-093919

PRINTING HISTORY:
June 1999 (60,000)
September 1999 (25,000)
December 2001 (20,000)

Cover Design by Ron Wiggins
Typesetting by Joe Vantaggi on a Power Macintosh 8500
Printing by Offset Paperback Manufacturers, Dallas, PA

Printed in the United States of America

To my sons Jude, Buddy, and Xavey.
I gave them the whole nine yards.

ALSO BY BUD MACFARLANE JR.

PIERCED BY A SWORD
CONCEIVED WITHOUT SIN

HOUSE OF GOLD

BUD MACFARLANE JR.

SAINT JUDE MEDIA
CLEVELAND, OHIO

Foreword

You won't read a more timeless novel than the one you are holding in your hand—even if you are reading it one hundred years after it was first published.

It offers suffering. I know that sounds strange, but you will love the suffering inside these pages. It's honest, authentic, gut-wrenching. It's real suffering. You will understand soon enough.

I am twenty-two years old. I've helped my father edit three novels and Bud edit two others. I grew up in Canada, in a family that loves books. A family of storytellers. I love all kinds of stories, but this story cannot be categorized, it can only be experienced.

During its harshest and most brutal scenes, my heart was filled with tenderness and hope. I felt that I was *right there* with Buzz, Ellie, Mel, and the Man.

The Man? I can't wait until you meet the Man.

Like everything in this book, he's real, hard to describe, and the definition of cool. He's still with me. Right now. And I like that.

I believe this is Bud Macfarlane's best work. It is one of a kind, and will never be duplicated, not even by Bud himself.

It offers the cross. Can you take it?

JOHN D. O'BRIEN
1 MAY 1999
FEAST OF SAINT JOSEPH

Acknowledgments

My gratitude to my dedicated editors, especially John O'Brien, Thomas Case, Chris Lyons, and Carol Kean. This is your book, too.

My thanks to Joe Vantaggi, our talented typesetter, and Ron Wiggins, who created the luscious cover. Matt Pinto for planting the seed. Dave Targonski for the galvanizing theme. Ed "Elroy" Mulholland for giving me a title that was also a sure rudder. Dr. Scott Van Oosten for the chiropractic advice. Ron Curley for running "interference" during the storm.

Critical contributions came from Thomas Breznak, Christina Brundage, Mark Dittman, Father Mike Gurnick, Tedd Imgrund, Judith Johnson, Grace Kneeshaw, Anthony LaPlaca, Jeannine McDevitt, Tim Novecosky, Garth Pereira, Mary Rowe, and Theresa Weber. Thanks, guys and gals.

I especially want to thank the hundreds of priests, nuns, deacons, and brothers who prayed for me and continue to pray for all those who will read this book. My thanks to all the CatholiCity Citizens who prayed for me as I toiled.

My Little Flower, thanks. Keep smiling.

Thanks, Bill Whitmore, every novel I write is a legacy of your hard work. Thanks Al, Terry—you know why. Fred and Carolyn: you too!

Thanks to my smart, practical girl, Bai. The grace that saves souls never comes cheap.

Preface

The following story has the same characters as my second novel, *Conceived Without Sin*. You should have no trouble following along even if you haven't read *Conceived*. If you want to read the first book, please write in for a free copy from my publisher.

The backdrop of this novel is a catastrophic computer problem. Even pessimistic experts concede that the electric grid probably can't go down in one day. The optimistic experts don't think it can go down at all. As with the deadly virus in King's classic novel, *The Stand*, please feel free to consider this story's computer bug a literary device. Please take me at my word: my goal was not to convince you anything about computers one way or the other.

My purpose was something else.

Parents beware. I wrote this story for adults. Read it before you give it to your young-adult children.

Blackstone, Brixton, and Bagpipe are creations of my imagination. In the real world, the Magalloway region of New Hampshire is pure, undeveloped—and inaccessible—wilderness. The statue, Our Lady of the Rockies, is real. Her builder wrote a book about her; my publisher has listed where you can get a copy in the back of this book.

You can tell yourself that it's only fiction. Something to kill time. Yeah, that's what you can tell yourself. As for me, I saw what follows with my own eyes, then I wrote it down.

BUD MACFARLANE JR.
13 MAY 1999
FEAST OF THE ASCENSION

PART ONE

Empty Womb

"They shall be mine," says the Lord of Hosts,
"my treasured possession on the day when I act,
and I will spare them, just as in compassion
a man spares his son who serves him.
Then once more, you shall see the distinction
between the righteous and the wicked,
between those who serve God and those who do not."
Malachi 3:17

All the stories have been told,
of kings and days of old—but there's no England now.
*The Kinks, **Living on a Thin Line***

The only security is courage.
François La Rochefoucauld

I can't explain it, the things you're sayin' to me—
it's goin' ya ya ya ya ya ya ya.
Because I'm a twenty-first century digital boy;
I don't know how to live but I've got a lot of toys.
*Bad Religion, **21st Century Digital Boy***

Where did you leave your baby?
Bleeding in her bed, her ghost has come to stay,
Oh you can try, you can chase her away.
*Fastball, **Which Way to the Top***

Chapter One

Getting Out of Dodge

Nine years after Buzz Woodward failed to commit suicide on a dark and stormy night on a beach in New Jersey, he was having a hard time trying to convince his wife Melanie that they had to put their cozy little house in a suburb of Ohio on the market.

He was failing again. After all, this was the house Mel's mother had given them as a wedding gift. How many guys had no mortgage payments these days? Only rich guys like Buzz's best friend, Sam Fisk. And Mel's mother was no big fan of Gwynne "Buzz" Woodward. If the ReMax sign went on the front lawn, Melanie's folks would get out their sharp knives, for sure.

His job as a massotherapist—a massage therapist—did not bring in much money, and it always seemed like there was never quite enough milk in the fridge for Markie. And then there was the cost of the night classes in chiropractic. No way was Buzz *ever* going to Mel's folks for that. Sam was helping out with a little loan. The kind with no terms or interest rates or payments due, God love Sam—and Ellie, his stunning wife.

Buzz was *not* planning to be a masotherapist forever. And how many guys had trouble with their mother-in-law these days?

Pretty much the same as throughout history, he supposed.

He stood there on the pink rug with years of stains on it, leaning back on his heels, spouting facts and figures and theories gleaned from Sam Fisk and the Internet. His son Markie, four, was crying at his feet; Packy, only fourteen months, was sleeping soundly in Mel's hard, freckled arms as she sat on the cruddy old couch Buzz had salvaged from the garbage in Birdtown. He was still finding treasure in other people's trash—proud of it, despite the superior looks from Mel's folks.

The marriage, his second, had been a good one. Like his first marriage, now annulled for almost a decade, there had always been a lot of shouting over the years.

He and Mel, however, had grown comfortable within each other's temper. Now—it was now—with Melanie *not* shouting, that Buzz got that same feeling he had gotten on the jetty in New Jersey.

That no matter how this whole thing turned out—sell the damned house and move, not sell the house and die like a dog—he was taking *a long walk* on this baby.

But first he had to convince Mel to take the long walk with him. He stopped shouting. He paused as she looked up from the baby.

Oh, that thick, defiant red hair making a jailbreak from her freckled brow. No modern goo could incarcerate it. No electric curling iron could rehabilitate it. The big, burly man, now a full eighth-grade-boy's-worth overweight, suddenly wanted only to sink his hands into that rebellious hair, and to kiss her, and make another boy like Markie or Packy, and give this unknown third a nickname no other kid in Lakewood had.

Never marry a redhead, Markie, he thought, amused, reaching down to rub the boy's crewcut.

Mel saw the amused look in his eyes. The shouting-man was gone. She loved the way he switched moods so unpredictably. One minute a raving preacher on how a computer glitch could wipe out half of mankind, the next, the guy who saw a man's face portrayed in the holes of the electric socket on the wall.

"What's really going on with this computer thing, Buzzy? What's the truth?" she asked calmly.

Markie had found a working power screwdriver under the TV table, and had settled down, too. She knew her husband hated it when she called him Buzzy.

"If there's even a one-in-a-hundred shot that Sam is right, we gotta sell the house. Hey, on a completely different subject, I was just thinking, maybe we could have an appointment, tonight."

He smiled his most rakish smile. They both looked quickly at the little boy to confirm that he had not understood the code.

Then she frowned. Her libido had gone to Mexico after Packy was born, just as it had done after Markie. It was that bedamned breastfeeding that Ellie had taught her. Sure, the kids were calmer, got sick less often, were born farther apart, and she loved it, she really did, but nobody had mentioned beforehand that her sex drive would go into park and remain there for almost two years.

He read the frown. "No harm in asking, is there?"

"I guess not, but not tonight. Unless you insist. I can't help it if my hormones are on vacation."

He sat down next to her.

"I don't insist."

She looked at him closely. He was really serious about selling the house—he had resorted to the Puppy Dog Look.

Mel did not know the first thing about computers and embedded chips or programmer shortages. But she knew that Sam Fisk was always right about these things, and that Buzz, despite the low-rent crewcut, and scratching by on three or four masotherapy fees a day, was about the smartest man she had ever known.

He had a degree from Notre Dame, after all, and had put himself through college by picking food from dumpsters while working two jobs. Just the same way, he was going to be a chiropractor on a shoestring. No trust funds and preppy clothes for her Buzz.

His mother had left him as a child, and his alcoholic father, long since passed away, had been no help either. Her Buzz, big strong Buzz, with twice the brains and three times the energy of the lazy boys coming out of John Carroll down the road, was remaking himself into a chiropractor.

She had no doubt.

With God's grace, he had beaten alcoholism—twice—and somehow ended up a whole human being, standing on his own sturdy feet. She knew he would meet any challenge when it came to her and the boys. Some of the girls who had gone to Magnificat High with her had already been dumped by their money-and-status-obsessed former husbands.

Those Mags chicks had married suits; she had married *a soul*.

Like most satisfied wives, she knew that her man was like no other man. Unique. Just for her. The kind of man you follow to hell on earth, if that's what God wanted—which He sometimes did.

His one-man shouting match was over as quickly as it started. Melanie didn't mind the shouting; only a person with hot blood could understand enough to marry another. This passion would drive them to do whatever—whatever, mind you—was required to…to survive the coming calamity. In the pit of her stomach, where the bile flows, she knew he was a rock on this.

The house you grew up in! the red-haired part of Melanie protested.

Better Homes & Gardens was not coming by for that photoshoot anytime soon, Mel told herself. The block was turning over fast, and property values were dropping on this side of town. They wouldn't get much for the house.

At their weddings, her sisters had all been given enough money to buy a house. Mel, the last to get married, had been given the Lakewood house because her parents, long since migrated to the tony suburb of Bay Village, were tired of maintaining and renting it. She sometimes wondered if her parents had given the house to her for unspoken reasons relating to their disappointment that she had married Buzz.

He kissed her cheek, a brotherly prelude to nothing.

"I'll call the agent tomorrow afternoon, after I get to the clinic," he said finally. "But only after I talk to Sam one more time. This house represents all the money we have in the world. The sooner we turn it into money, the sooner we can turn that money into something that will be worth a damn after the stupid computer bug hits."

"I'll never understand," she mused, shaking her head, "how a Catholic as devout as you can say 'damn' so much."

He looked at her with an impish smile, but said nothing. He got down on the floor with Markie, who smiled brightly, and showed him how to insert the business end of the screwdriver into the back of the television set. They hadn't used the blasted thing in years—except to watch Buzz's beloved videos.

Packy reattached himself to his mother's little breast. She was a sprite of a woman. Two years younger than her husband, gravity's relentless effort to pull her bones and skin into the earth was taking its effect. Sam, even his drop-dead beautiful Ellie, the Johnsons, the Man, the Pennys, the Lawrences, Bill White and Brian Thredda—everybody in their circle was starting to show their age. When Buzz and the guys played their annual "Buzz Bowl" backyard football game on Thanksgiving, it took them almost a week to recover. It was called *pushing forty.*

"People are going to think we've lost it, you know, Mel. Get ready for that. Even our friends."

"There's no way to get ready for that," she told him a bit sharply, still looking down at Packy.

Packy. The name had been Buzz's idea. Only Buzz had the nerve to christen a child Blaise Pascal Woodward and then nickname him Packy.

Her tone gave him something to ponder.

"Nobody's immune from peer pressure," Buzz observed. He put his hand on the screwdriver in Markie's hand to guide it. "Here, Markie, like this."

He turned back to her.

"This thing will catch on sometime next year," he continued. "But this year, no way. Sam is way ahead of the curve again. I remember when he was years ahead on the Internet and people thought I was crazy for having an email address."

They knew he was referring to her parents.

"I ignored the skeptics when I married you," she said.

"I know, darling, I know. Let's pray our Rosary. It's getting late, and I've got to study," he said wearily.

✝ ✝ ✝

For Buzz, there was something really cool about being a nothing-special-nobody—an alcoholic/failed-suicide-attempter/divorced-annulled-remarried/screw-up from New Jersey—with the prerogative to breeze into the corporate offices of a millionaire.

Today he walked right by the smiling receptionist, waved at all the computer nerds hunkered over their workstations, then strolled directly into Sam Fisk's office like he owned the place.

"I'm not gonna hurtcha, Sam!" he cried out in his best, crazed, sing-songy Jack Nicholson voice after he closed the door. "I'm just gonna break every bone in your body."

Sam didn't even look up from his computer.

"Hi, Buzz. Marcie stocked the fridge with RC Cola yesterday. Help yourself."

Buzz grunted and walked over to the cleverly-hidden mini-fridge built into the east wall.

RC Cola, he thought. *Stands for Roman Catholic.*

Presently he plopped down on the green leather couch beneath a built-in bookcase filled with leatherbound books. Ellie had a thing about leather.

"I remember when your office was filled with OfficeMax furniture and Wal-Mart bookcases, Mr. Fisk."

Sam replied with a good-natured smile. For ten years Buzz had been throwing barbs, yet Sam was still completely impervious to teasing.

"Ellie says we need the facade, as she calls it, when the head honchos come into town to visit," he replied seriously.

"Ellie runs your company from her basement office in Bay Village."

"And she does a grand job—and she's not even on the payroll. I'm just the figurehead. I like it that way. I haven't really done any work here in three years besides learning how to fly the corporate plane," he exaggerated.

He looked up. "We've had this conversation a hundred times. Let's just skip it. I assume you're here about the computer bug again?"

He saved my life once, Buzz thought. *He's trying to save it again.*

Buzz leaned forward, clasped his hands together under his chin, his elbows on his knees, and waited for Sam to look him in the eye.

"One more time, Sam. Are you certain you're right?"

"Yes, Buzz, in my own way, I'm perfectly certain. Put your house on the market. I thought we already discussed this. Is Melanie giving you a hard time?"

"The scary part is that she didn't make that big of a stink," Buzz replied with an arched brow. "Oh, we shouted a little— actually, I did the shouting. She must have heard something in my voice. Fear, maybe? It used to be her mother's house. I'm calling the realtor this afternoon. Any progress with Ellie?"

Sam furrowed his brow and looked back to his computer.

"She's still doing research. She wants to talk to Bucky. He might be retired, but he's still got a lot of contacts in this town. Businessmen. Political types."

Sam returned his attention to his email. It had always been this way, and Buzz was not offended. Sam worked at work— even when Buzz dropped in.

Buzz slouched back into the cushy sofa, then turned his head to look down at the Flats, fifteen stories below. Tourists and professionals bustled on the boardwalks along the harbor lined on both sides with nightclubs and bars. They were doing a decent lunch hour trade. Sam held himself with perfect posture in an extra large swivel chair, all six-foot-six of him splayed out like an octopus missing four legs.

Click, click, clickety-click. The sound of computer keys was so much more pleasant than the old typewriters, Buzz observed.

The office was quite tasteful. Rich burgundy wall-paper; plush green carpeting. Mahogany furniture that looked as if a crane had been needed to haul it to these heights. The company had originally been called Edwards & Associates, but seven years ago Ellie had convinced her husband to change the name to just-plain-Edwards. She had read in one of her business books that shorter names were more easily recognized for *national* companies.

Before Ellie, the company had been doing fairly well serving the Midwest, with the majority of key accounts in northeastern Ohio. In that first year after the wedding, the Fisks had a house on the lake in Bay Village and were pulling down over three hundred thousand a year in combined incomes. Both had been driving Hondas to convince themselves they weren't going soft—and that the primary reward of running a company was providing employment for two dozen associates. They were part of the new entrepreneurial class—the new elite who refused to wear the monkey suit in a corporate zoo.

Buzz secretly believed that Ellie also thought the short version of the company name would look better on the backs of the jerseys of the four peewee baseball teams Sam sponsored in the inner-city leagues.

Keep Edwards regional? Ellie knew Sam could do better. He shortened the name.

She might be a dead ringer for Grace Kelly, but she has a business mind like a steel trap. (Buzz also believed she was the most excellent waltz partner in the world. Neither Sam nor Mel could waltz worth a prune.)

Yes, yes, *Ellie's* man was destined to go *national*.

So after futzing around doing 'research' for a year, Sam took his company national, and like everything else in his life, it just came to him, like water flowing down a giant, purple mountain.

His Opus Dei buddy, Bill White, who owned a large advertising agency in Cleveland, worked up a new logo. Against the seasoned advice of Ellie's father, Bucky James (who owned his own insurance company), Sam dumped the hardware division and went solely into *custom software solutions;* Johnny Traverse, Sam's longtime professional sidekick and salesman extraordinaire, called on some giant manufacturers of *whatever* in California and Texas.

Hard work. Great leadership. Great plan. Great service. Great programmers. Great sales team. Great timing. Bingo bango bongo, two years later Edwards made the *Inc.* Five Hundred. It was now pushing one hundred handsomely paid employees.

And for every major strategic decision along the way, Sam had been several moves ahead on the chessboard—in an industry known for rapid change. In certain circles—especially among his competitors, his ability to project into the future was legendary. The lanky exec pulled the trigger on these decisions with an eerie confidence, a detached nonchalance, a carefully measured repose. The future, which was a thick fog to most mortals—even other successful computer entrepreneurs—was often crystal clear to Sam.

"I earn my living by thinking about things and making decisions," he often explained to Buzz in a sheepish tone.

Aside from requisite visits to the CEOs and CIOs of his clients, he spent most of his day in the office—reading online discussion groups and conducting email correspondence with programmers and other businessmen. Often he looked out the window and…pondered. Sometimes he tinkered with code—but he claimed it was a form of procrastination and that his own programmers had surpassed him years ago.

He rarely talked about work at home, except for "official" conversations with Ellie during working hours. At the time

he founded the company, he had promised himself that he
would work Saturday mornings for the first seven years, which
of course he did with plodding zeal. A few years ago, on the
first Saturday after the first day of the eighth year, Buzz
dropped by the Fisk house out of sheer curiosity. Ellie served
flapjacks and maple syrup and Sam didn't bring up Edwards
one single time.

That was Sam Fisk.

Edwards dominates its niche, Ellie had mentioned to Buzz
one time. Buzz had only a vague idea what that actually meant.
In confidence, Sam had estimated to Buzz that Edwards was
worth around twelve million dollars.

*All this effort so Ellie, the Super-Catholic-Chick, could
give away over half what Sam made every year,* Buzz thought
now. *They've got a regular system going, those two. To think
she was barely going to Mass on Sundays when I met her.*

None of the employees, not even Johnny Traverse, who
owned four percent of the company, knew that Edwards was
on the block. Sam had explained to Buzz that brokers sold
companies like his blind to the Merger and Acquisition departments of giant corporations all the time. High-tech companies were especially dear to the market.

All this swirled in Buzz's head as he sat in Sam's office.
Sam was really, truly, actually selling his life's work. Everything had been so normal when Sam first called Buzz one
evening and asked him to look into something as harmless-
sounding as a computer glitch.

"I want your take on it," Sam had told him with nary a
hint of Armageddon in his voice, then rattled off a few
websites. "I'm deeply concerned."

That had been three weeks ago.

Deeply concerned. Hmmn.

That night Buzz started browsing the Net after the family
Rosary—Markie was just starting to join in, God love him—
figuring he would spend a leisurely hour or two online.

He stayed up until four. He overslept the alarm the next morning. When Buzz stopped by Edwards a few days later, he was more than merely *deeply concerned*.

Buzz had been sitting on this same couch in Sam's office…

✝ ✝ ✝

"Can it really happen, Sam—the whole grid? No telephones. No food delivery. What are the odds?"

"I believe there is a sixty percent chance for a complete, prolonged collapse of the infrastructure, and a thirty percent chance for a depression worse than the Great Depression—because the world economy is more global this time around. Those are rough numbers."

Sam wasn't kidding or smiling with those big teeth or anything. Dead serious. *Deeply concerned* again. He, Sam, computer magnate. He cracked one bony knuckle against another.

"But Sam, that only leaves ten percent for nothing much happening. Whose projections are these?"

"These are my personal *conclusions*. They are not projections. No one can project the future accurately. I draw conclusions based on necessarily incomplete data. That's why I gave you percentages. These conclusions help me make decisions about what action we can take *now,* before the future happens."

There was absolutely no hint of pride or arrogance in Sam's voice. He might as well have been describing the day's weather. Sam read the skepticism on Buzz's face.

"Look Buzz, I've been researching this for a long time. It all started when a client in Arizona asked me if Edwards was planning to go into millennium bug remediation. I have known about the problem since I was programming punchcards back during my IBM days. Remember, I started out in mainframes. We all knew about it. None of us thought it was a big deal—

we assumed that the boxes we were using would be replaced by now.

"I began calling some of the engineers who work for our top clients—guys who design and install microcontrollers—what we call black boxes in the industry. These embedded chips are the real threat. They're in everything. Most can't be reprogrammed. Most can't be replaced—no matter what you'll read in the press when they catch on to this. The factories that made them are long gone.

"The layman does not have a grasp of the scope of the problem. The vast majority of the executives at the companies who hire Edwards are not technically sophisticated when it comes to computers—that's why they hire Edwards.

"Thinking only about short term earnings and their effect on stock valuations, executives will continue to ignore meaningful remediation until it's too late. When they finally face the problem, the demand for consulting companies and programmers will far outstrip supply.

"Every company and government agency in every industry in every country is going to have failures of millions of embedded chips, countless millions of computers, and billions of lines of code—*all at the same time.*

"Oh yes, and the vast majority of PCs and their applications also need to be fixed. There is no way all these things can all be addressed on time. Did you know that a huge percentage of software projects are completed late, or are never completed?

"Our current infrastructure has an expiration date, Buzz. Edwards will be worthless on January 1st, 2000. If I view this from a pure financial perspective, selling the company while it still has a perceived value is my only rational course of action."

He paused, then once more turned to his computer screen.

The intercom buzzed. He told Marcie to hold the call. Governor Taft could have been on the line, but when Buzz was in the office, Sam had Marcie hold the calls. Sam turned back to Buzz.

"So I first looked into this problem strictly to find out if I should move Edwards in the direction of remediation—not to find out if the infrastructure was at risk. Although I was fairly certain we could make money on remediation, I wasn't sure if I was willing to tool up for a market that would disappear a few months after all the code had been fixed—"

"But you found yourself staying up late, doing more research than you expected," Buzz interrupted.

"Just as you did for the last few nights, Buzz."

Sam shook his head.

"I began contacting the best programmers in the country. I speak their language. I compared notes with old-time hackers, elite RPG guys—" Sam paused, realizing that Buzz would have no idea what RPG was, "and other computer languages my young geeks on the other side of that door have never heard of, much less studied."

Sam drew a deep breath. It was not often he spoke at such length.

"I now believe that five hundred years from now, when people recall our century, this computer problem will be the first thing they remember, followed by World War II, the Great Depression, and of course, Pope John Paul II."

This last assertion had shaken Buzz. Sam making sweeping historical statements was like, well, Buzz *not* making them.

"I don't know what to say. How do you react to the end of…everything?" Buzz had asked.

Usually, there was a slight hint of humor in just about everything Buzz said. This time, he heard the edge—the edge of panic—in his own voice. The faces of Markie and Packy quickly darted into his mind's eye.

"Get out of Dodge, Buzz."

"Huh?"

"We need to get out of Dodge," his friend repeated, more slowly this time. "Move away. The cities, the suburbs…are not going to be safe. Chris is going to be ten next year. I don't want him to have to see—the problem—first hand. It could become dangerous."

"Run? Run to the hills?" Buzz had asked, his voice sounding far away, incredulous.

"I'm putting Edwards on the block. I met with the kind of business brokerage which sells my kind of company last week. I'm going to a seminar with them next week—"

"Is this Sam Fisk I'm talking to—"

But Sam, uncharacteristically, interrupted his friend, forcing himself to finish, and Buzz to listen.

"—and Ellie doesn't like it one bit. I'm selling Edwards against her wishes. I'm waiting for her to make up her own mind. Pray God she comes around. No one can make that woman's mind up for her."

"But you love Edwards. Ellie loves it…"

Ever since the medical problems, when they were forced to accept that Christopher would be their only child, growing Edwards so they could give money away to charity had been like a…life preserver.

"My heart is not in Edwards. When you come to your own conclusions—and I'll try to help you—your heart won't be in this paradigm either.

"Since we were born—since *everybody* was born, we've all flicked a switch on the wall and the light came on; turned the faucet and hot water came out…and ever since my father died, well…"

Sam Fisk was lost for words for a moment. He looked at the little bronze crucifix he kept on the modem next to his computer, shaking his head. The crucifix was a reliquary containing a tiny piece of bone from the bodies of Saint Anthony of Padua and Saint Francis Xavier.

"Buzz, it's vital to me that you're with me on this. You, me, Mel and Ellie. Our Lady brought us together. I still remember when you rammed into me on the Rocky River courts like it was yesterday. Do you remember that? Remember when we met? I didn't know it then, but it was Our Lady bringing you into my life. I can't face this without you."

Sam's voice actually cracked at the end. Sam the former atheist. Sam, he of two emotions: calm and comatose. All these years later, it still jolted Buzz when Sam talked Catholic like that. Talking about the Blessed Mother. He was one of the most devout souls Buzz had ever known, leaving his friend in the dust spiritually years ago—at least that's how Buzz felt about it—yet Sam rarely talked about his faith. He lived it.

And that was that. Oh, they discussed the matter for another two hours. Sam had Marcie put off seven important phone calls. Sam shot down every objection Buzz could conjure. They called baby-sitters and set up dinner at Nate's with Mel and Ellie that night, for more talk, talk, talk. During the meal, Sam limited himself to explaining the problem to the two women—and steered well clear of his decision to move out of Cleveland.

The technical issues flowed right over Mel's head. Ellie came up with the same objections Buzz raised earlier that day, but was not convinced by Sam's counter-arguments.

For the rest of the world, hell on earth was a little over a year and a half into the future. For Buzz and Sam, the gas burners, set temporarily to simmer, came on that day.

✛ ✛ ✛

Buzz turned onto his back, and looked at the blank, gray ceiling. Mel's skin exuded an unseen afterglow. For a change, the baby had not woken up in the middle of the festivities. She now gently moved him to his crib, which was attached to the bed. She and Ellie had removed one side of a normal crib and had somehow managed to velcro it to the bed. Mel pulled herself up to sit Indian-style next to her husband.

Other couples smoke cigarettes after, he thought, his own inside joke, one he repeated to himself every time. *Mel gets a back rub.*

He sat up, then quickly repositioned himself to a kneeling position behind her. He placed his hands on her shoulders and began the massage.

"I married you for these," she whispered to him—repeating her own favorite phrase—then let slip a tiny groan as he felt for the tightness, then did his thing.

He had the gift. He had strong, disciplined fingers. Growing up, Buzz had been an unusually strong child and young man—a powerful, if limited, athlete. Then, before his career in masotherapy, his arms, hands, and fingers had been built up beyond reason from handling tens of thousands of packages as a UPS driver. If he chose, he could bring a strong man to his knees with a handshake.

"Yeah, I know. You love my hands, not me."

"That's right, Buzzy."

Buzzy again. What was a guy to do?

"So what brought on the Tiger Lady?" he asked, referring to their activities moments earlier.

He knew her eyes were closed. His were open, although he was really "looking" through the tips of his fingers at the muscles in her back. She was much tighter than usual. Their little master bedroom was fuzzy with vaguely perceived grey outlines.

He waited. One good thing about them: they both liked to talk. No communication problems here.

Still, she didn't answer him for several minutes.

"Nightmare," she finally explained, then yawned. "I guess I was so frightened I needed to know I wasn't alone. All of me needed all of you."

She found his hand, and pulled it over her shoulder, giving it a tender kiss.

"In the dream," she continued, "I was in the basement of our house. It was smaller than our real basement. It smelled awful. Markie was older, and whining in that way we both hate. 'Mommy, I'm hungry!' he cried over and over.

"Markie was starving. Really, truly starving. His stomach was bloated out like those poor African children you see on television. You were nowhere to be found. I was in a panic."

She shrugged off his massage and twisted to face him, placing one arm on his shoulder to steady herself.

"Buzz," she mouthed with a barely audible voice.

He let his hands fall to his knees. It was closer to sunrise than they had realized. Outside the dawn was breaking, and he could make out the features of her face now—but not the freckles.

"Yesterday," she continued, "I agreed to sell the house on a purely intellectual level—because I trust Sam and I trust you. It's different now. I don't want to risk what happened in my dream happening in real life. I'll hate moving, for sure, but I'll go. I'll do whatever I have to do to protect the boys."

He put one hand on her cheek. "Honey, it was only a dream. The Book of Sirach says only a fool pays attention to his dreams."

"Can we just skip the Sirach for once? It's the only book in the Bible you ever quote. Didn't Joseph have a dream telling him to take Mary and Baby Jesus to Egypt? Besides, you're the one who wanted to get out of Dodge, not me."

"Somehow I thought you would go along with it but drag your feet," he snorted. "That was my master plan for getting out of following Sam to God-knows-where. Now our only hope is that Ellie continues to stonewall."

Buzz was admitting that he really didn't have the expertise to make a hard decision about the technical aspects of the problem. He, too, when it got down to it, was trusting Sam's judgment.

"Well, I'm in," she said with finality. "Ellie might be strong, and we both know she's willing to go toe-to-toe with Sam on this, but in the end, he'll convince her."

"How can you be so sure?"

"Because Sam is Sam."

He closed his eyes and said a little prayer, the kind with no words, where your soul just kinda dances a two-step in the direction of heaven. *Lord!*

"Good," he tried to sound firm, in his best Head-of-the-Household voice, as he lay back down.

She slid down next to him, half his size, and arranged herself in his nooks and crannies. Her kisses glanced off his lips, his cheek, his neck, then she nestled her chin on his shoulder. They held each other in this way, awake, under the K-Mart covers for another hour until the alarm rang.

Where are we going to go? Buzz asked himself.

✝ ✝ ✝

"Montana," Sam informed him two days later from across the antique oak table in the kitchen of the Fisk home.

Behind Sam, Lake Erie stretched out like a calm blue comforter. Their house wasn't large—a three bedroom Cape Cod, forty yards from the cliffs which winter winds and summer storms wore down a foot or two every year. Except for refinishing the hardwood floors, the house was virtually untouched from the day they bought it.

The rage in Bay Village was to pay huge sums for small old houses on the lake, then tear them down to be replaced by enormous Ego Domes, as Buzz had taken to calling them. There was an Ego Dome on either side of the Fisks' house—and fortunately, these monstrosities were hidden by equally ostentatious landscaping.

Sam and Ellie's lawn, pockmarked by occasional bald patches surrounded by flat grass and a spattering of indifferently maintained oaks and malnourished pine bushes, seemed antique by comparison.

Sam's son Christopher was at his iMac in the small den off to the side of the kitchen, engrossed in a game. The tall, thin boy, blond like his mom, was already following in his dad's footsteps; Chris had programmed and published three simple shareware games online—with a little help from Sam.

Markie was sleeping over at the Pennys, and Packy was sound asleep on the couch in the living room.

Ellie walked over from the counter, holding a pot of coffee. She was wearing faded jeans, a dark blue polo shirt, and her favorite set of 'everyday' diamond earrings. She was keeping her hair short this year, and her bangs hung over her brow, unkempt, with a lone set of strands coming over one of her brown eyes. She blew at it from her lower lip.

Despite their friendship, and despite having known Ellie for several years, Mel bore a familiar expression, an expression Buzz had seen on many female faces when they saw Ellie Fisk:

How does she do it? How does Ellie manage to look so striking without any apparent effort?

"Montana? That's really far away—yes, El, thanks, I'll have another cup," Buzz said. In the mode of the Irish, he had already poured cream into his cup to accept the coffee.

Sam pulled a color computer printout from a folder and held it out; Mel snatched it. She held it up so she and her husband could both see it. It was an image of a statue of Mary, Our Lady of the Rockies, in Butte, Montana.

Ellie plunked herself down next to Buzz to see the picture—or to be on the opposite side of the table from Sam. It was hard to tell.

"Wow," Mel whispered. "She's incredible."

"Yeah, wow," Buzz seconded. "How come we've never seen this before?"

"I don't really know. I just saw it myself a week ago, surfing on the Net. It's as big as the Statue of Liberty, except this one is made out of steel and it's perched on top of an eight-thousand-foot mountain, straddling the Continental Divide. A group of local guys put it up in the Eighties—just regular welders and steelworkers. It's a dramatic story. The whole town eventually took part in the project. There's a book I'm reading by an incredible guy named Lee Royalle, who engineered the structure without the benefit of having graduated from high school. And he's not a bad storyteller, either."

Ellie placed her cup on the table with a jitter, a flash in her eyes.

"What is it?" Mel asked, not unkindly.

"Montana," Ellie said coldly. Her answer was directed at Sam. She was obviously trying to hold her temper. "You expect me to move to Montana? To leave our life behind? Montana is nowhere. Why can't we just buy a farm in southern Ohio to satisfy your computer-nerd fantasies?"

Ellie glared at Buzz, who looked down at his hands, suddenly feeling guilty.

Sam didn't answer her at first.

"Well, Sam," Buzz jumped in, "why Montana?"

"Ellie just said it for me: Montana is nowhere. I believe we'll be safest if we go as far from population centers as we can manage. I've been thinking about upstate Wisconsin—"

"—That's news to me," Ellie interjected.

For the first time in his life, gauging from the look in his friend's eyes, Buzz felt as if Sam were going to blow sky high.

Instead, the storm within him passed quickly, and Sam responded with serenity, "That's not fair. You have refused to discuss this with me while you continue your research—"

"—well I recently finished my research. I'm not going anywhere."

"Finished?" Sam asked, genuinely surprised.

"Yes. I could quote you twenty of Bucky's friends, and none of them think the bug is going to cause more than a mild recession. Some even think that it could be a boon to the economy as foreign money seeks safe haven here because doomsayers like you have got them scared out of their wits."

"Oh, I see," Sam replied.

He turned to Buzz and Mel. "Ellie has made up her mind about the computer problem. We won't move from Cleveland unless she agrees with me that it's necessary. She doesn't. I'm sorry I wasted your time. Sorry Mel. It was premature of me to ask you over."

Sam looked away from his wife. "But I'm still selling Edwards." He rose to his feet slowly.

An awkward silence ensued.

Buzz kicked out of his seat, then jumped up and got Mel's chair. He started to help put her windbreaker on. Mel and Ellie locked gazes for the entire interlude.

"Walk Buzz to the door, Sam," Mel ordered with a smile as genuine as a Clinton denial. "Ellie and I need to talk alone."

Buzz and Sam exchanged looks.

The men walked through the living room to the front door. Mel sat back down with Ellie. She saw that Ellie's eyes were now watery. She took her friend's hand.

"Please," Ellie whispered. "I don't want Chris to see me like this. I'm falling apart. Let's go out to the back deck."

"Sure thing, El," Mel replied. "I'll go grab your coat from the front closet. Take my coffee with you. I'll meet you there in a sec."

✦ ✦ ✦

"What's going on?" Buzz asked on the front porch. It was a chilly evening. The two men could see their breath in the air. It had been years since Buzz had yearned for a cigarette. He wanted one now.

"Ellie's under a lot of mental stress," Sam replied. "I think the shrinks call it cognitive dissonance."

"Huh?" Buzz turned and leaned back against the stone railing, then began to put on his gloves. It was a small porch, and Sam was right in front of him.

"She's holding two contradictory views at the same time," Sam explained. "She's read the same evidence I've read, and she's heard all my reasons, *and* my counter-arguments to her objections. She knows I'm right. She's too smart *not* to know I'm right—on some level. Yet, she doesn't want to accept the truth because she doesn't want to move—and who can blame her?—so she's grasping at straws from her father's friends, who, frankly, don't know the difference between a computer and an infrared toilet at a truck stop."

Buzz laughed. Sam tucked his head sideways and squinted in agitation.

"My my," Buzz managed between laughs, "aren't you the amateur psychologist. Hey, I thought that was my job.

"Listen Sam, how's this for an analysis. Bucky's friends are right about the computer bug, therefore Ellie is right. Your wife knows that you are wrong, and it's quite rational for her to believe that you've lost your mind, and now she's really pissed.

"Let me use more clinical terms. She is *expressing strong dissatisfaction* that you're going to make her move two thousand miles away to the middle of nowhere near a town named after a man's backside.

"Butte? Who the hell moves to *Butte?*

"She is perhaps a tad *disenchanted* that you're willing to throw away everything you two have built together since you got married. Oh, and you're going to ruin my life and family while you're at it. I think that about covers it."

Sam nodded slowly. He gazed up his long driveway to the peaceful streets of Bay, imagining what those well-manicured avenues would look like without street lamps.

"That is a reasonable alternative analysis, Dr. Buzz. But you don't believe it, do you?"

"No, not really!" Buzz declared with a slightly manic pitch, throwing his hands up in the air.

He turned to look down the driveway with Sam, imagining troops and gangs and starving children wandering the streets.

"Hey, I wonder what my little Mel is saying to your El on the back deck?" Buzz hugged his own shoulders.

"I have no idea," Sam replied.

"There's a perfectly warm house between us," Buzz observed, "and we have to decide if we're going to ruin our lives while freezing out here on the porches. I wonder how long they'll make us stay out here?"

After forty minutes, Buzz went around back to get an update. Mel told him to buzz off, and that she and Ellie were going back inside to talk in the kitchen.

Ellie waved and gave Buzz a wan, happy smile.

Buzz and Sam decided to go to Joe's Deli with the cellphone and wait for the women to hash things out on their own.

Chapter Two

Whiskey Island Rules

The following evening, Buzz stood in his backyard watering the grass. Several weeks earlier, he had taken down a giant oak tree to make more room for playing whiffleball with Markie, who was just beginning to show interest in learning how to swing a bat. Teaching Markie how to hit had been one of those iconographic dreams of fatherhood which Buzz had spun to Mel when they were courting.

He had the tree guys cut and split the tree into three cords which were now stacked against the back fence. Just weeks earlier, Buzz had trekked to Builders Square to buy topsoil, fertilizer, and grass seed to begin the first battle in what he had described to Mel as the Lawn Wars. It had taken him an entire Saturday: filling the hole, tramping down the dirt, raking it, then seeding. The directions on the grass seed bag had cautioned to water often during the first crucial weeks.

Since the problem had come up, Buzz found himself watering the little five-by-five foot patch two or three times a day. As soon as the water soaked down, Buzz felt an uncontrollable urge to water it again. The tiny, lime green shoots were growing taller, greener, and stronger.

He dreamed of a world without electricity.

Mel opened the kitchen window. "Buzz, you're gonna kill that grass!"

He did not answer her. He was in his own world, preparing for the New Paradigm, as Sam called it—a world without electricity. A world where trains and planes and automobiles were a thing of the past.

A world where most of the populations of the Western world had died from starvation and disease, and like serfs, the survivors were spending most of their time trying to grow something to eat.

Mel came outside and stood beside him, her hands on her hips. Yes, she loved him, but he was always late. Dinner was getting cold. His lack of consideration for her schedule was a cross she bore.

"I *said* you are going to kill that grass if you keep watering it so much. And dinner's ready."

"Oh, uh." He shook out of his reverie. "What?"

"Dinner's ready."

"Great. I'll be right in. I'm almost done. Did you say something?"

"Yes," she repeated with a sigh, "you're watering the grass too much. Do you realize this is the second time since you came home? You've been like this all week. Why are you doing this?"

He looked down, as if for the first time. The patch *was* a bit waterlogged. He released the handle on the nozzle.

"I guess I just want to see something live. I want to see something grow."

✝ ✝ ✝

Buzz yelled "Hey!" at the top of his lungs as he came to the table in the cramped kitchen nook. Packy laughed with gusto. Buzz shouted "Hey!" again, even louder, bugging his eyes out at Markie, making a scary face. Both boys laughed again.

Melanie rolled her eyes. Buzz called it Startle Training. From the earliest possible age—usually as soon as the babies recognized sounds and were able to smile—he began daily efforts to sneak up on them and frighten them with loud shouts. Buzz would then laugh as if it were the funniest thing in the world. It took a few weeks of repetition, but now, the boys would invariably giggle when he attempted to frighten them with his loud, booming shouts or animal cries.

"When my boys grow up," he had explained, "they won't get nervous or freak out in times of sudden danger. They've had Startle Training."

Yes, she loved him, but wasn't quite sure if she loved him for this. The boys did seem to enjoy it, but somehow she doubted that the best parenting books had a section on Startle Training. Perhaps, a parent did need to begin the training early. Though he did this every night when he came to the dinner table, his shouts never failed to give her a jolt.

"Let's pray," he intoned slowly after he sat down. "You lead, Markie."

Markie, a perpetually moving bundle of muscle and flesh, transformed himself into a little monk, folded his hands, dropped his head, closed his eyes, and said grace perfectly. As always, Packy observed his parents and brother in prayer, and just as grace ended, brought his hands together, pleased with himself. Sometimes he clapped. He was an excellent clapper.

"So did you talk Ellie into moving last night? What did you talk about?" Buzz asked before plunging a huge chunk of chicken breast into his mouth.

He was a world-class speed-eater.

"That's between me and Ellie," Mel answered with a small smile.

"Shouldn't be any secrets between a husband and his wife," Buzz said, looking at his food.

"A good friend never breaks a promise of confidentiality," Mel rejoined, still cutting chicken into little pieces for Packy.

By the time she finished getting Packy's food ready, she knew that Buzz would be done with his dinner. Melanie was accustomed to this state of affairs.

"Oh," Buzz said. "Then she's agreed to move."

"I didn't say that."

"You implied it."

"How could you possibly infer that I implied that?" she asked him.

He was right, of course. This drove her crazy, how he knew her so well that he could tell what she was thinking. Other wives complained that their husbands were out of touch; had no clue what was going on in their minds. For Mel, it was just the opposite. There was nothing she could hide from him. Sam knew the future. Buzz could "guess," as he called it, what she was thinking.

Yes, she loved him, and she supposed she loved this about him.

It's not wise to dwell on why I love Buzz, she told herself. *It might remind me of all the things I don't love about him.*

Often what she loved and didn't love about him were the exact same things.

"You know me, little Mel," Buzz explained matter-of-factly. "I just know. I'm glad you convinced her to get out of Dodge."

"I don't think I convinced her at all," Mel partially broke her promise, although with a feminine strategy. "Men just never understand women. She needed someone to listen to her. She's terrified. To Sam it's all a matter of logic and reason."

If I tell him some of the truth, then I don't have to reveal the whole truth.

Buzz gave her a look which clearly asked: *So what's wrong with logic and reason?*

She read him. "Did it ever occur to you or Sam that Ellie might not want to make a decision out of fear, even if the situation is truly, logically frightful?"

"I can't speak for Sam."

He was finished now. Two full glasses of RC Cola were sloshing around with the chicken in his belly. Mel was just starting on her peas. The chicken breast was cold.

He slipped down from his chair and layed back on the floor. He lifted his calves up onto the chair, and continued to speak to his wife, looking up at her. He did this every night, claiming he was more comfortable and that it was a good position for digestion.

She closed her eyes and sighed.

"And you wonder why Ellie doesn't want to move out of Cleveland with us?" she observed.

"Huh?" he asked.

"Forget it."

She was used to his ways. She continued her previous explanation, "Ellie needs time to adjust psychologically."

"What about you? What do you need?"

She laughed.

"I had my dream, remember? Mommy I'm hungry. That was enough psychological adjustment, thank you very much.

"Besides, I've come up with a great way to put it out of my mind. I just refuse to think about it. We're going to move, and I'm going to help, but I'm not going to think about why. I'm going to make believe we're just moving like anybody else moves. I'm going to tell myself normal-sounding lies like, 'I've always wanted to move to Montana.'"

"Isn't that called denial, Sweetie?" Buzz asked, then, "Let the baby out of his highchair, wouldya?"

She did this. In seconds, Packy had slithered down and was riding horsy on Buzz's chest.

"Whatever gets me through the night, Buzzy. At least I'm not watering the lawn eight times a day."

"Sounds like a plan to me. You're willing to move, but are purposely in denial as to why. I'm watering the lawn. And Sam…and Sam, he…"

"Sam is Sam."

He pulled his legs off the chair, and deftly positioned the baby on his knees. *Airplane!*

Packy squealed. His drool came down on Buzz's shirt. *The trick,* Buzz thought, an expert dad, *is to keep that drool from going in my mouth.*

"Did I ever tell you about the time me and Donna and Sam went to the beach in New Jersey?"

"Like all your stories, yes, many times. But tell me again."

"Forget it."

He laughed, and snuck under the table and grabbed Markie's legs, making growling noises. "I'm gonna bite your belly! The lion is hungry!"

"No!" Markie shrieked with false terror, meaning, essentially, *Please go right ahead.*

Mel shook her head. *Boys will be boys.*

It was the same every night. Yes, she loved them all. Her three little boys.

✛ ✛ ✛

Sam was snoring. His wife rose from the bed and padded into the bathroom, flicked the light, and gently closed the door halfway.

Ellie took a hard gaze at herself in the full-length mirror. She was wearing a smock, as Sam called them, for reasons she never fully understood. Perhaps his mother had called plain cotton one-piece pajamas *smocks.*

No, that couldn't be. He lost his mother when he was a child. Me, Buzz, Sam—motherless children all.

She stepped closer and looked into her own eyes.

Who was this girl before her? She still thought of herself—of Mel, of Marie Penny, Kathy Lawrence, her woman friends—as girls.

But they weren't girls. They were moms. Front and center. First and foremost. Top to bottom.

Am I looking at a mom?

She placed her hands on her stomach, and yearned for a working womb the way a paraplegic yearns to walk.

This was a useless place to go, but she would go anyway. Chris made her a mom. Of course. And she hid her yearnings well. From Sam, from the girls, from herself. She was thirty-eight. It was a physical impossibility that she could conceive a child, but even if she could, that hypothetical part of her life as a woman—the part with a precious eight-pound bundle, a bundle worth more than all the gold in all the vaults in all the world—the part with nursing, strollers, with quiet times on the bed with just her and a baby—was passing by so quickly, so inexorably. They had taken out one ovary. The other one—she couldn't ever, ever, forget the phrase the doctor had used, thinking she was out of earshot—her remaining ovary was *shriveled up.*

Shriveled up. Not a day went by. Not a day.

Thirty-eight. Pushing forty. Soon, she would not even be able to *hope against hope.*

She shared everything with the other moms—except the yearning. Mel, Marie, Kathy—all they ever seemed to talk about was their children and having more children. They were proto-modern Catholics, part of the new generation of believers—still a minority—that loved children, loved the *idea* of children, loved mothering, and embraced the very cross of motherhood as if it were the True Cross of Christ. They loved 'being open to life' more than life itself.

Perhaps other generations had embraced motherhood, but none against a culture so hostile to children.

Pope John Paul II had led the way. In the vast Ocean of Death that was the late twentieth century, this new breed of mothers flew the standard of life on the masts of their little arks.

Weary of her own image, she looked back to the bedroom. Sam's feet hung over the end of the bed.

Mel married crazy Jack, she thought.

And I married the Beanstalk.

And like the beanstalk of the famous fairy-tale, her husband's lofty top poked up into another world. A world of certainties. And there was a giant bug up there.

Fee, fi, fo, fum, I smell the blood of an IBM.

She smiled at herself.

Is he right? Is Sam right?

She knew Bucky and his friends were wrong. She had heard it in their voices—the ignorance, the smug denial. They had written Sam off so casually.

Sam was *never* wrong. *Never* about computers.

Did Bucky actually believe that she would doubt Sam?

She had fooled her father into thinking just that while researching the bug. She loved her father, but he had always underestimated Sam.

During her whirlwind courtship, others saw only Sam's awkward features and pockmarked complexion, and wondered why Ellie James, who could have had any man she wanted, chose Sam. Ellie had seen the promise of something unique: a man capable of greatness.

And so humble, so considerate.

Greatness and humility together.

How rare was that?

Sam is never wrong.

Only a fool would discount Sam's unerring success for almost two decades in the industry. As if he had done it by chance! The fools.

Of course he was right. Of course the lights would go out, with all the repercussions which Sam so dryly listed.

"Why don't you put it on a spreadsheet," she had suggested to her husband with only the teensiest bit of sarcasm.

"Do you really think it would help?" he asked her right back, clueless. He always treated her thoughts and suggestions and ideas with such gravity.

Of course he was right. He was Sam Fisk.

She had no doubt that given another ten or twenty years, he would have become a billionaire. Another Bill Gates. Only a fool could fail to see that.

But the world is filled with fools.

"They're going to party hearty right up 'til the rain starts falling, just like in Noah's times," Buzz had said about the millennium.

You got that right, Buzz.

She felt the yearning again.

It was not really a feeling. It was something that was not there and could not be ignored. A lack.

An absence.

Fertility was a house of gold, and she was on the outside, looking in. A house of gold.

So when Mel and Kathy and Marie talked about children, Ellie played the role of excited friend to the hilt. After all, she had Chris and Edwards and her prolife charities, and the True Faith and the nice house in Bay Village and a Dodge Durango with leather seats.

They all just assumed, as she wanted them to, that she was comfortable with, and resigned to, not being able to have another baby.

Not another child. Another baby.

A house of gold.

That was exactly what her womb was not.

Her soul cried out: *Give me love. Give me hope. Give me strength. Immaculate Mary! Jesus!*

Her passionate prayer ran out of words.

Sam. Her gangly saint. He was the reason she kept up the front for the other moms. For years, she had successfully avoided the trap of her empty womb becoming the subject of conversation in her devout social circles. She had seen just that happen with other barren women—whose infertility soon came to subtly dominate the phone calls, the Rosary groups, the private little promises that "we're all praying for you."

That was not for Ellie. It was not her way.

As much as infertility defined her marriage, she could not bear the thought that it might define how she was viewed by those she loved most besides Sam and Chris—her friends.

She felt in her gut that she had a right to be known as Just-Ellie. Not as Ellie-Who-Can't-Have-A-Child.

In the early years, when they took her aside and asked if she had ever considered adoption, she had brushed them off with false casualness. They never had an inkling that Christopher had been an "accident," an unplanned surprise from the honeymoon. To think that at the time she had regretted becoming pregnant because she had been so wrapped up in running her own fledgling consulting company.

"We don't feel that is where God is leading us," was what she told them when they suggested she look into adoption. It wasn't a lie. She most certainly did not want to adopt, and did not believe God wanted that for her. Sam broached the subject just once, soon after the operation. She told him the truth and he never brought it up again. That had been so *Sam*.

Instead, she and Sam gave hundreds of thousands to Catholic adoption agencies which served couples who did have that calling. She couldn't force herself to want something she didn't want.

But there's really more to it, isn't there?

There was someone who should never, would never, could never, know about her deepest desire.

For if she told her friends how much she wanted to have another baby, it might get back to Sam. And she could never let that happen.

She loved him too much to allow him to think she was disappointed about being barren. Not that it would lessen her value in his eyes. That was not Sam's way. She just wanted him to believe she was happy. That she was satisfied with the cards they had been dealt.

Is that too much to ask? And I am satisfied.

I am.

Her spiritual director knew, and he had agreed with her decision to…carry this cross in her own way.

Which brings you back to the computer problem, she thought now.

Chris and Sam. Her world: Chris and Sam.

In the nuts and bolts of it as a technical issue, she had no problem accepting the idea that Sam was right about the bug. But she did have an enormous problem facing the possibility of losing Sam and Chris.

Unlike Sam, she had gone to the next level beyond the immediate repercussions of the computer problem. She had already deduced that no matter where they moved—to Montana or Alaska *or wherever*—the world was going to become a hard, cruel place.

Nasty, brutish, and short, she had read somewhere once in another context, and the phrase came back to her now. She was an intelligent, practical girl.

And that a simple flu could kill her husband and son in a fortnight without modern antibiotics. Or a gang of thieves enraged by their wealth. Or good old-fashioned warfare. Or any number of things. Surely Buzz could draw florid, bloody pictures for the group to ponder.

She was too objective to kid herself about them apples, and all them apples was rotten.

Maybe I just don't have enough faith? Maybe God will protect us. Angels will strike down our foes!

And maybe not.

She was spiritually mature enough to realize that God never promised happiness in this world. The Blessed Mother had told Saint Bernadette exactly that at Lourdes.

She knew full well that God might so choose to take Christopher and Sam away from her, and that she would have to accept that reality—in order to keep her hand on the plow.

Faith? Now that's faith, Ellie dear.

Hadn't Buzz taught them all about the cross? His suicide attempt had somehow allowed Pure Grace to bring Sam from atheism to faith in an instant on that dark, horrible, and mystically glorious afternoon so many years ago.

Is that why you told Melanie on the deck? To force yourself to carry the cross?

Last night, Melanie had been the perfect friend when Ellie took down the facade and told her about her ardent desire to have a baby and her deepest fears about losing Sam and Chris—that and more. Mel had listened, and later, hugged, shared tears, and held her in that way only women understand.

Now Mel knew, and had sworn to never breathe a word to Buzz or Sam.

If only I had more faith.

But faith was a gift from God. You couldn't just add more of it to satisfy your taste—like adding sugar to coffee. Who was she to question how much faith God gave to her?

What was that scripture Buzz always quoted?

"No man who puts his hand to the plow and looks back is worthy of the Kingdom of God."

I have a plow. Yes, that's enough. Not a house of gold, but I have two priceless diamonds.

She was at peace with her life, her decision, despite the yearnings.

Indeed, she had thrown her *whole* self into supporting Sam's rise to greatness, giving money away to the Catholic charities and apostolates ignored by the traditional philanthropists (even in charity, they were entrepreneurs), and enjoying an uncomplicated life with Christopher, her precious gem. Her Chris—like having a miniature version of Sam. How could she complain?

So don't complain, Ellie. I won't complain. She steeled herself. *I will not complain.*

She counted her blessings. She had Chris. She had Sam. She had Buzz and Mel. She had the Johnsons, the Pennys, the Lawrences. She had her beloved Catholic faith; she was consecrated to Immaculate Mary.

She had lake views and comfortable shoes.

Don't be silly.

Looking at herself again in the mirror, she realized that she still had her looks—plenty enough to turn a man's head. Excellent skin. A few gray hairs, but nothing noticeable.

One time, just last summer, Ellie had been walking across the street on her way to Huntington Beach when a gawking driver actually rammed into another car at the red light. She had seen the whole embarrassing episode with her own eyes.

Men could be such cads.

She rushed away, of course, and never told a soul.

Ellie had always been coldly objective about her looks— and like many virtuous women with this gift, she avoided trading on it. From the first moment, she had been thrilled to offer this part of herself to Sam.

Everything for Sam.

Even bearing this cross in this way was for Sam.

It was always worse at night. She chastised herself for allowing herself to wallow in it.

She walked deliberately to the bed, hesitated for a second, then slipped under the covers, snuggling her back up to Sam's. She closed her eyes, and imagined a golden house on a golden hill. She opened her eyes to rid herself of the image.

Enough already! Go to sleep.

This computer problem was bringing out the best and worst in all of them. She had a vague intuition that this was a fore-shadowing of things to come for the multitudes, but the insight escaped before her mind could grasp it.

Ellie Fisk had worldly riches, status, intelligence, beauty—everything an American girl could want.

And she would trade it all for a baby.

✝ ✝ ✝

The sun was setting on Lakewood.

Markie ran ahead of Buzz and Melanie around to the back of the Pennys' two-story house and was soon mixed into the teeming throngs of Penny, Lawrence, and Johnson children. The Pennys had seven children, and the Lawrences eight—all under the age of fourteen.

Two of Mark and Maggie Johnson's three girls were teen-agers who played the role of overseers. Their oldest daughter was going to marry a Thomas Aquinas College man and lived in California. Their only son, Seamus, was eight, and like his father, already towered above other boys his age. His best friend was Christopher Fisk, who was almost as tall. Unlike the Woodwards, Pennys, Fisks, and Lawrences, Mark and Maggie were beyond forty, yet still a few years away from *pushing fifty*.

The adults crammed themselves onto the front porch.

Cigars and bottled beers abounded. The houses were all close together on this typical Lakewood street, but the Pennys' house was a world of its own. After dumping his RC Colas into a cooler in the kitchen, Buzz came to the porch. Mel rose from her sturdy plastic chair, and after Buzz sat down in it, she sat on his lap. Packy was in the living room, toddling with the other smallest children, in view and earshot through a window on the porch wall of the house.

✝ ✝ ✝

A Penny Party. Kids. Cigars. Beer. And for Buzz, cola and chewing gum. Wolfe Tones wafted in from a cheap stereo somewhere in the house.

The rules were simple: bring the kids if you had 'em. Bring your own beverage. Share your cigars. Use Buzz's Zippo, which, since Buzz had quit smoking years earlier, was a ceremonial heirloom kept between parties on the Pennys' mantlepiece. Discussion of Chesterton was required. Belloc encouraged. C.S. Lewis optional. Anything Catholic a must. Unabashed bashing of Democrats, Clinton, liberals within and without the Church was never frowned upon. Thumbing of noses at the New World Order considered a bonus.

Perfect.

The reasons and ways and where-hows to make them all such a tight circle of friends were now long forgotten. Jimmy Lawrence and Tim Penny had grown up together. They shared the same classrooms and after-school memories from kindergarten through Ignatius High and John Carroll. Each had married his sharp, pretty, devout high school sweetheart.

Buzz entered the group originally as a friend of Mark Johnson, who shared with him a mutual friendship with Bill White. (Everyone called him Opus Dei Bill, except when he was in their presence.)

Opus Dei, literally the *Work of God,* was a Catholic organization which emphasized the need to seek sanctity in daily work.

Mark Johnson was an FBI agent, a Naval Academy graduate, and a former All-American football player who had moved to Cleveland almost a decade earlier. He played basketball with Sam and Buzz.

Tim Penny worked in middle management for an insurance company, and Jimmy Lawrence was one of Cleveland's finest, though now he rode a desk at police headquarters rather than a cruiser in the mean streets. Mark met Jimmy during a court case years ago. Jimmy had introduced him to his best friend, Tim, and so the circle expanded. Mark's friends became Tim and Jimmy's friends, and vice versa.

Three more regulars to the Penny Parties would show up shortly—Tim's brother Bill (the Not Opus Dei Bill), the Man (a black Notre Dame grad whose real name was rarely used, and who was originally from Buzz's basketball circle), and the perpetual bachelor, Brian Thredda, who seemed to spend half his life accompanying the group's favorite priest, the noble Father Dial, pastor at Saint Philomena's, on trips to Rome and Europe.

Father Dial was a magnet for them all. In poor health for decades, this powerful homilist had been exiled to a poor parish on the outskirts of one of Cleveland's worst westside neighborhoods. Though many in the circle were registered as members of different parishes, they all belonged to Saint Philomena's in their hearts, often investing hundreds of extra hours per year in order to drive their children to his orthodox grammar school. Always financially strapped, he somehow managed to keep his simple, Romanesque church cleanly-painted, flowers blooming in its gardens, and the nuns who taught at his school well-fed. It was rumored he had friends in the Roman Curia at the highest levels—another reason for his frequent excursions to the Holy City.

Poor health, age, and a certain rock-ribbed inability to avoid calling a spade a spade in public had kept the bishop's ring off his finger. The hierarchy's loss had been this little circle of Catholics' gain.

Five years earlier, when Buzz had been one of the perpetual bachelors along with Brian Thredda, the Man, and Opus
Dei Bill, he had walked into a Penny Party and lowered his
gaze upon the elfin Melanie O'Meara. It was not love at first
sight for either.

Marie Penny had been hoping to match Mel up with Brian
or Bill (the Opus Dei Bill) that summer night…

✙ ✙ ✙

Buzz had not been as heavy then—and was in splendid
shape from playing pick-up basketball all summer long. His
crewcut was thicker, and less peppered with gray. Only a few
years earlier, he and Mark, Opus Dei Bill, the Man, and Sam
had teamed up for a Cinderella win of the city-wide charity
basketball tournament. His slopey shoulders matched his eye-
lids, and his penchant for giant, baggy black shorts, plain
blue T-shirts, and black socks made him an unenticing, almost fearful-looking man.

Buzz Woodward exuded: *Yeah, I'm strange, and screw
you if you don't like it,* which is exactly what his friends liked
about him. Marie and Kathy had given up trying to find a
woman willing to overlook his rank sociopathy. Not that Buzz
was rude or discourteous. It was just that he was…

…strange. And he knew it. And he didn't care.

So when Mel first saw him out of the corner of her eye as
she stood in the dining room picking at one of Kathy's half-
dollar-sized pizzas, her reaction was typical.

She was repulsed.

When he opened his mouth, and started—spouting—she
wrote him off.

Now take Bill White. He was trim, medium-height (and
therefore closer to Mel in stature), handsome in a classically
dark-haired Irish way, and the owner of a successful advertising company—and so Catholic! At least according to Marie
Penny. Now *he* was what Mel needed—and had dreamed of

since rediscovering her faith almost fifteen years earlier at the Newman Club of Texas A&M.

Not that she was any catch herself. The devout Catholic black sheep from a fallen-away Wasp family, she had given up on finding a decent Catholic husband. Then she met Marie and Kathy praying the Rosary in front of the abortion mill downtown. She had been twenty-nine at the time, but her freckles, mop of red hair, and tiny frame still gave the impression of a girl in her teens.

So it was to her and Buzz's great surprise when they fell in love that summer—slowly but surely. It was the Penny Party Dynamic that snared them. On the porch, during the often hilarious repartee among the men, she found herself laughing hardest at Buzz's outrageous jokes. He just plain broke her up.

She would always remember an observation he made on that very first night: "Women are so vain," he had said bluntly. "When a woman walks into a room, the first thing she does is measure how she looks compared to other women. Guys are fundamentally violent. When a man walks into a room, the first thing he does is figure out which of the other guys can kick his ass."

Not eloquent. But true—and subtle. And she also noted that Buzz could probably kick everybody's ass, except for Mark, who was taken. Though Brian and Tim would give him a run for his money.

His insights into human nature did not draw her to him, however (though she didn't mind his ass-kicking qualities). It was just that Buzz made her laugh.

Opus Dei Bill, on the other hand, sat to the side, rarely speaking. She began to wonder if there was anything inside Bill, who never looked at her in that way a woman wants to be looked at, even at social occasions. (She was wrong, of course. Inside, he was an intense cauldron of devotion.)

Besides, she thought, Opus Dei Bill was almost forty, and there had to be a reason.

Buzz and Mel's remarks to each other rarely went beyond Hello and Good Night. It took about six Penny Parties, but Melanie O'Meara found herself looking forward to them for a reason she could never quite articulate, or perhaps, could not admit to herself—she wanted an excuse to listen to the big slob.

Starting at opposite ends of the porch chair arrangement, she found herself sitting closer and closer to him as the summer drew on and the nights grew chillier. Until one party in August, she found herself with him on the same piece of furniture, an ancient aluminum rocker the Pennys had salvaged from some forgotten garage sale. Usually, the loveseat-sized rocker, which anchored the south side of the party-deck, was reserved for married couples.

Like many child-sized grown-ups, her perceptions and sheer adultness had gradually resized her mentally into the same proportions as others. Still, she was taken aback when she now saw how tiny her leg was compared to Buzz's massive thigh. His forearm, chastely resting several inches above her on the back cushion, was as thick as her shoulders.

She was stirred by the proximity, and for the first time, by the physical power of the man. It was a bit shocking—and also comforting. His presence distracted her from the conversation. For the first time, she wasn't really listening to the others, or even to him.

The topic tonight was whether Buchanan could ever be elected. Buzz, who loved Patty-B (as he was known in Penny Party Parlance) as much as the rest of them, gave him absolutely zero chance of success. The others gave him a longshot's chance.

"If he can just win New Hampshire again…" Tim Penny would begin…

Amidst the discussion (which always grew louder in direct proportion to the number of beers Tim downed—and rightly so), Buzz grew silent and lowered his arm onto her shoulder, then lowered his head to her left ear, and whispered,

"Later on, I want to tell you about the time I tried to commit suicide."

He returned his arm to its proper place (by her reckoning), and immediately began addressing the group about how the mainstream Republicans would just circle the wagons again on Patty-B if he even *did* win New Hampshire…

She looked at him with a disconcerted stare, noting the pleased look in the corner of his eye as he spoke to the others. Such confidence! Such nerve!

Had he really just whispered something to her?

Muttering to herself that she was chilly, she rose and left the porch. She spent the rest of the evening in the living room, watching the little ones, chatting with the older Johnson daughters. She spied Buzz looking at her through the window and averted her eyes, and then changed her seat to be out of his view.

In her gut, she flashed back to the same silly, repulsive nervousness that marked those stupid eighth grade Spin-the-Bottle parties her sisters had dragged her to—boys, yucky boys, trying to kiss her on the lips in badly-lit basements.

Yet, when he approached her at the end of the party, and asked her, with all the articulateness of a mule, "Well?"— she put up only token resistance.

The perpetual bachelors were gone, and only Mark and Maggie were holding out on the porch with Tim and Marie.

"Well, what?" she asked back, pretending not to have the slightest idea.

"I would be honored to buy you a cup of coffee. The night is young."

Honored?

She couldn't recall him ever sounding so…gentlemanly.

"The night is hardly young. It's two in the morning," she replied crisply as she fumbled with her jacket. "I have to go to Mass tomorrow morning."

"We can always go to the four at Saint Phil's," he offered, reaching quickly to help put her jacket on.

"We?"

He just smiled, sleepy-eyed.

I suppose this is what he thinks passes for charm, her red-haired side smirked.

But the part of her that wanted to get married someday, which figured that nothing ventured is nothing gained, replied, "Okay, I'll follow you in my car."

Which she did, to the Quick Mart on the corner at Franklin, where he picked up two coffees (somehow he knew that she took her coffee with plenty of cream), then onto the parking lot at the Poor Clares' convent on Rocky River Drive.

Oh, that first date at the Poor Clares.

✛ ✛ ✛

After he got out of the car, he said, "Follow me," then he led her to the all-night chapel, where they prayed before the Blessed Sacrament for several minutes, kneeling next to each other.

They weren't alone. Two sisters were in the mirror chapel opposite them, though Mel and Buzz could not see them.

As he left the chapel, he offered her his meat-hook arm, which she took, again surprised by his tender courtliness, looking forward to his next surprise. They strolled in silence back to his car, where the coffees steamed on the dash.

He did a Buzz Thing next: he started the car, and with a few deft turns of the wheel, had them facing in an odd direction in the lot, no longer aligned with the white parking spaces on the pavement.

"Why did you do that?" Mel asked, curious, feeling as if she had never really talked to this strange man before.

"I like to face Jesus. An old habit from my UPS days. He's right over there in the chapel. He knows we're here together. He's listening to us. A girl I could have married lives there with Him. She married Him instead."

Odd words, but like all the ones she heard from his lips, compelling. Compelling to her, and uniquely so. She could

not imagine any other woman besides herself caring about
what he cared about.

Facing Jesus. Yes, she cared about that. She liked facing
Jesus, too.

"Oh." She looked forward, nervous, feeling awkward, but
not afraid.

"He's our chaperone," he added.

He carefully opened the prefab lid on her coffee and blew
on it for her before handing the cup to her. She had a tremendous intuition that he was about to declare his love for her,
like some idiot.

She took a stab. "You're not going to say something dumb
like how you love me or anything like that, are you?"

He laughed to himself, and turned his shoulders, and took
a gentle knuckle to the tip of her chin, and turned her face
toward his. A vapor light from the lot cast yellow shadows on
them.

"Mel, there's one thing we're going to have to get out in
the open from the start—I rarely have any idea what's going
to come out before it comes out. And I'm nervous as heck
right now. I could say anything. Even that I loved you. Or
that I wished I worked in the salt mines on Whiskey Island
just so when I went to work in the morning I could say, 'Well,
back to the salt mines,' and really mean it."

This made her smile. She nodded.

Okay. Whiskey Island Ground Rules, she thought.

His round, almost Russian features, somehow had become—handsome. She stifled an urge to kiss him—a small
kiss on the cheek, the innocent kind of kiss a daughter stopped
giving her father when she became a teenager.

She did not kiss him.

His was a stark face. No visible scars, but she knew they
were there; he had the kind of eyes she had seen in war photos
in *Life* magazine as a child.

Everyone knew that Buzz had been an alcoholic, and that
he had tried to kill himself once—long before he came into
the group. It was known that he never dated. Though Mel

had never seen her, she also knew he had a teenage daughter named Jennifer who lived in Florida, and that she came to stay with him on rare occasions.

The suicide attempt was a topic she had never heard him discuss. It was the thing of whispers and snippets on the one or two occasions Marie or Kathy brought it up. The message had been clear: *Don't talk about it in front of Buzz. He doesn't like to talk about it. Mark Johnson was there on the beach, and saved him. Sam became a Catholic.*

The events of that night in New Jersey had taken on almost mythical dimensions.

"So, what happened?" she asked now.

"Oh yeah, *that*," he replied.

They both knew what she was asking about.

The Attempt.

"I'll get to that," Buzz promised her. "It's really not a big deal. That's why I want to tell you about it. That was another man, another Buzz—a man I don't even know anymore. A long time ago.

"But I do want you to know who I am, and that's part of it. But can I ask you something first? How come we never hear about your parents or your sisters at the Pennys? I know you have sisters. Tell me about your family."

Boy, that cut to it. The one thing she hated to talk about. Her family. That was what Buzz did—he cut through things, and into things—into lives.

"I hate my family," she told him honestly.

"Hate? Isn't that a strong word?"

She shook her head.

"Yes. It is. I love them, too, I guess. What choice does anybody have? But I can't stand to be around them. They're totally plastic. I think they're dysfunctional."

"What do you mean by plastic..?"

And so, for the rest of that odd first date, until the sun came up in the Poor Clares' parking lot, instead of talking about himself, he proceeded to ask her about herself, like no boy or man had ever asked her. He began with her family,

then her likes and dislikes, what she read, and why she was
such a devout Catholic, adding his own comments here and
there, revealing himself to her in his questions, until she was
aching for him to take one of her small hands and hold it
tight.

He never did get around to telling her about his suicide
attempt—not that first night.

They went to the 6:45 Mass at the convent. At the sign of
peace, he did take her hand, and in a way, never let go. They
began driving to the Penny Parties together, and he asked her
to marry him on Easter Sunday. They were married at the
Poor Clare Chapel, amidst their friends and family, the following summer.

✛ ✛ ✛

Luck. Destiny. Fortune. Chance. Serendipity.

It was Chesterton who observed that the funniest things
are those which are the most serious—like a man making
love to a woman. A man chasing after a white hat on the
beach is not nearly as funny as a man chasing after a woman.

Since charcoal first scratched across cave walls, the poets,
playwrights, painters, and pocket philosophers have tried to
describe the force behind that nameless faculty within that
allows a man and a woman to recognize that they are right
for each other.

On the night at the Poor Clares, Buzz Woodward and
Melanie O'Meara realized that the cosmic wheel had spun to
a stop and his ball landed on her number.

Of all the kinds of things that happen to people, the mystery of the moment when a woman first sees and accepts the
man as the one *who will be the father,* the one *who will enter
into her,* is the most singular and unrepeatable. For most souls,
if the night of knowing happens at all, it happens only once,
and will never happen again.

For the knowing leads to sacramental union, and the union
leads to babies—those genetically-blended omelettes of body

and soul—new endless beings, bursting with as much fresh pluck as the soul-fusion of man and wife. Every child is a one-hit wonder who can be torn apart by neither man nor God. (Just try to rip the father-part out from the mother-part of a DNA strand.)

In other words, Mel and Buzz had started a long walk down their own private road that would disintegrate behind them, never to be traveled again. Soon they would be accompanied by snot-nosed whelps who themselves were designed to start their own roads with a chosen *one.*

Then, the roads of multiple immortals intertwine, and the mind explodes, and the ponderer is forced to wait until heaven to comprehend how something as sublime as Buzz-Mel-Love could ever be stuffed into something as tiny as the relic of a saint, or expanded into something as overwhelming as the shining white eucharistic belt holding up the trousers of the Alpha/Omega.

The champagne goblet of romantic allurement can be gulped time and again, with a series of partners—but the bubbles dissipate and the tonic soon goes flat. Motel beds are soiled, but no road is traveled. No flesh is created. It's over as soon as it starts.

To indulge in even the first sip (without the willingness to swim in the sweat, beer, milk, blood, water, and tears of marriage) is to anticipate the death of the emotion.

Unlike the *real thing* Melanie O'Meara and Buzz Woodward discovered, chemical romance has no eternal ramification, no fertile firework exploding abreast the stars.

On the night at the convent, as Buzz blew on the coffee before handing it to his future wife, he was already hoping to teach his boys to headbutt, to snatch fireflies—how to place sacramental charge-sticks into their souls as if they were real-live Gumbys made out of plastic-explosive—to let them cut their own things down and do whatever other tasks a happy, unpredictable God might require.

The roulette-ball-landing can be longed for, but can never be planned. The hope for this unique moment is sometimes dashed for decades, over and over, never fulfilled, even for those sensitive souls who pine for its cosmic beauty.

Or the moment can come to inarticulate teenagers on the first skirmish, establishing a union which lasts a lifetime, then stretches forward in the vibrating lives of their progeny, multiplying into thousands of offspring within a deuce of centuries, peppering the globe—all from one single moment of *knowing*.

The heresy of modern romance is the illusion that moments with such staggering importance are anything other than guided and provided by Another.

Tis all pure grace, and only our last journey-step into heaven will unveil just how many times divine finger-touches landed on the heads of those who began the long walk hand-in-hand.

To desire another, but never experience the knowing, much less the merging, is worthy.

To be presented with another, then spurn the choice, is tragic. Both give poets grain for baking their bitterest breads.

Buzz and Mel did not think these lofty thoughts.

They didn't sweat the cosmos.

As they enjoyed their one moment—the feathery feel of Buzz's fingertips on Mel's trembling lip, the mundane (but, oh so personal) conversations, the good coffee, their Perfect Chaperone, the rolling down of windows to bring in the chill and make the warm hand-holding all the warmer, their inkling of divine serendipity—they simply lived it, as those who get a crack at it must.

It sure is hard to ponder the mysteries of life while living them at the same time. The mondo wave comes, and the surfer jumps up on his board, balancing, fearful and thrilled, and struggles to bring that baby home without falling off.

Mel said, "Catch me if you can."

Buzz lassoed her with a diamond ring.

✙ ✙ ✙

Buzz mentally returned to the party, unusually silent, thinking about the computer problem, and how in less than two years it could take all this away from him: the fun times, the backyard football games, the homilies by Father Dial at Saint Phil's, the kids playing together.

He was disconnected, looking at Tim and the others with new eyes. Sam and Ellie had always been—lofty—just not social types. Nobody would ever describe Sam as the life of any party. Maggie and Mark Johnson, older, and like Buzz, transplants to Cleveland from New Jersey, had never quite jibed with the seemingly ultra-serious devout Catholics in Ohio. In the first few years in Cleveland, Buzz and Mark had sometimes talked about the lack of normal, fun, yet completely orthodox Catholics in the area—until they found the Penny/Lawrence social circle. Finally—a bunch of regular guys who would just as soon take a drive to Jacobs Field as head to Saint Philomena's to catch a confession.

For Buzz and Mark, it was like finding an oasis—a peek at the Chestertonian Party of Heaven—where the music was playing and the beer was flowing on the Pennys' front porch.

Tim Penny was a lot like Buzz—except that he was normal. He was almost as big, carried a smaller paunch, sported light brown hair, and had classic Irish features. His distinguishing characteristic was that the back of his head extended a couple inches farther than most heads. The length of his head was in the 99th percentile, for sure.

Even so, it wasn't a particularly noticeable trait, but the Penny Head, which Tim shared with his brother Bill, and they with their sons, was sometimes a topic of conversation among the men. It was a given: all Penny men and boys required custom-fitted football helmets.

Like all of them, Tim Penny believed there were only three major sports—baseball, basketball, and football—and that every red-blooded American should be at least minimally competent in each. And by gosh and by golly, under his constant tutelage, all his boys were well on their way toward that honorable goal by age five.

Hockey, volleyball, skiing? Diversions, perhaps. Real sports, no.

Unless you were a Canadian, then you—but not an American—could consider hockey a major. But you also had to accept that football in Canada was an absolute joke.

Soccer was beyond the pale (although daughters could be given a dispensation).

Tim Penny lived for his wife Marie, and for his kids. His idea of a good day was one that started with Mass. His idea of a good evening was to come home from work and have his kids run to greet him, then dinner with the kids, then Nerf baskets with the kids in the living room—or whiffleball in the backyard, or throwing the football on the front sidewalk. His idea of a good night was one that ended with the Rosary.

At the parties, in the Great Irish Tradition, he often repeated stories about personal triumphs over the Culture of Death that came during everyday battles, such as the time the guys at work asked him how he could afford to have so many kids.

"Look out the window there," he pointed with pride. "See that ugly old orange Escort? *That's* how I afford it."

These stories, and similar ones shared by the others, might have seemed mundane to an outsider, but to those in the circle, the stories held great meaning—and rightly so. For devout Catholics in a modern world, every day was filled with challenges to a normal Catholic way of life. Normal—as defined by the group—was simply being open to having a large family, even if you weren't married (yet).

In a subtle way, all his friends were spokes in Tim Penny's wheel. It was his porch, after all, and he was the one who knew all the words to the Irish standards; it was Tim who quoted the Second Amendment or Chesterton word-for-word.

One time, early on, Buzz asked the group with utter sincerity, "What do you guys think of the Conspiracy Theory of History?"

"Are you implying that there is *another* theory of history?" Tim replied with a straight face.

Brian Thredda almost had his beer come out his nose he laughed so hard. Now, Buzz's question and Tim's answer were often recounted. The stuff of legend.

On this spring evening all these years later, with the millennium twenty months away, the wives had been gently shooed from the porch with conspiratorial looks from the men. Buzz found himself sitting next to Sam on the same aluminum rocker where he had begun his relationship with Mel, facing a tribunal of Tim, Tim's brother Bill, Opus Dei Bill, Brian, and Jimmy. Mark Johnson sat in the back, behind Tim and the others.

Tim cleared his throat, then carefully refreshed the burn on his cigar with the community Zippo.

Court was in session.

"What's this we hear about you guys leaving Cleveland?"

Oh crap, Buzz thought.

He had been dreading this moment. The bug had come up once before, and the group, like most groups, had written it off.

He looked at Sam.

Sam will explain, Buzz thought.

Before either could answer, Jimmy piped in, "Why are you running away?"

"Running away? Who said anything about running away?" Buzz asked defensively. "We're just moving. You guys should consider what would happen around here if the food supply chain stopped flowing—"

Buzz saw Brian, who was sitting near the door, farthest away, make a disapproving face. Brian was a successful businessman in his own right—he owned three popular restaurants in Lakewood. Sam was not as well-respected in this group as Brian.

"Let's say it does get that bad," Brian conceded. "I still don't see why you would want to move away. This is where you have your friends. Why not stay here?"

"Yeah," Tim piled on. "If it turns out to be as bad as you think, we can all deal with it together, right here in Cleveland. Or we could all be martyrs together."

Sam cleared his throat. "I don't see how starving to death makes anyone a martyr. Are you really suggesting that all our boys deserve to starve to death when steps could be taken to avoid it?"

That was too serious. Too—realistic.

"I'm just saying there's little chance of that ever happening," Brian replied. "And if it does, at least we would all be together."

"The important thing is that my children go to heaven," Tim said seriously. "Maybe we will all die because of it— though I think that's a remote possibility—maybe not. But I'm not afraid of my children dying."

But what if God wants them to live—to grow older and have their own children? Buzz thought, but didn't say.

A long minute passed.

"You could come with us," Buzz suggested to them all.

As soon as he spoke, he regretted the words.

Tim shook his head. "And what would I do for a living in Montana?"

It was a reasonable question. It answered itself. What would any of them do? Buzz hadn't given a thought to what he would do. There was Sam and Sam's money when he sold Edwards. None of the men here, though they had good jobs, had a lot of money. The kids had taken care of that. Most of their professional contemporaries—their careers peaking during middle age—lived in larger houses in so-called better towns, their wives driving shiny new minivans for their one-point-eight children.

Only Brian, who was single, had financial options. And he gave a substantial portion of his income to Saint Philomena's. (Tim had once joked that Father Dial should rename the grammar school after Brian.)

Suddenly Buzz felt—unlike himself. Normally, his words to his friends flowed easily. In his gut, he knew defending his

position was useless—useless—even though Buzz also knew
he was right. He was stung because they implied he and Sam
were cowards for "running." Real men don't run. He forgave
them quickly, because he loved them.

They were right: he *was* running. He was afraid.

But he was right: he *should* run. He *should* be afraid.

And wasn't Tim also right, according to his own lights?
Why should he and his friends run from a danger that was
going to be everywhere? A danger he neither understood nor
believed in? Leave the town where he grew up? Pull his kids
from the only decent Catholic grade school in the area? Leave
Father Dial?

All based on Sam Fisk's conjectures.

In April of 1998, to the normal person, good Catholic or
bad, the millennium bug wasn't a credible threat. And even if
it was, it was a mild threat—not the kind which required that
you obliterate your roots.

Wasn't that the magic of the Penny Parties—that they were
all tied together like roots beneath the surface of a huge oak
tree?

Mark Johnson piped in, "Sam, I respect that you understand computers. And I'm still doing my own research. Even
if the lights go out for two months, that won't necessarily
mean they won't get things going again. I've got my little ten
acres in Oberlin. We could all hole up there until the worst is
over. Why Montana?"

"Yeah!" Tim practically shouted. "We can all hole up at
Mark's farm! It's only twenty miles away. Jimmy, you've been
talking about getting something out by Mark's little place for
years…"

Jimmy nodded.

"But not a real farm," Jimmy explained. "Kathy's always
wanted something small—a few cows, a few chickens—for
the boys in the summer."

There was always something calming about Jimmy when
he spoke.

"I wouldn't exactly call what I have in Oberlin a farm," Mark added. "It's a run-down shack. I doubt it's been farmed for forty years."

"We could get some sacks of rice down at Sam's Club, ride it out?" Tim suggested to the whole group, warming to the topic.

"How would you go to the bathroom?" Buzz asked.

"I could install a septic system," Brian threw in.

"We could do that," Jimmy added. "But you don't even need that. Not if you're just a-holin' up. When I was a little boy, and we visited my aunt's place in Michigan, we all used a privy. All's you need is a shovel—dig a hole. That and a bag of lime…"

And the group was rolling now—building an imaginary retreat for a six week crisis. Buzz and Sam were off the hot seat. Soon, imaginary kids would be having imaginary snow-ball fights in the fields of Mark Johnson's not-really-a-farm out in Oberlin. It was all a pleasant diversion.

Buzz looked at Sam. Sam gave a little, barely perceptible shake of his head.

It's not worth arguing when you know you can't win, Sam's eyes told him.

Mel stuck her head into the window from the living room.

"Hey guys, it got kinda quiet out there. What plots are you hatching?"

"Funeral plots, honey," Buzz whispered back, under the din of the new conversational thread.

Bill Penny was now standing in the middle of the porch, his hand over his heart, pledging allegiance to the United States of Mark's Farm. Another beer popped open. The laughter was back.

"Buzz, Markie's getting whiny. I think we should take him home."

"Okay," he told her without enthusiasm. He was inwardly relieved.

Rescue! Buzz thought.

Buzz rose from his chair.

It was official: Mark Johnson's not-a-farm was sufficient to take care of any possible woes that might be caused by a computer bug.

Someone took up another subject, an old favorite. Who was the greater American: John Wayne or Jimmy Stewart? (Hands down: Wayne, but Opus Dei Bill, normally quiet, could always be counted on to make The Case for Stewart.)

"I guess I should go get my wife," Sam said to no one in particular.

A few minutes later, standing next to their cars, the Woodwards and Fisks decided to meet at Sam's house.

Chapter Three

Dirty Croquet

"Trying to talk to somebody about this thing is like telling a mother she's not doing a good job raising her children," Melanie observed as they sat at the kitchen table in Sam and Ellie's house. "No, that's not right."

She bit her lower lip, struggling to find her point.

When they got back to the house, Buzz and Sam soon discovered that Mel and Ellie had been confronted by the other wives about their plans to move away from Cleveland while Buzz and Sam had been grilled on the porch by Tim and the others.

"No. You're onto something here," Ellie spoke up after a moment of reflection. "Here's another way of looking at the problem. Let's just suppose you were Maggie, and you heard that Sam and I were moving away out of fear for Christopher's life—all because of a computer problem. Let's grant that from her point of view, the worst it can cause is a depression, and at best, the computer bug is probably just some hyped-up non-event. Okay?

"By our decision to move, by our actions, we are saying to them, even if we don't say it straight out: 'If you don't move, your children are probably going to starve to death, or die from some other horrible cause—violence or disease. If you allow this to happen to your kids, you're not fulfilling your responsibilities as a parent.'"

Buzz banged a fist on the table. "I get it. Right, Ellie. If I'm Tim Penny or Mark Johnson, well, I know I'm a good dad, and a good dad would never put his children in such danger, therefore—"

"Therefore, it *has* to be a non-event," Ellie finished for him. "It's got its own kind of circular logic."

They all turned to Sam. After all, he had convinced the three of them to move.

"And therefore," he said quietly, "Buzz and Mel, Sam and Ellie have gone crazy."

There was something in his voice, something sad.

"What is it, honey?" Ellie reached for his fidgeting hand.

"Don't you see what this means?" he continued. "It means they'll never investigate. And they'll never change their minds if they don't investigate. The more we try to convince them, the stronger they'll resist. The problem really isn't that they're *in denial* about a computer bug. Nobody is dumb enough to deny that the computers need to be fixed. Real denial is when you reject something you know is true—like the widow who makes believe her husband is still alive.

"The problem here is that the average person rejects *the premise* that a computer problem can *cause a collapse.* If they reject that premise, then they relieve themselves of the responsibility of investigating it. And how can we blame them: who wants to face something as ugly as mass starvation, chaos, and disease? Better to reject the premise and sleep soundly at night.

"Maybe we're technically right about this thing—but maybe the sane people are the ones who ignore it. At least they'll get to enjoy the next year and a half—even if it means they won't prepare and they'll probably…" he couldn't finish.

They'll probably die, Buzz finished in his head. He could tell that Mel didn't quite get Sam's point.

"I'll never accept that there is something insane about accepting the truth," Buzz said.

He pronounced each word slowly, with utter conviction, and looked each of the others in the eye, one by one.

"Maybe, Sam," Ellie said suddenly, brightly, as if coming out of days of pondering. "If we really get going on this, and if your company sells quickly, we can make preparations for our friends, too. Maybe they'll come up at the last minute, and we'll be able to take them in. Maybe we're supposed to be like an...an advance team. Maybe that's why God is inspiring us to do what we're doing—because we are willing and able to make preparations. Very few people have our financial resources."

"That's a lot of maybes," Buzz said, catching Sam's resignation like an airborne virus.

Sam's always right. They'll never come. They'll buy their five sacks of rice at Sam's Club and stick them in their basements or at Mark's 'farm,' then sleep soundly at night thinking they're prepared.

"Let's keep a positive attitude," Melanie added with false optimism, sensing that the men were weary. "There's still a lot of time left—more than a year and a half.

"Maybe the press will catch on, or the government will start telling people to make preparations. More information will come out. More facts. The Pennys and Johnsons are smart—real smart. As smart as they come. But they will catch on eventually."

Sam looked at her. He decided to tell her the truth—what he had already figured out.

"The press will never catch on," he began. "Oh, they'll have reports on the bug, more and more as the months pass by, but keep in mind that reporters are even more ignorant about computers and complex systems than the CEOs who hire Edwards. The press will add to the mass rationalizations, repeat the party line that it will only cause a bump in the road—and make it even harder for us to convince our friends. They'll add to the confusion with conflicting reports. You see the denial in our friends—reporters and editors are just as human.

"Right now, there is very little about the problem in the mainstream media. The best information is on the Internet. Mark and Tim aren't even online.

"As for the government, I would be surprised if those in charge at the highest levels—especially in the intelligence agencies which are supposed to figure this kind of stuff out—I'd be surprised if they don't know the truth. You can read it between the lines in some of the reports to the congressional subcommittee on the issue.

"They probably feel as helpless as everybody else. Suppose you're the guy in charge, and you start telling the man on the street the truth—there are only two possible outcomes. First, the man on the street ignores you, and you've just convinced him, as we've just convinced our friends, that you're a lunatic; or, second, the man on the street listens to you, and on the very next day—"

"—the bank runs begin, which doesn't help anybody," Buzz finished.

They were all on the same page now.

"So it's a Catch-22," Ellie summarized.

Buzz stood up and walked over to the wall next to the window which showed the view of the lake, which tonight, in the moonlight, was barely visible. He began gingerly slamming his forehead into the wall.

"Arrghh!"

"Right Buzzy, arrghh," Melanie said glumly.

Buzz stopped banging. He turned to his friends.

A heavy calm fell on them.

"And where does that leave us?" Ellie broke the silence, unaware that her right hand was rubbing her shirt below her stomach—her womb.

Again, they looked to Sam. He closed his eyes, then opened them, placing his palms flat onto the table, stretching his long arms.

"We move forward," he said calmly. "And pray for our friends, and assume that whatever preparations we do make, we're making for them, too. Buzz and I will fly to Montana next weekend and start scouting for a place to buy."

They spent the rest of the evening discussing what they would need to look for in a site. A farm? A ranch? On a mountain or on a plain? What would they do for power? Solar, wind, hydro, generators? What would they eat? Where would they get bulk food? How would they cook it? How would they heat their homes? Wood? Coal? Wasn't there a better fuel than wood—Sam had found a website run by a bunch of former back-to-the-land hippie-types extolling the virtues of solar heating. Greenhouses? Root cellars? Should they buy an existing farm and fix it up? Cows or chickens—or both or neither? Wait, why not stay in Ohio? Too close to population centers, that's right. Then how about Minnesota—or northern Wisconsin? Melanie wanted to know why not somewhere warm—New Mexico or Arizona. Hard to farm in the desert, and that's where everybody will be going—south, toward the warm weather. But it's so *cold* up north—Exactly. That's the whole idea.

It was a frustrating conversation. They felt lost, without bearings. Finally, Buzz suggested they all take a general area and do research. Sam for site location and off-grid electrical systems. Ellie took food purchasing, storage, and preparation. Melanie, farming and farm tools. (*What a hoot! Me, a farmer?* she thought.) Buzz took water systems, miscellaneous items as they came up, and ongoing research on the bug (he almost enjoyed the last).

None of them were experts. None had ever planned for the end of civilization.

✝ ✝ ✝

A week later, after Mass, Buzz and his wife were driving to her parents' compound, as he called it. It was an unusually warm, clear afternoon. Her sisters and their husbands would be at the house.

"You'll have to tell them soon, Mel. You don't want them finding out from our friends, or when the real estate sign goes up on Tuesday. And you don't want to tell them over the phone."

She didn't reply. She knew he was right. *Today is the day.*

Still, she replied, "They won't see the sign. They never drive by our house."

She held sets of stapled papers on her lap. They were a hodgepodge of reports about the computer problem which Buzz had printed up from several sites on the Internet.

They pulled into the driveway at the end of a cul-de-sac in an exclusive gated subdivision—Pheasant Hollow—and wound past spectacular rows of shaped hedges, wood-chipped faux hills, and trees bred especially for their current usage. It seemed like it took half a day of driving before Buzz and Mel were able to view the enormous house, which was set deep on a gentle slope. It was impossible to categorize the home architecturally—it was a modern combination of custom gables, three kinds of genuine pastel stone facings, arches, giant windows, small round windows, and six—not five, not four—garage door openings: two in the front, four in the back, on a lower level of the slope. Also accessible from the back: the indoor pool.

"Gamma's house!" Packy cried.

Oh, crudbuckets, Buzz muttered mentally as they pulled around to the back, *they've set up the croquet course again.*

Buzz steered their battered little Festiva alongside a spar-kling four-wheel-drive Navigator, a massive Town and Coun-try, and, of course, Howie's beloved Lexus, which he only drove on Sundays, or so it seemed to Buzz.

He deduced that Mr. O'Meara's super-size-me Mercedes and Mrs. O'Meara's Jag convertible must be in the garage.

This illustration of Kublai-Khan-Gone-Suburban, which, strangely enough, was no longer uncommon in any tony sub-urb of any American city, was a spawn of stock market profit—silicon chips, and emerging markets.

George O'Meara, now seventy-one and retired, had
founded his own private fund-management firm in the 1960s.
Back then, O'Meara had convinced ten men with nothing
better to do with a million dollars to roll the dice with him.
Today, an individual investor who desired to reap the growth
dividends from the now legendary O'Meara Portfolio needed
to cough up a cool sixteen million for the privilege.

The old man had once mentioned that the house was paid
for with *interest compounded from interest.*

The O'Mearas also owned a spectacular summer home
on forty acres on the lake in northern Michigan, and the perfunctory condo on a golf course in Florida for those getaway
weekends when the Cleveland winter became too oppressive.

"Please take the baby for me," Mel asked, still in the car.
"He's fallen asleep."

"Let's roll down the windows. We'll hear him cry if he
wakes up."

A look of horror came to her eyes. "My mother would
throw a fit."

Speak of the devil, Buzz thought, as Helen O'Meara approached the car from afar.

She was dressed impeccably in a white tennis outfit out-
lined with light blue lace. Ten years younger than her husband, she looked twenty years younger courtesy of the latest
advances in cosmetic surgery. Those scalpels and suction
machines were getting so good it was hard to tell Does She
or Doesn't She anymore. She was trim, healthy—physically
perfect in every matronly way. She shared a red mane with
her daughter—now undetectably phony—and little else. She
was tall, as was George.

It was family lore that an elf with unruly red hair would
be born to an O'Meara every other generation. This elf would
be male—and destined to be a brawler, a murderer, a drunk,
extortionist, con man, or some other unholy version of a man
found under the general heading of good-for-nothing. George,
given an extra Martini or two, would regale his family members with the stories of his infamous Uncle Sean O'Meara,

who robbed banks in the old country and ended his life rotting from syphilis in a gaol in County Galway.

Buzz had once been shown a portrait of Uncle Sean portrayed as a young man, and damned if he wasn't a tiny little streak of freckles with electric red screaming out of his scalp—a visual male reproduction of Mel, right down to the funny way he stood back on his heels with his toes pointed outward.

By Melanie's way of thinking, she had even screwed up by being born the wrong sex, messing up hundreds of years of tradition. She had been her mother's last child, the never outwardly acknowledged accident who came five years after Mrs. O'Meara's designated *final* daughter, Mandy—or perhaps George's final attempt to hit a boy on the dartboard of fertility. No harm done—George had two brothers, and there were four nephews to carry on the family name.

The O'Mearas weren't Catholic, despite the Irish heritage. They were fallen-away Episcopalian, "planted" in central Ireland by some forgotten English king during a century lost in the dustbin of history. Mel's conversion to Catholicism after taking a course on world religions at Texas A&M, however, had not been a heartbreak. It had been a practically expected disappointment.

What else should they have anticipated from the elfin terror? Thief…prostitute…ne'er-do-well…

…Catholic.

It was all the same.

Markie darted to his grandmother and received a hug, then headed toward Ashley, one of his older cousins, who was reclining in a *chaise longue* on the stone patio that separated the house from the vast green wonderyard.

Buzz and Mel had gotten out of the car; he was leaning back in, gingerly unlatching Packy from the childseat.

Helen greeted her black sheep with a closed smile and a debutante's peck on the cheek.

"Melanie dear! Just in time for hors d'oeuvres! I was just about to call and make sure you were all right."

The smile turned plastic.

"Good afternoon, Buzz."

You dirty pond slime who's not responsible enough to arrive on time for a simple family outing, Mel finished her imagined version of her mother's thoughts.

It was an old, old habit.

"I have to go back and see about the others," Helen O'Meara continued brightly. "Do you need Charles to carry anything?"

Charles was the butler. The O'Mearas actually, truly had a black butler named Charles. He was from the Virgin Islands.

"No, Ma'am," Buzz said with an ever-so-slight, sing-songy bit of Nicholson in his voice. "I believe I can handle it."

"Very well then," Helen countered, already looking away toward the house. She bounced off.

It was beyond Buzz how a woman her age could *bounce.* But that she did. It was there before his eyes, undeniable.

In five years, except for the one "private chat" with her mother the day after the engagement was announced, Mel had not actually heard a negative word about Buzz from either Helen or George.

Even at the time of the engagement, the slights had been oblique, *"This Woodward fellow doesn't seem to have the background required to provide you with a decent living. Are you sure you know what you're doing?"*

Her mother did not need to fire verbal bullets. The snobbery which sometimes descended into downright mean-spiritedness was conveyed by tone, inflection, silence, or body language.

Melanie often felt as if her parents communicated in another language altogether. A language where nothing is ever said—all is implied. A language in which yes means no, and no means yes.

O'Meara-speak.

Even now, as Buzz straightened up with the groggy Packy in his arms, Mel reflected that Helen had been turned slightly away from Buzz during the entire interchange.

The message was clear: *I will face you, yes, but not by one degree more than is required by convention. Now that I've done the minimum regarding social amenities, we're done talking for the evening, young man—until I am required to say good-bye.*

Mel wondered once again—as she always did—if the Treatment was conscious on her mother's part, or if it came naturally through breeding. It was a mystery.

As they walked to the exquisite stone courtyard just beyond the back of the house, already set with tables for an outdoor dinner by caterers, Mel reflected upon how Buzz had so easily read the unspoken O'Meara language from the very start.

In the beginning, he had been a full-time interpreter for his wife. He often translated for her during debriefing sessions after these perfunctory visits. His ability was a result of his gift for "guessing" about people, as he called it—a wonder-talent he possessed that was soon attested to by all who knew him well. After he was introduced to George and Helen for the first time, he had taken Mel aside and guessed the color, make, and year of both their cars, Helen's favorite novel, and their preferred restaurant.

Mel was certain her parents and sisters had absolutely no clue how well Buzz read them. They paid as much attention to him as they paid to their servants.

In fact, one of the great blessings of marrying Buzz had been this ability of his to read them for her. It liberated her. That another person she trusted could confirm to her for certain that her parents were, in fact, insane, and that this other person, Buzz, loved her, somehow was the final glue to secure her own sanity.

After five years, she was now fairly adept at reading O'Meara-speak. They had spun her in circles her whole life with that unspoken language before she even realized it existed. In the early years, the message was sent through an endless series of governesses, none of whom had lasted terribly long. (At age six, Mel had been forced to go to extremes to get rid of the German one—Greta was her name?—yes, she had set Greta's skirt on fire.)

The Governess Message had been clear: *You are an inconvenience. You are not supposed to be here, but as long as you are, I suppose someone must be hired to watch over you.*

Mel could write a book about it. *I'd call it: My Mother is the Anti-Christ.*

Salvation came in Texas, after she finally graduated from Bay High (she had been tossed out of three all-girl private schools, including Magnificat High over Christmas break during senior year). She had insisted on going to Texas A&M. Why there? The name simply popped into her head when her mother asked her about her college plans. At the time, Melanie had no earthly idea what Texas A&M was actually like, except that it was probably in Texas.

It was just a weird enough choice to throw George and Helen a curve. *Texas is far away. A four year hiatus from the Red Terror. Yes, let us ship Melanie off to…Texas!*

Mel did manage to come back to Cleveland for Christmas break—twice in four years.

When Melanie left for college, she was a pot-smoking, sexually-active, foul-mouthed problem child; and when she returned, she was a chaste, quiet, sober Catholic woman. She got a job teaching kindergarten for Saint Raphael Grammar School in Bay, which she did for three years before switching to Fr. Dial's school at Saint Philomena after running into the Pennys. She retired the day before Markie was born.

Let them all rot and die in the collapse, the red-haired part of Melanie spit, the years of the Treatment welling up as they always did when she set foot on their properties.

She spanked the child inside rather harshly. She detested this side of herself. There was no working through it. There was only…

…forgiveness.

I forgive them, she repeated for the millionth time. *I forgive mother. I forgive father. I love them. Dear Jesus, help me love them. They have no idea what they're doing, that's what*

Buzz always says. Roll with it. "Forgive them and roll." For-
give them and roll. That's what Buzz says. Oh, Sweet Virgin,
thank you for Buzz. I forgive them, and I ask you to forgive
me for despising them...

So today, she forgave and she rolled.

She was going on eleven years as a Catholic, and not one
of her confessions—hundreds now, because she went every
week—and not one failed to include asking God for the grace
to forgive her parents, and to love them, and for absolution
for hating them.

And so it came and went for broken Mel of the Bay Village O'Mearas. Hate and forgiveness. Terror and virtue.

It sure beats suicide or the crazy house. Forgive and roll,
forgive and roll.

Yes, yes, she and Buzz were the perfect match.

Buzz could lay on his back on the kitchen floor after he
gorged himself on her lousy cooking all he wanted. He too
had been broken; pure Catholic sacramental grace had patched
him back together.

And so she, and so she. Pure grace had patched her back
together, too.

The only difference was that Buzz had actually had the
guts to attempt suicide, whereas she, for all her rouge-headed
bravado before meeting him, had never been able to screw
up the courage to take a long walk off a short jetty.

And Buzz would have succeeded too, if his friends had
not saved him.

Melanie thanked God they had. She thanked God for Sam.
And for Mark, and for Tim and Bill and Jimmy and Bryan
and Marie and Ellie and Kathy, and for the stout holy one in
the convent, the Poor Clare, Sister Regina—once known as
Donna Beck.

Because when they saved Buzz, they had also kept open a
human window through which the rejuvenating breezes of
pure grace could refresh her soul; grace with the power and
promise that one day she might live as a healed, whole woman
through the sacrament of marriage.

✠ ✠ ✠

After the meal, Howard "Howie" Barnstable and Brooks Thornton, the husbands of Mel's sisters Melissa and Mandy, lobbied Buzz and George into a game of lawn croquet. Every man for himself. On previous occasions, although Buzz was not a master croquet player, his natural athletic ability allowed him to hold his own when the mallets and painted wooden balls were lined up on the immaculately mowed back lawn. He even managed to win the rubber match the last time they played the previous summer.

Howard R. Barnstable was a tall, thin reed of a man in his forties with a rakish smile and dark eyes and black hair freckled with gray—a scion of the Boston Barnstables, a Yale graduate with a Harvard MBA; he had climbed to the top levels of George's company.

Howard and Melissa O'Meara-Barnstable had delivered the perfect one-boy one-girl Wasp quota of grandchildren to the family. Simpson and Galen (Buzz always had trouble figuring out which name went to the boy and which to the girl) were teenagers now, and had already left for their own social engagements.

Brooks Thornton (*What was it with these first names that could pass for last names?* Buzz often wondered) was two years younger than Howie—also handsome in a preppy kind of way—and still sported a relatively long Groton haircut featuring his wavy brown locks. He had put on a few country-club pounds over the years. Brooks was a whizbang patent lawyer for one of Cleveland's finest law firms. Mandy had delivered one child before deciding to become an interior decorator.

The daughter, Ashley, a sweet little waif with fine auburn hair and finer features, was sixteen, and sported a tastefully pierced eyelid. She had been in and out of drug rehab centers since she was twelve, and was the only relative with whom Buzz could even remotely hold a conversation. He found the young woman's aloofness from her own family—even if feigned—refreshing, if not a bit depressing. Presently, she watched Markie on the sidelines while sipping a Gin & Tonic & Lime without the gin.

Croquet requires a surprising amount of strength. For true aficionados, the only permissible position for striking the ball was to crouch over it with the ball between one's feet in order to wallop or tap it after pulling the mallet back under one's legs. A "golfer's stance"—striking the ball from the side— was considered gauche and therefore forbidden on the O'Meara field-of-play. Buzz's ability to whack the ball accurately over long distances made up for his lack of finesse near the wickets and stake.

All four men were ferocious competitors. Age had caught up to George, however, who quickly fell behind during most games. Howie had been playing since he was a child. Brooks was a superior golfer and had a certain gift for making the pressure shot. Both husbands were master taunters—a practice not considered beyond the pale on the O'Meara field. All part of the game.

There was always money riding on the game. This bothered Buzz, who, unlike the others, could not afford to lose the minimum twenty dollar ante. But he had taken that hundred and fifty last summer, when they had outvoted him to raise the bet from twenty to fifty for the final match of the season.

"Say, gentlemen," George began, placing his glass of wine on the white-lacquered, wrought-iron table Charles had brought to the sideline for the occasion. "I propose that we add a little spice to the games this summer. Let's raise the ante to one hundred dollars per game."

"That's a bit steep for me, Mr. O'Meara," Buzz called from several yards away, practicing his stroke.

"Only if you lose," Brooks pointed out, smiling with good nature, as he warmed up beside Buzz.

"You're all bound to break even as the summer progresses, except for me, of course, unless you give me a handicap," George reasoned.

Handicaps were definitely not allowed in croquet. The others didn't bother to even shoot down the handicap idea. Surely George was kidding about that.

"I'm all for a C-note," Howie weighed in, standing beside George, Heineken in hand. "And I'm sure you can hold your own, Buzz."

Buzz whacked a practice ball thirty feet and directly through a brass, U-shaped wicket. *Yeah!*

He rarely gambled on anything. But he could feel that he was *on* tonight. He rolled his head a bit around his neck, feeling it crack. *Why not? I could go home with three hundred dollars in my pocket tonight. Maybe get something nice for Mel for Easter with it.*

"Then count me in," the big man said as he walked back to the sidelines to grab his cola. Charles had remembered to add a slice of lemon for him.

"Excellent," George told him. "Gentlemen, let's begin."

As the three others turned to enter the field of play, Buzz did not see George nod at his sons-in-law, nor see Howie wink at Brooks, who returned a knowing smile.

The game started out cordially. Buzz began well and was able to make it past the first two wickets beyond the stake. Brooks caught up during his turn, and using a common tactic, managed to hit Buzz's ball with his own, and took the option of placing his ball next to Buzz's, then with his foot on his own ball, smacked his own ball, and by extension drove Buzz's ball far off the playing field. This was called "sending" an opposing player's ball. Brooks then took his second bonus shot—a player received two bonus shots after tapping into another's ball between wickets.

George, as usual, methodically worked his way past the first wicket, then came short of the second. Howie caught up to George, and sent George's ball off the field, then caught up to Brooks. Buzz trotted thirty yards to his ball, and made a

nice drive to return to a competitive position, a few yards
behind Brooks.

Then, with a nod to Howie that Buzz saw, Brooks reversed
his direction, and tapped into Buzz's ball.

Hey! Buzz thought as Brooks again lined his ball up next
to Buzz's, placing his foot to send it. Strategically, this didn't
make sense.

"It's not against the rules," Brooks said jovially, as he
whacked Buzz off into the hedges near the property line. He
smiled at Buzz with a grin which Buzz could not read.

Now I'm really behind. For the first time, he realized that
he stood a good chance of losing one hundred dollars.

Brooks blew his next shot, ending up just in front of Howie.
George managed to come close to returning to the field-of-
play during his turn, but not close enough, in the croquet
equivalent of a bogie.

Instead of sending Brooks off-field, Howie elected to
glance his ball off Brooks's—called making a "roquet"—and
took a two wicket lead, making it to the stake where the game
began. He would now attempt to reverse back around the field
in order to win the game.

Buzz, leaning into the hedge, made a spectacular shot to
return to his previous position. Now there was still plenty of
course left to make a comeback with a few good shots—part
of the romance of the sport was this built-in comeback dynamic. If one could catch the leader, there was always the
possibility of sending him off the field. Then the new leader
would be in the same danger from the player behind him, and
so on.

Brooks caught up to Howie, but curiously decided against
driving him off the field. This was not too uncommon. Instead he chose to try to extend his lead, though Buzz wondered if this was the right tactic in this situation. He walked
up to Brooks. In a trick he had learned playing other sports,
he hoped the proximity of his physical presence could slightly
rattle the other player.

It was George's turn. He easily manoeuvred his ball to just behind Buzz with a nice shot through the second wicket, then tapped Buzz's ball. This would enable him to take two additional and much-needed free strokes for moving forward to catch up to Howie and Brooks. Then George did a curious thing. He elected to send Buzz off the field for the third straight time.

"George? What the hell—" Buzz said.

George's decision to send him truly sucked.

George came over and whispered to Buzz, "What's the matter, can't take the heat?"

"You know as well as I do that sending me was the wrong shot," Buzz replied with an edge.

"Temper temper. I'm not going to win this game," George countered calmly, raising an eyebrow. "I'm allowed to have my fun."

Buzz bit off a reply. *But you're supposed to try to win, not pick on me!*

"Don't let the old man bother you," Brooks called over happily. "I've seen you come from behind before, Buzz."

"Yeah, yeah," Buzz replied, then under his breath, "Screw you, George."

Howie was moving forward during his turn now, going past Brooks again, building a lead.

"What did you just say?" George asked sharply, raising his mallet slightly.

"Nothing," Buzz replied sullenly, looking at his ball twenty-five yards away, not far from the tables where the wives were chatting on the stone court.

"I heard you. And you call yourself a Christian," the old man said sadly, tsk-tsking, as he walked away from Buzz.

Huh? Supposed to be a Christian?

It was Buzz's turn again. He was hopelessly behind now. There was only one strategy left. Skip ahead without going through the designated wickets and then try to send Howie and Brooks off-field, then double back on the wickets to try to catch up. He would need help from whoever was second—

in this case, Brooks. He walked quickly to his ball, and over-shot only slightly. He was letting his anger—and the thought of losing that hundred—into his swing. By sheer luck—against the odds—his ball tapped into Howie's at the end of its journey.

Brooks whooped.

"Take that!" Buzz yelled from his distant position. "Pay-back time!"

He practically raced back to Howie's ball and sent it ca-reening to the hedges. Then he missed in an effort to roquet off Brooks's ball.

"Two can play at that game," Brooks chortled. "Thanks for giving me the lead." He quickly tapped Buzz's ball.

"There are still a few wickets left, Tiger Woods," Buzz replied, a bit more aggression in his voice than would nor-mally be called for. *Who could blame me? It's like they've all decided to gang up on me.*

Brooks promptly lined up and drove Buzz back to the hedges, not ten feet from Howie's ball.

Buzz was still standing next to Brooks when he caught sight of Howie, against all rational strategy, tapping into Buzz. Howie quickly lined up to send Buzz's ball again.

"Howie," Buzz Woodward yelled, "what the…*freak*…are you doing?!"

Howie didn't reply. He swung mightily and sent Buzz's ball flying past the stone court, almost all the way to the cars parked another twenty-five yards away.

Buzz, unable to control himself, let loose an excremental word.

"Not looking too good for the Christian," George offered sadly, clicking his tongue. "And Buzz, would you mind watch-ing your gutter mouth. This is a gentleman's game."

Buzz saw red. *A gentleman's game? I have a hundred dollars riding on this—farce.*

"And what does being a Christian have to do with any of this?" he asked George O'Meara, sounding unstable, and defi-nitely angry.

"It seems obvious, doesn't it?" George replied in a patronizing tone. "You fancy yourself this perfect Catholic, yet you can't seem to control yourself while playing a simple game. Now, pardon me."

George walked back to his ball and calmly blew his next shot, then looked up with a serene expression of resignation, as if to illustrate for poor, lowly Buzz the *proper* way to handle disappointment.

"Your turn," Brooks told Buzz.

Brooks was already in a crouch, eyeing his next shot. Howie had managed to get halfway back to the field. Brooks's lead was growing.

Bastards.

Buzz stormed off toward his ball. It took what seemed like ages to reach it. He was breathing hard—from the tension, not the walk. He looked down at his yellow ball.

I'll get back into this! he told himself, knowing it was hopeless. *It's as if they ganged up on me on purpose,* he repeated to himself, again.

Then, just as he was about to strike the ball, reality dawned on him.

They *had* done this on purpose.

A game of dirty croquet. Pre-planned, no doubt—right down to the hundred dollar ante—the whole nine yards.

He looked up and eyed them from afar. They were by the sideline table now, watching and waiting for him, Heinies in hand, smug as crud on a rug. Silently sharing their little secret.

Those bastards. Christian my ass.

Still, his realization did not mute the anger.

Buzz, New Jersey boy to the core, devised a plan.

First, he reared and fired a gargantuan shot, bringing him within striking distance of the playing green. He knew now he couldn't win—even if he played perfectly they would continue sending him. But he had to get closer to them.

He walked past his ball, and stood next to Howie, who was lining up his next shot, out of earshot from George and Brooks.

"Is Brooks in on it too?" Buzz asked knowingly.

"In on what?" Howie asked innocently, without looking up from the ball as he stroked it.

"You know exactly what I'm talking about," Buzz accused calmly.

Howie, holding his mallet parallel to the ground now, leaned his tall frame back on his heels a bit, then chuckled a cynical chuckle, as if to telegraph in unspoken O'Meara-speak: *All in good fun, asswipe.*

Buzz had all the confirmation he needed. Howie walked away, toward his ball and the others.

Bastards.

Buzz looked over to the women. The coffee in their cups was probably growing cold. They were oblivious to the friendly little game of Buzz the Piñata taking place on the croquet field. He saw Mel looking bored, nursing Packy at a table, but was unable to catch her eye. Helen was on her feet, heading toward the inside of the house.

Please forgive me, Mel, for what I am about to do.

Then, strangely, he surprised himself with this prayer: *Yahweh, make strong the hands of your chosen one. Lay mine enemies down before me.*

He placed his mallet on the ground, and walked toward the three men. On his last turn, Brooks had won the game easily.

Buzz approached them slowly, thinking of… *positioning.* The sound of their patter seemed far away. George's laugh died down.

The big, sleepy-eyed man with a crewcut stood squarely before Brooks, who was slightly shorter than Buzz. Howie, two inches taller, was to Buzz's right. George was standing on the other side of the iron table. The sun was just below the hedges now—darkness was falling.

"Pay up," Brooks said, with a tilt of his head and a squint, still holding his mallet.

Buzz nodded sagely, and moved his left hand as if to reach for his wallet, then...

...wheeled around and coldcocked Howie with a devastating punch squarely to the taller man's mouth and nose. It was a half-sidewinding, half-judo blow, and Buzz had put his whole thick frame into it, pulling it *just so* at the final instant. He had no desire to kill him.

Howie's eyes went crosswise, and he crumpled to the ground, out cold. There was a trickle of blood coming from his lip, and it quickly formed a rivulet onto his cheek.

The air had escaped audibly from George's lungs; he caught his breath, "My God, what have you done?"

Buzz, holding his fist in his right hand, turned to Brooks, who had now raised his mallet over his shoulder, hesitating...

Buzz stepped back—almost danced back—and raised his hands, palm upward, flicking his fingers in the universal *come on* gesture.

"You want a piece of me too, Brooks, you lying sack of scum?" Buzz taunted, a grisly smile on his face.

He heard Melissa scream and from the corner of his eye saw her and Mandy come running.

"Buzz!" George shouted. "Brooks! No!"

"Make up your mind, Brooks. You have the mallet. Take your best shot."

There was fear in Brooks's eyes; he still held the mallet menacingly in the air.

Melissa arrived first and fell to her knees next to her husband. She took his head onto her lap, and began gently slapping his cheeks in an effort to revive him.

Howie issued a low groan, then slurred, "What the..."

Brooks lowered his mallet, and dropped it to the ground.

"What are you going to do? Are you going to beat me up?" he taunted, his eyes now unreadable.

The emotions of the moment seeped out of Buzz with amazing speed. He lowered his hands.

George found his legs and came around the table and stood next to Brooks.

"Get off my property, Buzz. I'm going to call the police. And I expect that Howard will be pressing charges."

Mel arrived, still holding the baby. Her expression asked, *What in God's creation just happened here?*

Buzz took a step forward, and Brooks jumped a bit to the side.

He's as scared as a rabbit, Buzz thought, knowing the violence was over.

He reached between George and Brooks for his glass of cola. The matter of charges being pressed was the furthest thing from his mind. He took a huge gulp, then turned to his wife.

"I'll explain later," Buzz told his wife. "But first I need to tell your father something."

"Now you listen to me—" George began.

"No. You listen to me," Buzz interrupted.

A serene authority was in Buzz's voice. George's mouth slammed shut from the force of it.

"What did you do to my Howie?" Melissa, in tears, pleaded from her post on the ground, not quite worked up to anger.

"Melissa honey…?" Howie asked, coming back from the ether.

"Oh my God! What's happening?" Helen shrilled as she arrived at the group, completely clueless.

"Melanie and I have decided to move away from Cleveland," Buzz continued calmly. "She was afraid to tell you but I'm telling you now. Our original reason—a computer problem—doesn't really matter anymore, because the last thing on earth I'm ever going to do is let Mel or Mark or Packy anywhere near you people ever again. You're all—"

He hesitated, searching for the right word. But he couldn't find a word to describe their mode of evil. Perhaps the word didn't exist. He looked down at his sneakers: dirty, old, worn-out Cons. He noticed that George's tennis shoes looked as if they had come right out of the box this morning.

"You're crazy," George finally uttered, shaking his head, taking Helen's hand. His face, his eyes, his skin—looked worn and old and tired.

"Maybe so," Buzz replied. "Maybe that's why I see through all of you so easily."

He turned. "Let's get out of here, Mel. I'm feeling sick to my stomach."

He put his arm around her shoulder.

"Melanie?!" Helen mewed, a bit unhinged.

"Good-bye, Mother," Mel replied, no longer facing her, a unique brand of finality in her voice.

Buzz and Mel hurried away. He repressed his urge to run. When they got to the car, he quickly strapped Markie into his carseat. No saying bye-bye to Gramma tonight.

"You'll be hearing from our lawyer," Melissa called behind them.

Buzz began telling his version of the story before they got to the end of the driveway. He finished just as they pulled into their stump of a driveway in Lakewood.

"My parents didn't protest when you said we were moving away," was all she said.

✝ ✝ ✝

The police came to their door later that evening, and took down Buzz's side of the story, but did not arrest him. George had filed a complaint. For reasons they never discovered, Howard decided not to press charges and the drama ended without further incident. Mel heard later that Howie had not been injured beyond a fat lip and sore ego.

At Mel's gentle urging, a week later, Buzz wrote this short note of apology to her brother-in-law:

> Dear Howie,
>
> I'm sorry I hit you, and I'm glad you're okay. There is no excuse for me to resort to violence, regardless of the provocation. I hope you can find it in your heart to forgive me.
>
> Sincerely,
> Buzz

He wasn't very excited about sending the note, but agreed with Mel in principle that sending it was the right thing to do, so he swallowed his pride.

"I'll let pre-American Revolution Mohawks pull out my fingernails one-by-one before I ever pay up on that bet," he told her as he sealed the envelope.

"I don't think a bet counts if somebody cheats like that, Sweetie. And where do you come up with stuff like Indians pulling out your fingernails? Yuck!"

"Sorry, last night I watched Last of the Mohicans after you went to bed," he explained, followed by his shouting impersonation of Daniel Day-Lewis, "You stay alive! No matter what occurs, I will find you!"

The Woodwards were not invited to subsequent family gatherings at the O'Meara compound.

Chapter Four

The Other Woman

Sam and Buzz took the corporate plane to Montana. It took an entire day, beginning with pre-flight at six in the morning, and they stopped in Coon Rapids, Minnesota to refuel.

It wasn't a fancy plane—a used, twenty-two-year-old twin-engine Beachcraft Baron 58 with upgraded avionics, decent de-icing capabilities, and enough room to cram six skinny people into her cabin.

Buzz was cramped and claustrophobic in the cockpit next to Sam, who piloted with the same nerveless calm with which he guided his company; both were relieved when they climbed over the final mountain east of Butte.

Buzz's discomfort during the flight had not ruined, however, his amazement at the endless empty spaces that defined the state. The skies had been clear, and for what seemed like thousands of miles, the eastern third of the state was really nothing more than a huge, cold plain. There were very few trees, but plenty of mounds of dirt, dust, and sand, peppered infrequently with a small town here and there. The mountains began to dominate the state only after they passed the famous cowtown, Billings. He had not seen any farms, though Sam promised him that the real estate agent in Butte had been confident that there were several to look at within a two or three hour drive west and south of the city.

They stayed at the Fairfield Inn on the outskirts near the airport. There really wasn't a defined downtown in Butte. It was more akin to an organically laid out flower of rust and ramshackle buildings on a plain surrounded by seven mountain ranges. Incredibly rich copper mines serially owned by several different holding companies over the decades had placed the town at its location in central Montana. At one time, more copper had been clawed from beneath its rocky surface than from any other single place on the planet.

Settled primarily by Irish Catholic immigrants in the late 1800s, it was at one time known for having more "Sullivans than Smiths." It was said that in its heyday, Butte was more well-known in Ireland than was New York City. By the turn of the century, pollution from the huge smelting factories had killed off most of the trees in the town and surrounding areas. Back then it was rare for a miner to reach the ripe old age of fifty. Environmental regulations and foreign competition eventually drove the smelters out of business.

In recent times, Butte had become the butt of jokes—the Jersey City of Montana. It had failed to make any trendy magazine's list of Top 100 American Cities. Yet despite the harsh climate, the remoteness, and a Depression-era economy that lasted through the 1980s, its hardy, gut-tough sons had a love for their hometown that was esoteric—inexplicable to those who never lived there, except perhaps citizens of other maligned outbacks.

Butte, like the Jersey Citys and Garys and Fargos of the American landscape, was what it was and where it was. Her people held on to her the way you hold on to an old jalopy that served you well in your youth; you behold it as shiny and new as the day you bought it, overlooking its rust and sagging chassis. A view through the eyes of the heart.

Butte was still there, proud and defiant—in a world where silicon, not copper, was now the measure of economic value. The story had been told of the immigrant laddie from Butte who returned to the old country to visit his relatives after a lifetime choking and slaving in the mines. He caught ill during the trip. As his brothers, cousins, aunts, and uncles gathered 'round his deathbed, his last words were thus: "When I die, I want you to take me home, and bury me in Butte."

In the early Eighties, with its obsolete copper mines shuttered and unemployment rampant, there had been rumors of Butte becoming a ghost town right up until Our Lady of the Rockies climbed atop its rockiest, tallest mountain. On the very day after her statue was completed, a new company announced the purchase of the mines, along with plans to modernize and reopen them. Butte had enjoyed relative prosperity and a mild comeback in the years since.

Buzz and Sam emerged from breakfast at the Denny's next to the hotel to greet the real estate agent as he pulled up in his car. The ground was still covered with snow—not an uncommon sight in April, apparently.

Hugh Wiggins jumped out of his rusty sedan, then shook their hands. He was a short, portly man with big hands and a ruddy complexion. He wore a threadbare brown suit, and Buzz noticed that his shoes probably hadn't been shined in months.

They exchanged the usual pleasantries, then drove off, heading west on I-90. Sam sat in front.

Occasionally Buzz commented on the beauty of the natural surroundings—the hills, the buttes, the mountains, the occasional clumps of pines.

There really was a "big sky" here which gave false impressions of true distances. The mountains always seemed to be close and far away at the same time, especially to the north. It was a stark state—more high plain than either Clevelander had realized.

It rained on and off, like a shower faucet being turned by an unseen hand. The droplets rolled off the windshield like mercury. Buzz remarked about this effect, and Hugh explained that the air was especially dry in Montana. At one point, Buzz realized that he could see three separate rainstorms on the horizon in three different directions. Hugh called these localized storms "squalls." He added that out-of-staters often were impressed by this curious Montana phenomenon of "seeing the weather."

Buzz fell into a melancholic daydream, staring out the window, imagining the beams on the wooden electric-line poles to be oversized crucifixes, and the sun as laying her golden shrouds on the earth in the far-off places where he saw it was not raining.

·　"How come you chose this area?" Hugh asked eventually, a cheap cigar perched on his lower lip. The question had been gnawing at him ever since Sam's telephone call a week earlier.

Buzz caught Sam's gaze in the rearview mirror. They had agreed to keep mum about the computer bug during the search. They realized that bringing it up would just complicate things, and give the locals a reason to think they were nuts. Time for the cover story.

"I'm interested in building a corporate retreat—something different," Sam explained. "I've always wanted to have something in Montana, and my best friend here has always dreamed of owning his own farm. We are planning on marrying the two ideas. Mr. Woodward will live here all year round on the farm, and I'll come for summer vacation and to hold seminars during the rest of the year."

The explanation seemed to satisfy Hugh. Both passengers could feel his urge to ask the logical follow-up question, *But why Butte?*

After all, droves of rich folks and beautiful people were buying up ranches, farms, and mountainsides in Montana and Wyoming—in places like Walcott, Jackson Hole, and in the western valley surrounding Missoula, which had milder weather. But not near Butte.

Hugh showed them four properties that day. The first was a "small" ranch—300 acres—and the next two were larger, flat "wheat" farms on the plain whose main crop turned out to be hay, not wheat, which Buzz and Sam discovered after talking with the owners at each property. Apparently the big wheat cooperatives in other parts of the state had made local wheat farming unprofitable.

"Don't any of these properties have streams or rivers on them?" Sam asked when they were back in the car, frustrated, after checking out the third disappointing property in a row.

A river or stream had been a condition he had given Hugh over the phone.

"Uh, some do, but not these I'm showin' you today," Hugh stumbled for words. "Maybe some properties with uh, rivers, will come on the market in the springtime. It's still early in the season."

Buzz rolled his eyes. *Isn't it spring already?*

He felt a pang of futility in his heart. *This is all wrong! What are we doing out here in Montana? We don't know a soul.*

"Wait, there is one more place," Hugh suddenly offered. "It's not a proper ranch or a farm. But it does have a…brook on it, and a bit of tillable land. It's on the way back to Butte, not far from town.

"It's not exactly on the market, but old Harvey Stone has always been considerin' sellin' it. Even had it on the market a couple years back. I went to grade school with 'im."

So Hugh drove them to the property, which was located about three miles northeast of the city. It was seventy-five acres—seventy-two of which consisted of bare mountainside dotted with a few hardy pines. It featured a small, rickety farmhouse at the base of the mountain, and less than three acres of farmland. A small barn—hardly larger than a two-car garage—stood nearby. There was one cow guarded by four mangy dogs patrolling the driveway. Two old snowmobiles lingered by the front porch. White smoke drifted out the stone chimney. The house had black-slatted wood siding.

"Wait here." Hugh jumped out, then fearlessly cut a path through the yapping hounds and knocked on the front door.

"Is that the river?" Buzz asked, pointing to a slope behind the house. They spied a trickle of water barely a foot wide slipping down into a small pool by the barn.

"I sure hope not," Sam said.

Hugh returned to the car.

"Harvey's not home. He's probably out hunting. We could come back later."

Sam and Buzz shared a dejected look.

"No, don't bother. We're not interested," Sam told him. "Please take us back to the hotel."

During the short drive back, Buzz asked from the back seat, "Hugh, what have you got lined up for us tomorrow?"

"I'm still workin' on that."

In the rearview, Buzz saw Hugh shift his eyes a bit as he spoke. "Got a couple places in mind."

"Good," Buzz muttered. *Yeah, right.*

Sam remained silent.

They got out of the car and stood in the parking lot watching Hugh drive away.

"This isn't working out, is it, Sam?"

Sam shook his head.

"Should we even bother going out with Hugh tomorrow?"

Sam shook his head again.

"This sucks."

Sam nodded.

They returned to their hotel, washed up, then enjoyed a one-star meal of omelettes and clam strips at the Denny's before returning to their room. It was a standard-issue room, punched out of the same Xerox machine as every room in every mid-range hotel chain in the country. They might as well have been in Texas, or New Jersey, or South Carolina.

"Maybe we could find another real estate agency?" Buzz asked a sullen Sam.

"We could try. I called five last week, and believe it or not, Hugh Wiggins struck me as the most professional. By the time we track one down, we'll have lost a whole day. Even if we do find one, I get the feeling that nothing here is going to fit our parameters. And I've got to get back to Edwards for Monday's strategy meeting."

"Does this mean we're gonna have to come back to Butte next weekend?"

Sam looked at Buzz, then down at his hands.

"No," the tall man replied.

"Huh?"

"I'm sorry, Buzz. Montana is all wrong. Don't you feel it? We're like fish out of water here."

Buzz paused. "Yeah."

"Yeah."

They called their wives and told them the news: Montana was a huge detour. Ellie was not too pleased, Buzz judged by the look on Sam's face.

Mel was actually happy about it, though surprised that the men had made up their minds about Montana so quickly—without a clear-cut second option.

"Where will we look next?" Mel asked.

"I don't know," Buzz told her.

"Then I'll pray." God, he loved her.

Sam then called Hugh Wiggins and canceled the next day's appointment. The two friends sat on the edge of their hotel beds and prayed an unenthusiastic Rosary. Then Sam plugged his laptop into the extra jack, and began surfing the net to browse several "alternative energy" sites he had bookmarked.

Buzz called the front desk and got directions to the nearest Catholic church, then called the church and got a recording relating the daily Mass time.

Good, they have a Saturday morning Mass.

He walked to the window. It was dark now, and he could see the statue of Our Lady on her mountaintop. Actually, she wasn't standing on the peak—rather, she was perched on a natural platform next to the peak. Her builders had leveled off the platform at a place called Lamb Rock—after much blasting and heavy machinery work.

How did they get her up there?

He knew, of course. In four stages by military skylift helicopter. Lee Royalle's book, *Our Lady Builds a Statue,* had kept him riveted from start to finish with all the details.

When he had first seen the bluish-grey statue from the plane as Sam descended over the pass leading into Butte, Buzz had been mildly disappointed by her relative size. She was formed in the mode of Our Lady of Grace as found on the Miraculous Medal, with her arms outstretched as if to distribute heavenly grace to the world. Yet even a statue as large as the Statue of Liberty could be dwarfed by an eighty-five hundred foot mountain. Here, from the hotel room, she seemed tiny—the size of his pinky—far away, untouchable.

He walked back to the desk and flipped open the phone book. He found a single listing under "Royalle, L." He looked at Sam, who was immersed in the Web. He picked up the phone and dialed the number.

✝ ✝ ✝

"Sure, I'm Lee Royalle, who are you?" the voice at the other end of the line growled.

On a lark, Buzz decided to get down to brass tacks.

"My name is Buzz Woodward, I flew in from Cleveland last night. I want you to take me up to see the Lady."

There was a long pause at the other end of the line. "Is this a joke?"

"You are the guy who built the statue?"

A laugh. "Yeah, and you want me to bring you up there to see her? When?"

"Tomorrow is my last day here."

Another long pause. "Mountain's closed 'til spring, sorry." Buzz could tell Royalle wasn't much for long sentences.

"But there's a road—"

"Road's closed for winter. I tried to get up to see her my-self last week using my four wheel drive. No way. Didn't get two thousand feet. Been washouts during the thaw last month, and now it's all ice and snow up to yer hips. Sorry."

"But—" Buzz was out of ideas.

A long pause on the line. He heard a woman's voice in the background. "Who ya talkin' to, Lee?"

"Some crazy guy from Cleveland says he wants me to take him up the mountain to see the Lady!"

Buzz heard a womanly guffaw in the background.

Royalle returned his attention to the crazy guy from Cleveland. "Maybe some other time...uh, what did you say yer name was?"

"Buzz," Buzz replied glumly. *Montana: what a disaster,* he thought.

"Buzz then. Sorry. No way yer gettin' up to see that statue. Not in this weather."

The man, clearly growing angry, had punctuated his sentence with a foul word.

"Listen, uh," Buzz stalled, mildly shocked by Royalle's earthy language. Buzz wondered briefly why he was bothering to press on with this sudden Don Quixote request.

Then it came to him.

The man on the other end was waiting...for what, neither man really knew.

"Listen, Lee, I read your damned book. I feel like I know you. If you somehow got a friggin giant statue up on that mountain—you can sure as hell get me up there too if you put your friggin mind to it!"

A very long pause. Then a gruff laugh, and another curse word, this one coming with a good-natured tone.

"Okay there, Mr. Buzz from Cleveland. I'll figger out a way up. Meet me after Mass tomorrow at Saint Mary's."

By coincidence, it was the same parish to which Buzz had gotten directions earlier.

"Eight o'clock Mass, then," Buzz confirmed.

"Yeah, eight."

Both men paused. Buzz considered telling Royalle about Sam, but decided not to push his luck.

"So long," Buzz said.

Royalle hung up without saying good-bye.

Sam was looking up from his screen, staring at Buzz. "What was that all about?"

"We're going to see Our Lady tomorrow."

Sam actually smiled. His first of the entire day.

"Excellent. So how is he going to get you up the mountain?"

"I have no idea. He said he'll think of something. And
he'll get *both of us* up the mountain. No way I'm going up
there all alone with that madman."

Buzz and Sam sat in the back pew of the church during
Mass; Lee Royalle was sitting right in front of them. They
recognized him from the photos in his book. He was a thin,
wiry man, now in his sixties, with a slight stoop in his upper
back and neck, and a full head of salty brown hair. He wore a
Notre Dame Fighting Irish winter coat, which he did not take
off—a practice shared by the other Butteites at Mass, which
was well-attended. After Communion, Buzz noticed that there
were unusual Stations of the Cross that had been fashioned
out of bronze. He did not know that the very same Lee James
Royalle kneeling in front of him had been the sculptor.

Royalle turned to leave, and Buzz stuck out his hand. The
older man shook it, and Buzz couldn't help but notice the
disappointment in the man's face. Royalle's hands were strong,
with long fingers hardened with calluses.

Royalle looked to Sam as the churchgoers filed out past
them. "I hope you're Buzz."

Sam said, "Sorry, I'm Sam Fisk. This is Buzz."

Buzz tilted his head to the side and gave Lee his best Tom
Cruise *I Guess I'm Going to the University of Illinois* smile.
"Hello Mr. Royalle!"

Lee looked him up and down again and revealed the reason for his disappointment. "You weigh in at two-fifty, two
seventy-five, don't you, son?"

"More like two seventy-five," Buzz replied, a bit confused.

They made their way outside. It was cold and windy.

"You ever ride a snowmobile?" Lee asked.

His features, scraggly from years of hunting in raw
weather, became more distinct in the sharp sunlight.

Sam and Buzz shook their heads.

Lee Royalle of Butte, Montana, fresh from Holy Communion, spit a cussword foul enough to make a grandmother drop her stockings.

"That a problem, sir?" Buzz asked with his most courteous voice.

"Hell, we'll figure something out," he said as much to himself as Buzz. "Your tall friend plannin' to come up with us?"

"Yes," Sam answered.

Royalle cursed again, in a natural, almost happy sort of way. Buzz and Sam were already becoming accustomed to his expletives.

"Follow me. No, wait," he said, thinking, rubbing his chin. "Jump in my Ram. Hell, I'll drive you over to the damned mountain."

Minutes later, they sat three across in the pick-up, which was a muscular new Dodge, careening across town to the highway. Sam was in the middle, his mile-long legs bunching his knees up above dashboard level. Country music blasted from the sound system.

"How long 'til we get there?" Buzz asked.

"Huh?"

"I said: How long 'til we get there?" Buzz shouted.

"Huh?!"

Buzz gave up. It didn't seem to bother Lee that he hadn't answered Buzz's question.

Turned out Lee Royalle was hard of hearing.

Ten minutes later, Lee pulled up to the front drive of— Harvey Stone's farm. It was the same place Hugh Wiggins had shown them yesterday afternoon, right down to the mutt dogs, starving cow, and raging one foot "river." Except there were five dogs today. Lee turned off the engine.

"Harvey's usually off a-hunting on a sunny day like this one—damn!" Lee said with good cheer before beeping his horn.

The dogs came running, and started growling fiercely just beyond the truck doors.

"We've been here!" Buzz exclaimed. It just had to be a sign. But a sign that meant what?

"Thought you said you've never been to Butte?" Lee asked.

"That's right, but a real estate agent took us here yesterday. What is this place?"

Lee frowned as if it were obvious where they were.

They were at Harvey Stone's place. Right around the backside of the mountain with the road that led to Our Lady of the Rockies. He didn't bother to tell the crazy man from Cleveland this. My God, Our Lady sometimes sent him some real beauts.

Lee jumped out and ran to the house and walked in the front door, closing it behind him.

Sam finally spoke up, for the first time since after Mass: "Buzz, are you sure you can trust this guy?"

Buzz smiled widely. "If he can bring me up that mountain, I don't care. I kinda like him, don't you?"

Sam nodded, and cracked a big-toothed smile.

Sure enough, a fairly young man—no more than forty—thin, with a nice smile, who must have been Harvey Stone, Lee alongside, emerged from the house, and started fiddling with the two snowmobiles next to the porch.

Lee ran over to the truck. "I guess Our Lady wants you to get up this damned mountain today!" He ran back to the snowmobiles.

Excitement overcoming his fear of the dogs, Buzz jumped out of the truck. The mangy dogs gave him a sniff and a cursory growl, but they let him pass as he trotted over to the two Montanans.

"Harvey, this is Buzz," Lee said, not looking up from the snowmobile.

Harvey nodded. "Hi." Then returned to the job at hand.

"It conks out when it runs hot, so just leave it," Stone continued to Lee. "Harvey Jr. is out with the good sled today. I'll go up with him and get it later if that happens."

Buzz wasn't exactly sure he liked hearing these engineering details.

"Sure thing," Lee replied.

After another five minutes of adjusting this and priming that on the bigger machine, both machines were sputtering in neutral. It was clear that the larger black snowmobile—the one that "tended to overheat," was quite old—and was intended for Buzz. The newer yellow machine, which had started right up, was assigned to Lee, with Sam riding behind.

"Never driven a sled, eh?" Harvey asked Buzz.

"Nope. Got any advice?"

"Just twist on this handle to go forward. And don't fall off."

Buzz nodded.

Don't think about it. Just do it. Don't think about it. Just do it... he repeated to himself.

Now that Buzz's intense eleven-second course in snowmobile operation was fully complete, they all bundled up and prepared to conquer a mountain.

"Ever been on a mountain this high before?" Lee shouted over the rattle of the engines, buttoning his tan Carhartt coat around his scarf.

The Clevelanders shook their heads.

This seemed quite amusing to the mountain man, judging by his hearty laugh.

He twisted his throttle and drew away with a whir and a kick of snow. Buzz found his own throttle and gingerly began to follow. The first half mile of road beyond Stone's driveway was a gradual incline, wide and smooth, and the snow was packed down. Soon Lee and Sam were thirty yards ahead. Buzz zigged and zagged, and eventually got an uncertain hang of the machine.

Four of the dogs were barking and yipping on either side and in front of his sled, adding to the video-game feeling of the whole adventure. They left him alone a quarter mile up the road, and he imagined that their message was clear: *Good luck, crazy man! We're savvy, outdoor country dogs who grew up on this here mountain, and there's no friggin' way we're*

*foolish enough to follow you. You'll come back in a casket
and we'll howl then!*

Buzz was starting to notice how truly cold it was with the
wind. He was squinting, and pulled his Red Sox cap over his
eyes to brace against the elements.

How he regretted not bringing his heavy-duty gloves and
snow hat on this trip—and he had left his sunglasses in the
rental car at the church. As it was, he was thankful for the
leather work gloves he had found in the pockets of his spring
jacket. This morning, he had donned two layers of T-shirts,
one polo, and his Tabasco Sauce sweatshirt underneath the
jacket, as well as a pair of long shorts underneath his baggy
khakis. Unfortunately he and Sam were wearing sneakers.

The road narrowed significantly, and he saw Lee and Sam
dip into the pines. He followed them in, feeling more confident handling the machine. Soon, like tiny beetles climbing
along a groove on a peeled apple, they came out to the side of
the mountain.

He would look up to catch glimpses of the other snowmobile on the longer straightaways, but generally concentrated on watching and tracing the trail in the snow left by
Lee's machine. Occasionally, he had to slow, then steer around
washouts which left him with a scant yard or so of sturdy
path. Other times, he revved the engine and blasted through
drifts—reading clues from Lee's broken tracks.

Butte was significantly above sea level, so they hadn't
started at ground zero. He realized there was no direct way to
the top, as they switched back every so often in long, uneven
zigs and zags. As three thousand feet became four thousand,
and four became five, and the road which was cut into the
edge of the mountainside became narrower, and pine trees
less dense, he was simultaneously juiced by two emotions:
fear and wonder.

Fear of falling several thousand feet to his certain death if
he veered five or six feet off the trail; wonder at the most
breathtaking views of mountains he had ever seen in his life.
The whole experience was… pure …immaculate…

…like Our Lady. I'm going to see Our Lady!

He started grooving to the muse of the job at hand, enjoying himself immensely, lost in the little details of staying in one piece (*"And don't fall off!"*) while gustily grabbing as many glances from the path to the vistas as he could dare.

The machine broke down at seven thousand feet.

His ancient Ski-Doo suddenly lost power, and ground to a halt in a three-foot drift. Somehow, Lee sensed this and doubled back.

"She's just around the corner! Another mile, boys!" he yelled after killing his engine and freeing a few choice curses into the silent, pristine surroundings.

"What are we gonna do next?" Buzz asked, wiping ice from the hair around his ears.

"Just leave the damn things here. Get 'em on the way back down. Follow me. I'll break trail. She's not far now! She's expecting you! Don't disappoint her!"

And like a mountain ram, Lee scooted ahead in snow up to his knees. Sam and Buzz gave each other a look and a shrug of a shoulder, and had after him.

Twenty-five yards later they were huffing and puffing, each step a mighty endeavor. Lee doubled back again.

"Mountain air. Really sucks the life outta yer legs!"

He wasn't even breathing hard. He slapped Buzz on the back. "Move out, old man!" He darted off.

He's sixty-four years old, and he's calling me an old man? Well, he sure makes me feel like one.

Sam and Buzz trudged along, placing their feet in the trail Lee had broken, which varied from two feet of snow up to their hips. They stopped every ten or fifteen yards to catch their breath. They were on the backside of the mountain now, and the views led to…more and more mountains, as far as the eye could see. Lee was a half-mile ahead of them, sitting on a boulder by the side of the road above the snow.

No farms or ranches that way, Buzz thought.

"Come on, old man!" Lee called to Buzz. "She's just around the corner."

There was plenty of time to enjoy the scenery.

"Hear that?" Buzz breathed to Sam.

Sam stopped to listen. "Hear what?"

"Silence. Perfect silence."

Buzz was thirsty—so he ate snow. They decided to try to pray Hail Marys out loud to help with the pace, but they didn't have the lungs to keep it up.

It seemed like forever, but they finally caught up to Lee. The snow was not nearly as high anymore—up to their ankles. As they plodded around the next long, lazy turn, Buzz and Sam realized that the prevailing winds had blown most of the snow off the road in this section.

"Just a little ways more and we'll see her!" Lee encouraged them.

His energy was relentless, exasperating—and inspirational. It was slowly dawning on Buzz that this mountain man was a breed apart. Never in his life had Buzz so regretted being a New Jersey boy from the suburbs. He would have to redefine what he believed constituted that highly sought after trait of American manhood: toughness.

Lee is tough. I'm...not.

"Is she really just around the corner?" Sam asked between sucks of breath.

"You betcha. Let's go! Damn."

But Lee was no longer rushing out in front of them. He was matching their pace. The lighter snow really helped.

Then, in a matter of a few steps, they came around the back of the mountain and saw...

Her.

Our Lady. She was another quarter mile away, but she was magnificent. Buzz and Sam stopped in their tracks and gawked.

Wow.

She *towered.*

Again, Buzz thought: *How did you ever get her up here, Lee Royalle!*

The pride was evident on Lee's face. Sam put an arm around Buzz's shoulder. "I'm thankful we came to Montana."

"My wife likes to call her my 'other woman,'" Lee whispered.

And so she was. He had spent almost six years of his life spearheading the project to build her, welding and riveting her together, sheet by sheet, with his own hands, according to his own design.

He and his friends—most of whom worked at a welding company that had recently gone defunct—had put her together with virtually no money, out of scrap and salvaged parts, donated materials, and sheer will. Among other miracles, this man without a high school diploma had designed a true engineering wonder—an enormous structure fully capable of resisting or swaying with perfect aplomb against some of the harshest winds on the planet.

According to the moving account in Lee's book, the subplot about the building of the road that Sam and Buzz had just traversed was just as inspiring and magnificent as the erection of the statue. In their spare time, day after day, year after year, using borrowed Cats and bulldozers, a valiant handful of volunteers had frequently put their lives in jeopardy while building a road for a statue that none of them could be sure would ever be completed. Blasting away with dynamite, thousands of feet above the city, always at the mercy of the elements and treacherous inclines, they tamed a mountain which seldom wished to cooperate with their efforts.

Mountain men. Tough guys. Fellas with union cards who hadn't darkened the floor of a church with their shadows since grade school. Men who had no idea how the hell to play croquet. That perhaps was the most incredible and inspiring part of the story of Our Lady of the Rockies: she had taken hardened hearts of hard men, and in many cases brought them back home to the sacraments.

The man who first suggested putting a statue of Mary on the mountain had not even been a practicing Catholic. At the time, he had been a friend of the owner of the welding shop

where Lee was an employee. The man's wife had been scheduled to undergo a very risky surgery. He promised God he
would put a statue on the mountain if his wife lived through
the operation.

His wife recovered. The original plan had called for a life-
size statue. For some mysterious reason, during early design
stages, the size of the statue increased by a factor of twenty.
The original engineer and architect had dropped out shortly
after the project got underway, and both jobs had fallen into
the lap of Lee Royalle, who had already welded together a
single, enormous "finger" for display in order to help inspire
donations.

But all these years later, for Lee Royalle, the real miracle
hadn't been the road or the statue—the real miracle was that
a guy like him now prayed the Rosary and rarely missed daily
Mass, had written a book, and spoke in public about Our
Lady and her statue.

At the sight of her, Buzz, Sam, and Lee felt the import of
these miracles, then did what real men do.

They said nothing and moved forward.

✛ ✛ ✛

Snow drifts greeted them in the final hundred-yard span.
They could now see the huge plain that held Butte beyond
the statue, impossibly far below them on the steep side of the
mountain. Sam and Buzz were stopping every ten yards to
rest, despite Lee's goading. The Lady was now hovering over
them like a skyscraper.

With thirty yards to go, Buzz was a few steps behind Lee.
The Clevelander stopped and placed his hands on his knees.

"What'sa matter, old man?" Lee asked.

"Nothin'. I'll make it."

Buzz straightened up and stretched his arms. Ignoring his
protesting lungs and the pain in his legs, he began to run,
pulling his legs out of the snow with his knees high like a

lifeguard entering the surf. "Race ya!" he challenged as he passed by Lee.

Lee quickly caught up to Buzz with twenty yards to go.

"You'll never win," Lee laughed.

Even so, the older man was feeling the fatigue.

"Not unless I cheat!" Buzz retorted and with that, slammed his shoulder into the thinner man, knocking Lee into the drift.

"Hey!"

Buzz pushed forward, truly exhausted. To Sam, who was watching this contest with amusement, Buzz seemed to be plodding rather slowly, but Buzz felt as if he were bolting toward the statue.

Lee was up on his feet in an instant, and to Sam, appeared to be ready to tackle Buzz from behind, but Lee elected instead to pass the larger man in the last five yards.

Even though he had lost the race, Buzz still lunged head-first, right arm outstretched, to touch the statue, landing face-first in the snow.

He heard Lee laugh for what seemed like the hundredth time today. Buzz turned over on his back, and squinting in the sun, saw Lee Royalle and his fair Lady from this unusual perspective.

"Thank you."

Neither man was sure if Buzz was thanking Lee or the woman.

Sam finally arrived..

"Your friend is crazy," Lee observed sagely.

"I know. We hear that a lot." Then, turning to look up at the statue, added, "Thank you, Mr. Royalle, for bringing us up here. She's amazing."

Lee nodded, looking up at her again. She had been here over thirteen years, and he still couldn't pull his eyes away from her for long.

"I got the keys. Let me take you up inside," Lee said after a minute. "But let's go around front first."

"Great. Help me up," Buzz commanded, lifting both arms into the air. Lee and Sam each grabbed a hand and helped him to his feet.

Buzz and Sam had seen photographs, but nothing could compare to this. The statue began just below her knees, and for the first time they were able to observe the ingenious series of air vents seamlessly designed into the folds of her cloak under her arms. Our Lady's hands were larger than Buzz, and he pictured himself resting in them. Her shoulders, high above, were square in a muscular way; this was aesthetically appropriate given her surroundings.

Her face bore a strong resemblance to Lady Liberty, but was not as stern. She radiated strength, beauty, and perhaps, not oddly, motherhood.

Lee answered Sam's questions concerning her architecture with practiced ease. During the short summers, after the road was patched up, Lee led tours for the growing number of busloads of pilgrims. He told them stories about miraculous healings and conversions, including a story about two of the road builders who had seen an apparition of Mary—she was as large as the statue—on this very spot while they were leveling off the platform. She had said nothing to them. Both men had asked Lee to leave the story out of the book for fear that no one would believe it.

✢ ✢ ✢

Later they entered the structure and climbed series of shaky ladders amidst an amazing array of welded beams and steel supports. Pilgrims, who were not allowed past ground level, had hung hundreds of rosaries, statues, and notes on the inner walls below.

Sam, Buzz, and Lee prayed a Rosary together on the highest level, in the very head of the statue. With the sun low in the sky, the men left Our Lady, and trudged back to the snowmobiles.

"Go as fast as you can!" Lee shouted to Buzz after he fiddled and jiggered with the old snowmobile until it started. "It'll stall if you slow down."

Buzz took off down the mountain, elated and unmindful of the cold seeping into his toes and fingers. To his surprise, he found himself racing Lee within minutes of departing. Because he was carrying Sam, Lee's sled was slower than Buzz's. They were able to go much faster on the way down. Buzz opened up a significant lead, but Lee took a shortcut down a deer path to catch up. As the road widened near the bottom, Buzz opened her up all the way, sluicing around the switchbacks with an abandon that could be shared only by a true novice or a true veteran.

Lee bumped hard into a dip over a culvert, and both he and Sam went flying off their snowmobile. No harm done. They climbed right back on, but Buzz won the race to Harvey Stone's place.

And Our Lady of the Rockies had won his heart.

PART TWO

Bagpipe

The children woke up, and they couldn't find them.
They left before the sun came up that day.
They just drove off and left it all behind them.
Where were they going without ever knowing the way?
*Fastball, **The Way***

The beginnings of all things are small.
Cicero

When they kick out your front door,
how you gonna come?
With your hands on your head,
or on the trigger of your gun?
*The Clash, **The Guns of Brixton***

At that time Mary got ready and hurried
to a town in the hill country of Judea.
Luke 1:39

I was born on a storm-swept rock
and hate the soft growth of sun-baked lands
where there is no frost in men's bones.
Liam O'Flaherty

As I look into the gray sky, where it should be blue,
I ask why, why it should be so?
I'll cry, and say that I don't know.
*Deep Purple, **April***

Chapter Five

Ellie's Fiat

After their fifth straight meal at Denny's, and sore from the day's adventure, they showered, then crawled into bed before praying their second Rosary of the day. It was dark. Twenty minutes later, Buzz began sobbing.

"Buzz?" Sam called over with alarm, jolted from his drowsiness. "What's the matter?"

Buzz didn't answer, but his sobbing became softer.

"Buzz! You're freaking me out," Sam shouted his whisper.

Buzz got hold of himself.

"It just hit me; it just really, really sunk in," Buzz moaned. "We're not going to make it, are we? We're not going to live through the collapse."

"Buzz, I can't tell you what will happen to us."

"I was thinking about Markie and Packy," Buzz explained wearily. "And Christopher. They're so young. They're so—they've never known suffering, or even been to a funeral."

"That's why I want to get out of Cleveland," Sam replied firmly. "There are no guarantees that any of us will survive if we leave. But maybe we can go to a place where the breakdown won't be as chaotic. Where death won't be so…ugly."

"But I thought our goal was to survive," Buzz asked, a weak pleading in his voice.

He hated himself for sounding so weak. So unmanly. The sobbing had come from nowhere, disturbing him at his core. It had been years since a wave of depression—even trickles less severe than this—had broken in on him.

"We have a moral obligation to do whatever we can to protect our children, yes," Sam explained, laying on his back now, his hands tucked beneath his head. "It's not much different than smelling smoke in your home. It's on fire. You grab your children and run outside into a blizzard. Now you're outside in a blizzard without any clothes. I have no firm expectation that we'll survive. Moving away increases our odds, but not by much."

There was serenity in Sam's voice. His resignation was the opposite of weakness.

Buzz pulled his head up from his pillow and rested his chin under his arm. "So you have accepted the fact that you are going to die," Buzz told him.

"I accepted that fact when I became a Christian. I'm more worried that God will not be pleased if I didn't do everything in my power to protect Ellie and Chris. Accepting that the bug might cause my death makes it easier for me to make objective decisions, and therefore, to do a better job of protecting my family."

Buzz mulled this over for several minutes. Despite the macabre subject matter, he was feeling much better.

"And you call me crazy," he finally muttered.

"What was that?" Sam asked.

"Nothing. Let's get some sleep."

Yet Buzz could not fall asleep. A few minutes later, he spoke up again. "Sam? You awake?"

"Ummph?" Sam slurred from the far bank of the river of dreams.

"How does Our Lady fit in? Why did she bring us up the mountain today?"

He heard Sam snore in reply.

"Sam?"

No reply.

Buzz asked Mary instead: *Why did you bring us to Montana? Where do we go next?*

He heard no reply from her before falling into a dream…

He dreamed of a burning cabin in a clearing on a snowy hill blanketed with thousands of green pine trees. He did not know where he was—except that he was not in…Montana.

He was on foot, a mile away from the homestead, on an icy country road. The cabin was painted a soft golden brown, which eerily complemented the angry black clouds of smoke and yellow flames billowing out its shattered windows. He heard a feminine scream drift across to him from inside the house. He heard a baby crying, far away, but wasn't certain whether this sobbing was coming from the house or not.

"No use worrying about something I can't change," his dream self said. "I better get over there and help!"

In that strange way of dreams, he heard a voice, as clear as a child's conscience, say to him from the sky:

"Live free or die."

There was no time to dwell on the meaning of the phrase. He *had* to get to that cabin! Yet no matter how hard he tried to run up the road, the house would always remain the same distance away. He slogged in vain, bogging down in snow drifts, crying out, "I'm on my way! I'm on my way!"

He fell down. His hands were frozen, and he looked down as his index finger brushed his belt and— broke off, clinking onto the ice. There was no blood.

He struggled up, his hand numb. In his heart, he knew for certain he was too late. He fell into a snow drift, and let out an inarticulate cry of despair…

He fell into another dream.

The next morning, the words "live free or die" echoed into his thoughts when he looked into his eyes in the mirror as he shaved. The phrase sounded vaguely familiar, and he made a mental note to ask Sam about it over breakfast.

Maybe it's a campaign slogan?

Sam, also dimly familiar with the phrase, did not know its origin.

✝ ✝ ✝

They flew back the next morning after meeting Lee
Royalle for Sunday Mass. They stopped in Kansas City for
the night to break up the trip, planning to give Sam just enough
time to make it back to Cleveland for his Monday afternoon
meeting.

They did not set foot on Montana soil again.

✝ ✝ ✝

Fates can sometimes shift like cars in traffic. Ellie drove
with Mel in the Durango to Hopkins Airport to pick up their
husbands. After picking them up, during the first few minutes of the ride home, the wives could tell their men were
tired and dejected after their failed attempt to find a location
in Montana.

"Back to square one," Buzz commented sullenly, holding
Mel's hand in the back seat. Christopher was at school. Markie
and Packy were in the third seat.

"I never liked the idea of Montana anyway," Mel consoled. "Where do we look next? Sam?"

"Don't ask me. I'm the one who came up with Montana.
What was I thinking?"

"Don't get down on yourself," Ellie counseled. "Maybe
you should go back again—somewhere else in the state. The
Missoula area looks promising—I was checking it out on the
Net on Saturday. They have a nice group of devout Catholics
there called the Saint Gregory Guild. They bring orthodox
speakers in and run a Catholic bookstore. It's a very good
website. I even went into a chat room with the director, a nice
fellow named Rick Vinegart. We should go back to Montana."

"No," Buzz and Sam said at the same time, with jolting
intensity.

Pardon me, Ellie thought.

That capped the conversation for several minutes. There was heavy traffic near the NASA complex. They crawled along at the end of a line of cars stretching out on Brookpark Road.

"Looks like N-A-S-A is getting out early today for some reason," Buzz observed. Locals didn't call NASA *nasa* like the rest of America. They pronounced each letter in the acronym. Nobody knew why.

"I'm going to be late," Sam mused. "Maybe I should forget about changing at the house and we could turn around and go directly downtown."

"You still have time, honey. The traffic will loosen up in a few minutes," Ellie advised.

"Look Markie, an airplane," Buzz called out, pointing to the jet taking off parallel to the road.

"Shsshh, he's asleep," Mel cautioned with a whisper. Buzz turned around. It was so.

"Oh. Sorry."

"Hair pain! Hair pain!" Packy cried from his car-seat.

The thunderous sound of Pratt & Whitneys rumbled outside. They felt it more than they heard it.

The traffic was now at a complete standstill. To make matters worse, there was a U-Haul truck in front of them. Another American family moving. Perhaps the standstill was due to an accident. The U-Haul blocked their view and ability to diagnose the situation. Buzz was uncomfortable with the silence.

"Say, El," he broke in. "You don't happen to know where the phrase 'live free or die' comes from?"

She looked at him in the rearview mirror. "Sounds familiar…" She shook her head.

"It's on the tip of my tongue," Mel piped in, looking up to remember. She had learned that phrase in school somewhere—had been required to memorize it…

"It's a cool saying, isn't it? Maybe it's from a flag," Buzz added.

"I know where it's from," Sam said suddenly, a tinge of excitement in his voice.

"But yesterday you said you didn't know. Did you remember all the sudden?" Buzz asked.

"No. I never knew it until two seconds ago." Sam half-turned to half-face his friends in the back. There was a big smile on his face.

"Sam! Tell us," Ellie demanded.

"It's right in front of you, look." He turned back, then pointed to the U-Haul. "On the license plate."

"New Hampshire! That's right!" Mel cried out. Markie woke up in the back seat. "I had to memorize all the mottos of all the states in fifth grade. You know, that Missouri is the 'Show Me' state, and so on.".

"Momma?" Markie asked groggily.

"Sorry I woke you, Sweetie," she soothed him, turning to place a warm hand on his cheek. "Go back to sleep. Take a nap-nap." He closed his eyes.

"Nap nap!" Packy mimicked.

Indeed, the truck in front of them had New Hampshire plates. "Live Free or Die," the state motto, was raised in light green on the top of the plate.

"It *is* a moving truck…" Sam led them.

"Sam, you're not suggesting…" Ellie began.

"Why not?"

"Live free or die—perfect," Buzz explained, his everyday enthusiasm sliding back into his voice like a magazine locking into a handgun. "Traffic jam so we couldn't miss it. It all fits. It's a signal grace."

By *signal grace,* Buzz meant a sign from God.

He remembered asking Our Lady for help finding a place to go before falling asleep, but for some reason, decided not to bring this up. Then he had another flash.

"And Carlton *Fisk* is from New Hamsphire," Buzz added excitedly. Every Red Sox fan his age knew that. "Your name is Fisk. Or was Pudge from Vermont?"

Pudge was Carlton Fisk's nickname.

Either way. This lined up for Buzz—and, typically, for no one else. They made confused faces.

"He was an All-Star. A Hall of Famer," Buzz added. *Can't they see it?*

"Anybody been to New Hampshire?" Mel asked, moving forward from Carlton Fisk.

They all shook their heads, including Mel.

"Then let's definitely check out New Hampshire," she concluded. The men could not follow her logic, because, being a woman, she wasn't using any. "I want to go there. I can feel it. Can't you, Ellie?"

"I don't feel anything about New Hampshire. I think of maple syrup and that movie, what was it? On Golden Pond. I hate Jane Fonda. Sure was a pretty place, though. Sam?"

"It's sparsely populated," he offered the only thing that really came to his mind.

"This is quite scientific," Ellie observed keenly.

"We're going to move to New Hampshire," Mel said again, with more confidence than ever. "I can just feel it. I can feel something in those words: live free or die."

Her verbal fierceness gave them all pause. Her *tone* gave them all pause.

"Only a fool ignores a woman's intuition," Buzz offered.

He was already all for New Hampshire. The day had started with nowhere to go, with the millennium clock ticking. Now he had a destination, a place to go—a house on a hill—and he was heading for it. Some souls are born to leap toward destiny; others allow destiny to come. Buzz was the former; Sam the latter.

Yet both Sam and Buzz were partisans of woman's intuition. They had now been married for enough years to believe this fundamental truth of human existence. Learning to love the differences between man and woman is the apex of married wisdom.

"No offense, Mel, but my own sense of woman's intuition doesn't click," Ellie admitted. "New Hampshire is drawing a blank for me."

Traffic began to move. Ellie, always an aggressive driver, saw an opening, and, intimidating a tiny Jap car with her Durango, made a spot for herself in the left lane and pulled past the U-Haul. The three others searched the otherwise ordinary moving truck for clues, as if there would be a giant "New Hampshire and the End of the World: Perfect Together" advertisement painted on its side.

Then they looked at the vehicle in front of them. It was a forest green Dodge Durango. The exact same make, model, color, and year as the one in which they were sitting.

Ellie noticed first and gulped.

"Do you see it?" she murmured hoarsely, not finding her voice. They saw it, too.

It had New Hampshire plates.

"What are the odds?" Buzz asked softly, in awe.

Sam, in character, said nothing. He prayed a Hail Mary.

Tinted glass prevented them from seeing inside the duplicate Durango.

This is just too weird, Mel thought. But she could not deny the strong positive *thing* in her heart/gut/soul about *New Hampshire*—just as she had always had a strong negative *thing* about Montana.

If she could have put a word to the feeling, it would have been: *Destiny*—with a capital *D*. The kind of destiny which spoke of divine plans set in motion before one's conception; plans as fixed as the color of one's hair. Weighed down with a universal human spiritual blindness courtesy of Adam and Eve, Mel grasped none of these insights with perfect certainty. Thus is the dark lens through which we all chart our futures. At times more light escapes through the lens than at other times.

Sometimes, to nudge things forward, the Father throws in a license plate—or two.

"I like New Hampshire," she repeated, mantra-like, surprised by her own serene confidence in lobbying the group.

"Me, too," Buzz added, feeding off her strength, virtually unaware of his own distant sense of foreboding (his male intuition, and therefore, beyond his grasp). Had *New Hampshire* been etched into his heart at the moment he had been knitted in the palm of the Creator's hand? He did not know. He could not know, he would not know—until he lived it.

The congestion had indeed been caused by the space agency letting out early.

Bureaucracies always take vacation days and half days at the drop of a hat, Buzz thought. *It's probably My Pointless Existence as a Slave Sure Beats Dying Day.*

They were out of traffic now, beyond the space agency, and Ellie, driving like Ellie, hurtled past the other Durango in seconds. She whisked around onto 210th, forcing them all to lean into their seat belts like eggs in a carton.

Buzz never let Mel drive, and here was his proof.

"New Hampshire," Ellie said softly, to no one in particular. *Live free or die. Hmmn.*

Or die.

Was she willing to die for...*freedom?*

She had never looked at it that way. Freedom had always been something she had taken for granted, so much so that she never thought about it, except in the context of license—there was that word again, in another context. The modern culture had twisted freedom into a license to kill babies. Indignation over this perversion had driven her to fight back over the years—with her volunteerism, her organizational skills, with Sam's money, with her cool zeal.

What is true freedom? What does it mean to live free?

Was freedom Lady Liberty off the northeast shores of New Jersey? Or was it Our Lady of the Rockies?

Surely Our Lady's choice had been to *surrender* freedom.

Isn't that what her fiat meant? Isn't that what Jesus' death on the cross illustrated: 'Not my will but thine?'

The old yearning for a baby came back to her now with bitter force.

I am the handmaiden of the Lord, let it be done unto me according to Thy word, Ellie echoed the very words which had brought the Incarnation into time.

Those open-ended words had placed the Christ into the living tabernacle of Mary's womb—into a living house of gold.

Surely the Blessed Mother had been willing to die for divine freedom?

She said, Let it be done unto me! Ellie thought.

New Hampshire?

Let New Hampshire be done unto me, Ellie decided now.

With this simple prayer, Ellie resigned herself to New Hampshire's unknowable portents, and, she changed her life forever.

For the group *had* to agree as a whole. From the start it had been unspoken and understood that they each had a full veto on all important decisions for this project. Their friendship had always been governed by the willingness of each member to surrender to the greater good of the whole.

"Ellie? Ellie?" Sam asked. "We're here. At the house."

She was staring at the lake from the end of her driveway. She broke from her reverie. She wondered if she had missed any of their conversation while she was in her trance. Buzz and Mel sat silently in the back seat.

"Wait here and I'll get changed in a jiffy," Sam suggested to his friends. "That way the babies will stay asleep until we drop you off in Lakewood."

"Sure thing," Buzz agreed with a hushed voice and a wink. "We'll wait."

Sam carefully opened the door, folded his body out, and in consideration of the sleepers, half-closed the car door. Ellie pressed the overhead button for the garage door opener. As she watched him stride toward the house, the most beautiful woman in Bay Village resolved to talk to him later about—freedom. He would listen attentively—then confirm or probe her thoughts.

I need to talk with Buzz, too, she thought oddly.

She looked into her rearview mirror and caught his eye. He had been looking at her in the mirror as if he had read her mind. His eyes were dark, inscrutable, beneath sleepy folds. He nodded gravely.

"New Hampshire," he mouthed silently for her to read, squinting.

She looked away from him, toward the lake, with all its fertile promise, feeling her inner yearning yet again, a dull, numb throb this time. Ellie found herself wishing for once that this irrational desire for a baby would just go away.

Let it be done unto me, grace reminded her.

✝ ✝ ✝

It was May, 1998.

Calibrated by the sun since the first man and woman left paradise, all mankind awoke, worked, prayed or didn't pray, ate, recreated, then slept. To save time, man fashioned for himself machines. He carved from wood and chipped from stone machines for farming and hunting—spears and shovels. He used a handful of materials: wood, animal skins, reeds, clay, spit and mud. Eventually he clawed his machines from below the earth—first copper, then iron.

By our time, his machines were created by other machines. Countless materials were used—plastics, chemicals, alloys. These machines did not sleep.

They bowed to no sun.

Man was proud of his machines. They freed him from the inconsistencies of weather. He stopped storing in for winter because machines kept his foods fresh, warm or cold. Few stayed on farms; now *millions* lived in cities where machines churned below, amid, and above them. For the first time, man's home was itself one humming machine. Silence ceased.

The hum was everywhere.

By this sunny afternoon in May, as Ellie waited patiently with her friends in the Durango, mankind's most important machines had again become constituted from the most common of all elements: sand—silicon.

Silicon machinery used electrons to multiply mankind's labor—but at speeds incomprehensible by the proud men careening across the ether. Words to describe the speed at which these insomniac machines flashed entered the language of the common man: *mega, giga, cyber, hyper.* He uttered these words with a casual and confident sense of unknowing.

A subtle and barely-noticed era was established in a mere three decades—a single tick on the Clock of Time. Man began recording the value of his goods and labors—in short, his money—using invisible, digital air. He discarded gold, silver, and intricately printed papers in exchange for electrons on wired wafers.

It was now the era of electron money.

While modern man slept, machines performed the tasks of thousands of men. Machines kept him warm. Machines gave him light. Machines stored and cooked his food. Machines transported him. Machines multiplied and subtracted and divided for him. Machines diagnosed and cured him. Machines paid his bills. Machines obliterated his enemies on battlefields. Machines vacuumed his children from their mothers' wombs.

When his currency became the electron, his world became one single interconnected Machine. It was no longer possible to determine who was the master and who was the servant.

Yet, for all this Machine's microcosmic grandeur, for all its mighty works and sublime deeds, for all its complexity and efficiency, the Machine lacked one glaring quality.

It could not think a single thought.

It was utterly stupid. Many billions of idiot savants whirred and beeped and grinded and sweeped—but did not think. Electrons are not thoughts. To the extent man served the Machine which served him, he was a slave to a moron. The Machine could not think—but it could be possessed. And there was a ghost in this machine—a dark angel.

A dæmon of the ether.

Plugged in, smug, and coddled in May of 1998, mankind slept peacefully while his idiot-son machines slouched toward a permanent midnight.

✠ ✠ ✠

Three weeks later, they piled into Sam's plane, children and all, and flew to Manchester, New Hampshire. They rented a minivan. They had decided to limit their search to Coos County, north of the White Mountains. Off a map, Mel had picked a town called Bagpipe in the northeast corner of the state.

"Why so remote?" Buzz had asked.

"It has a Catholic Church and a full-time priest, and a few farms for sale," she explained. "And I like the name."

She had begun her research on the Internet, then made a few calls to real estate agents, chambers of commerce, and the regional newspaper, *North Country Guardian*.

Bagpipe was located on Route 29, several miles east of the First Connecticut Lake. They met a real estate agent in Errol, a woman of French descent named Anne, who was quite professional, and they fell in love with the first farm she showed them. Actually, it was raining fiercely the first time they saw the property north of town on Dead Diamond River Road. They elected to skip it and explore four other properties first.

Late that afternoon, they went back to the first property without the agent. It was called locally the Henderson Place, even though it was owned by a lawyer from Nashua named Ned Rockingham. His father, Ned Rockingham Sr., a widower, had kept up the farm until he entered a nursing home several years earlier. Ned Sr. had died and the property was now in estate. It had been a potato farm for over one hundred years. The property consisted of three hundred and forty acres, mostly timber, on a long slope, or "swell," that eased down to a little river with no name. The top of the Henderson Swell, near the road, opened up to twenty-seven fertile acres.

Next to the road was a small Cape Cod farmhouse that hadn't seen a coat of red paint in a generation, a dilapidated barn, a potato house, and an overgrown logging road leading down alongside the tillable land into a thicket of pines and hardwoods, then to the brook, and finally back up a steep, rocky hill—really a thousand-foot mountain. Beyond the peak of the mountain, called Henderson's Leap, was a view of no man's land—to Magalloway Mountain.

On the other side of the swell, to the east, beyond the farmhouse, was more thick forest, all the way to Azicohos Lake, then more miles and miles of pristine, undeveloped timberland stretching into central Maine.

Bagpipe was the last settlement on Route 29, which abruptly turned into a gravel road a mile north of the center of town. The route stretched all the way up to Quebec, but was not plowed during the winter beyond the Henderson Swell because it degenerated into a trail.

Bagpipe was the end of the line.

Its rail spur had closed in the 1940s with the advent of modern trucking. The town had a population of fifty-seven souls, one gas station-grocery-video store, one railroad-car diner, two churches, one town hall, one part-time policeman, a volunteer fire department with a thirty-seven-year-old fire truck, and a hunting lodge named Nobles patronized by fishermen in the summer and snowmobilers in the winter. Its one factory, which had once produced leather boots, had closed in the 1960s and now stood empty, shedding roof shingles, on the north end of town.

It had been settled in the 1830s by a Scotsman named Jonathan Noble, a retired Marine colonel—a veteran of the Tripoli Campaign—who had also founded the lodge here that still bore his name. According to the real estate agent, he had coaxed well-heeled hunters and fishermen from Hartford to Boston to his lodge; some had built vacation homes—called "camps" here—and one had opened the now defunct boot factory.

Eventually farmers came to scratch hay, potato, and winter wheat farms from the few patches of fertile soil, coexisting with loggers who harvested pine, beech, or maple that covered one mountain next to another all the way to the

Atlantic coast, or so it seemed. The State of New Hampshire or the logging companies with mills in Berlin and other towns to the south laid claim to the surrounding mountains, much of which had rarely been seen by human eyes from the ground, except by the most adventurous hunters.

By the late 1800s, the famous Balsams Hotel in Dixville Notch was prospering less than an hour to the southeast. Nearby Bagpipe had siphoned off some of the rather wealthy North Country aficionados until the bust of '29. The Balsams survived—Bagpipe did not.

Now, only a handful of dairy or hay farmers were left on the three or four dirt roads fingering out from the palm of the town. Most of the farmers hadn't made a dime in the last twenty years. Rockingham Sr. had been the lone remaining potato farmer. The hilly land and short growing season were not compatible with the technology and scale required for profitable modern farming.

The Fisks and Woodwards stayed at Nobles that evening. The charming old lodge had old furniture, old beds, and no phones in the rooms. They attended Sunday Mass in the tiny wooden Church of Saint Francis Xavier the next morning. The old priest, Father Raymond LeClaire, whispered his way through Mass, including a sound but uninspiring homily; his rubrics were correct and his disposition was obviously reverent. When they saw his eyes as he raised the host at the consecration, they knew he truly believed. There were three other families and two children in attendance.

They chatted with Father LeClaire afterwards. He was friendly, but not inquisitive, and perhaps a bit past his prime mentally. They didn't ask him his age, but it was obvious he was in his eighties. They did learn that he had grown up in Bagpipe, the son of a logger, and Buzz surmised that he must have been retired to his hometown by an understanding bishop in Manchester, the seat of the state-wide diocese.

After brunch at the local diner, Norbert's, with the agreement of his friends, Sam called the real estate agent and made an offer on the property; his offer was accepted that after-

noon after one brief round of negotiation. The farm was theirs
for a thousand less than ninety thousand.

They flew back to Ohio that afternoon. The cash deal was
closed two weeks later after the deed was searched and the
land surveyed. Sam subdivided and gave twenty acres, including five acres of farmland, to the Woodwards. There was
no zoning or planning board in Bagpipe, so the matter was
relatively simple and straightforward.

Ellie began contacting local contractors to build a road,
and she and Mel began planning their homes. They decided
to abandon the farmhouse in order to build three hundred
yards into the property, about halfway to the brook, in a patch
of grazing land beyond the farmland—for the pristine view,
for the privacy, and for the southern exposure. There was only
one other farm on Dead Diamond River Road, owned by a
newly-wed couple, the Samples. Their farm grew Christmas
trees, hay, and cattle. It was three miles down the road, halfway into town. A few camps, which were not permanent resi-
dences, also shared the road.

✝ ✝ ✝

"What do you mean you don't have any money?" Buzz
asked Sam in July, on the deck of Sam's house.

"It's not that I don't have money, it's that my money is
tied up in the business and in this house," Sam explained.

He had never spoken in detail about his wealth in all the
years Buzz had known him. Buzz had just assumed there was
a million or more dollars in the Fisk bank account.

"First of all," Sam began, "most of my wealth is invested
in Edwards. Almost all of it. The value of my labor over the
past eleven years is 'stored' in the company. Until it sells, I
don't have much cash to work with.

"Secondly, Ellie has been giving away more than half my
salary since we got married. While we try to live modestly in
our Bay Village home, there are taxes and expenses there.
We take that one nice vacation every year, of course. But

most of our monthly income goes to charities. Ellie also gave away almost everything I got from my father's estate, which really wasn't much. I have a substantial sum in Christopher's college trust fund—"

"Why don't you take that out?" Buzz interrupted tactlessly.

"It's not as simple as that. I would lose much of it to taxes. I won't belabor you with the details. I have taken all my money out of the market, and between that and what I had on hand, minus the cost of the farm in Bagpipe, we can just about swing building our new house and the improvements to the property—*if and when* our Bay Village house sells. At that time, I'll have some extra to help you out with your new home, and to stock up on supplies."

This news had rocked Buzz. It would be months before the company officially went onto the market—because of something called due diligence, according to Sam. If the word spread to the general public about the probability of collapse, the economy could take a dive from one day to the next, making the sale of Edwards less likely. The Fisk house had now been on the market for almost two months with no offers.

"We'll just have to trust God, Buzz," Sam added. "I'm sure He has a plan for the money. If Edwards sells, we'll have more money than we'll know what to do with. I'm sure Ellie has most of it earmarked for her charities. If it doesn't sell, it doesn't sell. Until then, we'll just have to wait until my house sells. At least your house is already gone."

"Yeah," Buzz agreed. He had actually gotten a good price for it—one hundred and ten thousand. Just enough to build a modest little home in Bagpipe.

"Trust in God," Sam repeated serenely, putting a hand on Buzz's shoulder.

His calm faith was almost as annoying as it was consoling.

✛ ✛ ✛

In August, Buzz and Sam made two trips to New Hampshire and one to Canada to line up contractors. Buzz visited two modular home companies in Quebec, bringing rough plans Mel had created on a home-design software program. Sam found a company in Berlin that manufactured custom, pre-cut post-and-beam homes, although it would have to be assembled on-site. He began working on Ellie's plan with a consultant there.

✠ ✠ ✠

In September they finalized plans for their homes, began buying solar panels, purchased a marine-grade diesel generator, lined up a septic system contractor, and then ordered pre-fabricated basement walls from a company in Massachusetts.

In October the construction of their driveway—a gravel road—was delayed when they discovered that their contractor, a good man, was juggling several clients during his busy season, and was only able to show up half the time.

Both families soon discovered that it was difficult to find subcontractors for electric, plumbing, and finishing work. As with almost all construction work, there were unexpected delays and red tape—getting a permit from the state for their septic systems and so forth. Most of their contractors had to come from as far away as Berlin to the south (over an hour and a half drive) or from Colebrook, over an hour to the southeast. Almost all the planning had to be done from Cleveland, which caused further delays.

By the end of September, the Fisks' house had still not sold. Edwards was scheduled to go on the market in January. Buzz and Mel placed the order for their modular home, which was now due to arrive in late October.

✠ ✠ ✠

The delays with constructing the driveway, then the septic systems, pushed back the excavation of the foundations into early November. The excavation was delayed when a rock ledge was discovered underneath Sam's building site. This had to be blasted. These developments delayed the delivery of Buzz's house from the modular home company; the two-bedroom ranch didn't arrive until mid-November.

Buzz and Sam flew to New Hampshire every other week. Buzz was missing his classes and had to drop out of chiropractic school, only six months shy of graduation.

Sam began supplementing Buzz's modest income because the big man was not able to take on as many masotherapy sessions at the clinic. He and Mel and the Fisks had been missing, much to their regret, most of the Penny Parties, although the annual Thanksgiving Buzz Bowl was held without a hitch.

✠ ✠ ✠

By December they were racing the winter weather. Their new water well had finally been drilled, but they weren't able to complete the complicated cistern and water lines stretching to the top of the hill (for natural water pressure) designed by an engineer Sam had found from Concord, almost three hours to the south.

Sam had convinced the group to forego hooking up to a power line from the local electric utility; the line would have cost a fortune to bring down from the road. They were then required to locate and hire specialized electricians from Portland, Maine, to install the custom solar/generator system Buzz had designed with the help of a consultant from Vermont.

The electric contractors from Maine came and went, but the system was filled with bugs. Frustrated, Sam fired the Maine contractors. The ground froze in late December, and the problems with the electrical system made Buzz's house uninhabitable until the spring of 1999.

The road to the farm became caked with snow and ice, although it was plowed and sanded with fastidious attention by the town, which shared a giant snowplow with Errol. The Henderson Place was almost six miles from the center of Bagpipe.

Their driveway became impassible without a four-wheel drive vehicle, as snow would thaw during brief periods of warm weather, then freeze into ice. Sam traded his Accord in for a 4WD Subaru wagon, which he gave to Buzz. Sam then leased a diesel GMC pick-up through Edwards, had a plow installed on it, and left it in New Hampshire at the jobsite.

The Fisks' home had still not sold going into the winter slowdown. The Bay Village market had gone soft, and Sam's asking price, although below what he would have wanted under other conditions, appealed to an extremely small percentage of prospective home buyers.

Despite their original goal of moving to Bagpipe before the new year, both families decided to wait until summer, when Sam's new house was scheduled to be ready enough for a move-in. They spent the rest of the winter and spring in Cleveland, doing research and buying supplies, which they stored in Sam's garage. The supply list was endless.

By February, Sam ran out of cash, and they decided to wait until the house sold before making more bulk purchases. The Fisks had to wait for Sam's paychecks now.

The Woodwards were also out of extra money. They had agreed beforehand to avoid credit card or mortgage debt, just in case the millennium brought a depression instead of a collapse, and in the event that Sam's business didn't sell at all.

Buzz continued his daily research on the computer crisis. As 1998 turned into 1999, the mainstream reports on the now infamous Millennium Bug became contradictory and confusing. But the facts he found as he dug deep into raw sources on the Net confirmed his worst fears.

Despite rosy press releases and website announcements from big companies, the mandatory SEC filings and insider user-groups revealed that most companies and government agencies were missing their deadlines, falling behind, scrambling to find programmers who just didn't exist, and generally mucking things up just as Sam had predicted.

Reports from countries overseas were even more disheartening. Asian countries, already mired in a severe recession, were ignoring the problem. Russia was a basket case, as usual. Some countries in the Middle East had even announced that they would not bother to try to fix the bug until after the new year, when they could discover which systems were infected.

Numerous government announcements and newspaper reports painted people who were making conservative preparations as extremists, and cautioned Americans not to take their money out of the banks.

It was clear to Buzz that the powers-that-be feared bank runs and were doing their best to convince Americans there was nothing to worry about. He felt ambivalent about this; the status quo, and the strong economy that came with it, after all, were making it easier for Buzz to complete his preparations.

Denial is your friend, he thought sardonically, *and it's your friend's enemy.*

✠ ✠ ✠

January, February, and March passed in a barrage of planning, discussion, family life, and trips back and forth to New Hampshire. They gave up futile attempts to convince their friends that the bug was a threat. Mel even began bringing the boys over to see their grandmother on the occasional afternoon—without Buzz, of course.

As for Buzz, his attempts via phone and email to convince his daughter Jennifer about the threat proved fruitless. Jennifer was now a freshman at Gonzaga in Washington State, and had been estranged from her father since she was a toddler. Jennifer didn't practice the faith, and, poisoned by her bitter, fallen-away mother, had always considered him to be a

religious fanatic. She hadn't called him "Dad" in over twelve
years. By her lights, it was clear that his views on the millennium bug made him an *extremist, survivalist* religious fanatic.

Her mother, Sandy, lived in Florida now, happily remarried to a businessman named Joey Caprizona, a Brooklyn
expatriate who owned a sprawling Chevrolet-Subaru-Mazda-
Kia-GMC-Yamaha-SeaDoo-Lexus dealership in North Palm
Beach.

When May of 1999 zoomed around, the Fisks' house in
Ohio finally sold, and to most Americans, the world pretty
much looked exactly how it had looked in May of 1998.

✠ ✠ ✠

When Melanie married Buzz, they had tried to conceive
a child right away and Buzz had hit the target on the first try.
After Markie was born, the on-demand, all-natural breastfeeding delayed Packy's arrival for almost three years.

Mel's fertility kicked back into gear in March of 1999. It
was a difficult decision, but they decided to try to postpone
their next child in order to avoid giving birth in January of
2000. In June, despite their best efforts to learn Natural Family
Planning on the fly, Buzz hit the target again.

Mel was pregnant.

Chapter Six

The Insurance Policy

"Oh honey," Mel said. "I'm so ashamed of myself."

"Why?" Buzz asked.

They were both looking at the little red plus sign on the pregnancy test. They had decided to see what was what after cleaning the dinner dishes.

"Because I never wanted to be the kind of woman who ever regretted being pregnant."

They were standing on either side of an island counter in the kitchen of their two-bedroom apartment on the second floor of a typical 1940s Lakewood double-decker. Buzz was leaning his elbows on the counter, his eyes level with Mel's. Packy was napping in the bedroom. Markie was watching a Gumby video in the living room. Moving boxes were everywhere. They would be heading to their new home in Bagpipe in one week.

He looked into her eyes for several long moments.

She wondered what he was thinking. He hadn't shaved in three days, and his crewcut was getting a bit too bushy.

How come I don't look into your eyes like this anymore? he thought. *Does this happen to every married couple?*

There was something *powerful* about looking into his wife's eyes. Something he had forgotten.

Yes, *that* was it.

"You're the one I love," he told her plainly.

This earned him an elfin smile. She leaned over and gave him a peck on a stubbly cheek.

"I know. But this baby will come in March of next year. Terrible timing, end-of-the-world-wise."

"I don't know about that," he said, still looking her in the eyes. She looked down at her hands. "We tried to learn NFP. I still think it was the night we rented You've Got Mail—"

"Oh stop!" she gasped, then slapped him on the arm.

"Ouch. What I mean is, we were open to life, and if you're expecting, then we'll just give God the benefit of the doubt. This child is meant to be. Maybe he'll be a bishop or a saint or a carpenter with ten children who each have ten children— and by using NFP we were screwing around with his destiny. We'll just have to trust God."

"How come you always assume they're going to be boys? Trust God, trust God, trust God—you're starting to sound like Sam," she observed after a moment.

She turned and placed the plastic test-square on a shelf in the cabinet. He side-stepped the counter and snatched her arm, then spun her around, pulling her into his embrace.

"And what's so bad about trusting God?" he asked, lowering his forehead to touch hers, his voice low and intimate.

She refused to look up at him.

"Nothing."

"Come on, Sweet-Sweet," he urged softly. "Tell Dr. Buzz vhat iz dee problem?"

She turned her head, pulled out of his embrace, and walked out of the kitchen.

"I said nothing!" she called behind her, stifling tears. *He's not going to see me cry.*

He saw her go past Markie to the outside balcony.

He looked up at the light fixture on the ceiling. There was no use trying to talk when the scarlet fire was blazing.

He followed her out and found her on the wooden bench, crying silently, hugging herself. He lowered himself to the bench next to her and gave her what she really needed.

He held her, and said nothing.

They moved to New Hampshire four days later. The Fisks were set to move after the Fourth of July. Edwards had not sold yet, but the economy was humming right along, and Sam insisted that it was just a matter of time before an offer came in.

✝ ✝ ✝

It was a chilly evening at the Rocky River courts, and all the hoopsters had gone home except for two six-foot-six friends. One, beyond the foul line, was thin and lanky. The other, standing under the rim, dressed in sweats, had the well-muscled, Olympian physique of a decathlete. From afar, this herculean specimen seemed as limber as a thirty-year-old. He was, in fact, in his mid-forties, a former All-American football player.

The lanky man launched a graceful jumper with slow, perfect form. The ball clanged off the rim; the massive one, Mark Johnson, enveloped the ball into one enormous hand, then effortlessly zipped a pass out beyond the foul line to Sam Fisk, who in one smooth motion fired again.

Swish. Another pass. Swish.

"That's ten. My turn," Mark called out, keeping the ball, then dribbling past his friend as they switched positions. Mark's first three jumpers clanked off the rim.

He never did have a good shot. The ball always felt like a pebble in his fingers. Years of weight-lifting had not destroyed his coordination, but his touch was now almost completely gone. He had taken to wearing contacts to make the basket less blurry, and wore a brace on his left knee—an old injury.

He managed to sink three of his next seven. The drill was complete. The giant and the beanstalk sat down on the old wooden bleachers next to the court to imbibe the perfunctory Gatorade, sweat dripping from their brows and chins.

Mark had called Sam at work and asked for this one last night of hoops before the Fisks moved to New Hampshire. Sam had been much too busy with preparations and trips to New Hampshire to play pick-up this year. Mark, and even

Buzz before he moved away, and the Man, had kept up the hallowed tradition of summer hoops in Rocky River.

Opus Dei Bill White had retired a few years earlier, blaming an increasingly debilitating back condition. Those who remained were of course older, and a bit slower, for sure, but were still good enough on their best nights to reel off a few wins against the quicker, younger players who dominated the regular games here.

But time had taken its toll; two years ago, the Man had ended an era by abdicating his role as Rocky River Court Judge to a younger man with the unexciting and unmysterious name of John.

On some nights, a few of the other oldtimers could still be heard telling new players about the legendary team consisting of Mark, Sam, Buzz, the Man, and Deadeye Bill White. The Scaps.

Buzz had rustled them all together ten years ago, and Ellie had come up with the name: The Scaps (short for scapulars, which Buzz, Mark, and Bill always wore while playing). The Scaps had won the most exciting game in the history of Cleveland's annual charity tournament, the Revco Ten Thousand, against another legendary team from the East Side, the highly-favored Infernos, led by Cleveland hoop legend, Dante "the Italian" Curry. It seemed as if the whole city had seen the game between Dante's Infernos and the Scaps on cable TV.

In local basketball lore, the upset had been the basketball equivalent of a high school team beating the NBA Champions.

"That's Mark Johnson. He got over twenty rebounds against the 'fernos, who never knew what hit them. And there's Buzz Woodward—he shut down Curry *and* he nailed a forty-five foot bomb to ice the game!" In fact, it had been a thirty-five footer, but the distance grew with the years, and Dante had scored almost all the points for the Infernos.

"And the Man, he was the captain. Did you know he won a national championship playing football for Notre Dame?

What's the Man's real name? Boy, you *are* ignorant! Yo, *no-body* knows his real name, 'ceptin' *his mama*. Most folks don't think the Man even *got* a real name. And lemme give you some advice, snot-fer-brains—don't you go asking 'im if you wanna keep playin' on *his* courts."

Still, it had been so many years ago.

The years between your mid-thirties and your late forties were like dog years, Mark thought now.

Mark and Maggie Johnson. He the FBI agent. The other Catholic Power Couple besides the Fisks in the social group. Pioneer homeschoolers—Maggie had founded the first Catholic homeschooling association in the area, and was well-known and respected in the diocesan offices. Four children, three older girls all turning out well and a boy, the apple of Mark's eye. Mark's son Seamus was Christopher Fisk's best friend.

As Sam sat next to Mark now, it was hard to imagine that Mark's marriage had been on the rocks ten years ago, just before he met Sam Fisk. Mark had put in for a transfer to Ohio to take a less-demanding assignment in the white-collar crime unit. This enabled him to rebuild his marriage by spending more time with his wife and children, and to be closer to his boyhood friend, Bill—Opus Dei—White.

Mark was now director of the unit, and basically rode a desk. In recent years, for the sake of his family, and with no regrets, he had turned down two offers to head more important posts outside of Cleveland, effectively ending any lingering ambitions for a more successful and better-paying career.

The sun had set now, and the vapor lights were flickering on. A lone jogger passed on the path on the other side of the courts. These were two men who spent most of their lives doing, not saying. The Gatorade bottles were empty.

"How's the knee?" Sam asked finally, breaking the awkward silence.

"It's only pain," Mark said, a familiar doxology.

A minute passed. Mark stood up and stretched, keys in hand, as if to leave, resting his weight gingerly on his bum knee.

"You came to ask me something," Sam leaned back on the wooden plank behind him.

"It's about the damned computers," Mark stated.

"Are you still a skeptic?"

"Yes."

"So, what is there to talk about?"

Mark looked over Sam's head, uncharacteristically avoiding his eyes. He sat back down. There, that was better. They could both look at the court together.

"I've been hearing things in the office. You know, a lot of bureau guys are ex-military. Seals. Delta Force. Black ops. We all have contacts."

Sam didn't respond, asking *And?* silently.

"And there are some interesting conversations going on around the water cooler. Did you know the National Guard is preparing for a national deployment in December?"

"In fact, yes, I did know that." Sam nodded. "Buzz told me he read something on the Internet about a nationwide drill last month. There were official denials after leaks from concerned guardsmen. Then some kind of statement about anti-terrorism."

"That's the official version. It was purportedly an anti-terrorist exercise. Inside word says the operation was bug-driven. Tell me something, how many terrorist organizations have the resources to attack the entire United States at the same time?"

"The question answers itself," Sam replied gravely, but keeping his voice light.

There was a lull.

"Seamus is gonna miss Christopher," Mark finally said.

"You can always come visit."

"Yeah, we'll have to do that later this summer, after you get settled in," Mark replied.

Both men knew this was a script, and that there would be no visit.

"And we'll come back to Cleveland. I've still got Edwards to run until it sells. If it sells."

"Right," Mark finished.

He turned to Sam, looked him in the eye, opened his mouth, then closed it. Hesitation was not a Mark Johnson trait.

This bug has a way of throwing people off-balance, Sam thought.

"Mark, I know what's eating at you. There's still time to do something, to get ready."

"It's not that, Sam. I've been thinking about doing a few things out at the Oberlin place. Storing up a few—emergency supplies. Security items, if you get my drift."

Security items, thought Sam. *Guns. Ammunition.*

Buzz had been bugging Sam about this very kind of security item. *Mark is an FBI agent, after all.*

"You can't eat gunpowder," Sam observed sagely.

"Maybe not."

"There's always New Hampshire—"

"Maggie would never go for it. I know her. She can be pretty hard-headed..."

"Kinda like Ellie?"

"Worse than Ellie."

Both men chuckled. Maggie had thrown Mark out of the house for several months, way back when, before they met Sam.

"Besides, it doesn't make any sense for us to run off to New Hampshire. It's too late, for one thing. And what would I do for a living up there?

"The nearest FBI office is in Manchester. Then I've got Sarah's tuition at Thomas Aquinas College, Angela starts at Steubenville next year, and Meggie's thinking of going to Magnificat High. I'm going to have to mortgage the house again come fall."

So you have been thinking about it, Sam thought.

"The housing market is soft," Mark continued, starting a new thread. "Seems like more and more houses are going on the market. Makes me wonder if this bug isn't starting to get under the skin of some other families—but nobody is admitting it out loud.

"Maggie knows two Protestant families from her home-schooling group who're doin' just what you and Buzz are doin', only they're goin' to Wisconsin. Sayin' God told'm to bug out—and half their church is bugging out with 'em."

Sam noticed that if Mark talked in long paragraphs, by the end, he sometimes reverted to his clipped New Jersey accent. Buzz was the same way.

"My house was on the market for a long time before it sold," Sam stated, rubbing his chin.

"Sam, I don't know much about computers. I'm just a dumb jock with a shield, but…" Mark was lost for words.

"But it's all so overwhelming, right," Sam finished for him. "It's impossible to prepare for the end of the world."

Mark affirmed Sam's statement with silence. Then, after a minute, as if finishing the thought, added, "But that hasn't stopped you and Buzz from trying."

"I'm pretty sure that what we're doing is what God wants for us," Sam explained. "Our spiritual director has been in our corner since day one. God has helped us find a perfect location, and helped us build two houses under difficult circumstances.

"You have no idea how hard it is to build up there. Contractors are scarce, and the few good ones are extremely busy during the short summer season. We're not going to finish half the project we planned.

"Even so, I am certain that what we're doing is *not* what God wants for everyone. I'm sure of it. It's too hard. Maybe He got me and Buzz started on this…this project," Sam always had trouble *naming* what they were doing, "…because I could afford it and because Buzz was just crazy enough to go along with it. You know how he is. Ellie and I wouldn't dream of doing this without him and Mel."

Ask him now, his instincts told him. Sam decided to go for it.

"And we could sure use a guy like you with us."

Sam, a subtle businessman, relaxed, waiting with an inner knowing that silence was his ally at this juncture.

"I appreciate the offer," Mark didn't hesitate. "But no can do. Maggie. I just…can't."

"I understand. I've accepted that our friends can't follow us. I was shortsighted enough to think some of you might last year, when we got started. Moving is just not God's plan for most people because it's not practical. You've got those tuitions, eh? Ellie still thinks you and the Pennys and the rest are going to come up to New Hampshire at the last minute."

"Maybe we will," Mark Johnson offered with a tone that was almost—sweet, but really wasn't. Guys like Mark were definitely not *sweet.*

"You know that's not true. If that were true, you would store your food and security items in Bagpipe, not Oberlin."

On rare occasions, even with friends, Sam felt it hard not to call a spade a spade.

"Fair enough. Then what happens next?" Mark asked.

"Trust in God."

"That's a given."

"I used to think so," Sam said. "Now I'm not so sure. I haven't been a Christian as long as the rest of you. This whole project has been the greatest thing that's ever happened to my faith, Mark, it really has been. Things have always come easy to me—at least that's what Buzz always tells me. And he's right. I've lived a charmed life—success, great friends, the most beautiful wife in the world, an incredible son, and after meeting Buzz and you and Bill, finding the true faith. What a surprise! But Buzz is right: it all came to me. There has been no struggle, no cross."

Now it was Mark's turn to wonder and wait. Sam was not given to monologues. *This damned bug sure brings out things in people,* Mark thought now.

"For the first time," Sam continued, "I've run into something that won't come to me. Buzz may or may not have told you this, but I don't believe we'll survive up there. Maybe our odds are better if things do fall apart, and maybe Christopher, Mark, and Pascal will have a better chance of making it, but I don't expect to live. As sure as I know the crash is coming, I'm also sure I'm too soft to make the adjustment to the new way of life—"

"—you're not soft, Sam," Mark interrupted.

"Let me finish," Sam said firmly.

Mark was taken aback. He had never heard this kind of passion in Sam before—or heard him come so close to raising his voice.

"Sorry, man," Mark apologized.

Ten years ago, Mark might not have apologized, and he knew it. *The difference between thirty and forty?* his ego piped in.

"No, I'm sorry," Sam returned to his normal tone. "And I forgot what I was talking about."

"You were talking about a new way of life," Mark prompted, his curiosity truly piqued.

"Yes, a new *paradigm*. Or, as Buzz calls it, the new springtime. He eats, sleeps, and breathes this stuff. Whatever you want to call it—a new way of life, a new paradigm—I simply do not believe that I am…suited. But this realization is also forcing me to trust God, not myself, in order to be able to accept the unknown. My prayer life has never been stronger. Ellie and I are totally committed to our spiritual director now.

"Maybe that solves the mystery of why God would want us to leave everything behind. He's not asking this of us in order to insure that we survive—instead, God wants to find out if we *can* leave everything behind.

"Some days, the whole project is so overwhelming that I wish I were in your position; you don't really have the professional or financial option to get out of Dodge."

Sam took a deep breath.

Mark reflected that there were still levels of Sam Fisk that he had never seen before. This realization jolted him. It became all the more difficult to write off Sam Fisk's ideas so casually, as Bill White had done—although Mark was sure that Bill would never dream of doing so in front of Sam.

Mark picked a long strand of grass at his feet, and plugged it into his mouth.

And when I picture what this town would be like after three weeks with the water off and the lights down and the grocery store shelves empty, I wish I had your options, Sam.

Mark had seen firsthand the underbelly of society during his early years in the bureau. Except for Jimmy Lawrence, another cop, Mark doubted that his friends, even Sam, had any clue how ugly it could get under the right—make that *wrong*—conditions.

Maybe Buzz. Buzz had the imagination. Folks in the suburbs feared the residents in the inner cities. No one said that out loud, of course. But it was there. Agent Johnson had not the slightest doubt that the now placid—yet amoral—residents of the suburbs would turn into animals under desperate conditions. Law enforcement, rightly or wrongly, gave most of its practitioners a healthy respect for Original Sin—and an experience-based skepticism that Joe Sixpack would magically morph into Mother Teresa when the toilets stopped flushing and his stomach rumbled.

"So what happens next?" Mark asked again. Both men sensed there was one more mystery left in this conversation.

"Let's pray, brother," Sam suggested, sitting up.

He wrapped his arms around the basketball on his lap. Mark folded his hands and bowed his head. Sam waited for him to begin. In any group of men, even a group of two, Mark was the unspoken leader.

"Saint Michael the Archangel—" Mark began, and Sam joined in, "—defend us in the day of battle. Be our safeguard against the wickedness and snares of the devil. May God rebuke him, we humbly pray, and do thou, O Prince of the Heavenly Hosts, by the power of God, cast into hell satan and all the evil spirits who prowl about the world seeking the ruin of souls. Amen."

"Amen," Sam repeated, opening his eyes. *Trust in God.*

Their man-to-man was over.

Or was it? They stood up, and walked to their vehicles. Mark had an old pick-up truck—*de rigueur* in Avon Lake, where he had moved four years earlier to be able to afford a larger house on a full acre—and be a bit closer to Oberlin, where he planned to settle for his retirement.

After they started their engines, Mark rolled down his window and signaled for Sam to do the same.

"Yes?" Sam asked.

"I was just thinking—where do you park your plane?"

Sam thought it was an odd question.

"You mean the company plane? Uh, usually at Burke Lakefront."

Mark nodded. "Ever think of parking at the county airport out my way?"

"Not really; that would be too long a drive from Edwards. I usually leave from the office. Why?"

Mark smiled. "Just curious, is all. Give my best to Grace Kelly."

"And give my best to Maureen O'Hara," Sam rejoined.

It was an old exchange, even though Maggie, an Irish brunette, only remotely resembled O'Hara.

They drove their separate ways.

✝ ✝ ✝

Later that evening, Mark called Bill White.

"What are you doing for the new year?" Mark asked his boyhood friend.

"I'm going to be at my firm's annual New Year's party. I've invited all my customers."

"No preparations—stocking up food, that kind of thing?" Mark pressed.

"The Red Cross has advised that we keep three days of food on hand. I already have that in my apartment. Have you been talking to Buzz again?"

Mark paused at the other end of the line.

"Sam Fisk thinks it's going to be pretty bad," Mark said finally.

He respected both Bill and Sam's judgment.

"Sam is a talented businessman, Mark. No one's sharper. But he's also a computer guy at heart. He's a lot like my programmers here. Computer guys always think of everything in terms of computers. There's a lot more to the world than computers. Sam's belief in the ability of a computer glitch to cause a collapse is equal to his ability to make preparations.

"My agency is compliant—and has been since February. Nothing to it. Most of my clients say they're getting ready. I'm expecting nothing more than the equivalent of a winter storm. My biggest client owns the largest stock brokerage in Cleveland, Mark, and he's forecasting a boom during the first quarter of 2000. But we've been over this before."

"What about Buzz?" Mark asked.

It was a pregnant question. They had both known Buzz since before Mark moved to Cleveland.

"I love Buzz. We all do, but—"

"But?" Mark asked.

"But Buzz is a UPS driver. His head is filled with wacky theories he reads off the Internet. I hate to put it that way. But he believes every end-times prophecy and Marian apparition that comes down the pike."

"That's just not fair. I've never heard Buzz say that this computer thing is part of the end times. Nor Sam. They both think it's a secular problem."

"Yes, it is a secular problem; that's my point," Bill reiterated. "But he and Ellie, too—both have a *predispostion* to expect tribulations and calamities from all their books and tapes—you have to admit that.

"American know-how is going to take care of it. We invented computers; we'll fix them. Europe isn't far behind, no matter what Buzz's Internet crazies tell him. They handled the Euro conversion just fine."

Bill White's clipped tone revealed that he was growing impatient—a bored professor repeating a lecture he had given before.

"Thanks," Mark finished. "I just needed to hear some common sense. So you're throwing a New Year's party?"

"And you're invited, of course. A millennium only rolls around once every thousand years. Ha ha." This passed for a joke in Bill White's book. "And one more thing," Bill added, as if a thought had just struck him.

It hadn't. He had been waiting for the right moment to lower the boom on Mark's doubt: "The pope has promised that the New Millennium will bring a new springtime to the Church. That's hardly compatible with a computer bug causing the end of the world. Don't you think the pope would warn Catholics if something that horrible was coming?"

"Is that really his job? Didn't you just say it was a secular problem?" Mark countered, imagining what Buzz might say. "John Paul II is hardly a technology guru. And I read the pope's encyclical on the New Millennium. You're quoting him out of context. There were a lot of *if-then* statements in that document, if memory serves me correct. *If* Christians live according to the faith, *then* a new springtime will come.

"Seems to me the Holy Father was throwing down a challenge, not making predictions," Mark continued forcefully, finding words that surprised himself. "And I read on Catholicity.com that Cardinal Ratzinger, when asked about the encyclical, commented darkly that pruning is necessary before a flower can bloom. Maybe what Sam and Buzz are doing is avoiding some of the worst parts of the pruning."

His articulate reply caught Bill White off guard, as revealed by the long pause which ensued.

"I'm following the pope when it comes to the year two-thousand," Bill said, as if this explained all, as if it showed clearly that Sam and Buzz were patently wrong.

You didn't counter my points, Mark thought.

Mark had merely been playing devil's advocate, hoping that Bill would lay his doubts to rest. This conversation was not going as planned.

"Sure. Me too," Mark agreed, but with mental reservation. *The pope has not discouraged Catholics from making prudent preparations.*

A Bible passage, a proverb, floated into Mark's consciousness. *The prudent man sees danger and flees, while the fool does nothing and perishes.*

"Good," Bill replied, letting it go. "Look at the clock; it's nine-forty-five! I've got to get some sleep."

Bill's clockwork habits were the stuff of legend. If he wasn't brushing his teeth by nine-forty-seven, his world would collapse.

"Good night then, buddy," Mark responded.

Bill or Sam? Which one should I believe?

After the phone call, Mark went into Seamus's bedroom and stood over the bed, watching his son sleep. Mark shook his head, prayed a Hail Mary, then went into his own bedroom and jostled Maggie's shoulder.

"What is it?" she yawned.

"I want to make some preparations at the Oberlin place," he told her.

"Have you been talking to Sam about that computer thing again?" she asked drowsily.

"Yes."

"Fine. Now let me go back to sleep," she pleaded.

✦ ✦ ✦

He hedged his bets. Mark Johnson was not a man of means. His preparations cost a few thousand dollars, which he took from his modest rainy-day savings, figuring that this damned bug might just be the Mother of All Rainy Days.

He did not feel it was necessary to involve Maggie, who was busy. His preparations, which he weighed alone and carefully, consisted of the following things, which he accomplished with a few hours of research on the Internet, a few phone calls to place orders, six Saturdays of work, one phone call to Buzz, and one phone call to Sam.

He first installed a big lock on the door and on the lone window in the cabin—it wasn't more than a shack, really. Pouring buckets of water on the roof, he located three leaks, then added a few tar shingles that didn't quite match color.

Working with Seamus, he roughly insulated the little cabin with fiberglass which he left showing. In the paper, he found a small woodstove at a housesale, and jerry-rigged the installation at the fireplace that was already in the cabin.

He squirreled ammo (shotgun, handgun, hunting rifle), and four gold coins (which his father had given to him as birthday gifts, one each year, during his four years at the Academy) under the floorboards. He picked up four used but clean fifty-gallon drums from a fellow who owed him a favor. He filled one with gasoline and "life extender" additives (he already owned a small Coleman generator, which he moved to the cabin). He filled the other three drums with sacks of rice he procured at Sam's Club.

The most expensive item, a new handpump for the abandoned—but still active—well on the property, required the help of the Man to install one Saturday. (After discovering on the Internet that handpumps were backordered at most suppliers, he called Buzz, who knew of a Catholic supplier in Vermont who had set aside a few extras for "good families.")

Mark stocked in his small game traps, most of his hand tools, and some basic over-the-counter drugs such as aspirin and cough syrup. A thermometer. Hydrogen peroxide. Two new hunting knives of the highest quality. Two sets each of new thermal underwear from Lands' End for himself, Maggie, Seamus, Meg, and Angela. He didn't plan for Sarah to come—

she now had the last name of a bright young Catholic fella in California.

Two cases of "six day" holy candles that he had asked Father Dial to bless. Six heavy-duty scapulars from the Rose Scapular Company. One crucifix. One framed photograph of the Little Flower. Waterproof matches. Four twenty-gallon propane tanks—he already owned a small propane camp-stove. A cast-iron dutch oven (which, to the uninitiated, looked like a huge skillet with a matching cover). He mentally set aside a place on the shelf and floor for their winter boots, sleeping bags, and heavy coats, which he would keep at the Avon house until—and if—he came here.

He spent one weekend foraging in his woods for fallen timber, cutting it with his chainsaw, then splitting it himself, teaching Seamus along the way. This gave him four cords, and he had two additional cords of seasoned oak delivered; he covered these with old plywood sheets.

A case of twelve small Tabasco sauce bottles from Sam's Club. A split case of six bottles of Maker's Mark and six Jameson Irish, respectively (a man had to have his pleasures after all, and heck, they would make great trading items in a pinch).

A Bible. A new *Catechism of the Catholic Church.* His paperback volumes of Butler's *Lives of the Saints.* His favorite Catholic novel by that guy from Notre Dame. Salt. Olive oil. Sugar. Honey. He didn't go overboard on these latter items—a few bags or bottles each. Finally—again from Sam's Club—a few cases of soup, canned fruit, and canned vegetables to break the monotony of the rice. Powdered milk. Three large cans of Chock Full o' Nuts coffee.

The cabin already had an unplumbed sink and a few pots and pans in the rough cabinets. A rickety old bunk bed, built into the wall. He added two portable, inflatable camp sleeping cushions. He went out back and poured a few sacks of lime into the privy, which hadn't been used in years, and was in surprisingly good condition.

When the time came, he planned to bring his security items, his family, the winter apparel, and ten fresh cartons of Marlboros for trade.

The cabin was set off from the road, unseen behind a stand of trees. He had cautioned Seamus to work in silence when outside, praying to Our Lady. The driveway had been overgrown with weeds for years, and he was careful to drive off to the side of it when it was practical. He thought better of adding new "No Trespassing" signs at strategic locations. Except for the new shingles, which he had carefully dusted with a few handfuls of dirt, the handpump (which was around the back anyway), and the newly-stacked cords of wood, the cabin did not appear all that different than when he first began his project. He had talked to no one about it except the Man, Buzz, and Sam.

On a chilly afternoon in September, when he was finished, he called Sam for a favor. Sam promised to do his best to comply.

"What have you been up to out there?" Maggie asked him one time.

"Just buying a little insurance."

Chapter Seven

The Man

At Saint Philomena's, the Man received the Sacred Host on his tongue, then swallowed it before returning to his pew. He knelt, bowed his bald head, and offered his Communion for Buzz, Mel, and their children. Then he began an intimate dialogue with the God in his stomach. The thin black man had been offering up Communion as an act of gratitude for Buzz since his conversion, the year the big lug had brought him back to the practice of his faith.

The Man looked up at the priest, and smiled. It had taken a hard head to crack a hard egg.

For that is what the Man had been: a hard egg. A hard case. A private, broken, silent wind passing over the earth, alone but not lonely, before Buzz barged into his insulated world in the summer of 1993 to pop open the carbonated top of the universe.

Before Buzz, the Man had lived a solitary life. The last of seven children, born to a forty-five year old mother who died of diabetes when he was in second grade, he had not known his own brothers and sisters as peers, but rather as distracted surrogate parents. His next-oldest sibling, his sister Irene, had been eight years older than him. His mother's death had hardened his father's heart—perhaps the already sullen boy had reminded Cameron Smith of his wife. His mother had taken the boy to Mass on Sundays, even perhaps prayed the Rosary as he fell off to sleep in her arms (the Man's memory was fuzzy about this), but Cameron, a devout agnostic, had not continued the practice of the faith after her death. As the father goes, so go his children.

The Man was the odd-brother-out who had dropped off the face of the earth thirty-some years earlier when he had taken that scholarship to Notre Dame. His three brothers and one sister still living resided in Virginia, retired after careers in the civil service and middle-class bliss. Except for his father, none of them had bothered to contact him in years, though Irene had tried with Christmas cards addressed to the hotel (where he worked as a concierge) before she died in an auto accident in 1974. Her funeral had been the reason for his last trip to Virginia.

The Man remained unmoved by his alienation from his family. Only his father, a judge in Alexandria, had stayed in touch with the occasional phone call before his death from complications related to Parkinson's in 1990, the year the Man had won the Revco Ten Thousand Tournament with Buzz and Buzz's friends. The funeral had taken place on the day they won the tournament, and he had missed the funeral to honor his commitment to the team.

He was not uncomfortable with his seemingly obsessive desire to be alone—a desire that had simply been a part of him since, well, since before he could remember. In grammar school and high school, he had been the contented loner. At college—oh, that had been easy, he a black at a Catholic college dominated by middle-class white kids, further insulated by the mystique of his athletic prowess. And because he was black and did not go to church then, his dorm rector at Howard Hall and the other students had assumed he was not a Catholic. In fact, his kinfolk were Catholics in Maryland since before the United States was born, from a rare line of black freemen who traditionally worked as accountants and clerks for Catholic merchants in a state founded by Catholics seeking religious freedom. In the areas surrounding the capital, there were still many Catholic churches attended by generations of blacks—segregated, to be sure, from their prejudiced white brethren right up until the 1960s.

Why had he played sports? Certainly not for the camaraderie. For the love of the game, yes. The field of play was the perfect arena to simply be what he was without complicated relationships or intimate communication. Even before Notre Dame, on the many athletic teams on which he participated, he had formed no friendships, cemented no bonds.

Ara Parseghian had recruited him because he could cover and tackle and return kicks—not because he was popular with the other players.

On the field of play, the others interpreted his aloofness as the mysterious coin of leadership—and perhaps it was—but the Man accepted his *aloneness* as simply the way he was designed. A fact, not a choice. Leadership, that impossible-to-define virtue which caused mighty struggles for most men because of their desire to be liked or their desire for power, had been a natural, easy skill for the Man, who cared nothing of the esteem of men. Leadership was a requirement for order and a sure path to winning, and in situations where lesser men failed to step up into the breach, the Man had led.

The same attribute had made him the undisputed king and judge of the Rocky River courts in the early Seventies after he settled in Cleveland and landed the position with the elegant Stouffers Hotel. A few of the white boys on the courts, trying to be hip in that pathetic way whites mimic black lingo, had taken to calling him the Man.

"You the man!" they had clamored after his patented, silky drives.

The mystique of the nickname had evolved slowly and organically, and it suited him and made his life easier. In the early years, a few others had known his real name, but all had forgotten it by the time Buzz had shown up as a high school player. The nickname allowed him to indulge in the one social passion of his life—athletics—yet remain an island unto himself.

Besides Buzz, there had been one other to pierce his private world. The girl. The shy one at Notre Dame. Maryann O'Connor, who shared her own *aloneness* in common with him—and his passion for history. She was a frumpy brunette with bad skin and thick glasses. She had a fashion sense that barely rose above a partiality for comfortable gray sweat pants and indistinct shirts. Her only apparently bold assertion of personality had been her habit of wearing the brown scapular outside of her blouse. (He never discovered that wearing it next to her skin caused rashes.)

Starting when he was a freshman, and she a sophomore, they had read books in silence near and often next to each other every night in the history section in the library. During his freshman year, they had merely exchanged looks. During his sophomore year, they began to say hello to each other; and she, to grace him with a delicate, bashful smile, as sweet and disarming and to his surprise—welcome—as a warm day in February.

It was obvious to him that she did not know or care that he was a key player on the only team that mattered on campus. By his junior year, they were sharing books, and had two classes together in the history department, even though her major was the little-known General Program of Studies. GPs, as they were known amongst themselves, studied the seminal texts of Western Civilization using the classic seminar method.

For all he knew, she had no friends either. She was an intensely devout Catholic. She suggested he read Cardinal Newman, Belloc, Augustine, Waugh , Knox, Chesterton, and others. Before Maryann, as a student of history, he had taken the Catholic Church for what it plainly was: one of the dominant forces of human history, if not the premier force of history in the West, at least since the time of Constantine.

Because of Maryann, these great minds proved to him that if there was one true Church, it had to be the Catholic Church because it alone could demonstrate a direct line to Saint Peter, along with a purity of doctrine unchanged for two thousand years. He just didn't get Chesterton. The Man was incapable of understanding paradox. The skepticism of the modern philosophers, such as Sartre and Russell, also had their appeal. He returned to his histories.

Yet briefly, because of her books, he had gone to one confession, and then to Mass several times (alone, of course). He had dimly anticipated that something might "happen" to him during Mass, but nothing did, even after Communion.

He felt nothing. His senses, ever alert, registered no difference in himself or his environment. He fell back into an indifferent, if open-minded, agnosticism. She did not know of his brief fling with the sacraments because he never told her. She graduated after his junior year, went to Stanford for her masters, and he never contacted her again.

During his last conversation with her, on a sunny day in May, standing next to the Father Sorin statue on the North Quad, she had told him a curious thing—and the only personal thing said between them in three years: "I love you. I'll always pray for you."

Then she stepped forward, eyes watery, to give him a hug that he returned half-heartedly, embarrassed. She stepped away, looking down.

"Good luck," he had replied.

Sometimes, when he picked up Chesterton or Belloc or Augustine, he remembered her words. What kind of love had she meant? Boy-girl love or soul-soul love? Or both?

He would never know on this earth.

He had not loved her—at least not in those ways.

All these years later, he realized, with Jesus in his belly, that he had been destined for a life of solitude and prayer, probably as a religious, and that his neglect of the faith as an adult had closed that option. Perhaps he had even been meant to be an abbot.

He would never know in this world.

Today he was retired, fifty-one, earning a modest income from the money he had saved after decades of working at the hotel. His outwardly social career had been another clever way to hide his true self.

The Man was not aloof with the customers, of course, but his relationships with them, even with patrons who had known him for decades and fancied themselves "in" with him, had been strictly professional. His smiles were cool. His warmth was studied and directed toward the goal of service. He was in their worlds but not of them. The history books which lined his little home not far from Saint Philomena's Parish—these were his true companions.

Before Buzz, history, populated with its epic and tragic characters, seemed more real to him than his very self. There they were, these heroes and villains, in black and white, *on paper.* They had *been.* By their very deaths, the figures of history had become *real.*

Then came Buzz…

✛ ✛ ✛

It was 1993. Late August. Soon the Rocky River courts would shut down for good as the sun leaped lower across the evening sky and the chill winds of autumn descended from Canada into Cleveland. Another successful and satisfying reign as the Man of the courts was drawing to a close.

Dante Curry, the legend from Little Italy who had played the heavy-favorite-foil to the underdog Scaps three summers earlier, slowed by a severe knee injury which never quite mended, had taken to playing with "the Team," as Buzz's band of players was now known on the courts, making this summer's hoops all the more fun. Even Tim Penny, who was cautious about spending time away from his family, showed up for a run now and again.

The Scaps had worn on the Man's resolve for solitude all summer, but he had held them off again without too much effort. Mark Johnson, Buzz, Sam, Bill White—they kept inviting him to their summer gatherings after the games at Tim Penny's, or to Mark Johnson's place for beer, or over to Buzz's apartment for videos.

The Man really liked that Mark Johnson. The Man and Mark shared that unique thing—that leadership quality, that *I-don't-give-a-damn-because-I'm-moving-forward-and-you-can-follow-me-or-get-the-hell-out-of-my-way* quality.

Yet despite turning them all down, for the first time in his life, if only for the summer on the courts, he began to associate with these other men as equals, and he looked forward to seeing them for the games.

But he did not accept their invitations. His refusals became a ritual unto themselves. He politely declined, then walked alone to his Oldsmobile and drove home.

Then, dammit, Buzz had followed him home one September night without him knowing it, and discovered where he lived. Two months later, the Man opened the front door on a chilly Sunday morning in November and found Buzz reading his *Plain Dealer,* sitting on the wooden Adirondack chair on his porch.

"How did you get here?" the Man had asked, with not a bit of anger in his voice.

"I drove," Buzz replied, not looking up from the Sports Section. "Can you believe the Cavs lost again? They should trade Ferry."

"I don't follow the Cavs. May I please have my paper?"

"Sure thing," Buzz replied, handing it over. He had his beloved Pepsi with him—a whole six-pack.

"Thank you, Buzz."

The Man took the paper and closed the front door without a word, smile, or grimace. Buzz stayed on the front porch for two hours that Sunday, even though the Man ignored him. What was he supposed to do, call the police?

Buzz returned the following Sunday, at seven in the morning, reading the sports before the Man awoke, sipping Pepsi.

"Those pathetic Cavs," he said. No *hello.* No *Can I come in?* "Lost again. Ferry barely even plays."

"I don't follow the Cavs. May I please have my paper?"

"Can I keep the Sports Section?" Buzz asked. "It gets pretty boring out here with nothing to read. And have you noticed that Pepsi and Coke don't taste the same since they switched from sugar to corn syrup? It's a conspiracy."

The Man easily held off a smile. *That is true about Coke and Pepsi. They taste awful without sugar. Buzz, you really are a one.*

He took the paper, but left Buzz the Sports Section. Buzz stayed for three hours. The Man watched him out the corner of his eye through the lace under-curtains from the kitchen as he ate his Cream of Wheat. When Buzz was done with the paper, he left the porch briefly to get a religious book from his car. The Man spied a picture of the Mother of God on its cover.

The next Sunday—same thing. Buzz berated the Cavaliers. The Man let Buzz keep the Sports Section again, but did not speak to Buzz or invite him in.

When the Man left his house to jog or run errands in the car, he did so via the back door, and did not greet Buzz as he pulled his car by the front porch.

The fourth Sunday, Buzz didn't show up. The Man was relieved—and vaguely disappointed.

On the fifth Sunday, there he was again. Reading the Sports Section.

"Cavs won!" Buzz shouted. "Mark Price had thirty-seven points!"

"I don't follow the Cavs," the Man said.

"Why do you keep telling me that? I never said you did." *That does it. Now I'm pissed.*

"What are you doing on my porch every other Sunday?" the Man asked.

"Reading. Praying. Do you mind?"

"Yes. I have to ask you to stop doing this. You obviously think you're going to wear me out and convert me or something. Don't think I don't know what you're like. I like playing hoops with you, Buzz, and some of your friends are very classy," the Man paused, letting the small insult—*that Buzz was not classy*—sink in, "but you can't come here like this. I'm not interested."

"Interested in what?" Buzz asked back, grinning.

This boy is a lunatic. The Man sighed.

"Just go home, Buzz. And don't come back."

"Okay," Buzz conceded, his smile fading. Then, "But can I finish the Sports Section before I go?"

The Man didn't answer. He calmly closed the door. Buzz only stayed for an hour that Sunday.

And promptly returned the following Sunday, the Sunday before Christmas. Reading the paper, bundled up in a heavy winter parka, his hands enclosed in woolen mittens. It had snowed the night before, and it was windy and cold.

When the Man opened the front door, he was genuinely surprised to see him—more surprised than on the first Sunday. Buzz was having trouble negotiating the paper with his thick mittens.

"Good mornin'!" Buzz shouted. "Cavs didn't play last night. Jacks won, though."

"I don't follow the Lumberjacks." The Man's voice was colder than the current wind.

"Me neither," Buzz said. The Lumberjacks were the local minor league hockey team. "Hey, I'm getting tréjà-vu, you know, tréjà-vu—that strange, eerie certainty that I've done this exact same thing twice before."

The man ignored the Buzzian observation or joke—or whatever it was.

"You've got to stop doing this," he said plainly.

"No, you've got to stop doing this," Buzz replied, looking up, looking the Man in the eye for the first time since this bizarre chess game had begun.

"Don't make me call the police," the Man said with a slight snarl, throwing back his shoulders.

"Then call them. I'll come back next week."

"I could get a restraining order."

"Then do it."

"Calling my bluff?" the Man asked.

"Yes. So call the police. Bring the full weight of the court system to bear on your best friend in the world. I'm going to finish reading my paper."

"You're not my friend. And that's *my* paper," the Man snapped, lightly hopping from foot to foot. He was standing in his pajamas behind the screen door.

"Then I'm going to finish reading *your* paper," Buzz said in a sarcastic tone. Then to himself, looking at the paper again, under his breath, "I couldn't name three players on the Lumberjacks."

"Have it your way."

The Man closed the door. And called the police. As if impelled by a sixth sense, Buzz leapt from the porch like a cat and drove off in his battered Festiva a minute before the cruiser arrived.

"Do you know this man who came to your porch?" the officer asked a few minutes later.

"Yes, I play basketball with him."

"How long have you known him?"

"Almost ten years. But not socially."

"Has he made any threats or violent actions towards your person?"

"No," the Man replied honestly.

The officer made a sympathetic boy-people-can-be-weird face. "Then call us if he trespasses again."

Buzz showed up the following Saturday, the day before Christmas. The Man didn't open the door. He called the police first. Then he came to the door, wearing a coat.

"Hi!" Buzz greeted him cheerfully, as if he had been invited over. He wasn't reading the paper. He stood facing the Man at the door.

"I've called the police again. Would you please leave? I'm going to get a restraining order next. Please, stop doing this."

"You stop doing this," Buzz replied once again, genuine sadness in his voice.

"Stop doing what?"

"You know exactly what."

"Spell it out for me," the Man insisted, ice in his voice.

"Shutting me out. Shutting everybody out."

The Man didn't reply. He opened and closed his mouth.

"When the police come," Buzz continued, "you're going to have to tell them to arrest me."

The Man thought about this.

"What do you want from me?" the Man asked.

"Right now, a cup of coffee—I'm freezing. And somebody to hang out with on Sunday."

There was a childlike honesty in Buzz's voice. He did have a way…

…and the Man found himself being—swayed.

"What about your friends?" the Man asked.

"They've got families. I want to hang out with somebody like me. Another loner—"

You don't know the meaning of loner, the Man thought. *Or do you?*

The police cruiser pulled up behind Buzz.

"Police are here," the Man informed him, keeping his poker face.

Buzz heard the door of the cruiser opening, and the sound of the police radio popping, but didn't turn around. The Man looked over Buzz's shoulder and recognized that this was the same officer as last week.

"Well?" Buzz asked.

"Excuse me, sir," the policeman asked the Man. "Do we have a problem here?"

Buzz turned to half-face the officer, who was now at the bottom of the porch steps.

"Hi," Buzz said with a pleasant smile and a wave, then looked back to the Man. *Hail Mary, full of grace, please let the Man save face…*

There was a long pause.

"No, officer," the Man replied. "We're just fine. Sorry to bother you."

He saw Buzz break out in a triumphant, joyful smile—
ear to ear, forehead to chin.

"Are you sure?" the officer asked again, looking at Buzz
carefully.

Scanning for a weapon? the Man asked himself.

Why did I call the police? It's only Buzz, for Pete's sake.

"No, we're old friends. We're okay," the Man said with a
rare smile.

"Okay. If you're sure." The officer returned to his car.

"Come on in, Buzz."

"Thanks."

Buzz walked in the door, and noticing the boots and shoes
on the floor nearby, took off his own boots.

The Man's home was a study in simplicity and durability.
A heavy-duty set of matching couch and easy chair. A large
Philco television with a cherry cabinet—obviously many
years old.

Books everywhere in solid, cherry or darkly-stained oak
bookcases. Browns, blacks, soft yellows, with a touch of orange on the patterns of the heavy curtains. When the Man
bought something, he bought sturdy. He bought traditional.

"I don't have any coffee in the house," the Man explained
gruffly.

"That's okay," Buzz said, pulling a small bag of beans out
of his coat pocket. "Brought my own java. I know you don't
drink coffee."

"How did you know that?"

"Don't tell me that in all these years you've known me,
you haven't noticed that I just know things about people?"
Buzz replied, his coat off now. "Where do I hang this?"

"Give it here."

The Man hung the coat on a hanger in the front closet.
Buzz noticed there were four other jackets neatly arranged
there, and a black fedora with a white band resting alone on
the upper shelf.

"I thought I was immune to your famous gift," the Man
observed before turning to face Buzz.

"Nope. I know all about you," Buzz answered.

"You do, do you?"

"Yup."

The Man made no reply.

Buzz followed him into the kitchen. The Man retrieved his percolator from a cabinet and gave it to Buzz, who began to put together a pot of coffee. The Man decided to break his routine—what the hell—and began to scramble eggs. He poured them on an old, perfectly-cured cast-iron skillet.

They ate breakfast in silence. Buzz read the Sports Section. The Man read the news.

Forty minutes later, Buzz thanked him for breakfast and left.

He came back every Sunday through February, and they shared silence and the newspaper. On the first Sunday in March, Buzz arrived to find a pot of coffee made with his favorite brand—Eight O'Clock—ready to go.

On the second Sunday in March, Buzz mentioned that there was confession at Saint Phil's after the noon Mass.

"And you want me to go?" the Man inquired skeptically.

"Yeah. We could argue and talk about it for months on end, and you could start calling the cops again, or you could just skip the silent mystery man thing for once and make it easy on me and just go."

"How come you're so sure I'll go—now or ever?"

"I'm not. I'm just throwing underwear against the wall and seeing if it'll stick. Well, then again, I am *pretty* sure. I've seen the books on your shelves. There sure is a hell of a lot of Chesterton in this house."

"And some C.S. Lewis," the Man pointed out.

"You're a believer."

"Intellectually," the Man conceded.

"You're a believer," Buzz repeated, boring in on him with his sleepy eyes.

The Man looked away. This was unusual for him during their rare conversations.

A believer or a coward, the older man thought. *An old coward.*

The conversation ended. Fifteen minutes later, when the Man reached into the closet to get Buzz's woolen Red Sox jacket (with leather sleeves—a Christmas gift from Sam and Ellie years ago), he also grabbed his own coat, then drove in silence with Buzz to Mass at Saint Phil's. The Man didn't receive Communion, but afterwards he went to confession— for five minutes.

"That was fast," Buzz remarked in the car on the way back to the Man's place.

"Bless me, Father, for I have sinned," the Man suddenly repeated, jolting Buzz. "It's been twenty-six years since my last confession. I haven't gone to Mass during that time, and I've been a pride-filled loner who has rejected my own family and alienated every person who has ever been a friend."

"Bet that threw him for a loop," Buzz commented.

"He asked me why," the Man offered. Things were suddenly—loosened up—inside himself. This was certainly different. Unlike his confession during college, *something* had definitely *happened.*

"You don't have to tell me," Buzz said. "But I'm dying to know."

"I told him I didn't know why I was that way. He asked me a few more questions, but there's not much more to say. Then he absolved me."

"Can I ask you something?" Buzz asked.

The Man paused. They were at a red light. Buzz turned to look at him.

"Okay," the Man replied.

"Would you put this scapular on?"

Buzz pulled it out of his pocket. It looked old. In fact, it was almost five years old.

"It's the same one Donna offered to you at the Revco Ten Thousand. You didn't want to put it on then. She's been praying for this day for four years. She asked me to bring you back home the day she went into the convent."

The Man stifled an urge to cry. Still, his eyes watered up pretty darn quick. Buzz looked back to the road to preserve the Man's dignity—but he still held up the scapular.

The Man took it.

✛ ✛ ✛

Buzz came to visit the following Sunday—and also "dropped by" for dinner on every Tuesday and Thursday.

He knew above all things that the Man was a creature of habit. Sometimes he brought Mark Johnson along. The Man started—only by a relative measure—to open up in conversation, and even to enjoy himself. He found that Buzz was well-read—surprisingly well-read—and could actually hold a decent conversation about history. At first, besides Sister Regina—formerly known as Donna Beck—who received the glorious news of the Man's reversion by letter from Buzz, only Mark Johnson knew about this turn of events in the Man's life.

Buzz, Mark, and the Man became friends. Mark began stopping by on Tuesdays with Seamus for dinner. Sometimes, they all watched a video which Buzz would rent. Only westerns or war movies.

The Man fully returned to the practice of the sacraments, and began methodically working his way through the classics of Catholic spiritual life: the Little Flower, Saint John of the Cross, Saint Francis De Sales, Saint Teresa of Avila. He took to the devout life with ease, and soon had Father Dial as his spiritual director. In Father Dubay's timeless work, *Fire Within,* he found a key that unlocked the door to the endless Trinitarian universe within and without—the basics of contemplative prayer.

He remained on the surface as he was below the surface— quiet, private, reserved—a bookworm. But now he was a *Catholic* man of solitude. He was the only person in the world whose presence actually calmed and quieted the hyperkinetic

Buzz Woodward, so Buzz also drew a peculiar strength and peace from their friendship.

The following summer, when Bill White invited the Man over for a gathering with the Johnsons after a run on the courts, the Man shocked him when he accepted the invitation. Soon he became a silent but reassuring regular at the Penny Parties, where he insisted on being called Hal. His name was Hal Smith. His odd nickname was reserved for the courts, he explained, not for friends. They all still couldn't help but refer to him as the Man when he was not with them.

After all, Hal Smith *was* the Man. And now he was *their* man. And Jesus was *his* Man.

And so it came to be that it was the Man who suggested to Buzz over Sunday breakfast the following summer that he might-maybe-should consider starting something up with that little redhead friend of Marie Penny—Melanie O'Meara.

"She's too high-strung for me," Buzz scoffed.

"That's what you need," the Man replied.

"But she can't stand me."

"She doesn't know you. Give her a try. You're both lonely. You're both, uh, different."

"You meant to say *crazy,* didn't you," Buzz said with a firm certainty, sipping his coffee.

The Man didn't reply.

"I'm just not ready to get married again," Buzz continued. There was a long pause.

"His ability to delude himself is amazing," the Man observed to his newspaper, shaking his head.

But later, during the wedding and reception, the Man grinned endlessly, like a proud father, and bragged to one and all (after several glasses of wine) that he had played the matchmaker.

And that is how Buzz helped save the Man's soul, and, later on, how the Man came to save Buzz's life.

✢ ✢ ✢

In the months before Buzz and Mel moved up to Bagpipe, Buzz frequently tried to convince the Man to move up
with them. Their last conversation was the most frustrating
of all.

"You mean you *believe* that the bug will turn the lights
off but you *still* want to stay in Cleveland?" Buzz asked.

There was a serenity—a down-home holiness in the Man's
voice when he explained. "Buzz, you can run, but you can't
hide. God is everywhere. He is here in Cleveland, and He'll
take care of me. This is my home. I understand that you're
doing what you think is best for your boys. But God has made
it clear to me that He wants me to stay here."

Buzz didn't exactly hate it, but it was annoying how the
people he converted became holier than he was by a factor of
ten. These few years later after his conversion, the Man was
fasting three days a week, attending daily Mass, teaching a
night course in contemplative prayer at Saint Phil's, and spending two hours a day in prayer before the Blessed Sacrament.
It was known that he was considering entering the Trappist
monastery in Utah where he spent his vacations every winter.

"So God told you, huh?" Buzz almost taunted. "Maybe
my kids need you up in Bagpipe. Did you mention that to
God?"

The Man closed his eyes.

"You're praying right now, aren't you?" Buzz was surprised by the bitterness in his voice.

They were sitting on the Man's porch. The Man did a funny
thing—something that would have amazed Buzz and the Man
himself in the old days.

He reached over and took Buzz's hand.

They watched a beat-up Caddy filled with Puerto Ricans
cruise slowly up the street.

"It's understandable that you're all nervous about leaving
your friends behind, Buzz. You've been keyed up lately. Moving is stressful. Have you been losing your temper with Mel
again?"

Buzz nodded.

The Man had become a spiritual director of sorts for Buzz over the past five years. How the tables had turned.

"The devil works through our weaknesses," the Man explained. "You've been under spiritual attack."

"From every direction," Buzz conceded. "All our plans in Bagpipe have been disastrous. The water system is screwed up. The electric generator is always breaking down. I'm not a potato farmer. Mel is dreading the move.

"It's sinking in now that we're really, truly leaving. This computer thing really sucks. I thought you, or maybe some of our friends would follow us up. Instead, the Dow breaks ten thousand and the gravy train just keeps-a-rolling. People think we're nuts. Sometimes I wonder myself."

The Man gave an understanding nod to the street.

"What about Sam?" the Man asked. He took his hand away.

"He's like you. The perfect saint. He expects to die up there. I thought the whole point was to try to survive."

"What about you?" the Man asked.

"I'm not ready to die."

"We don't always get a choice about things like that," the Man observed.

"What are you, friggin Gandhi? You ready to die for your people? Like the people in this neighborhood give a rip about an old black guy like you?"

The Man laughed. He laughed every once in a while now.

"You'd be surprised. There's plenty of saints in this neighborhood. You're a racist, Buzz Woodward," the Man chided.

Buzz let that drop.

They sat together for a while, then made their good-byes. The Woodwards were leaving the next day. The moving van had already taken their furniture, and they were staying with the Fisks.

"I love you, Hal," Buzz said as they hugged on the porch, wondering. Because he believed that he might never see his friends again, he was finding it easier to tell them he loved them.

The man was like a black stick of muscle. Skin, bones, and muscle.

"I love you too, Buzz. Thanks."

✝ ✝ ✝

A week later, the boxes were everywhere in the Fisk house—big ones, wardrobe boxes, little book boxes. The new owners were coming the day after tomorrow. Christopher was asleep. It was past three in the morning, and Ellie was startled when Sam found her looking in the full-length mirror in the bathroom.

"Whatcha doin'?" he yawned.

She turned and he saw the tears in her eyes, and he fully awakened into concern.

"Crying," she told him. *About the children I'll never have.*

"Jittery about the move? Second thoughts?" he put a hand of long fingers on her cheek and gently rubbed a tear with his thumb.

"That's right," she lied.

"Is there anything I can do to help you?" he asked, innocent sincerity in his voice, searching her eyes.

How this made her love him all the more.

"Make love to me."

He pulled her to himself, then took her back to the marriage bed.

Chapter Eight

The Disaster

The Fisks and Woodwards spent the rest of the summer and fall trying to fix up the "disaster," as Buzz referred to their homestead in Bagpipe. They eventually got the generator/solar/battery system working, but were unable to set up a wind turbine as planned because they ran out of money.

By the time Sam's company was sold to a gigantic British firm in late October—with the money due in December after the lawyers got through—it was too late to apply his millions to the farm and the town. The proceeds from the sale of the Fisks' home and what was left over after Sam cashed in Christopher's college fund had just about covered their costs. Sam took to telecommuting—providing consulting advice to his old company for a relatively modest salary.

Buzz's efforts to plant a garden proved frustrating. His tomatoes and other vegetables died—something to do with the soil acidity, or so the locals told him down at the diner. They had managed to install decent wood cookstoves, and with a little hunting around, Buzz found a hand-pump for the extra well that got drilled in September. They had managed to order enough bulk food to feed fifty adults for a year—wheat, rice, beans, and lentils packed in plastic buckets stored in the Fisks' basement.

The bright spot of the whole endeavor for Buzz was Markie. Never had Buzz spent so much time with him. Buzz realized that his long hours studying and going to classes at night in recent years, with large amounts of quality time for

Markie only coming on weekends, had cheated the boy out
of a proper relationship with his father.

Now, for the past six months, Markie had a chance to hang
out with his dad and Sam and Christopher during their many
outdoor and indoor projects, chatting away, fetching tools and
hugs all the while. In stature, the tyke had taken after his
mother—a slight build with sandy brown hair, and freckles
in abundance. He had nothing like the rounded shoulders and
thick thighs of his father. His knees were wider than his thighs.
Big daddy had taken to calling him "my peanut."

Packy was still breastfeeding—and monopolizing Mel—
so Markie ate up the attention from his father. Every week-
day, Buzz woke him early, dressed him, then took him to Mass
and breakfast in town. As he loaded him into the Festiva,
Buzz never failed to be amazed by his tininess. Markie barely
weighed more than Packy, though he was longer and much
more coordinated, of course, than his impish younger brother.

Markie was earnest, not impish, and filled with spiritual
insight. *Even my son is holier than me,* Buzz often mused.

"Daddy, can I ask you sumthin'?" little Markie would always politely begin after Mass, holding his father's hand as
they walked down the breathtakingly sparse main street of
Bagpipe toward the diner.

After so many years in Cleveland, with its big Midwest-
ern sky, Buzz was still not visually adjusted to having a pine-
covered mountain dominate every angle and view. Bagpipe
resembled a pioneer town in Alaska more than a quaint New
England hamlet. There were no carved wooden signs and
antique shops here, or bustling tourists from New York and
Connecticut running around looking for genuine maple syrup
and lobster doodads for the mantelpieces (though Norbert's
did sell plastic, moose-shaped key-chains, which hung on a
faded cardboard display next to the register).

"Sure, Peanut," he would complete the doxology. "Fire
away."

Markie would always wait for the Fire Away, then, making believe that he had a gun in his free hand, he would make

shooting motions and noises. Exhibiting a genetic gift shared by four-year-old boys worldwide, his gun-sounds were precise and lifelike. This never failed to crack Buzz up. Then, after the laughter, the question would come.

"Daddy, do bad guys always go to hell, like that bad guy in that movie?"

"Which movie?"

"High Moon." Markie meant *High Noon*.

"You mean Frank Miller."

"Yeah, did that bad guy Miller go to hell?"

"I don't rightly know. God told us not to judge."

"But he took the wide road, so he has to go to hell," Markie observed.

Buzz paused. The Gospel today had been the one about the road to hell being wide and well-travelled.

Markie continued, "And the road in the town was wide. There were four guys on it. The policeman—" he was referring to the character portrayed by Gary Cooper, the marshall, "—he took the narrow road to the barn. He was holy."

"That sure makes sense. But maybe the bad guy didn't go to hell."

"You mean he got grace?" The kid was quick.

"Yeah, maybe the bad man asked God for mercy right before his heart stopped beating."

"Good. I prayed for him."

"You did?" Buzz said, touched. It was a teaching moment. "Markie, you realize that movies are make-believe, don't you? Frank Miller never really existed. He was just an actor."

"Of course I know *that*," Markie replied. "But it's never a bad thing to pray. That's what Mommy says."

Buzz rubbed his mini-crewcut affectionately.

That's right, kiddo.

They came to the door of the diner. It was eight-thirty, and warming up. Father LeClaire would be along shortly. He had breakfast here every day, too, right after Mass, and sometimes sat and enjoyed Buzz and Markie's company, repeating the same stories about his youth over and over. Buzz didn't know many locals yet, except for the plumber-farmer, Tommy Sample, who had worked on their homes, but he was getting to know the good Father.

"Yeah, maybe he got grace," Markie said, screwing his eyebrows, speaking with the gravity only a four-year-old can muster. That *Me-and-My-Dad-Agree-So-It's-True* tone.

"Daddy?" he asked again.

Buzz grunted, and reached down to lift his peanut up over the big curb and carry him into the restaurant.

"Daddy, were you ever a bad guy?" Markie asked.

He was so small in Buzz's arms. Buzz thought of what was coming and was frightened for him.

"A long time ago. Before I met your mommy. But never as bad as the guy in the movie, Peanut."

"So you got grace."

"Sure did," Buzz reassured him with a big smile, then a kiss on the neck as he pulled the door open, bell ringing. "God gave me a whole boatload of grace. Then He gave me you."

Markie looked his father dead in the eye, uncorked a joyful smile, then buried his head into Buzz's neck and hugged hard.

✛ ✛ ✛

In November the telephone rang and everything changed. Mel was in the kitchen, trying once again to bake bread in the woodstove now that it was cold enough outside to run the temperature up inside. She wasn't doing very well. It was taking forever to form a lump of dough and flour into a recognizable loaf.

Buzz was outside splitting wood with a hand-axe, while Markie watched, when the phone rang.

"Woodward Bakery, how may I help you?" Mel mugged into the handset.

"Er, this is Sister Regina," the nun on the other end of the line said uncertainly. "Perhaps I have the wrong number?

I called information for this number. I would like to speak with Buzz Woodward…"

Mel laughed.

"You must be Donna! Oh, I'm sorry, I mean Sister Regina. This is Mel, and yes, Sister, you've got the right number. Buzz is outside splitting wood."

There was a relieved pause. "Have I called at a bad time?"

"Not at all."

Another pause.

"Sister?" Mel asked.

"Yes?"

"I thought you weren't allowed to make phone calls? I mean, I've been hearing about you for years from my husband, but you've never called us before."

"This is…an unusual exception. I feel like I know you, Mrs. Woodward—I've been praying for you every day for five years. Buzz sent me a photograph from your wedding, and although I do not have it anymore, your face is etched in my mind."

The sister's voice was husky—like her stocky build. Mel's impression of Sister had been gleaned from photos Buzz kept of her from her pre-convent days.

"Please call me Mel."

Mel felt awkward. From the way Buzz, Sam, and Ellie talked about her, even though they had only seen Donna twice in person since she entered the Poor Clare Convent—and both those times separated by a screen—Sister Regina never seemed more than a doorway away, as if she were in the other room, waiting to come in and join the conversation. For Mel, who hadn't really known the former Donna Beck, she was a ghost. A person who had passed on to another world.

Plus, there was always the shock of hearing the voice of a contemplative. They had an alarming way of sounding, well, normal, as Donna—er, Sister Regina—did now.

"And thank you," Melanie continued. "We really need the prayers. And we pray for you every night during our Rosary. Things have been so crazy around here. Buzz calls this the

Bagpipe Disaster Area—" she heard Sister Regina laugh, "what with the stock market crashing last week, and stories in the papers about people clearing the shelves at Sam's Clubs, the new banking laws—the whole country is jittery, even up here."

"The computer bug," Sister explained matter-of-factly.

"Yes, the computer bug."

There was a pause.

"Maybe I should be talking to you instead of Buzz," Sister suggested cryptically.

"I'm all ears," Mel stated quickly.

"Do you know what an extern is?"

"Yes, that's the nun in your convent assigned to do tasks that require interacting with the outside world."

"Then I don't need to explain. I have been assigned as a temporary extern for my monastery by the Mother Abbess. For a special assignment. That's why I need to talk to Buzz. I need to ask him—to ask both of you—for a big favor. I might as well ask you first, and let you explain to Buzz, then you can pray and decide. I need for you to present my request to Sam and Ellie, too."

"Are you coming to visit?"

"No, that is not possible. The phone will have to suffice."

"Then shoot," Mel blurted.

Her curiosity was growing and she wondered if using the word *shoot* was somehow impolite. She left the dough on the counter and sat down at the kitchen table. "I'm ready."

"Well…" Sister Regina paused again. "Where to start? Okay, well, a few months back, Sam took the liberty of ordering an elaborate solar-electric system for the convent. You understand—for just in case. It has arrived. And by the way, thank you for the wheat. We bake our own bread, so if we need to set something up for the poor during the…troubles, we'll be able to do our part.

"But we have no idea how to set up these solar panels. There are boxes and boxes here of wires, batteries, special light fixtures—something called an inverter—plus these large aluminum frames, and the panels. We have no idea if the frames go on the ground, or the roof, or what.

"We've tried calling local electricians, but with all the craziness going on, they're all booked up, and the fellow who helps us with our maintenance is afraid of, uh, messing up the system…and…"

"And you need some advice?" Mel asked.

This was becoming interesting. Neither Sam nor Buzz had mentioned donating solar panels to the Poor Clares. One of a thousand details that had fallen through the cracks.

"We need more than advice." Sister paused again. "This is not easy for me to ask, but I might as well come right out with it."

Is she requesting this under obedience? Mel asked herself during Sister Regina's ensuing pause.

"Do you think that Sam or Buzz would be willing to come back to Cleveland to help us set up the system?" the nun continued. "Mother believes that if the computer problem proves to be serious—" *serious,* a euphemism for so many possible outcomes "—then we'll need the lights for the public Adoration Chapel. For the people who will be coming to us at all hours. For the…bread lines and the kitchen. This is so weird even talking about these kinds of things."

Mel took a deep breath. "I'll ask Buzz."

"Don't feel obligated to do anything. You and the Fisks have been so generous to us over the years…"

"Sister, I don't feel obligated. It's just with the airlines announcing special schedules starting next month, the mandated slowdown of the factories—"

"Look, maybe you shouldn't ask them at all…we can forget this phone call…" Sister backtracked.

Mel felt like a selfish heel. But in the pit of her stomach, she felt the same call of destiny she had felt when she first saw the license plate with the words *Live Free or Die* during the traffic jam near the NASA complex in a time that now seemed like another world in another lifetime.

"Please don't worry about it, Sister. I'll talk to them. Oh! My bread is burning! Could you hold on?"

Mel put the phone down on the table, then rushed to the oven and pulled open the door. Smoke poured out. *Arrrghh!* The bread inside was a blackened brick. She went back to the phone.

"Sister? You still there?"

"Yes, I'm still here."

"Let me call you back after I talk to Buzz and Sam. And could I ask you for a favor?"

"Shoot," Donna said.

"Could you pray for my parents? They haven't spoken to us in months. And for Ellie's father—"

"—Bucky."

"Yes, Bucky. He's been very cold to Ellie since she moved away. He thinks the computer problem will amount to nothing."

"I understand completely. To be honest, I also have some questions about it. But praying is my job. Maybe if nothing serious happens—" there was that word again "—Ellie'll be able to patch things up with her father next year."

"I hope so, Sister. I hope so."

On the monitor, Mel heard Packy begin to stir from his nap. "I've got to pick up the baby. God bless."

"God bless."

✢ ✢ ✢

Sam was thrilled to hear the news about the solar-electric equipment. During a meeting at his kitchen table that evening, he explained how he had ordered it in June, offering to pay triple the retail price if it could be delivered before the end of October. A savvy supplier in Nevada had set aside a few systems in order to gouge well-heeled customers. Sam was happy to be gouged. Such preparation-oriented products had long since become back-ordered beyond the millennium. Buzz was seeing used woodstoves owned by denialists (the majority who believed that the bug would not cause long-term problems) offered on Internet auction sites for up to five times the price of new stoves (which were also extremely difficult, if not impossible, to find). Millions of people were now vying to purchase tens of thousands of items.

"It's a long drive, but I'll go to Cleveland," Sam offered. Christopher was sitting next to him.

Ellie instantly got that familiar, troubled line in the center of her forehead. "No way. You're terrible with electric."

It was true. For all his talent with computers, Sam was an awful electrician.

And, she thought selfishly, unable to control her emotion, *I don't want you down there so close to the date turnover.*

"Then Buzz should go," Mel offered.

"Yeah, I'm the man for the job," Buzz confirmed. "If, as Sam says, it is the same system that we have here, I'm confident I can set it up, especially if there's no generator involved. It will take several days, maybe a week. I'll drive down and be back before the Feast of the Immaculate Conception. That way I don't have to worry about the airlines if there are any delays."

After so many projects on their homestead coming in late, or not coming to completion at all because of delays, screwups, and lack of expert help, the group simply assumed there would be delays in completing the system in Cleveland.

"I should be back in a week," Buzz finished.

"What if martial law is declared and they don't allow you to drive back?" Ellie asked.

She saw the look of concern on Mel's face. *So it's okay for Buzz to go, but not Sam,* Ellie's conscience chided.

"There's been no hard evidence of that kind of thing happening before the date change-over, despite rumors on the Internet," Sam interjected. "The government wants to keep people calm—and rightly so. They barely avoided panic when they were forced to restrict cash withdrawals last week. The last thing they need is more panic.

"If they start restricting travel, the country would grind to a halt and people would really get nervous."

"At this point, I don't think we can guess or assume anything," Buzz observed keenly, elbows on the table, folding his hands and tapping the tips of his index fingers.

He looked at Mel.

"Are you sure you're okay with this?" he asked.

"No," she told him honestly. "Of course my heart wants you to stay here. But my head thinks you should go. It would help a lot of people if the lights stayed on at the convent. A lot of people are going to head toward the Poor Clares when things go rotten."

Buzz nodded gravely. "What do you think, Chris?"

They had taken to asking Chris for his advice. Partly because they wanted to draw him into their plans as the millennium approached, and mostly because he often had interesting insights. It was Chris who had successfully lobbied his father to install a second well with a hand pump a few months earlier as a backup to their primary well, which depended on an electric pump.

"Could any of your friends in Cleveland help out, Uncle Buzz?" Christopher asked. He pronounced each word clearly, and had a calm, even delivery—just like his father.

"Hey! The Man is a pretty handy guy," Buzz mused enthusiastically. "I think he might even know electric. And I'm sure Mark could help me set up the frames on the roof. That's a great idea, Chris. I'll call them tonight."

"If you can get help, then you'll get back here faster," Ellie added, still feeling a little guilty.

"We've still got a lot of preparation to do up here," Mel said. "Right up until the new year."

They all nodded. Wood to split. Woodstoves to cure and grow accustomed to. The snows had already started, and the day following a storm, it was often impossible to get to the end of their driveway, much less to town, without Sam's snowplow. It seemed as if every project, large or small, took two or three times longer because of the weather. Painting a wall could be set back a whole day if Buzz was forced to drive to Berlin to get paint supplies in bad weather.

"Right," Sam summarized. "So we're all agreed. Buzz leaves tomorrow. Buzz, you get that system set up, give our love to Donna, get back fast. We'll hold the fort for you up here in the meantime. Let's see, today is November 29th. With any luck, you'll be back by December 5th or 6th."

Sam had never gotten out of the habit of referring to Sister Regina as Donna.

"Sounds like a plan," Buzz seconded.

Ellie nodded and reached for Christopher's hand under the table.

Mel stifled an urge to throw up. She was showing now— already having switched to her fat-pants. It struck her as strange that she would feel nauseated now, for her morning sickness had abated in October.

Maybe it's not the baby, a prophetic, not altogether pleasant little voice told her. *Maybe it has to do with Buzz. Maybe he won't come back.*

She shrugged it off, rose from the table, and excused herself. She hurried to the bathroom, knelt before the toilet, and dry-heaved twice.

No way he won't come back. No way, she reassured herself. *It's not like the transportation systems are shut down.*

The feeling passed by the time she returned to the table, and she wrote it off as nerves.

✝ ✝ ✝

On an unusually warm, late fall day, Buzz pulled into the parking lot of the Poor Clares on Rocky River Drive and looked at the large building in front of him. It was a self-contained dormitory, church, kitchen, laundry, and garage all wrapped up in one, with additions and improvements implemented over decades.

Ten years earlier, Sam and Ellie (before Sam's conversion to Catholicism, Buzz remembered now) had donated most of the money required to expand the adoration chapel, which was, in effect, three churches in one—one for the public, and two, hidden from view, for the sisters. The nuns would attend Mass in a second chapel off to the side of the public chapel, and spend most of their day in prayer in a third chapel—a mirror room opposite the public chapel, whose center wall shared a monstrance containing the Sacred Host which could be viewed from either side. Buzz noticed that the newer red bricks that made up "Sam's Addition," as he always thought of it, were almost faded enough to blend in with the older part of the structure.

Beyond the building, on the other side of twelve-foot walls of ivy-covered brick, there were five acres of well-manicured grounds, with trees and paths and lawns and gardens, which the sisters maintained themselves and used for recreation and outdoor prayer.

It was almost noon. He was dog tired, and his eyes burned when he held a blink closed. The drive from Bagpipe had taken three extra hours due to bad weather in Vermont and western New York. He had been traveling for twenty-seven hours, including a short stay at a fleabag motel in a forget-table town off I-90 between Rochester and Buffalo. There was no cruise control in the Festiva—its odometer had clicked past the two hundred thousand mile mark on this trip—and his right leg was stiff from hour after hour of holding down the gas pedal.

He jumped out of the car, and spent a few moments stretch-ing. He had called the Man and Mark Johnson from the road, and they were due to arrive in the afternoon—earlier if Mark could get off work. Mark had also invited Bill White to help. Bill had promised to come by in two days—on Saturday, even though he was still of the opinion that the bug was much ado about nothing.

He looked up and saw *her*. She was practically running toward him, her brown habit billowing as she came around toward the parking lot.

"Donna!" he cried out. "Uh, Sister Regina!" he corrected; he hurried toward her.

When she reached him, without thinking, he grabbed her in a bear hug and pulled her off the ground, and began twirling her around.

"Buzz! What are you doing!" she protested.

She hadn't figured on this much affection. She hadn't been embraced by a man in almost a decade—not even by her father during his visits.

He was oblivious to her protests.

"My little one! My little one!" he repeated over and over again, finally lowering her to the ground.

He was surprised how light—and solid—her figure, muffled beneath the flowing garment, had felt.

She glared at him, looking up at the windows of the building to see if they had been seen during his uninvited frolic.

"What?" he asked her, clueless. Then it dawned on him. "Did I break some kind of rule? Am I not supposed to hug you like that?"

She rolled her eyes. "Buzz! Oh, forget it. There is not exactly a rule. Nobody goes around bear-hugging Poor Clares, is all, so they never wrote down a rule to forbid it. Just forget it—and don't do it again. No offense. Hey, it sure is great to see you."

"Sorry, kiddo," Buzz said contritely.

His contrition washed quickly back into delight at seeing her again. It had been five years since he had seen her last. He had introduced Mel to her after the honeymoon—and that time there had been a screen and ten feet between them.

"You've lost some weight," he said. "You're almost skinny now."

"I really haven't paid attention. The life here has been good to me. We don't own a scale, so I have no idea what I weigh," she explained.

It struck him how she sounded the same as before she went into the convent. It was as if he expected a contemplative to forget how to have a conversation. But there was also something radically different about her.

Her eyes. They shined. They glowed. They jumped out at him.

The two old friends stood awkwardly, looking at each other. She lowered her gaze.

"Your eyes are…striking," he told her.

It was as if the Lord was looking through her at him.

Maybe He's doing just that. He didn't exactly feel comfortable with this thought.

"That so? Well, so are yours."

"How so?" he asked.

"Yours are…the same. I've noticed that it's normal for people's eyes to change as they get older. It's so seldom that I meet people I used to know, and when I do, it jumps out at me. My mother's eyes have changed—so have my father's, my sister Cindy, too. Yours haven't."

"Is that good or bad?" he asked.

His arms felt like useless branches at his side. This was a weird conversation, but then again, that's what they had always specialized in.

She looked up and smiled. "Who knows? This is a bizarre conversation."

"Sure is—just like old times!" he practically shouted it.

She turned serious.

"I miss you," she said, looking down again.

"I miss you, too, little one." He shuffled his feet.

Now *she* felt like hugging her old friend, her Buzz.

"So how is Mel? How are the boys?" she asked, raising her eyebrows. "Did you bring pictures?"

Her tone was much lighter now.

"No! Shoot. And I meant to bring some." He would regret this gaffe even more later on.

They made small talk. On the concrete path next to the front steps of the building, he described Mel and the boys to her in technicolor. He told her about the homestead, Sam, Ellie, and little man Chris.

Eventually, he asked. "So what's next?"

"Follow me to the garage." Keys materialized from secret folds in her habit. Buzz half-expected to see her yank out a solar panel, too.

"All the boxes are there," she said as she started walking. "Afterwards, I'll introduce you to our new Mother Abbess. She's looking forward to meeting the infamous Buzz Woodward."

✝ ✝ ✝

It turned out that the Man knew a lot about electric. He had the knack, and had rewired his own home, and done work for the hotel. Except when she initially showed them around the monastery and the various rooms where they would work, and consulting with them about various details, Buzz did not see much of Sister Regina.

Sister Francesca, a civil engineer in her former life, had been assigned to maintain the system, and as the final step in the installation, she would be taught by Buzz how to maintain the batteries and program the inverter. He had been doing these tasks for the system in New Hampshire since May. During her infrequent breaks, Sister Francesca, a slight woman with a flat, open face reflecting her Polish ancestry, came to watch them build the system.

Refilling the deep-cycle batteries with distilled water and learning how to program the inverter, which converted AC power into DC power, and vice versa, while regulating the flow of electricity into the batteries from the panels, was the most complicated part of maintenance.

In Mark's garage, Mark and Bill fashioned a fairly complicated box out of plywood and two-by-fours to house the array of batteries, and brought it to the monastery on Saturday morning.

The purpose of the box was to capture dangerous hydrogen gases emitted during the charging of the batteries—and to vent these gases to the outside of the building. By late

Saturday afternoon the Man and Buzz had the inverter hooked up. They wired various controllers for the solarvoltaic panels in the basement, where the battery box would also remain. Then they installed the batteries inside the box.

They planned to install the sixteen solar panels on the back roof of the convent—three stories high—on Monday. The trickiest part of the system was installing DC wiring from the basement to the kitchen, the common room, and chapels. This was followed by attaching super-efficient DC light fixtures.

The advantage of the solar system was simplicity. Once installed properly, it had no moving parts to wear out, and the batteries could last for up to seven years if they were well-maintained. The disadvantage of solar power was that it did not produce much electricity by modern consumption standards. The sixteen-panel system Sam had purchased would produce only four or five kilowatts per sunny day. The sisters would be fortunate to be able to minimally light the critical parts of their physical plant for twelve hours a day with that much power.

The more sun, the more power. On cloudy days, the panels would produce practically no electricity. The purpose of the batteries was to store whatever power the panels did produce. Two or three cloudy days in a row could run the batteries down to a preset shutdown level.

Buzz explained to Sister Regina that a normal "off grid" solarvoltaic system would often be hooked up to a generator as a back-up for filling the batteries. The convent did not have a generator, and it was now virtually impossible to buy one. Even so, he pointed out, a generator was only as useful as the fuel needed to run it. There just wasn't enough time to find, integrate, and store a significant amount of diesel, propane, or gasoline for a generator anyway.

Buzz called Mel every morning and every evening, giving her updates, and they marvelled together over how the project was going so smoothly and remaining on the tight schedule. Buzz stayed at the Man's house, visited the Pennys and his other friends at the end of the day, and went to the 6:45 Mass at the Poor Clares every morning.

Things were going so swimmingly that they decided to skip work on Sunday because it wasn't necessary. On Sunday, he attended Mass with the Man at Saint Phil's, and by appointment, went to Father Dial for his last confession before the millennium. He and the Man spent Sunday with the Mark Johnson family, hanging out with the kids, and talking collapse. On Sunday afternoon, Mark took him to his cabin in Oberlin, and Buzz was impressed with its simplicity and practicality.

Mark took Monday off from work, and along with the Man, came to the convent early in the morning. Mark had rustled up some scaffolding from his friend, a contractor named Joe Kemp. They all deemed it safer than climbing ladders to the french roof, which, fortunately, had a relatively flat pitch. If all went well today, Buzz would be on the road in time to return to New Hampshire for the Immaculate Conception holy day, his favorite day of any year.

By noon, they had set up the scaffolding, and had run the power cord for their drills through a window in one of the dormitory rooms, which the Poor Clares called cells. Sister Regina had plugged the cord in a cell wall herself. She taped the other end of the cord to a pole, then lifted the pole out the window to the Man, who was on the roof.

"Excellent weather!" Buzz shouted to the sister from the private grounds below. It was crisp, around thirty-eight degrees, clear, and sunny. No wind. The best anyone could expect for a Cleveland December.

"Of course!" Sister Regina shouted back down. "We've had thirty-two Poor Clares praying for good weather ever since the panels arrived."

After Mark and the Man installed the fairly elegant aluminum frame designed to hold the panels on the roof, they spent nearly two hours carefully bringing the panels up the scaffolding, one-by-one. The panels were about forty pounds each, but bulky, constructed of multiple layers of photovoltaic cells sandwiched between glass, with stainless steel frames. If they dropped one and broke it, the entire system would have to be reconfigured.

From the ground, Buzz lifted a panel to Mark, which Mark then passed up to the Man. Then they all climbed a scaffold level, and repeated the process. Once a panel was on the roof, Mark and the Man secured it to the frame, slowly and carefully. They climbed back down for the next panel.

This is going too well, Buzz thought, alternately praying Hail Marys and the Saint Michael Prayer under his breath. *Thank you Jesus!*

Mark and the Man negotiated the roof like mountain goats. Buzz, who had always been afraid of heights, was happy to let them do the roof work, though he was itching to see their handiwork.

It was an easy task to wire them all together once the final panel was installed. Because the sun was shining today, each panel would be "live." That is, generating electricity. The voltage was mild. It was the combination of all sixteen panels working together that made them effective.

The final step would be to turn on the inverter, see if the batteries started charging, and then switch the DC lights on around the monastery to make sure they were working. It was decided, so Buzz could return to Bagpipe sooner, that the Man, a quick study, could show Sister Francesca the rest, and would remain on call if needed to troubleshoot bugs in the coming weeks.

"How's it going up there?" he called up.

Buzz waved at Sister Regina.

She was monitoring the progress now from the dorm window on the third floor, listening to the sound of footsteps above her on the roof, and taking in this one last chance to hang out with Buzz.

After all, Buzz, if you're right about the bug—if Sam's right—I may never see you again.

Oh, she still loved him. But no longer with any romantic intentions. Sister Regina had made her final profession of solemn vows more than three years ago. The person attracted to Buzz romantically had been another person, someone called Donna Beck, during the dog years. Buzz was one of those things—maybe the most difficult and important thing—she had given up to possess the Pearl of Great Price, her spouse, Jesus.

Yet he was not a thing; he was flesh and blood. There's a difference, she reflected now, between giving up clothes and cars and careers and giving up a friendship. Her sentiments today were noble. But she felt a pang to see him below, heavier now, but still pulsating with energy. After he recovered from his suicide attempt, she had prayed for years that he would heal enough to be able to marry again, and she was sure that Mel was God's answer to her prayers.

She felt responsible.

She saw Buzz, but she couldn't see the evil whispering to him, cajoling him.

Take a look, Buzz. Get closer to Donna one last time and take a good look. What could be wrong with that?

Just a little nudge.

Buzz looked up at Donna; she was leaning on her forearms on the ledge of the window, a few yards to the left of the scaffolding, and he felt an odd longing. This longing was too vague and dusty and old for him to put a conscious finger on it.

Maybe I could climb up to the top scaffold and pull my head over the roof and watch them finish? he asked himself. *And maybe say boo to Donna, too.*

"I'm coming up, you guys!" he called.

Always impetuous, ignoring his fear of heights, he bounded onto the lowest scaffold, and began to climb the monkey bars to the next levels.

"Better stay there," the Man called down, unseen. "No need to come up here. We'll be done in a few minutes."

"Coming anyway!" Buzz yelled back.

Two minutes later, he was at Sister Regina's level.

"Hey big guy," she called over, beaming.

What a lovely smile. He burned it into his memory. It was a nice photo: she in the window, happy, filled with love. He felt good.

"Hey, Sis," he laughed. "One more level."

"Be careful," she cautioned. "It's a long way down."

He glanced below, and yes, she was right. Buzz got that awful, pithy feeling of anxiety known well to all those with the fear of heights, then looked back up with a shaken grin.

"I'm not afraid of heights," he puffed with bravado. "What I'm really afraid of is hitting the ground."

She giggled. *Same old Buzz.*

Oh, how she missed his goofiness.

He reached up for the bar on the last level of the scaffold, and pulled himself up into a sitting position on one of three two-by-tens serving as the "floor" of the scaffold.

It *was* kind of scary up here.

Don't look down.

He stood up, managing to ignore the shakiness he felt in his knees. Vertigo.

Just one peek over the roof, see the panels, then I'm done, he told himself.

Instead of climbing up by using the metal bars on either side like a ladder, he would instead just pull his head up over the top by taking hold of the gutter a few inches above his eye level. It looked solid—made of some kind of stone.

Don't grab that! Buzz's guardian angel shouted through his conscience.

It was too late for angels. Free will could be a real bummer to angels assigned to guys like Buzz.

"Honey, I'm home!" he shouted to his friends on the roof. He reached up for the old terra-cotta gutter with both hands, and began to pull himself up.

Sister Regina, only a few yards away, heard the cracking sound.

The gutter gave way.

Buzz Woodward, his wife and children eight hundred miles to the east, disoriented by the sickening feeling of the gutter pulling away from the roof into his hands, reverted to his instinctual sense of balance, and took a step backwards…

…past the two-by-ten, into thin air.

"Mark!" Buzz cried, flailing, the gutter in his left hand now, his right hand reaching for the metal bar to the right.

By an inch the bar was too far away, and it slipped out of his reach, and now he was falling, falling, and his left ankle caught into a bar on the next level of the scaffold, and his body spun around…

…as Sister screamed…

…and the Man cried out…

…as Buzz hit the back of his head on the next level. *Crack!* And he spun again…

And he continued his fall, toward the mortal coil, his back toward the ground like a cat without the instinct to right itself, and toward a black dark unconsciousness, into a rosebush that finally broke the fall, the last image in his mind that of the blue sky spinning like the bottom of a backyard pool, the last sound that of Donna's screams, and his last anguished thought:

Mel! Oh Mel…

PART THREE

The Long Walk

Lead kindly light, amid the encircling gloom
Lead Thou me on
The night is dark, and I am far from home
John Cardinal Newman

Kathryn: Mr. Cole, do you know why you're here?
James: Gotta good memory—have a tough mind.
*James Cole to Kathryn Railly, **12 Monkeys***

Violence is just—when kindness is vain.
Pierre Coreille

But don't you worry 'bout a thing, Mama,
'cause I'll be standing in the wings
when you check it out—when you get off your trip.
Stevie Wonder, ***Don't Worry 'bout a Thing***

Suck it up and go.
Al Rotella

People travel to wonder
at the heights of the mountaintops,
at the huge waves of the sea,
at the long courses of the rivers,
at the vast compass of the ocean,
at the circular motion of the stars—
and they pass by themselves without wondering.
Saint Augustine of Hippo

Chapter Nine

Baby Steps

Buzz Woodward dreamed of a golden house on a golden hill covered with golden barley; a house with many glimmering rooms. It was summertime.

It's made of solid gold! he exclaimed, excited and happy.

In this dream, his body was far away from the golden wonderhouse, and he was on his hands and knees on a dusty country road. His soul was able to leave his body and float toward the house, and, hovering in the air, he peered through the crystalline windows into each room. He saw babies resting on shimmering silver blankets, sleeping peacefully.

Newborn babies. Black, and yellow, and white babies. There were icons on the walls—the kind of icons found in Orthodox churches. Virgin and Child icons. The faces on the Madonnas were so peaceful...

He knew the names of the babies. All of them, their names he knew, as if their names were written on his soul. Alexandra Bradley, Ivan Vostapovich, Travis McCormick, Seth Squires, Jose Ramirez, Lu Won Chi, DeRon Jackson, Hilda Schindler, Jonathan Briggs, Marika Popov, and...

...Mark Woodward, Buzz's own son. Buzz's heart skipped a beat. His Mark was here. The expression on his face was one of perfect serenity.

Markie! Wake up! It's me, Da Da! My Peanut!

But Markie did not wake up. This alarmed Buzz.

His dream-soul was instantly sucked back into his body, and now the golden house was far away. He was again on his hands and knees, on the dusty country road, and suddenly, pain was infused all over his body, as if he had been lashed thirty-nine times with a cat-o'-nine tails. He screamed.

He was wearing a red-checkered shirt and khakis, and felt his own blood dripping down his sleeves from the wounds on his back. He heard a voice that sounded like Mark Johnson, deep and strong:

"It's only pain, darlin'."

Where had he heard that before?

I must get to Markie! It's only pain! And where is Packy? Where is Mel? Where is...my other child?

Perhaps they were in the golden house, too, waiting for him?

With great effort, ignoring his pain, which had now spread into his head, into his joints and bones, he pulled himself up and crawled toward the house.

There was no sound in this dream. Just blue skies and silent breezes.

It seemed to take forever, and his dream-self was vaguely fearful of waking up, but eventually he reached the long drive-way, perhaps two hundred dream-yards from the building, and instead of going down the driveway, he left the road and made an angle toward the house into the barley.

I'm coming, Markie!

Incredibly, even though the pain remained with him, he was becoming...*accustomed to it.* He pressed on, still on his hands and knees, his vision blurry, the barley brushing against his face and forearms. No sounds but his own thoughts, which focused on one objective:

The house of gold.

Finally, Buzz was at the door. He pulled himself up to a kneeling position, and endured incredible pain when he straightened his back, forcing him to pause and lean his fore-head on the warm, golden door.

It is made of solid gold!

He reached and knocked, but the door did not open.

He pulled himself up, ignoring the pain in his ankle and the excruciating pain in his head. He gripped the doorknob, opened it, and…

✞ ✞ ✞

…opened his eyes in the real world. It was a dark place. He was in a bed, on his back, covered with two blankets and a comforter. His nose was cold. The room was cold. It was a small room, and through the corner of his eye, he saw a sliver of daylight escaping in.

He felt hunger pangs. His mouth was parched. He tried to raise his head, but was met with a throng of pain in the back of his neck before any actual movement occurred.

He gave up.

He tried to move his head, but felt a strange pain in his face; he saw a pouch hanging from a portable metal stand next to the bed in the bit of light between him and the window. It looked like a coat rack.

There was slender plastic tube leading from the pouch to his…

Nose!

It was not a pleasant feeling.

Feeding tube, he thought groggily.

With great effort he turned his head to his right, and saw the outline of a person—man or woman, he could not tell— sitting on a chair in the corner, head nodded down into his or her chest, sleeping.

Where am I?

He tried to croak these words. A groan came out instead.

The person lifted his or her head, and leaned forward.

"Buzz?" It was a woman's voice. Very familiar.

He groaned again.

"Buzz! You're awake. Oh, thank you, Jesus." The woman rushed over to the side of the bed. She was wearing a brown habit.

"Do you recognize me?" she asked, taking his hand with her left, and placing her right hand on his forehead with unmitigated tenderness.

His eyes focused and he saw tears streaming down her cheeks. *You are..?*

"Do you know who I am?" the woman repeated.

A look of concern came to her face. Her white headpiece hid her hair from him. The large forehead, the open, brown eyes…

"I know…you," he croaked, more a breathy whisper than words. "You're my friend, Donna."

She nodded.

"Do you know your name?" she asked.

"Of course," he replied. He grinned, but it felt unnatural. "I'm Buzz Woodward."

The words were coming more easily now.

"Welcome back," she said happily. "Hold on."

She rose and went to the window, and slowly opened the curtain halfway. He cringed. But he forced his eyes open.

"Do you know what year it is?" she asked.

He tried to form an answer to the question. He couldn't.

"I don't know. What happened to me?"

"You fell. It's the year two thousand, Buzz. It's March."

He saw her hesitate.

"Sam was right. The lights are out," she continued.

Two thousand! Lights out.

It all came back to him. The solar panels. The climb on the scaffold. The image of the spinning sky on his way down.

He pulled himself away from these disturbing memories, and looked carefully at her. For the first time, he saw that her skin was pallid, her habit loose around her face, and that there were bags under her eyes.

"Donna?" he found his voice, and it sounded far away to him. She turned to face him.

"How's Mel?"

In the light of day streaming through the window, he saw a worried look dawn on her face.

✜ ✜ ✜

He had woken up in a small room on the first floor of the monastery. Sister Regina left him and came back in a few minutes with the Man by her side. They removed the feeding tube. After helping Buzz to a sitting position—which caused great pain in his head—she helped him sip warm sugary water through a straw in a plastic cup.

Over the next few hours, as his mind slowly but surely regained its normal clarity, she told him, in fits and spurts, about the horrible events that had taken place while he was in the coma.

Immediately after his fall, he had been rushed to Fairview Hospital, where it was confirmed that he had a severely bruised ankle and a concussion that had left him in a coma. Buzz remained in the Critical Care Unit until the day after Christmas. Sam and Mel had flown in from New Hampshire to be by his side.

A great debate had taken place among Sam, Mel, Mark, and the Man over whether or not to try to fly or drive him to the regional hospital in Colebrook, New Hampshire. But all the doctors had insisted that such a trip might kill him. Mel had gotten hysterical, and only her responsibility for the boys and Sam's pleadings convinced her to return to Bagpipe by rental car, with Sam driving, two days before New Year's.

When the new year arrived, the millennium bug caused the power grid to go down almost immediately across the world, first in Australia and Asia, then India, the Middle East, and Russia, then across Europe, the Atlantic, and finally, the United States, Canada, and South America, then back across the empty, vast Pacific Ocean.

Cleveland turned frantic in minutes as the reports came in that "Australia has gone black." Something about an embedded chip with the bug, inadvertently overlooked by the engineers, in almost every electrical plant in the world.

The details were fuzzy—lost in the relentless downward spiral of dire events as things fell apart and the center did not hold.

People abandoned their plans for wild New Year's Eve parties and raided local grocery stores. Grocery store shelves emptied within hours, and riots broke out everywhere—in the cities, suburbs, in rural towns, according to the news reports. The power went off in the Cleveland area three hours after midnight.

Radio announcements from government officials, broadcasting from stations using back-up generators, had urged the people to remain calm, and reassured them that the power would come back within a week. The banks were closed for a "temporary holiday," and the President himself warned that the National Guard, already deployed in major cities "just in case," would shoot looters on sight. A state of national emergency was declared, and the president and governors of the states, by authority of executive orders, placed into law since the times of FDR, took authority over fuel, food, and telecommunications, such as they were.

Rumors abounded, including that a nuclear weapon had gone off in India near Bombay. In a move that surprised most citizens, FEMA, the Federal Emergency Management Administration, already had plans in place.

Even so, radio and television broadcasts became spottier and spottier (and without power, televisions were useless); those citizens who did not have heat were encouraged to go to local high schools and elementary schools for temporary shelter.

Most people did not follow these directions; they stayed at home or tried to leave the city. The highways and roads out of town, especially those heading south, were soon clogged with traffic, even before the National Guard was ordered to close off the main arteries to allow "emergency and relief access." Cars broke down or ran out of gas. Soon it was impossible to drive anywhere beyond the city.

It was cold during the first few days of January, and most citizens chose to stay at home and wait for the power (and water) to come back on, burning what wood they could get their hands on in their fireplaces, wearing winter coats indoors, and subsisting on the food stored in their own cupboards. After all, most people had a couple weeks worth of rations on hand.

On the Thursday after New Year's, the electricity returned inexplicably—for ten minutes. This caused many fires as appliances came back on and shorted out. The fire departments were overwhelmed. It was rumored that many fire trucks failed to operate because of the computer bug. With the 911 and phone systems down, it made emergency response all the more improbable. Buildings burned to the ground.

The more immediate problem was what to do with Buzz. Sam and Sister Regina had secured permission from the Mother Abbess (who felt responsible for his suffering) to move him to the convent, which was done with the help of Mark and the Man. Mark had bribed a worker at the hospital with thousands of dollars in cash given to him by Sam to "supply" the medical devices and feeding pouches that were used to keep him alive. Sister Regina Beck didn't know how these supplies were procured, but then again, she did not ask Mark, either.

Ironically, the solar-electric system that Buzz had helped set up had been used to refrigerate some of the packets during his down time. Buzz had woken up with less than three days of feeding bags left.

By the end of January, the food and medical supplies at the FEMA shelters had run out. Generators ran out of fuel. National Guardsmen left their posts to go to the aid of their families—and who could blame them? Radio broadcasts stopped. People everywhere were beginning to starve, and a nasty winter flu, normally controlled by modern medicine, began to race through the population like wildfire.

Four of the older sisters at the convent had already died from pneumonia. Sam had also donated several thousand pounds of wheat to the convent during the previous summer, and word got out quickly to people in the surrounding neighborhoods. The nuns did not even bother to try to grind the wheat and bake it. They soaked it in cold water, added molasses or honey and distributed it from their garage as a kind of primitive gruel. Those supplies ran out in less than three days.

The Mother Abbess had kept back a small amount of the food for her sisters, but that ran out by mid-February. Some local Catholic families, patrons of the Poor Clares, and fearful of the collapse, had stored up food in their homes, and despite their own hunger, brought what they could to the nuns. The chapel was packed, night and day, with local pilgrims praying for God to end this strife He had not caused.

The dim DC lights in the convent stayed on and did their job. Two retired priests took up residence in the rooms next to Buzz, along with the Man, who abandoned his home the day after the lights went out to help care for his friend.

The priests heard confessions for hours on end. They offered Holy Mass for crowds overflowing out of the chapel onto the convent grounds. There was a rumor that a single morsel of hastily-baked Eucharist would feed an adult for a day.

With the unplowed roads blocked with abandoned or wrecked cars, and gasoline non-existent, an exodus had begun for those with enough energy to walk.

"I'm going to Amish country," was a refrain heard often in the suburbs, referring to the many settlements in the areas to the east and southwest of Cleveland.

Rumors, rumors, rumors. It was not known what happened to these people, or what they found. Sister Regina told Buzz that she suspected they didn't find much. How could several hundred Amish farmers take care of the needs of tens of thousands of people?

The city folks—those who survived the first wave of rioting—headed for the suburbs, and finding no food there, hunkered down in public buildings that were now useless. Gunshots were heard, mostly at night, everywhere.

Where were the police? Without gasoline for their cruisers or electricity for their own communication systems, many had gone home to fend for their own families.

It was a quiet chaos. Many survivalist types had feared violence and riots, and yes, these had been an element of the breakdown. But as it turned out, people were too hungry, sick, and cold to do much more than burn furniture in their fireplaces (those fortunate enough to have fireplaces) and ration what food they had into smaller portions until…the pantries were bare.

A particularly frigid February made forays outside, especially after dark, dangerous or deadly. Many of those who had prepared by storing extra food supplies faced a gruesome choice: hide the food from starving neighbors, or be discovered and face the wrath of those same neighbors. Touchingly, at least from Sister Regina's point of view, most chose to share, according to the stories being told by the hundreds of pilgrims coming to Mass.

No one dared bring violence to the nuns, who were universally recognized, along with members of thousands of other churches around the world, Catholic and Protestant, for taking in the lonely, the dying, the sick, the hungry, the orphaned, the widowed, and the downtrodden.

People everywhere were also starving for news. What Clevelander did not have several relatives who lived somewhere else in the nation? Or across town, which now seemed a universe away.

Since the regular radio broadcasts had stopped—and even those still on the air were difficult to trust—it simply was not known what was going on in Europe, in New York, in Colorado—and in Buzz's case, in New Hampshire.

Sam, Ellie, and Mel, watching the darkness slowly make its deadly way across the world, had sent a stream of emails to the Man in the final hours before the electricity and telephone lines went dead.

They all contained the same theme:

"We're okay. We're trusting in God. We love you. When you wake up, come to us when it's safe."

Without explanation, on the fifth day of January, Mark Johnson and his family disappeared. Buzz and the Man suspected that he had gone to his place in Oberlin to ride things out.

Anywhere there was a stream, or brook, or outdoor running water, people could be seen with buckets and pitchers, trekking back and forth to get drinking water. Most homes had bleach, and it was quickly learned by all that a few drops could be used to purify water. Those lucky enough to have fireplaces gathered snow and ice from their backyards and melted it.

Men, women, and children who had showered and bathed every day for their entire lives had now gone without a bath for weeks.

Refugees, fewer as the Ides of March approached, were everywhere, on foot, most heading south.

People had already started to drop in the streets.

Corpses, many still nursing diseases, were stored in backyards—covered with tarps or stones if possible—to await the spring thaw for burial.

What had been a large city surrounded by a dozen large suburbs had degenerated in a matter of weeks into hundreds of disparate neighborhoods. Some neighborhoods had even set up crude roadblocks using abandoned vehicles, with sentries taking turns to block passage. Refugees were told to walk around.

The denial about the crash that existed before the Troubles, as they became known in the Cleveland area, did not abate. Yes, it was no longer possible to deny that the lights had gone out, and only the insane would debate that the computer bug had been the cause. But now, the denial took the form of March Madness, as the Man aptly named it.

"Things will get better in the spring," people told themselves. "The authorities will come with food. It will get warmer. If we can just hold out."

None of these people dared to admit the awful truth: the infrastructure for growing, fertilizing, harvesting, processing, storing, delivering, and selling food was gone. An intelligent man could deduce that the world's summer harvest of 2000 would be a tiny fraction of the harvest of 1999.

Others, more realistic, realizing they would be dead by spring, and cold and lethargic, simply gave up struggling, took to their beds, and waited for death.

Others, a minority of grim realists, began to do what the most desperate have done throughout history. When faced with starvation, they reenacted the deeds of some of the citizens of Leningrad during Hitler's siege in World War II:

They became cannibals.

The worst disease of all, dubbed Captain Breakers by a person whose name would be lost to history, was manifested by millions of souls. Captain Breakers took many forms, but all its forms shared this in common: the modern mind, raised from birth with no care or concern for procuring daily bread, accustomed to artificial light at the flick of a switch, now forced to go cold turkey from what had been dozens of hours a week of television, bereft of the false identities supplied by one's occupation (I'm a lawyer; I'm a truck driver; I'm a nurse; I'm a house painter), unable to accept the death of friends and relatives and—God, oh-God-no—not the children, the babies, the little ones—this modern mind simply turned off.

Off, like the lights. Captain Breakers.

And thus, suicide. Irrational bursts. Fits of sobbing. Running. Running in the streets toward destinations unknown or destinations dreamed—to the South, to Florida, to Columbus, to California, where the lights really, really truly *must* be on and the food grows right off the trees. Anywhere but here, where reality bore down like a giant unseen anvil on mental shoulders too weak to hold up to the agonizing strain. Breakers were everywhere.

This is the world Buzz found when he woke up: a world coming more and more to be dominated by insanity.

But none of this mattered to him.

Buzz had been insane once himself, and thus inoculated, was not disturbed when Hal and Donna (she allowed him to call her by her old name when she was alone with him) described all these things.

✛ ✛ ✛

Three days after he woke up, they sat together in his little room, the svelte black man and Sister Regina on wooden chairs, and Buzz on his bed.

"I've already lost thirty pounds, so I must begin the journey soon, or I'll become too weak," he told them. "I'm now two-fifty. I can probably go down to one-eighty."

"I'll go with you. There is nothing for me here," the Man offered, his tone hard.

"Okay," Buzz accepted, holding back a tear. This was true friendship.

"What if you die out there? At least wait until the weather gets warmer," Sister Regina protested, anxiety apparent in her voice. "Hal can forage for food here and you can build your strength."

"There is no food here. Or at least I don't think Hal and I are willing to kill for what food there is. I will probably die on the long walk. But I will die if I stay here. My life is not the issue. You pray for me, as long as you live, and I know that I will see Mel and my boys again." Buzz finished his speech.

Buzz succinctly defined the moral parameters and the overarching goal of his journey—his long walk, as he called it, to his personal house of gold.

The stocky nun opened her mouth and closed it. There was no use arguing. In her heart, she didn't want him to stay, and she knew him. She knew he had to go after his family.

They shared a silence.

"Then we leave tonight," the Man said. "According to plan."

✙ ✙ ✙

The plan the Man had referred to had been hatched before the millennium. The day Sam and Mel drove back to New Hampshire, the Man had decided that he would help Buzz return to Bagpipe if and when his friend came out of the coma.

He had moved his extra food from his home to the convent—mostly canned goods bought from the local grocery stores, and survived by strictly rationing it for the past two and a half months. He had also purchased two large, nylon backpacks and simple hiking supplies: hunting knives, wire traps, camp cookware, a small Bible, lightweight sleeping bags, a small tent, a bag of one hundred Miraculous Medals, two large bottles of vitamins, four extra-heavy wool scapulars, a retractable fishing pole and reel, an ancient rugged Forest Service compass, a wind-up Baygen flashlight, twelve gold coins which Sam had given him, and one thousand rounds of ammunition for his .22 Ruger rifle—his "rabbit gun." The rounds came in two bricks, and weighed but a few pounds.

Buzz did not own a gun, and even if he had, it would have been in Bagpipe. Both men already owned high-quality hiking boots—Caterpillar brand. For clothing, they had two extra pairs of wool socks, Lands' End thermal underwear (which Buzz had been wearing the day of his fall), Thinsulate gloves, black Polartec fleece hats (which Buzz insisted on calling *goupaleens*), one T-shirt (Buzz's had *Tabasco* screened on his, and Hal had his decade-old Scaps shirt from the championship year), and one heavy cotton long-sleeve shirt they planned to wear under two layers: a sweatshirt covered by a wool sweater.

The Man had been given the foresight to buy two expensive, but thin, lightweight winter "climbing" jackets rated for subzero temperatures. Buzz's fit loosely because of his weight loss, making it easier for him to wear his layers beneath.

A week after the blackout, Tim Penny had walked two miles to the convent with his oldest son to pray at the chapel and to visit Buzz. He had given the Man Buzz's careworn brass Zippo, and two tin bottles of lighter fluid for the journey.

"Marie told me to tell you she knows he'll wake up, and that we've got the children praying," Tim promised.

He knelt next to the bed and spoke to Buzz in an emotional whisper, "You wake up now..." his voice cracked.

"You hear me? You wake up! And no 'I told you so.' You and Sam were right, and there have been times I wish we were up in Bagpipe. Our neighborhood is getting crazy. My job is gone. But we've got a few weeks of rations left. We're heading out in the morning with all our gear, on foot, with Jimmy Lawrence and Brian Thredda, for Findley State Park, where we used to go camping. You remember that first time you went with us? When we kept that fire going all night long? If you can hear me, Buzz, you keep that fire going. Do you hear me? You keep that fire going."

Tim had prayed in silence for several more minutes before rising to leave.

The Man had not heard from the Pennys since the visit. There was now nothing left for him in Cleveland.

At two in the morning, Buzz limped out to the front steps of the monastery, all loaded down, waiting for Sister Regina. The Man stood silently by as Buzz shook the hand of the stout little nun. Her hand was warm, his cold, like the air around them.

"I love you, my little one," he whispered hoarsely.

His head was aching. His ankle was sore, but able to hold his weight. He was thankful that it hadn't been broken in the fall.

"I love you, too," she replied, leaping up to hug him impulsively, carefully avoiding throwing her arms around his neck; the stitches had been out for weeks now, but the area was still tender. She got his shoulders instead. He was still strong—like a big piece of furniture.

They pulled away quickly.

She turned to the Man, who was holding his Ruger on his hip, barrel facing toward the sky. His brown eyes, narrowed to slits with a slightly yellow outline, were unreadable, impenetrable.

She had seen that expression many, many times before, in her previous life—when she had watched him on the court, when he was playing for the win. His game face.

You take care of my Buzz, she ordered him with her eyes.

He nodded back, then looked up to the concrete cross on the top of the gable over the steps.

Sometimes there was nothing more to say.

She watched them walk into the darkness.

✛ ✛ ✛

Both men knew the area well. It only took them an hour to walk north through Lakewood to the lake. They stayed on the back roads. The partial moon supplied enough light to guide them. Finally, they climbed down to the boathouse of the Westside Sailing Club, nestled below the cliffs on the rippling shore of Lake Erie, out of sight.

It was a tall, almost gothic, three-story wooden structure with wrought-iron outdoor staircases and balconies overlooking the water. The front door had been busted in, but there were no squatters—weather on the lakefront during Cleveland winters could be brutal. There were plenty of signs of looting in the abandoned building—furniture was overturned, the kitchen shelves had been emptied. Outside several of the pleasure boats had been sunk at their docks—why, it was anybody's guess. Perhaps by a storm.

The frozen lake had only melted a week earlier—though there were still jagged, flat floating rafts of ice glimmering in the moonlight. The water was calm.

The Man led Buzz down to the basement, and past all sorts of junk and flotsam to a back room. They took off their coats, and together, knocked over a large bookcase filled with old paint cans. There was a door on the wall revealed, a pad-lock secure.

"Good," the Man grunted. "Now if I can just remember the combination."

"You're kidding, right?" Buzz asked.

The Man didn't answer. After three or four tries, the lock clicked open, and Buzz shined the flashlight over the Man's shoulder and saw the jerry cans—fuel for the Man's boat.

Half an hour later, they were zipping away in the Man's Waverunner—a little boat with the same kind of engine used for jet skis. They headed directly north for a long interlude before the Man turned right, and east.

"Hal, can I ask you a question?"

"Keep it down," the Man whispered dryly. "Our voices will carry over the water. You'd be surprised."

Buzz wasn't sure if he was kidding or not—they were at least a mile from the shoreline, and there wasn't another boat or ship in sight.

"Okay," Buzz whispered. "How did you know we would be making this trip? I mean—storing the gasoline for the Waverunner, the supplies, the backpacks."

"The Lord told me."

"How did He tell you?"

"I was in front of the Blessed Sacrament at Holy Angels, three months ago, and I was told in my heart to store the fuel and buy the supplies."

Buzz was amazed. "How did you know what size jacket to buy me?"

"I just knew."

"That's not very specific."

The Man kept his eyes on the gentle swells in front of the boat.

"As horrible as the world seems right now," the Man stated, "we're already in the new springtime. The Lord will speak clearly in the hearts of His children from now on."

He seemed to be speaking to the lake, not to Buzz, with a certainty that was—riveting.

"But why?"

"It's not our place to question God," the Man explained, but said no more.

They traveled slowly to maximize fuel economy, and to make the least amount of noise. The journey stretched on for just over four hours—almost one hundred and forty miles. By heading directly east, the arch of the east side of Lake Erie came to meet them. The temperature had fallen below freezing, and towards morning, the wind and the waves began to kick up. Buzz dry-heaved only twice, thankful that his last meal, a can of chicken noodle soup, had already been digested and therefore the calories had not been wasted.

✛ ✛ ✛

Hurrying to avoid being seen, and with some effort, they pulled the Waverunner onto the rocky shoreline, and then into a thicket of trees. They covered it with leaves. The sun had been up for more than an hour.

There were no homes on the waterline. The Man guessed that they were located somewhere past Erie, perhaps as far as Dunkirk, New York. Using the Man's compass, they walked southward into the woods, which was not dense, except for certain patches of thick, low pines, which they walked around, rather than fight.

"I knew we forgot something," the Man whispered.

"Wha's that?" Buzz asked breathlessly. He was limping noticeably.

"Machetes."

The two men found a deer path, and the going was easy. They soon climbed over a wire fence and crossed over an empty stretch of Route 5. They knew that Interstate 90 would not be far away now. The woods gave way to a farmer's clearing, and they saw I-90 perhaps a quarter mile in the distance. They retreated back into the woods, then made camp. They had agreed to pass major highways only under nightfall.

While Buzz set up the tent, the Man disappeared into the woods and set his three traps. He came back. They decided they were too close to the highway to start a fire, even in daylight, and Buzz crawled into his sleeping bag. The Man sat sentry, bundled in a sleeping bag, the Ruger leaning on a large oak tree beside him. He whispered a Rosary with Buzz, who fell asleep during the third decade. The Man finished alone, then spent the next two hours in a semi-contemplative state; alert for danger.

Alert for God.

At noon, he woke Buzz, and they switched places.

"I don't know how to use this rifle," Buzz told him.

"Shssshh, keep it down," the Man scolded him softly, shaking his head. "Just holding it might scare away a bad apple."

With the Man asleep, Buzz tried to pray, but was distracted by the itchiness of his neck wound. He picked at the scabs under the bristly hair in fits of irritation. (Sister Regina had cut it the day before with a pair of scissors—barberhood was not her calling.)

He noticed smoke coming out the chimney of the farmhouse to the east, although he saw no people come outside, and wondered if they should drop by and say hello. The Man would not like that idea.

"No interaction with strangers, if we can help it," the Man had said, laying down the ground rules.

The hours crawled by slowly. Buzz wished for a portable Sony TV with a video player, then scolded himself for the thought. What use was it to long for something that was impossible?

Strangely enough, this gave him hope. Videos were now impossible, but walking across the country to Mel and the boys was not. They had already come a long way in just one day. If his strength and his ankle held out, then built up *(What are we going to eat?),* the Man had estimated they could make twenty miles a day. Divided into seven hundred miles, and with no delays, that was only thirty-five days.

If I just have water, and a morsel here and there, plus two Centrums a day, I'll make it.

He prayed out loud in a whisper. "Jesus, I trust in you." Then he tried to picture Mel and Markie and Packy and Sam and Ellie and Christopher. He regretted more than ever leaving his photographs in Bagpipe. He didn't have one picture of his family in his wallet.

As always, he prayed for his daughter Jennifer, and for her mother, Sandy.

He realized that Mel had probably already given birth, and if he and the Man made good time, and the weather got better, as it must with spring approaching, perhaps he could arrive before the baby's first smile.

This gave him hope. Yes, something to shoot for. As the sun descended an unseen stairway toward the western horizon—towards Cleveland, where Donna lived, and where he knew he would never step foot again—he idled away his final hour of sentry duty pondering names for his next child.

Thomas, Jude, Maximilian, Gwynne Jr.—No! Never!—Anthony, Josemaria…

All his favorite saints…

…Bernadette, Catherine, Helen, Melanie—No! Never!—Therese, Grace—yes, Grace, that was a lovely name for a girl—Grace Woodward, I like that. We'll ask Sam and Ellie to be the godparents.

Again. They were already the godparents of Packy. (Mark and Maggie Johnson were Markie's.)

Buzz forgot to check his watch, and the Man woke up by internal alarm—"The Lord woke me up." He checked his traps, and found a rabbit. It had died while they slept, and he tied it to his belt.

They hiked across the hayfield to the interstate, which was abandoned, except for an overturned, burned-out tractor trailer about a half mile west. The man pulled a small wire clipper from Buzz's backpack, and used it to cut the wire fences on either side of the interstate. They crossed another empty field and headed for the woods, and in another half hour, walked across Route 20, which was also abandoned, and backtracked southeast until they found their target: Route 60. There was an abandoned gas station at the intersection. The sun was setting.

They decided to walk along the side of the road in the woods to avoid other travelers, even though they had not seen a single person for almost twenty-four hours.

Occasionally, they saw dim lights emanating from the farmhouses or homes that were located on Route 60.

"Twenty-two miles to Gerry," the Man confirmed, checking his Triple-A map. "Then we cut east into the wilds to get to the Allegheny Reservoir."

The moon was covered by clouds, and the darkness made it difficult and slow to navigate the trees on the side of Route 60. They had trouble finding a path alongside the road. Buzz was afraid that he would injure his sore ankle by stepping on an unseen rock or fallen tree branch. It was very difficult to figure how far they had come since leaving Route 20.

"Dinner time soon," the Man said. He had not uttered five sentences all day.

"I'm thirsty," Buzz told him. Their only canteen, last filled in Cleveland, was empty.

"Let's keep walking then," the Man suggested.

A few minutes later, they came around a lazy bend, and in a deserted stretch, heard the gurgling sound of a stream flowing down a small hill and passing beneath the road into a concrete pipe. Buzz quickly limped over and reached down to imbibe—

"Hold on!" the Man warned.

He came over, filled the canteen, and took out a small, plastic bottle shaped like Our Lady of Lourdes; he tapped a drop of clear liquid into the canteen.

"Holy water? That's excellent," Buzz observed.

"No, bleach. Sister Regina gave me the bottle. There might be traces of holy water mixed in, though. Double protection. Now drink."

Buzz took the canteen and drank. He felt good—hungry, but good. *I wouldn't have gotten ten miles out of Cleveland without the Man.*

"Let's press on. Dinner can wait," the Man said, looking around.

"Right," Buzz agreed. He didn't want to appear weak to the Man. *Boy, my ankle is killing me.*

"How come you never talk?" Buzz asked.

The Man did not answer.

Inwardly, the Man had the creeps. He did not like this road. But he did not know why. Was it the Lord speaking to him? He wasn't sure.

But he pressed on, knowing it was taxing Buzz's ankle, thinking there was no other choice. *It's a hard world. It's a hard world,* he told himself.

Their path became more hilly. They were forced to leave the scrub and walk on the road. Buzz had developed a painful rash between his thighs.

No Johnson & Johnson's baby powder here!

Strict silence. Just when Buzz felt that he could go no further, he spotted a cane—a real, ivory handled, walking cane!—on the shoulder of the road. It was slightly cracked, but serviceable.

They needed water; they came upon a stream. He needed help walking; he found a cane.

He half-expected to find a bottle of baby powder on the shoulder.

They came upon a sign: Sinclairville, 2 Miles. Gerry, 8 Miles.

Dinner time. Sun would come up soon. They moved away from the road, just below the top of a hill, near a rock formation—"Never camp or walk on the crest of a hill; enemies can see your silhouette even at night," said the Man—who promptly left Buzz to forage for wood.

Using the Zippo and some dried grass, they soon had a small fire going. Buzz marveled at the Man as he quickly cut three branches to form a spit, gutted the rabbit, then cooked it for dinner, which they supplemented with one Powerbar each. The Man had stashed the bars with the gasoline at the boathouse.

The Man took sentry, they whispered their Rosary, and Buzz fell asleep despite the dull throb in his neck and his ankle, encouraged by their progress.

The Man plucked a long reed of grass with his thin, black fingers, stripped it, then pinched it between his cheek and gum. He began to pray. One line.

Lord, we'll never make it.

Later, during Buzz's sentry shift, he dozed off. He awoke facing the barrel of a shotgun.

Chapter Ten

The Postmen

"Wake up, boy. Do you mean harm?" a voice asked Buzz, who found himself peering into the business end of a shotgun. He was wearing overalls and a thick, blue-checked shirt, and rubber boots.

It was daylight.

Buzz snapped awake. It took him a second to orient himself. *What? Who? Where am I?*

"Hal!" he called out.

"Boy, you didn't answer my question," the man with the shotgun said.

"No harm! We mean no harm!"

Buzz thrust his hands in the air. The Ruger was on the ground at his side. Shotgun Guy reached down and picked it up, then took a step back.

Hey, that's our gun! Buzz thought.

He started praying the first words of the Saint Michael Prayer over and over again. *Saint Michael the Archangel, defend us in the day of battle…Saint Michael the Archangel…*

"I'm coming out," the Man's deep voice came from the tent. "I'm unarmed. Everyone just relax."

The Man, bent over in a catcher's crouch, stepped out of the tent, hands in the air. Buzz was amazed when he saw a relaxed, friendly smile come to his face.

"Good morning," the Man said. "Can I put my hands down? I assure you we mean no harm. We're just passing through."

Shotgun Guy didn't answer, but honored them with a skeptical look, then turned his head halfway toward the road, yelling, "There's two of 'em, Norm!"

Buzz and the Man looked and saw a box truck on the road with *Propane America* lettered on its side.

The man who must have been Norm popped his head out of the truck, the morning sun shining off his bald pate. He looked about as old and gray as Shotgun Guy. Buzz placed them in their fifties.

Buzz found his voice. "We're just passing through, mister. Honest. My wife is stuck in New Hampshire, and we're walking there."

Buzz saw the Man roll his eyes.

"Well, it's the truth," Buzz explained to the Man, shrugging his shoulders.

Saint Michael the Archangel...

"Which way you headed?" the Shotgun Guy asked Buzz.

"South, toward Gerry," the Man answered quickly, lowering his hands. "Then east to the reservoir. We're trying to get to Route 6 in Pennsylvania eventually."

Buzz opened his mouth and allowed the following to come out: "So if you're planning to shoot us, then shoot us. If not, and if that truck you and Norm are drivin' is really working, maybe you can take us on down to Gerry. My ankle is killing me."

Norm had worked himself most of the way up the hill.

"What's up, Larry?"

"Says they need a lift to Gerry…"

Norm smiled a big smile. He had all his teeth, and somehow Buzz knew they would be okay. *This is not a scene from Deliverance.*

"They armed?" Norm asked.

Larry nodded, keeping his eyes on his quarry.

"You got any more guns?" Larry asked.

Buzz and the Man shook their heads. Buzz lowered his hands.

"No they ain't," Larry told Norm. "Not anymore."

Norm completed the last few steps to reach them. He was wearing dungarees, and a white sweatshirt under a Buffalo Bills winter jacket. He stuck out his arm and greeted Buzz and the Man with a handshake and a cordial smile. Buzz noticed Norm wince as he straightened up, and then favor his weight on his right foot.

"Things have been confusing around here. We're on patrol. I'm Norman Bates—I know, I know, just like the movie— and I'm sheriff of Gerry. We had to make a run up today to get Mrs. Halberstram. She's ailing, and you'll have to share space with her in the back of our truck if you really need a lift to Gerry. She's got the pneumonia."

As he said this, Buzz noticed the Motorola radio on his belt.

"We're headed that way," Norm continued, "but that's about as far as we can take ya. Just allow us to carry your twenty-two 'til we get there, if you don't mind."

Buzz and the Man nodded.

"Put that damn Remington down, Larry, before you get somebody hurt," the sheriff told his deputy.

He turned back to Buzz and winked. "Where you boys from?"

"Cleveland," Buzz answered.

"Heard any news?"

"We just left there two days ago," Buzz replied. "We'll fill you in on the way down. It's not going well."

Water, cane, ride, Buzz thought.

And that is how Buzz and the Man received a free ride in a propane (not gasoline) powered utility truck to a one-traffic-light (now out of service) town called Gerry, New York, Population 854 (before the crash, it was 992).

✠ ✠ ✠

When they got to Gerry, Buzz and the Man made a bee-line for the Catholic church, Saint Thomas More, and spoke with the local priest, a young man named Terry Lang.

The Man prayed in church for almost an hour, while Buzz answered questions for the sheriff and some of the townspeople at the police station.

By the time the Man got to the station, Buzz was in the middle of adjusting Norman Bates's back. Bates had been in a lot of pain, and felt like a new man.

Buzz followed by adjusting Shotgun Larry, then two other residents. In exchange for this treatment he and the Man received six potatoes, courtesy of a Bible-toting farmer named Norman Bates Sr., who had planted double his usual crop in anticipation of the breakdown.

The town had quickly set up roadblocks and patrols when the lights went out, and so far, the nasty strain of pneumonia, which apparently was not limited to Cleveland, had taken more of a toll than starvation.

The flus, Buzz thought as he cracked another back. *They used to sweep through the world, wiping out millions, before the advent of modern medicine.*

As a boy in New Jersey, he had walked to school by cutting through an ancient graveyard. He often wondered why he would see entire families listed on gravestones—parents, three, four, or five children sometimes—all with the same year of death carved neatly into the marble. Now he knew.

The flu. Such a pleasant little word.

Would invisible monsters with names such as smallpox, malaria, rheumatic fever, polio, and typhoid pick up their wide-brush brooms and again begin sweeping bodies off the surface of the earth?

"Boy, my back hasn't felt this good in ages, Dr. Woodward!" Norman told Buzz later. "Wish we had a chiropractor in town."

Wish we had a drug company here, too, Buzz thought.

Buzz did not feel it necessary to correct the sheriff. After all, Buzz had not said that he was a chiropractor, only that he knew chiropractic medicine. In fact, he had been practicing basic adjustments on real patients at the clinic for over a year.

In the afternoon, Buzz adjusted and massaged three dozen residents of Gerry. The following afternoon, loaded down with an entire sack of potatoes, some dried meats, and even a roll of toilet paper, they were escorted fourteen miles east by a young man named Sandy Garciapara (Buzz had adjusted Sandy's mother's back), who knew the hiking trails, to almost halfway to the Allegheny Reservoir. One resident, the owner of a small medical supply store, even gave Buzz a form-fitting canvas brace for his ankle.

The moon was out, and Buzz was chatty as they walked on a path heading south beside the reservoir.

"Don't you see it?" Buzz asked. "It's Divine Providence. Your outdoorsman skills and my chiropractic training are going to get us to Bagpipe!"

The Man grunted.

"What's the matter?"

"Nothin'," the Man said.

✝ ✝ ✝

Buzz awoke to find the Man digging into the soil with his hunting knife next to an overturned rock. Buzz rubbed the sleep from his eyes. It was still very cold.

"Worms?" he asked the Man. "Can we eat them?"

"And Jesus told them to cast their nets on the other side of the boat," the Man quoted. "Thought we might take half a day to rest. Have some fish for breakfast. Extend our rations."

And so they fished. The Man caught three catfish in five casts, which they fried and consumed right at the waterline. Far away, to the north, there was a dingy with another fisherman on it. Buzz waved. The man waved back.

Wiping his mouth with his sleeve, Buzz sighed. "I miss coffee. I really miss coffee."

The Man honored him with a grunt.

"Do you miss anything, Hal? You know, from the old world?"

There was no hesitation in the reply.

"Daily Mass."

Buzz felt small. *And I'm complaining about not having coffee.*

"God's handiwork is all around us," Buzz observed.

"Where?"

"The forest. This reservoir. The sun. The air."

"Oh."

Reed of grass in his mouth, the Man reclined back on his elbows and closed his eyes, then took in the warming rays. Buzz layed all the way back, his hands clasped behind his head. During the night, his headache had receded for the first time in the journey.

"On the day the lights went out, I rejoiced, Buzz. I praised God," he said calmly, his eyes still closed.

This threw Buzz.

"But all the death, the disease. The suffering." It seemed an obvious point to Buzz.

"Four thousand unborn babies were aborted in the United States every twenty-four hours last year. Even more snuffed out by the pill and IUD. When the lights went out, that ended. Whether they know it or not, the breakdown is an answer to billions of prayers by millions of pro-lifers over twenty-seven years. So I rejoiced."

Well, Buzz thought, thinking about the pill, *maybe we don't need those drug companies after all.*

"Buzz, can I level with you?"

"I'm insulted that you would even ask."

The Man rolled his eyes.

"The question was just a way of starting a serious conversation."

Buzz didn't reply. *I already thought it was pretty serious.*

"Buzz, the Lord has blessed our trip. But our good fortune can't last. God won't undo free will. The good weather is coming. People are in shock now, but they'll come out of it. Fifteen, maybe twenty percent of the population has probably died by now. With more to come. One day we're going to wake up to another Shotgun Larry, and this one is going to pull the trigger."

"I don't want to think about that," Buzz replied after a moment.

"You've got to think about it. You're depending on me too much. I'm not going to make it to Bagpipe. You've got to get mentally and spiritually ready to go it alone."

"You can't know something like that," Buzz responded, trying to keep his voice calm.

"The Lord let me know before your coma. I didn't know the details then, and I don't know them now. I don't believe I'll live to see the end of April."

Buzz could only think one thought, which came to him as a visual image: *Mel on their wedding night, on the bed, in the Stouffer's Hotel, her skin glistening in the lights reflecting in from the streets of Cleveland.*

"Look Hal, no offense," Buzz snapped, "but have you ever considered that some of these sure-fire things the Lord has been telling you might not be from the Lord—that they might be from you; that they might be coming from your subconscious? Exactly how did the Lord tell you that you'll die before April 30th? Did you hear actual words?"

It sounded like a rebuke. And it was.

The Man was not offended.

"The Lord doesn't tell me things like a mere human being would tell you something. He talks to me like a God would talk to somebody. It's a way of knowing in your heart. God don't need no *words*. God *is* a Word."

The Man's tone plainly conveyed to Buzz that all this was so patently obvious that it was barely worth mentioning.

Buzz felt, perhaps unfairly, that the Man might as well have been ending every sentence with: ...*got that, moron?*

"You're worried about Mel," the Man continued. "I'm telling you this...truth...for her sake, so you'll get ready. You're worried that you won't make it to Bagpipe without me—when you should be worried that you can't make it to Bagpipe without *the Lord*."

Got that, moron? Buzz heard, essentially missing everything—the Man's point, and the Man's motive.

Buzz took a deep breath. He looked at his friend, whose eyes were still closed, still perfectly relaxed.

"Maybe I'm worried about you, too, huh," Buzz responded after a moment of reflection. "Maybe I just don't like the idea of you dying. I mean, what would I do for a point guard on the Scaps?"

The Man chuckled politely—but didn't address Buzz's fear any further.

The conversation, which seemed to have more words than all their conversations so far, ended.

Dear Lord, don't let the Man die! Why would you allow the Man to die?

They cleaned up, took turns napping under the cover of the trees away from the waterline, then headed out at noon.

✝ ✝ ✝

Over the next two weeks, the weather became warmer, even for the mountain terrain they were crossing. They made their way south to Route 59, then east on 59 until it met up with Route 6.

Buzz and the Man brought news from town to town, trading chiropractic for food, and almost as important, receiving directions and advice on which back roads and hiking paths to take that paralleled Route 6. Mount Alton, East Smethville, Burtville. If the towns had Catholic churches, which every third one did, the Man would plunk himself down in front of the Blessed Sacrament, often convincing the local priest, if one was available, to expose Jesus in the monstrance. If there wasn't a Catholic church, he sought out the local preacher, and they prayed together.

"Where two or more are gathered in His name, there He shall be," the Man explained. "If I can't have Jesus present in the Host, I'll get Him present with another Christian."

"What's with your friend?" the locals would ask Buzz as he adjusted their backs and healed their pains, often setting up cushions on a coffee table in the post office or town hall on Main Street (and every town in this part of Pennsylvania had a main street named Main Street—it was a law or something).

"The Man is holy—that's about the only way I can explain it. It's like travelling with a Black Mother Teresa, or Mister Teresa, or whatever, I swear," he would explain. "The best thing your town can ever want is to have the Man praying for you. And believe me, he's praying for you right now."

These tough little towns, most having been in a low-grade depression since the 1930s, seemed to be scraping along. As the two friends worked their way further east, deeper into the mountains, the killer flus and pneumonias seemed to have taken less of a toll.

Hunters hunted; fishermen fished; the few farmers whose farms dotted the mountain countryside, many of them Christians who had prepared for the worst, had stored in more food than normal—potatoes, winter wheat, even corn.

Buzz noticed another important factor which favored the rural areas: no city sewage or water.

Practically every town had its share of wells and septic systems. Jerry-riggers rigged. It gave Buzz hope that Bagpipe was also hanging in there.

Many of the towns had set up roadblocks on either side of Route 6. When he and the Man came to these, Buzz preferred to let the Man do the talking—he had a disarming gift—Buzz thought of it as *charisma.*

The Man, ever the cryptic saint, when asked by Buzz about this unexpected talent, explained that the Holy Spirit put words into his mouth. And this made perfect sense to Buzz, for it seemed less the words—which were always direct, simple, and clear—than the *power* behind the one speaking them that gave them so much impact.

"Pay no mind to this here rabbit gun. It's just for hunting. If you want, you can hold it for us while we visit. My friend and I are just passing through," the Man would say with a smile, his hands open. "And we've got some mail for y'all."

Buzz noted that it wasn't all Holy Spirit. The Man, whose diction and English had otherwise always been measured and perfect, never used the Southern term *y'all* except at the road-blocks.

Skeptical country deputies and sentries would melt like snow in a sunbeam. Buzz would then trot out letters attesting to his chiropractic skills from the mayors or police chiefs of the previous towns.

Later on, Buzz would get his talking in with the townsfolk, brazenly telling one and all about the Catholic faith. Christianity was making a comeback, judging from the reactions Buzz received. Stripped of their jobs and material comforts, many were turning to religion. It was also touching and comforting how easy it was to connect spiritually with the devout Protestants they met along the way.

Maybe this isn't so bad, Buzz thought at times.

If they let him, Buzz would tell stories to their children in the town square or local school. Stories from the Bible, or classics like Little Red Riding Hood.

Sometimes he made up stories about spaceships, purple dogs, and planets made out of pancakes with Aunt Jemima hiding in the core, ready to grant wishes if the daring adventurer-children would just be willing to take a sip of her magic syrup.

The children, deprived of their Nintendos and antiseptic videos, ate these verbal treats out of Buzz's hand.

Buzz and the Man were almost always rewarded with food. Thereby encouraged, and less wary, they began walking during daylight hours, usually on the grassy shoulder of the road to alleviate the pounding on their knees and joints.

As for refugees they met along the way, at the Man's suggestion, they established a "policy." Buzz and the Man would share half their food, no matter how little or how much they had on them, and Buzz would offer to adjust their spines. So far, only one man, alone and ragged, had given them a fright.

Buzz saw him approaching from afar (his eyesight was much better than the Man's). With a sixth sense that the Man attributed to the Lord, the Man had pulled his Ruger off his shoulder before the crazy vagabond came within a half-mile.

Buzz prayed and the Man glared. The vagabond, dirty and eyes buggy, walked right past them without saying a word.

"Got the devil in 'im," the Man explained after the strange vagrant had passed from sight. "Don't let it bother you. Sometimes there's nothing you can do."

As if that explained everything.

"Do you think he'll double back?" Buzz asked, looking over his shoulder.

"The man or the devil?"

"Either one."

"The Lord has not revealed that to me."

"Thanks. I feel much better now."

Though they often felt the pangs of hunger, it seemed as if every time they would run out of food between towns, they would walk over a hill and find a fishing pond or a lone farmer with a bad back willing to trade a can of beans; or they would wake up with a rabbit or squirrel in the Man's traps.

✟ ✟ ✟

For all his life, from his earliest drives from New Jersey to Notre Dame during college, to his occasional jaunts from Cleveland as an adult to visit his uncle's shore house on Long Beach Island in New Jersey, Buzz had privately thought of western Pennsylvania as the Badlands.

Many a time as he rolled over Interstate 80, he saw in the Badlands deserted, desolate misanthropic mountains, yet not without their own strange elegiac beauty.

Twice he had experienced freak accidents in the Festiva, including one—a blowout—with Sam and Donna, that could have easily taken their lives.

Then there had been that ride across the state on his way down to the shore, drunk out of his mind, on the way to his suicide attempt. Thankfully, most of that ride was a blur to him now, but it was a Badlands Blur if there ever was one.

Now, during this journey toward Bagpipe, as he lost weight, as his ankle and head wound healed (the headaches were almost completely gone now), and his legs became stronger, the wide muscles in his already impressive thighs like rocks, he was realizing that the Badlands weren't so bad after all.

Unable to resist the Man's serene silence and constant recollection in "the Lord," Buzz found himself being drawn into a deeper union with God. In the early days of the long walk, he had mildly resented the Man's silence, and had somehow imagined that he would pass the time by talking his way across Pennsylvania.

The Badlands had become Goodlands for his soul. The only sore point was the slow pace of the journey.

✛ ✛ ✛

On the road on a sunny day in April.

"Hal, do you know what day it is?" Buzz asked, trying to hide a smile.

"Sure. Saturday."

"Yeah, but what day of the month?"

"Fifteenth," the Man said, not smiling.

"So, did you pay your taxes?"

Now the Man smiled.

✛ ✛ ✛

Sleeping on the floor of the town hall in Watrous, Buzz dreamed he was in a balloon floating over the mountains of Pennsylvania. The bright yellow balloon carried him in an old-fashioned wicker basket, replete with sandbags for ballast. The floor of the basket was made of a single, pure silver plate.

Pretty heavy material for a balloon, his dream-self thought.

Hands on the rail, he peered down, and to his frightened surprise, he saw himself and the Man walking along an empty road, thousands of feet below.

That's us! That's Route 6!

He heard the dulcet voice of a woman behind him.

He knew that voice!

"Buzz," she said.

He turned. He was mildly disappointed. It was not Mel. It was Ellie, dressed in an 1800s get-up: hoop dress, a gazillion layers of fluffy white lace shifts beneath, an Easter bonnet on her head.

As always, Ellie Fisk was a stunning beauty. Her skin soft, healthy, perfect. Her eyes radiant, brown and sugary as fudge. Her golden hair—light, whispery in the wind. The curve of her jaw, just right, just so, just...

"I love you, Buzz," she told him.

"I love you, too," he replied impatiently. *Of course I love you, you're one of my best friends in the whole world. Now let's get to the point!*

"Where is Mel?" he asked breathlessly. "How is she doing? Do you have any news?"

Ellie looked down at her hands.

"I love you, Buzz."

She began to weep bitter tears.

He went to her and took her by the shoulders, shaking her roughly. "What's wrong, Ellie!? What's the matter? What's wrong with Mel!"

"You're hurting me."

He let her go, and she crumpled to the silver floor.

"Angels will not come to save us," Ellie moaned between sobs.

The balloon started rocking and shaking, the wind kicked up violently, though there was no sound except his own dream-breathing and Ellie's joyless sobs.

Dream Buzz had a sudden urge to jump out of the balloon.

An easy way out.

He threw a leg up on the railing.

"No! Buzz no—not the jetty! Not again!" Ellie cried
through her tears...

...and what he saw below was no longer the verdant
mountainsides of Pennsylvania but the whole world as one
enormous badlands—a burning ocean filled with cities en-
gulfed in flames. Buzz saw widows and orphans, and sundry
souls writhing in pain. A world without hope. A world of the
future.

Then his dream-gaze saw the ancient balcony of Saint
Peter's Basilica, in the midst of the world aflame. The square
was filled with the enemies of the Church. They were mock-
ing the Holy Father. He was a short man, with brown skin.
And in the crowd, a boy with a rifle, with hatred in his heart,
taking aim.

No! Buzz cried...

And he fell into another dream...

✝ ✝ ✝

...as the Man dreamed of a faded green farmhouse next
to a barren, empty hayfield that had apparently been cut down
many winters earlier, then poisoned. There were several dead
bodies scattered in the field, all of them shot, all of them in a
line of sight from the dilapidated farmhouse. He found himself in the woods, just beyond the field. His sister Irene and
Buzz were with him.

In that strange way of dreams, he was able to see the faces
of each dead body. Their expressions in death were tranquil,
pacific. They were dressed in the garb of the ancients—robes,
white robes stained with scarlet blood. An angelic voice read
off their names for him, one by one, with great importance of
tone:

Saint Stephen.

Saint Paul.

Saint Lawrence.

Saint Isaac Jogues.

Saint Paul Miki.

Saint Theophane Venard.

Saint Maximilian.

And several more.

Each one a martyr. The hair stood up on the Man's dry, sinewy arms. *Fear.* Pure fear filled him and overflowed out of him.

"What's holding us up?" Buzz asked behind him.

Then the dream-Man saw…well, *the Lord.*

The Lord was on the other side of the field, dressed in a seamless tan garment, just like in all the movies, except now, there was a flight of nine enormous angels in array behind Him, in a giant forest populated by majestic, golden trees with silver leaves.

He smiled at the Man, and motioned at him: *Come with me, Hal!*

"But Lord, I'm afraid," the Man protested.

"What are you saying?" Buzz asked behind him. "Do you see somebody in the field?"

It's worth it. You'll be with me forever, my good and faithful servant. The living shall envy the dead, the Lord promised in dream-telepathy.

Despite his fear, the Man stepped into the barren blood-field, Buzz and Irene following him. Far off, in the green farmhouse, he heard the crinkly sound of glass breaking, and through the corner of his eye, he saw the barrel of a shotgun thrust out the broken window.

Keep your eyes on me, the Lord told him. *You can walk on water…*

Yes, Lord, the Man replied, getting the hang of things. *Of course, Lord…*

And the Man continued to walk forward, into another dream…

The Man woke up in a sweat, crying out. Buzz, next to him, also woke up, and turned on his side.

"Hal, what is it? You okay?"

"Nightmare," the Man said. "Nothing. Just a nightmare."

Buzz yawned. "Me too. Been happening for days now. Wanna pray?"

"Yeah."

So they prayed the old reliable, the Saint Michael Prayer, then began another Rosary. They were snoring by the third decade.

✛ ✛ ✛

A few days later they attended a sublime Sunday Mass celebrated by a bent, devout octogenarian Jesuit named Tim "Tiny" McInerny. Buzz adjusted his back, but he remained bent. (Buzz thought: *You can't unbend a Jesuit.*)

They rested for the afternoon at Mount Pisgah State Park, where they went fishing. They were making good progress, and were now just east of West Burlington, still on Route 6.

There seemed to be more refugees heading west as they got further along into eastern Pennsylvania. These refugees passed along rumors about a "reorganization" of the government taking place in New York and New Jersey. Details were sketchy. There was something about needing a special new card containing a chip in order to receive food.

Neither Buzz nor the Man liked the sound of this, and were wondering if they should head north. Route 6 would soon be taking a southeastward turn at Route 220, which continued down along the Susquehanna River toward Scranton.

The distances between the little towns they passed through were becoming shorter. They decided they would take mail no further than Rummersfield, then depart from Route 6.

Carrying the mail had been a big hit, and along with Buzz's chiropractic abilities, a great source of security for them. Even the towns that refused to take them in accepted the mail, gave them safe passage, and usually gave them mail for the next towns down the line.

The day was beautiful; it was a spring afternoon, and both men noticed the trees were beginning to bud. To save time, they were taking a back road, off Route 6. It was quite warm, and they tied their coats around their waists.

They came over a small crest and there it was: a man-made roadblock constructed with natural materials. Several large oak and maple trees had been cut to fall athwart the road at the bottom of the hill. No one was standing guard.

"What do you think it means?" Buzz asked.

"I don't like it. Maybe somebody doesn't want us to continue on this road," the Man assessed.

Buzz had come to place great weight in the Man's judgments. Buzz's attitude did not affect the Man either way.

"We could double back to Route 6. It's only five or six miles," Buzz suggested.

It struck neither man as strange that Buzz could now so easily append the word *only* before the phrase *five or six miles*.

The Man pulled out his compass, carefully taking a reading. The silvery instrument looked like a white eye in the pink of his palms.

"See down there," the Man pointed with a nod of his bristly chin. "If that dirt road just before the roadblock continues eastward, it could take us back to Route 6. It's getting late, and if that road does go east to 6, we'll save a day or more."

There were many trees in this area, but with their view from the crest, they could see clearly that the dirt road went straight a mile or more, punctuated by a single farmhouse within sight. They had come to trust the Man's compass and sense of direction more than any map, or even the verbal directions from town-dwellers.

Farmhouses. Or sometimes "single subdivisions," as Buzz called them—that is, private homes, not quite farms, set alone on a plot near the road.

These could portend good news or bad news. Often, they were empty, their owners having fled to the local town. Other times, the occupant or occupants would come out, holding a

rifle or shotgun, and watch the two travelers pass by until
they were out of sight.

Buzz would always wave meekly, avoiding eye contact,
as if to say both *Hello* and *No Need to Fear Us.*

More often than not, the Man and Buzz felt the eerie touch
of unseen, wary eyes watching them from inside the nooks
and crannies of the buildings.

Less often, but refreshingly, the owners would come running up to them, with skinny children trailing behind (an overweight child was a rare sight nowadays), looking for news, or
begging for food, or just seeking human contact.

One time, about two weeks ago, while walking on a moon-
lit night, they had heard the distinctive report of a shotgun
come from a dimly-lit cabin set a hundred feet from Route 6.
It was probably a warning shot aimed over their heads. Buzz
and the Man had run as fast as they could for a mile, laughing when the adrenaline wore off, if only because laughing
was better than crying.

And because Buzz liked to laugh.

In general, though, twenty or thirty Saint Michael prayers
per day seemed to be their best defense against the Farmhouse Enigma—another Buzz phrase.

"Oh, here comes another Farmhouse Enigma," he would
say when they spotted a house on the road ahead. They would
automatically (but fervently) pray to Saint Michael and move
forward. It was either impractical or geographically impossible, because of the mountain terrain, to go around every
Enigma. They had no choice but to plow forward.

Today, with the sun an hour from the western horizon,
they reluctantly decided to take the dirt road.

An hour later, the road had narrowed into a path barely
wide enough for them to walk side-by-side. At the crest of
the last hill, they had spied what they believed to be Route 6
a mile or two off in the distance, and felt relieved. They could
make it there, no sweat. Just another hill or two to traverse in
between.

Until the road stopped cold. There was a stand of woods, a walking path leading into the growing darkness. Like mice deep into a maze, they vaguely regretted they had not turned back at the roadblock.

They looked at each other and silently decided to move forward. Going off-road like this had proven difficult several times in the past. The brush could thicken, making progress slow. They could run into a river or wide stream, forcing them to get wet if they crossed, or, just as annoying, forcing them to walk alongside the bank until they came to a bridge or a stretch narrow enough to leap over.

Buzz stopped.

"Hal? Did you hear something?" he whispered.

"Ssshh. Could've been a deer…or something."

The Man, reacting to his instincts, took the Ruger off his shoulder, checked his load, then took the point.

They stepped lightly. Fifty yards later they came to an opening. They crouched and surveyed.

It was almost completely dark now.

There was an old green farmhouse—a salt box frame with clapboard siding, a hundred yards to their left. Its windows were darkened. There was no telltale smoke coming from its stone chimney. There was a hand-pump near the front door, and behind the house, a red barn. The field in front of them, which stretched for about a quarter mile, had obviously been plowed by tractor a while back, probably last fall; perhaps it had been corn. Neither Buzz nor the Man had any farming experience, but the organic, light-gray stubble in neat length-wise rows before them looked familiar—almost Ohio-ish.

There was no sign of life.

Far away, they heard a cow moo.

"There's livestock in that barn," Buzz mouthed in ultra-low super-whisper mode.

The Man nodded. He held his index and middle fingers to his eyes, then pointed toward the farmhouse.

Look over there…

Buzz looked. He saw nothing, then shook his head.

The Man had seen something in the window of the house. A shadow moving within a shadow. His senses, already heightened, ratcheted up a notch.

He put a hand on Buzz's forearm, holding it steady, signaling for Buzz to remain entirely still.

They listened, waiting, completely motionless for several minutes, chests heaving imperceptibly, the Man's eyes fixed on the window. He saw nothing in the shadows. *Maybe I was imagining things.*

Without moving, he whispered to Buzz, "We can't wait here forever. I'll go first."

"We can still turn around."

The Man shook his head ever so slightly. *If we're being hunted*—and he was sure in his bones this was the case—*they will follow us.*

There was no way to explain this to his friend. *We might as well make a dash toward Route 6. It can't be too far ahead.*

"Game time," he whispered soberly.

Buzz nodded. *Just like on the courts.*

The Man meant: *Stay cool. Get ready.*

An image of the Man on the Rocky River courts, slipping like black mercury down the lane between two giant defenders flashed into Buzz's mind.

Their eyes were adjusting to the darkness now, but clouds had come overhead. There was not much ambient moonlight.

"I'll go slow, then signal you to follow by swinging my right hand down, like this, palm open," the Man instructed. "Then you go full speed. Watch your ankle in those furrows. Got me?"

His voice was businesslike, and except for the ultra-low whisper, exactly the same as hundreds of times coaching Buzz on the courts.

"Yeah," Buzz whispered, his eyes widening. He tried to control his breathing.

"It's probably nothing," the Man reassured him.

Right, Buzz nodded. *Saint Michael the Archangel...*

The Man took a deep breath, and coming out of his crouch, still leaning forward, his Ruger floating comfortably in both hands in front of him, made his first step out from under the cover.

Buzz split his attention between the farmhouse and the Man, who quickly scooted a third of the way across the field.

A little voice spoke to Buzz: ...*to your right. Look to your right.*

He shifted his gaze, and in the woods beyond the field, on the opposite side of the farmhouse, he spotted..it. *A flash of glass.*

A rifle scope? A night-vision goggle? Buzz couldn't know this for sure. But there was somebody there!

What should I do? Call to Hal, who was halfway across the field? *Run forward?*

He decided to do both.

"Hal! To your right!!" Buzz hollered with all his lungs, the veins on his neck straining, then moving forward, thighs churning, knees high, quickly gaining to full speed.

The Man turned to his right.

The sound of a rifle report came from the woods to the right, where Buzz had spotted the hunter...

...and the Man was spun around by the impact and flopped to the ground.

"Noooooo! Basstaarrds!" Buzz screamed, hearing another gunshot over his voice as he did so, loping almost halfway to the darkened clump of his friend, who was barely scuddling around on the ground...

To Buzz's left, at the farmhouse, the distinctive jingle of breaking glass...and the business end of a shotgun thrust out the window where the Man had seen the shadow move...

...and Buzz was suddenly at the Man's side. The Man was struggling mightily to pull his backpack off.

Another rifle shot.

Buzz's backpack, parallel to the crossfire, thumped instantly, but Buzz quickly assessed that he had not been hit. He dove into a furrow, dirt punching into his mouth.

"You shot? Let's go! Hail Mary!" Buzz reached to pull the Man up, but the Man shook him off.

"We're safer separated! Keep running!" he growled at Buzz. "I'm okay! I'm right behind you! Go now!"

…the force in the Man's voice hit Buzz like a hurricane wind.

Man's right, so go! his instincts—and his angel—convinced him. *Mel!*

Buzz leaped up and galloped toward Route 6.

In one quick movement the Man pulled himself up onto one knee, sighted his Ruger, and calmly squeezed off five rounds in the direction of the rifleman in the woods, then rolled toward Buzz, then back up onto one knee, and repeated his cover fire—three rounds. He had two rounds left. He kept Buzz in his peripheral vision.

Buzz was almost beyond the field. *Good.*

The Man took off after him, zig-zagging toward his friend.

Buzz watched in amazement as the Man came toward him. There were no more shots from the woods, but the shotgun was roaring away. Four blasts, then a pause. Four blasts, pause. (Buzz deduced the pause was for reloading.)

Maybe the Man got the guy in the woods.

Maybe not.

Both Buzz and the Man knew intellectually that shotgun accuracy at this range was suspect, but it didn't lessen the sheer terror of being shot at. Buzz was now certain that he himself had not been hit.

Watching the familiar, silky gait of the Man, unburdened by his backpack, as he ducked and feigned, streaking toward him, gave Buzz hope.

Come on come on come on! Only a few more yards!

Surely the Man would not be able to run like this if he had been shot.

He's okay!

There was an unintelligible shout from the green farmhouse.

Seconds stretched into psuedo-hours, and then the Man was with Buzz, diving the last few feet into the bramble.

"Let's move out," the Man said, breathing heavily. "Stay close!"

And so they ran, as rabbits and deer and squirrels run, with the fervor and zeal only the hunted share, through the thick and the thicket, toward what their instincts told them was the east, toward Route 6, toward *safety*, which could only be defined as:

Not here.

They ran and they ran. For minutes, then tens of minutes, their legs strong, their bodies hard, built up by weeks on the road, mentally trained to trust each other by years on the courts together; Buzz with loping, virile power; the Man with darting, light strides, the deftness of a butterfly.

They stumbled up a small ravine and burst from the woods and onto a road.

"It's Route 6!" Buzz shouted.

The Man didn't stop. He ran right by his friend.

So Buzz followed, catching up, both of them truly winded now, but at a healthy jog, side by side, in the darkness.

After five minutes, the Man said between breaths, "Hold on."

Buzz stopped abruptly.

They bent over, clasping their knees, sucking air.

"Let's jump back up into—" the Man paused for a breath "—into the woods here. Behind that big rock. Where we can monitor the road."

The Man was already rummaging into Buzz's backpack for ammunition in order to reload his Ruger.

"Safer that way," he finished.

"Sure. Up the hill then," Buzz agreed, then spit. "You okay?"

"Yeah, I'm great," the Man replied.

And so they left the road and climbed up behind the huge granite rock, which itself was surrounded by low pines and

bushes. Buzz pulled off his backpack, then poked his finger
into the two bullet holes.

Oh Mary! Oh Jesus, God. Bullets! Thank you! Mel!

Disturbed by the manic incongruity of his thoughts, Buzz
forced himself to calm down by repeating, slowly:

Thank you, Mary. Thank you, Mary...

They sat with their backs to the rock, facing uphill, away
from the road. The Man, rifle at the ready, peered around to
his left, toward Route 6.

They waited this way, their breathing gradually slowing
along with the adrenaline rush, alternately praying and replaying the event in their minds, until sleep felled them.

Chapter Eleven

Hard Cold World

When Buzz woke up, he first noticed the strange smell. He did not recognize it. Over the past weeks they had both gotten used to the odors of their unbathed bodies—to the point that they didn't notice at all.

The frantic run during the escape had drained Buzz completely, and he had slept soundly, beyond dreams, during the warm night. He had snuggled next to the Man while he was asleep, his head nestled on his friend's shoulder.

What is that smell?

He straightened up, feeling sore all around, noticing his surroundings in the morning shadow of sunlight.

Reflexively, he began his morning prayer: *Dear Jesus, I don't know what will happen to me today, I only know that nothing will happen to me that was not foreseen by You, and directed to my greater good from all eternity. I adore Your holy and unfathomable plans—*

—the pungent smell barreled up his nostrils, interrupting his prayer.

Last night came back to him quickly, along with the gripping emotional fear the events had provoked. He wondered now if they were really out of danger.

Ask the Man what to do.

He jostled the Man's shoulder. His friend groaned a far-away groan.

"Wake up, Hal," he whispered. "It's morning."

The Man turned his head, and with great effort, opened his eyes. He smiled.

There was an angelic peace in his smile. But there was something wrong. His expression of peace became troubled.

"Buzz, your hands," the Man whispered hoarsely.

Buzz looked down at his hands, and saw…blood!

Some of the blood was dry, cracked and darkened, but a lot of it was new, liquidy, dripping down onto his forearm, which was also covered with small scrapes and bruises suffered during last night's scramble through the thicket.

How could these little cuts have bled so much? he asked himself, confused.

Blood—and something else—had been the source of the unusual smell.

Buzz looked from his hand and forearm to the Man's stomach, where his arm had been moments earlier while he had been asleep.

"Hal! You're bleeding!"

"Been shot," the Man said weakly.

Buzz gingerly opened Hal's jacket. The shirt had already been partially torn by…the bullet.

The blood was coagulated, hiding the bullet hole, but a gnarled piece of flesh was protruding out—

Buzz could not bear to look at it. His focus shifted frantically to the Man's eyes.

"Let's fix you up!" Buzz cried out.

"Shssshh," the Man cautioned, his voice alarmingly weak. "They could have followed us. Following our trail. Might have dogs."

Pathetically, the Man tried to sit up, and made an effort to hold the Ruger at attention, looking away from Buzz, toward the road below.

Buzz spoke with a clear voice. "We're going to dress that wound. Let me help you. Lie down! Now!"

The Man ignored him, and continued looking down at the road.

"Don't bother," he replied evenly. "I'm going to die today. Today is the day of glory."

"No!" Buzz shouted.

Buzz scrambled around the Man and the grey rock, slipping down the hill, then pulled himself back up to face him. "You can't die! I won't let you. No freakin' way!"

The serene smile returned. He carefully placed his Ruger onto his lap, winced, and lifted a hand to Buzz's face, now covered with dirt and scraggly beard, touching it tenderly. Buzz thought of his own mother—the mother he had never known.

And Mel.

Buzz tried to speak, but the Man's eyes held him silent. Tears welled up.

"Listen to me—" the Man began.

"No," Buzz interrupted with a croak.

"Listen to me!" the Man said forcefully—as loud as he could, which was not loud at all, wincing again, coughing from the effort.

Buzz looked down. The reality of the situation was striking him now, placing a heavy weight on his soul.

The Man is dying.

"Buzz, I have something I must tell you. We don't have much time. The Lord has spoken to me. Today is the day of glory. But He has a word for you—"

The Man began to cough violently, and his torso pitched forward. Buzz awkwardly crawled toward him, then carefully put his arms around the Man's shoulders, holding him until the coughing subsided.

The Man allowed himself to be lowered into Buzz's lap. In all their trials, as Buzz now wondered if the Man would last even a minute more, none of their long silences had matched these few moments.

There were no birds singing, or jets in the sky, or breezes ruffling the pines or leaves together. It was completely silent, except for the Man's shallow breathing.

Dear Sweet Jesus, not the Man! Not the Man! Buzz prayed, looking down at the beautiful ashen face of holiness.

The Man opened his eyes, which were more yellow than ever. His physical vitality on the trip had hidden from Buzz until this moment that the Man was well over fifty, of another generation. Buzz realized that he had never adjusted the Man's back, or even offered. He felt immensely guilty.

The Man had been so *strong*.

"I see the Lord!" the Man exclaimed softly. "He's coming for me. I see Mel, too! She's with Him."

He's seeing things, Buzz thought disjointedly.

"No, stay here," Buzz sobbed, unable to look at his friend, unable to look away. "We've got to go to Bagpipe. You and me. Sam and Ellie are waiting for us. Mel and the boys are waiting…you and me, we're a team…"

The tears came in a steady flow now. Buzz tried to control the shaking of his own body, welling up from his belly, in an effort to reduce the stress on the Man.

He took his hand and forearm and wrapped it around the Man's neck, resting his hand just above the wound.

How did you ever make that run last night?

"He's a-coming on a cloud!" the Man cried.

The Man was not with Buzz anymore, and was gazing up toward the empty blue sky.

He was an old man having a vision, in the arms of a young man dreaming dreams.

"O Sacred Head…surrounded," the Man sang low, slowly, tunelessly, to Buzz, "by crown of piercing thorn…"

"No, no… no," Buzz begged. "Stay here, Hal. Stay with me—"

The Man's body stiffened. His gaze shifted toward Buzz. The Man was suddenly *here* again.

"Buzz, listen to the Lord. Can you hear Him?"

The Man coughed harshly.

Buzz shook his head, knowing, in that way of soul-knowing, that the time had come.

"Oh…oh…I love Him so," the Man confided. "Today is the day of glory. He says you gonna make it to Bagpipe…that's great news, isn't it?"

"Huh?" Buzz asked, his heart skipping a beat. "He says what?"

"…make it to Bagpipe…" the Man repeated.

Then, his voice shifted, and became strong, the voice of Another: "Keep your hand on the plow, my son."

"…the plow?"

"The plow," the Man whispered weakly, the voice of the Other gone. "Yes, the plow…He has a heavy plow, for a big man, all ready…to go…for you…" the Man's voice was fading quickly, "He's a-saying that He…wants *me* to go with you…Amen, Sweet Jesus…I'll go! I'll go… with Buzz …to… Bag-… …pipe—"

And Hal Smith's last breath left his lungs. And his eyes lost their light. And his soul left his body.

And Buzz, alone, shaking uncontrollably with huge, silent sobs, held on to the lifeless body of the Man, unable to let go.

Hail Mary, full of grace. Hail Mary, full of grace. Hail Mary, full of grace…

✝ ✝ ✝

An hour later, the sobbing had ceased. The stimuli of the weight of the body, and the blood on the shirt, and the feel of the Man's frizzy hair under his chin, and the smell of no-life, gradually seeped in.

What to do next?

Don't freak out, for one thing, he steeled himself.

That was number one on the list.

Stay sane.

He gently moved the Man's body off his lap. He stood up, leaning on the rock, averting his eyes from the corpse. He noticed how sore his ankle had become—must have taxed it during the run last night.

You can't afford to go crazy. Keep your hand on the plow. That's what the Man says. Keep your hand on the plow.

Yes, a heavy weight was on his soul, just as it had been during the dark, terrible days before his suicide attempt, but now there were…*others* depending on his sanity. He had taken a sacramental vow.

Mel, Markie, Packy.

He had travelled on *that* road—the road of the insane—before.

No way, don't go there, Cowboy. Gotta stay tuned.

Gotta pray.

So Buzz carefully, methodically folded his hands, his hip against the rock, the corpse at this feet, and then closed his eyes.

Do the simple prayers. The ones that come easy. It's been a hard day so far. No need to get fancy.

Buzz prayed three Hail Marys. He concentrated on each word. He felt nothing.

But his faith gave him hope beyond mere feelings.

"I see Mel, too!" the Man's strange words drifted back to Buzz.

The Man was hallucinating. Sure, he was. Had to be. He lost a lot of blood. Or maybe he saw Jesus with her in Bagpipe, with Sam and Ellie and the boys…yeah, that's what he saw.

Good. Excellent.

Buzz wondered about what to do next. He looked around, up the hill, then down to the road. There were light breezes coming in from the south now, and he welcomed the sound of their songs in the leaves.

What to do next? He closed his eyes, and prayed the prayer that has no words. The prayer of a child, a movement of a soul with no power of its own.

A list of things to do came unbidden to his consciousness—as if infused from another being. This, in fact, was the case. Our Lady, having heard his prayers, and shared his tears, prompted her broken son with this partial list:

…Feed the hungry.

Clothe the naked.

Bury the dead…

Bury the dead. He had his answer.

✝ ✝ ✝

His following hours drained into a numb series of activities. Buzz forced himself into his tasks, directing his focus on his actions, on the movements of his hands, on the worn wooden handle of his workaday plow.

He took an inventory of his tools. He still had the canteen, the ammunition, the compass (which the Man, with keen foresight, had slipped into his pocket during the gun battle...), a sleeping bag, the bleach, one hunting knife, one snare trap, the gold coins, the sharpening stone, the needle-nosed pliers, a few items.

Unfortunately, the mini-tent, the fishing pole, the screwdriver, the Bible, the camp cookware—had all been lost in the abandoned backpack.

He still had the Zippo, but the cans of lighter fluid were lost.

Buzz took the Man's scapular from the corpse, scraped off the dried blood, and placed it around his own neck. He found a Saint Benedict medal in the Man's pocket, and put it in his own pocket. To his surprise, Buzz discovered a first-class relic of Saint Thérèse of Lisieux, the Man's favorite saint, in the other pocket.

Using the hunting knife to strip two fallen branches he found on the floor of the woods, which he fastened together using his and the Man's socks (pulling them off the Man's feet had been—something to not remember...), along with his sleeping bag, Buzz fashioned a crude, Indian-style stretcher. He loaded the body onto it, and began the most challenging walk of his journey—dragging it by the open ends of the two branches along the highway. It took seven hours, and it was almost sundown, before he came to a town whose name he forgot.

There was no Catholic church there, so he passed through, his hands raw with blisters, the muscles of his thick, undefined forearms swelling against the weight of the load.

It's only pain.

He found a stream, and washed himself and his clothes in the ice cold water. It took him a day and a half to reach the next town. This town had a Catholic church, Saint Gregory the Great, maintained by an old, starving priest named Father Antonio Mastreoni, who agreed to say the funeral Mass.

But first, Buzz found a local carpenter, and paid him a gold coin to construct a crude, plywood coffin.

To earn a meal from the town, Buzz forced himself to play the role of jovial chiropractor, but could not bring himself to tell the stories to the children.

During the funeral Mass that evening, feeling numb to all emotion, Buzz gave this eulogy to a church empty except for himself, the priest, and the Lord in the Blessed Sacrament:

"Hal Smith was a practicing Catholic and he was my friend. I'm sure he likes the fact that he is being buried from a church that has a statue of the Little Flower.

"For the last six years of his life, during every waking moment, he loved God with all his mind, with all his heart, and with all his soul. He was the best point guard in the history of the Rocky River courts. His love was so great that he laid down his life for me. He was a perfect saint. He was the Man, and there will never be another."

As he walked back into the town from the cemetery, having buried the casket alone after the old priest left, staring down at his dirty boots, Buzz heard the tinny *ring-ring* of a bell.

He looked up and saw a black kid, no older than seven, riding a bicycle toward him, a brown package in the basket attached to the front of the handlebars.

"Hi mister!" the kid smiled and waved, zipping past.

Bicycle, Buzz thought.

✝ ✝ ✝

The nights were the worst; that's when he missed the Man the most. Buzz tossed and turned. Every sound startled him.

He would sleep on his back, the Ruger on his chest, the hunting knife unsheathed next to his thigh. There were only so many Rosaries he could pray.

"I see Mel! She's with Him!"

He made a great effort to turn his mind from this—this *thing,* but these words of the Man kept coming back to him, draining Buzz's spirit.

Mel.

On most nights his terror finally led to exhaustion, and he awoke feeling dirty, hungry, then started walking east. He drank water, but he felt weaker and weaker in body and soul. There was little fat left on his body for reserve. He estimated that he was now below two hundred pounds.

The Amazing Millennium Diet, he joked ruefully.

He tried to hunt, and one time, shot a squirrel.

After two days with nothing substantial to eat, he found a dead cat, limp but not stiff, on the white line in the center of the road.

Tastes just like chicken, he joked blackly. *Sure it does.*

He skinned it and broiled it on a spit, just as the Man had taught him with the squirrels and rabbits, and forced himself to consume the gamey strands of flesh—and with greater effort, willed himself not to regurgitate it.

Mel. Markie. Packy. With each chew.

Eventually, trading time for calories, he learned to sit in the forest off the road for hours, waiting for a bird or a squirrel, perfectly still, his ankle aching, and he became better at shooting them.

Mechanically, before he came into the towns, he would shave his whiskers with the blade, using a brook or puddle as a mirror if he was able—*Mel, Markie, Packy*—preparing like an actor before a performance.

Yes, most men had beards now, he told himself. He knew his clean face made the best impression.

He was physically and emotionally drained almost all the time, but he was still as smart as they come.

Buzz accepted the crude fact that God had probably made him this way—smart—in order to survive this particular trip. This gave him little consolation.

The living will envy the dead, an insistent voice sometimes tempted.

He had loved—and still loved—the Man too much to envy the Man's day of glory.

So he cleaned his clothes, and shaved his face, and pasted on a smile as if it were a false mustache before he entered the towns.

The illusion complete, he would perform his easy-going spiel for the sentry or the mayor or the local strongman or the sheriff, feigning energy and confidence; praying wordlessly before the tabernacle if there was a Catholic church. Then he would adjust spines in exchange for food. Though now he spoke only when necessary to perform the act, and always, he felt a low-intensity jolt when he came out from the therapy sessions into the sun, or into the moonlight, and the Man was not there waiting for him.

Lately, the rations he was given were smaller and smaller— a chunk of stale bread, a bruised potato, a piece of cheese. But also, on more occasions, there was a piece of fresh fruit, a tomato, a slice or two of newly-butchered venison, a handful of nuts.

Sometimes, even during the day as he walked, erotic images of his wife would slipslide into his imagination, but he was not aroused. He would make great efforts to picture Markie and Packy in his mind's eye, but their faces had become blurs. Their names became disembodied words. He would try to remember times he had wrestled with them on the pink carpet of the Lakewood house, but he could not conjure up their faces.

He turned northeast on 706, and in a little town called Brandt, he traded his extra five-hundred-round box of ammo and a gold coin for an old, sturdy mountain bike—including two extra inner tubes, a patch kit, and a homemade wire basket large enough for his pack.

It was early May.

It rained less often. The weather had turned. He lost track of the days on the hand-drawn calendar in the little notebook the Man had left him.

Perhaps because of the starvation everywhere, there was a thinning of refugees on the main roads, although one time he pedaled right through the center of a gaggle of eight or so in one group—men, women carrying babies, and children.

They had called at him and cursed him, but he plowed forward, wordless, the hardened look in his eyes breaking their column. Who wanted to mess with a crazy man with a Ruger on his shoulder?

The long, sometimes steep hills were not easy to climb with the bike, so more often than not, he walked it up, then glided down the declines.

He was making better time, not as concerned about what harm might come his way. He was alone and at the mercy of fate. Either the Man's prophecy that he would reach Bagpipe was true or it wasn't. He would find out, he supposed.

Shoot me, or take my possessions, or do whatever, Buzz thought as he pedaled toward the next wanderer within his sight on the road. *I'll roll right through you.*

And so he did. Sometimes it seemed as if these others— many carrying their own psychological scars on their sleeves—did not even see Buzz as he whistled by within arm's reach of their ragged, thin bodies.

Mel, Markie, Packy. His mantra.

Buzz felt like a machine, and he was. Soul-sick, driven, manipulative, brows furrowed when alone on the road, dreamless.

Lonely. Mourning. Missing his friend more than he missed even his wife or his sons, and feeling guilt because of it.

Then he rolled into the town of Blackstone, off Route 30 in the Catskill Mountains southeast of Albany.

✚ ✚ ✚

Oberlin. Mark Johnson thrust the shovel into the pile, and threw a clump of mud onto Maggie's grave.

It was raining. Seamus took the shovel from his father's mighty hand, then followed suit.

"You finish, son," Mark said. "I need to spend some time alone. Pray for your mother, then look in on Meg."

The boy nodded as he began to bury his mother's body. Were those tears on his cheeks, or were they just raindrops?

Have I raised another Johnson robot?

It was hard for Mark to tell, for his son did not speak very often nowadays. Sure, the boy jumped to do anything Mark asked of him. Would take a bullet, no doubt, but he otherwise sat silently in his corner of the shack, pretending to read that stupid paperback.

Accompanied by far-off thunder, Mark lifted one foot after another until he was behind the shack, and raised his hands into the sky, palms open, the rain pelting his thick, handsome features, running through his bristly auburn hair, down his back.

It's a hard, cold world, Lord.

And so it was.

Why can't I cry?

It wasn't because he hadn't loved her. His love was true, and had been until the end, when her stovepipe breathing came to a halt, and her phlegm-filled lungs had finally been overtaken by the pneumonia that had taken her while she was in his arms. He was proud of her—the way she fought until the end, for Seamus and little Meggie's sake, despite the blow of losing Angela the week before to the same killer virus or bacteria or whatever it had been.

He let his arms drop, then sat on a wet stump, oblivious to the water. Time to think. Thinking, not bravery alone, won wars.

He couldn't kill what he couldn't see.

His rice and his gold coins and his aspirin and his hardware had proven pathetically, perfectly, powerless before the unseen scourge that had destroyed the lungs of his wife and daughter.

His wary foray on foot into downtown Oberlin, that den of witches and warlocks, rifle at the ready, had been a pitiful joke.

The two skeletons standing shift at the college infirmary had actually laughed at him when he took out the gold coins and asked for medicine...

"Penicillin? Antibiotics? Sure, coming right up," they had mocked, making a big show of checking a cabinet and a drawer. *"Oops! All gone! We'll call you when the next shipment comes in. Get it? We'll call you. On the phone!"*

Ho ho ho.

A hard cold world like this didn't deserve a woman like Maggie. She had remained soft and warm, inside and out, to the end, praying, offering it up, making him promise to remain strong, promise to protect Seamus and Meg, claiming to see the Blessed Mother at the very end, mixing her cries of physical agony with those of spiritual ecstasy.

She had died well, like a Johnson. He was proud of her.

Why couldn't he cry?

Because he knew the whole tragedy had been his fault. That bastard Sam Fisk had been right all along. Mark knew beyond doubt that his own pathetic little insurance policy had been hubris, a miscalculated, insignificant failure.

Mark was not an emotional man, and this helped him bat away the temptation to hurl his anger at Bill White for this predicament. Bill had been sincere in his role as devil's advocate to Sam Fisk's doom and gloom—Bill had given Mark nothing but the straight poop, at least by Bill's lights.

God have mercy on his soul, wherever Bill was by now—most likely in a grave or praying above one.

Maggie and Angela were dead because of Mark's lack of judgment and foresight, and he knew it. He had gambled their lives on a *bump in the road* or an *ice storm*—to recall those bitter rationalizations that came so glibly to every tongue before the horrors—and had lost.

He could have sold his house, quit his job, spent all his savings. Moved to Bagpipe. Scratched out a living up there somehow.

Woulda-coulda-shoulda. That kind of thinking was not like a Johnson.

He rejected all temptation to bellyache.

Taking out a policy for a total collapse had seemed too expensive at the time. Plus, he had felt so smug about the water pump, the rice, the ammo, the coins, the woodstove.

He, the Great Mark Johnson, had been *ready.*

Ho ho ho.

Ready for what? Certainly not ready for anything.

Not ready for this.

And in a day or two, no doubt, little Meg, cheated out of the first bloom of her womanhood, would follow Maggie to heaven because of his error. The waterlogged breathing had already begun in the twelve-year-old's lungs.

He could carry her somewhere, looking for medicine. He was strong. But where? In the rain?

Better to pray for a miracle, which is what he did night and day, to fill the silences. He accepted that Maggie's grace-filled death had been an answer to his prayers—just not the answer he had wanted.

Yet he did not *feel* helpless.

He was too tough, too faith-filled for that.

He *was* helpless.

And so he mourned the only woman he had ever loved, ever married, ever shared his magnificent body with, ever sacrificed his precious ego for, ever wanted, or ever needed.

He had only the Immaculate Virgin now, and *she* was with his Maggie.

He sat motionless in the warm rain, a breathing statue.

He accepted the plain, undressed fact that losing control was not an option. Maggie's memory would be *defiled* by the mere consideration of giving up or giving in. Seamus and Meg were *hers,* too, and he owed it to her to do everything—everything—in his power to save them.

He could mourn Maggie proper later—if there *was* a later. And if there wasn't a later, he reasoned in faith, he would be with Maggie, anyway.

So he set aside thoughts about his only true love, Margaret Johnson, and methodically sifted through his own mind, praying for inspiration, looking to find a way to save Meg and Seamus.

He accepted the reality that he could not expect to hole up in Oberlin indefinitely. His rice and ammo would not last forever (he had already given a portion of both to three neighbors who had asked politely). He could maybe bag another deer, but the game would thin out quickly as others took to the woods in search of protein. Besides, he had no way to store the meat beyond a few days. He was already out of salt, and was pretty sure that even if he did have salt, he didn't really know how to safely dry and salt meat.

Then there was the security issue. He and Seamus were already standing alternate shifts at guard duty. That kind of thing would wear on the boy eventually. On the other hand, Mark couldn't stay awake twenty-four hours a day. He had already been forced to shoot one poor sonufabitch—two weeks ago—who had shown the audacity to slither up Mark's driveway, shotgun in hand, at three in the morning. Mark, crouching in a shadow at his cabin window, had tranquilly squeezed off two rounds, and later, buried the corpse in the woods, off his property.

The defensive killing had not bothered Mark's conscience in the least. The intruder had been trespassing, had a loaded weapon, and the time and manner of his approach had been more than probable cause.

Even before the Troubles, Mark might have shot him. He had shot and killed a drug dealer once during his early years in the Bureau, back when he had worked the streets.

It was getting warmer, and the survivors from the city and the suburbs would be coming out to the country soon enough.

Those city boys'll be out here three days after they've scraped and scavenged every calorie off the shelves in the suburbs. And the meanest ones'll get here first.

Nope, Oberlin was definitely not a viable long-term strategy, though with the woodstove, the well, and his stockpile of food, he figured they could hold out well into the summer, barring unforeseen security problems.

Barring unforeseen security problems.

There was the rub. It was out of his power to *bar* security problems, all right, and when they did come, they would definitely be *unforeseen*.

Mark was a man of wisdom. While he would not hesitate to kill in self-defense, he was also fully aware that those who lived by the sword usually died by it. There was always some bad guy out there with better aim and a bigger gun.

What about New Hampshire?

That was crazy.

Maybe Buzz was crazy, maybe he wasn't, his most trusted inner voice told him. *There's crazy and then there's crazy. It's a different world now.*

It sure is, Mark thought.

He rejected the foolhardy idea out of hand. There had to be a *local* option.

What if there isn't?

There just had to be.

Do you mean local—local like this little retreat you set up here in Oberlin that killed Maggie?

So where? *Not here.*

He knew the idea of staying here was a temptation he must resist. He could not allow himself to be *lulled* by its familiarity and comforts (yes, for a fellow like Mark Johnson, three daily meals of rice, frigid water from a hand-pump, and a hole out back for a commode was plenty comfortable).

Staying here was the *soft* option. Why else would that scumbag have come crawling up the drive, locked and loaded and ready to rumble? Everybody was after *soft*.

Maggie deserved better than *soft*.

Then what?

It was a hard, cold world.

Mark Johnson was a hard, cold man.

He would have to come up with something.

Time passed. He rose from his perfect stillness and returned to the shack to hold Meggie, to cherish as much time with her as he could before she left him.

Chapter Twelve

Blackstone

New York State.

Off the beaten path of interstate highways, the town of Blackstone nestled at the bottom of a hill. It had seen its best days in the mid-1800s, when its paraffin factory, closed in 1910, had employed three hundred and supplied a world that lusted more and more after electric bulbs.

A handful of mountain farms in the surrounding hillsides stood barren, waiting for a harvest of sweet potatoes and yams that would probably not come this year—the farmers had no diesel left for their rickety tractors.

Buzz Woodward stopped on his bicycle, and gazed down at the town from the road. He briefly considered moving along until he spotted white smoke puffing from the chimney of a white clapboard building that he deduced must be a church of some denomination or other. It was too far away and there were too many trees for him to see if there was a telltale statue on the grounds.

Maybe it's a Catholic church?

He needed a confession more than food. The bitterness in his heart about losing the Man was starving his spirit.

Mel, Markie, Packy...

An old Clash tune drifted into his head: *Should I stay or should I go?*

You need a confession, his angel whispered.

Maybe there was a priest down there.

Buzz decided to find out. The dull ache of hunger in his stomach, and the decline of the road into town, sealed his decision. He listened.

Yes! He heard the sound of a brook.

He jumped off his bike, walked into the woods, and found it running parallel to the road, a quarter mile in. He methodically went through his routine of cleaning himself, including, as best he could, blindly trimming his crewcut. The style was his link to the past—and without the luxury of bathing, his scalp remained less miserably itchy.

His back wheel clicked as he glided slowly up the main street. There was no roadblock or sentry here, just the usual empty storefronts—Unique Antiques! Mrs. Donut, Johnson's Shell and Service, Three Penny Diner. There was no traffic light, and only one paved road running perpendicular to the main street (this time, however, it was named Oak Avenue—he was no longer in Pennsylvania, after all). The other road was Church Street, and as he cycled through the ghost town, he noted that there were two other churches—a tiny Church of the Nazarene and a gray, stone First Presbyterian Church of Blackstone, the Reverend Nathan Hawthorne, Pastor (if the glass and steel sign was still accurate).

He pulled up to the front steps of the third church, the last one on the block, sandwiched between two residential homes with overgrown grass (a common sight now that lawn mowers were museum pieces).

Our Lady of the Angels.

There were three bicycles parked here, and he arched his neck to look around to the back of the church. No cars. An abandoned U-Haul trailer stood alone, its doors swinging open.

Buzz heard the sound of a man's voice coming from inside the church.

The priest.

He climbed the steps, opened the door, and saw a man at the lectern who was reading out loud. Behind the reader was a skinny, bald man in a suit, sitting in the sanctuary. Buzz was immediately disappointed at their glaring lack of Roman collars—they probably were not priests.

There must be a priest here! Buzz deduced as he saw the monstrance on the altar, exposing the Savior. His disappointment shifted to elation.

"—the light shines in the darkness—"

The bespectacled man behind the lectern stopped reading and looked up from his Bible. His seersucker suit was clean and obviously well-pressed, and he had a little paunch.

"Well hello, stranger," he addressed Buzz. "We're just finishing a prayer vigil here. You're welcome to join us."

Buzz looked around and saw that the little church was packed. Every space in every pew was occupied. There were children, adults, old folks. Teenagers knelt in the side aisles. Their clothes hung loosely on their limbs, but their faces were clean; their clasped hands were not shaking. Some were even shaven.

Buzz nodded, smiled sheepishly, and found a place in the back behind the last pew, where he knelt on the carpet.

"The light shines in the darkness," the preacher continued. "But the darkness has not overcome it."

The man closed the Bible, put his hands on the lectern, then shut his eyes.

"Dear Jesus, we believe in You and we love You. Turn not Your ears from our heartfelt pleas. Heal Your daughter, Sister Emmanuel, so she may continue to lead our town in Your Holy Will. Amen."

The congregation echoed the man's amen, and all raised their heads from prayer. Those in the back who were kneeling stood up, Buzz included, and those on the kneelers sat down.

"Amen," the man repeated. He sat down in a chair in the sanctuary, and the skinny man behind him rose and came to the lectern.

"Thank you, Pastor Ellison, for that beautiful homily and Word of God. Our service is almost over."

"Will we be laying on hands, Deacon Samuels?" a young male voice called out from somewhere in the front.

"Yes, certainly." Samuel's eyes shifted to a spot in the front of the church. Buzz could not see who he was looking at.

Pastor? Deacon? Is this really a Catholic church?

But there was a monstrance. Yet it just didn't feel Catholic. Maybe it was Anglican. But the sign had said *Our Lady of the Angels Catholic Church,* hadn't it?

"Is this a Catholic church?" Buzz asked the pimply-faced teenage boy standing next to him. The boy gave him a funny look, but nodded.

Some in the congregation were filing up to the front now. Buzz saw a wheelchair as it was rolled to the center aisle before the altar. The wheelchair held an old lady wearing a religious habit.

This must be Sister Emmanuel.

The old nun's eyes remained closed. Buzz knelt in the center aisle and watched. He prayed a Hail Mary, then, *Lord, please heal this woman.*

A dozen others from the congregation gathered around her, including Pastor Ellison, and laid hands on her—on her head, her shoulders, her hips, her torso—and proceeded to pray in silence over her for what seemed like a long time to Buzz. Over ten minutes.

No one left the church. Those remaining in the pews returned to their knees and prayed.

For the first time since the Man had died, Buzz did not feel alone.

Without any cue, the laying on of hands ended, and the congregation began to file out past Buzz, who remained kneeling, his eyes closed, unwilling to abandon the deep state of recollection he was experiencing.

When he opened his eyes, there were seven people remaining in the front with the sister. The Sacred Host had been removed from the monstrance—Buzz caught a last-second glimpse of the man who had been called Deacon Samuels closing the tabernacle.

He must be a Catholic deacon, he surmised.

Buzz slowly walked up to the nun and her friends. He carefully genuflected before the tabernacle to his right.

They looked at him. He looked at them.

"My name is Buzz Woodward. I'm a Catholic on my way to New Hampshire to get to my family. I practice chiropractic medicine. Maybe I can help."

The astonished look in their eyes floored him. They broke out in huge smiles.

"Hello, Mr. Woodward," the pastor said, sticking out his hand.

Buzz shook it firmly. The pastor was no doubt surprised by the strength of the grip, just as Buzz was surprised by the weakness in Ellison's. Beneath his seersucker, the man was skin and bones, despite the small paunch.

"Sister has a broken back. She fell. At least we think it's broken. We have no doctors here. Can you fix her?"

There were three women and four men around him, and he looked at their faces. Despite their cleanliness, he saw bags beneath their eyes, and sunken cheeks on their faces— the same sorry breakdown indicators he had seen in every town.

The nun's eyes were still closed.

"I'm sorry, I don't think I can fix something like that. Is she conscious?"

"Sometimes. Not right now," an older woman with gray hair spoke up. "She's been asleep for two days."

"Are you a priest?" Buzz asked the pastor.

"No," Ellison replied calmly. "I'm the former minister of the church down the block, although my entire congregation and myself are now members of the Catholic Church. I recognize Sister Emmanuel as a true woman of God. An anointed prophet. She told us you would come."

"She what?" Buzz asked.

"A month ago, when most of the food ran out, before the Miracle of the Eucharist, Sister Emmanuel told us to expect a big man with a short haircut to come to Blackstone, riding a bicycle. She called you a man of sorrows, and told us that you were a healer, and that you would be an instrument of the mercy of God for this town."

His words hit Buzz like a medicine ball. He stepped back, plopped down on the pew, looked at his hands, then looked at the sleeping nun.

"She must be mistaken," he mumbled, as much to himself as to his listeners. "I'm no healer."

"But you are a chiropractor, no?" Deacon Samuels asked.

Buzz shook his head, dazed.

This doesn't happen. This doesn't happen, he told himself.

The woman with the gray hair came and sat down next to him. She put a frail arm around his shoulders.

"I'm Donna Melville. Sister Emmanuel is my older sister. Our brother Mark is the priest here. He's not well…two weeks ago he had a stroke. He's no longer able to speak, or say Mass."

Buzz's hope for confession gurgled down a drain in his heart.

"Father Mark and Sister have held this town together since the troubles, mister," another man, younger than the rest, with an open face, and thin black hair, explained. "Sister said you would come. Sister said you would heal."

"But I'm just a chiropractor," Buzz protested. "But even that's a lie. I know what I'm doing, but I never finished school. I've been trading adjustments for food all the way from Cleveland…until the Man…until the Man…"

"Who's the man?" Ellison asked, coming to kneel on one knee in front of Buzz, placing a bony hand on his leg.

"Huh?"

"The man. Who is this man?"

"Oh. His name was Hal Smith. He was traveling with me. He was shot. He…didn't make it. My friends in Cleveland, we always called him by his nickname, the Man. It's a long story."

Buzz was finding his voice. Their hands on his shoulder and his leg felt…good. Warm. Accepting. Comforting.

"Can you help us? Can you help Sister?" Donna Melville asked.

He raised his head. Words came to him.

"Now is not the time for talk," he said firmly. "Now is the time for action."

He found his feet, left the comfort of their affection, genuflected again, and crouched beside the wheelchair, ignoring the soreness in his ankle.

She was ancient, the skin on her hands and face a city map of wrinkles. She appeared to be sleeping, her head resting on her chin.

"How old is she?" he asked.

"Ninety-one," said the man with the black hair—his name was Roy Mulholland.

"If you bring her to a table, or even a bed, I can perhaps give her some comfort, a shoulder massage, adjust her neck. I can do that for you," Buzz said evenly, looking up at them.

✚ ✚ ✚

There was a firm bed in the tiny kitchenette behind the sacristy. Buzz decided against moving her when he saw the bed, fearful of exacerbating her back injury. She remained asleep and her pulse was strong, though her breathing was thin.

"She can sleep like this for ten, fifteen, sometimes twenty hours straight," her sister explained to him in a whisper. "Even before she fell."

"Where is the priest, her brother?" Buzz asked.

"In the rectory," Deacon Samuels responded.

"I want to see him first, before I begin. I want my soul to be clean before touching a holy woman."

"But he can't speak to you," the deacon responded.

"I know," Buzz replied somberly. "But I would like to see him anyway."

The deacon led him to the rectory, where Father Mark Melville was sitting in a chair, staring at a blank television. A large painting of the Divine Mercy was on the wall behind it.

A young man, a teenager no older than fifteen, dressed in denim shorts and a T-shirt with the words *Marie Bellet Rocks* screened on the front was sitting on the couch, reading a thick book called *Strangers and Sojourners.* He looked up at the visitors and smiled.

I've read that, Buzz thought.

The deacon made the introductions, and the shy young man left the room.

The room was small, with an old, comfortable couch, and several bookcases jammed with religious books. There was a brown rug with intricate white designs on a wooden floor beneath their feet. One bookcase was devoted completely to Catholic videos and audio tapes. Buzz walked around the room, glancing briefly at the titles, and recognized many.

"He takes food, thank goodness," the deacon explained nervously. "What little we can bring him. We have to mash it up. He drinks water from a straw.

"But he has lost weight. He was a heavyset man in December. He doesn't recognize any of us anymore, or respond to questions. Sometimes he counts to ten, or cries out when we try to move him. We're all afraid he'll catch the flu, or have another stroke, or will waste away without a proper diet."

Buzz could believe this, having lost over eighty pounds himself since before the coma.

He crouched next to the old man, who was wearing the standard uniform of a priest: black pants, an open, black cardigan sweater, a black shirt with a Roman collar. The clothes hung loosely on his body. Buzz saw a child's bib on the stand next to the easy chair.

The priest sported thinning, jet-black hair which contradicted his eighty-nine years on earth. He had a long, thin nose, and Scottish folds over his eyes. The only gray was on the flecks in his beard and mustache, which were neatly trimmed. It was obvious that his personal needs and appearance had been taken care of by others.

From behind, as if reading Buzz's mind, the deacon said, "The whole town, even the Nazarenes, vie for the honor of caring for him."

There was no reaction in the priest's brown eyes when Buzz looked into them.

What have you seen since 1910, old man?

"Do you trust me to be alone with him, Deacon?" Buzz asked, looking up to Samuels, who was still standing in the doorway.

The deacon nodded. "Call me Bob. I'll be right here in the dining room with Tommy if you need anything."

He turned and left, closing the door behind him.

Buzz took a deep breath. *No harm in trying.*

He recalled a story that Father Dial had once told during a homily. While on a trip to Rome, a man had collapsed from a heart attack, right in the middle of Saint Peter's Square. The priest had watched helplessly for a moment as a doctor from the crowd attempted to restart the man's heart.

Then, while the doctor was counting out loud, compressing the man's chest in and out, Father Dial had leaned over the dead man and whispered into his ear: "If you can hear me, I'm a Catholic priest. If you have any sins that you are sorry for, tell Our Lord now, and I will give you absolution."

Father Dial had then given the absolution, making the sign of the cross over the man's head. The man did not recover, despite the efforts of the doctor.

Maybe it can work in reverse, Buzz thought.

"Can you hear me?" he asked the old priest.

No response. Buzz got down on his knees, and shut his eyes tight, and rested his folded hands on the arm of the easy chair.

"Bless me, Father, for I have sinned," he began earnestly. It was in confession when he felt most like a little child. "It's been four weeks since my last confession." He had gone, along with the Man, in a little town called Rush.

"One two three four five!" the priest counted with vigor.

Buzz's eyes snapped open, startled. There was still absolutely no cognition in Father Mark's eyes. But he had spoken.

Maybe he does hear me.

Buzz closed his eyes again.

"I'm not sure if it's a sin or not, but several times at night, or during my walks, I allowed my imagination to linger on sexual images of my wife. She's in New Hampshire. Nothing came of it…my body is, uh, not working, in that department."

He half-expected to hear the priest begin to count again.

Jesus hears me even if this priest doesn't.

"But what I'm really sorry about is giving in to the temptation to despair during this journey. When the Man died, I didn't blame God or anything—I mean, God didn't shoot him—but I, uh, this is hard to explain—I know what I did in my heart was wrong. I gave up—inside. I was angry with God for letting the Man die. I miss him.

"Many years ago, I promised God that I would never despair again, so I broke that promise to God, too. That's it.

"Oh yeah, and I haven't prayed my Rosary like I should.

"For these and all my sins I'm sorry, Father. Amen."

Buzz waited for a minute, his eyes closed. He felt a warm, dry hand come to rest on his own. He opened his eyes to see Father Mark's hand there. There was no expression on his face; he was still staring past Buzz toward the television.

"One two three?" Buzz asked hopefully…

"One two three four five…through the ministry of the Church…six seven eight…I absolve you…nine ten. One two three four five six!"

All the words had come out clearly, tonelessly, the words of the absolution in the same counting cadences as the numbers.

Buzz gulped as he heard the words.

The priest's expression had still not changed at all, but this did not stop his penitent from bursting into tears.

Buzz kissed the liver-spotted hand over and over. He felt that he was kissing the hand of Christ. *Oh thank you, Jesus, oh thank you Jesus, thank you!*

"One two three?" Buzz asked again.

No response from Father Mark.

In that inner way of knowing, Buzz knew the sacrament had been consumated.

What is my penance? he asked his Lord.

Keep your hand to the plow, the Man's words drifted back to him from the past.

Fair enough.

He rose, walked to the door, and opened it. The deacon and the boy were sitting in silence, their heads bowed in prayer, at the dining room table. They looked at Buzz.

Well? they asked silently.

Buzz decided not to tell them about his unusual confession.

"Bring me to Sister Emmanuel."

✙ ✙ ✙

Fearful of moving her, Buzz decided to work on her in the wheelchair. It was not an ideal set-up, but they carefully shifted her forward on her chair, and her sister unbuttoned the old nun's habit, revealing her thin, cotton under-blouse.

Buzz asked the men to leave the room. Donna Melville stayed behind, at his side.

He used his hands to explore the nun's back for several minutes. Buzz had treated many malnourished patients during his journey, but none so old, and none whose skin was so completely bereft of muscle. She was bone and nerve.

You're starving.

Using his fingertips as eyes, Buzz looked for signs of subluxation. He concentrated on the upper part of her spine. It was obvious that her lumbo-sacral below was severely traumatized, and he was loath to apply pressure there.

It was impossible to tell if her back was truly broken without the benefit of X-rays, but he guessed it probably was. Either way, there was nothing he could do about that.

At least I can realign her atlas.

He gently massaged her shoulders, then told Donna, "I'm going to adjust her neck now. You'll hear a sound we call cavitation. Don't let it startle you. It's the sound of nitrogen escaping, releasing pressure from her nerves."

Standing behind her, holding her head with both his hands, his fingers outstretched under her jaw, he slowly rotated it to the right, and in a quick movement, he gave her a cervical-rotary adjustment. Then, the same to the left. He saw Donna wince at the sound of the muffled crackling.

"It's okay," he told her. "It went well."

He continued to massage the paltry muscles in her neck and shoulders, feeling worthless as a healer. There was nothing unusual at the ends of his fingers—no heat, no tactile sensations other than the ordinary ones that came with the practice of his art.

"I'm going to show you how to massage her arms," he whispered. "She is not asleep. She is in a coma. She may not come out of it. Not without nutrition. Even so, I advise you to exercise her arms and fingers at least twice a day. Here, I'll show you."

She nodded. He spent some time showing her how to massage her sister's arms, calves, and feet.

"It would be dangerous to teach you how to adjust her neck. She is too frail," he told her.

"What is her prognosis?" Donna asked bravely.

"Remember, I'm not a doctor," he told her.

"Your opinion, then," Donna pressed, obviously dejected by his earlier statements.

He motioned for her to walk away from the patient, toward the corner of the room, out of earshot.

"In my opinion," he whispered, taking her arm. "She will…pass away…soon. Perhaps within the next twenty-four hours."

Donna looked away, a cloud coming over her eyes.

"She really held this town together?" Buzz asked, unable to think of anything else to say.

The old woman nodded, and brought her hand to her mouth. Buzz, feeling distant, like an actor playing doctor, gave her a chaste embrace. She seemed smaller and frail in his arms.

"She said you would heal," he heard her whisper, blank disappointment, rather than accusation, in her voice.

Were you expecting her to rise from the chair and walk? Buzz asked himself, not unkindly.

He pulled away, and tipped his head down to see into her eyes.

"I'm sorry, Mrs. Melville. I can't work miracles. I'm just a chiropractic school drop-out."

✛ ✛ ✛

Later, he was treated to a dinner of onion soup with very little onion at the Samuels' house. Mrs. Samuels, a woman named Dolores, was all smiles, but few words. It was clear to Buzz that she was putting on a show for his sake. The deacon was all questions about his travels. He alone seemed to be rising above the news of Buzz's prognosis, which had spread quickly, that Sister Emmanuel would probably not recover.

There was a perpetual prayer vigil at the church now. The hundred or so citizens of Blackstone took shifts in groups of five or six, praying for her before the Blessed Sacrament.

After the meal, Buzz followed the deacon to the den. The sun had set now, and there was no light in the room except for a six-day church candle. There was a small bar in the den, and the deacon opened a cabinet behind it, and held out an unopened bottle of Bowmore Mariner, a fine, single malt Scotch.

"I've been saving two of these," he told Buzz.

"Go right ahead. I'm a recovering alcoholic, so I'll have to pass."

The deacon frowned. Buzz sat down on a stool at the bar and smiled. "Water?"

Bob Samuels opened the bottle and poured himself a careful fingerful. He then gave Buzz water from a reused plastic milk jug.

"To the Faith," the deacon toasted, holding up his crystal glass.

"The Faith!" Buzz said with real excitement, wondering where his enthusiasm was coming from. Perhaps the normalcy of this scene—being indoors, sitting in a den, having a conversation. Except for the candle, he could imagine doing just this before the lights went out.

Samuels, a true aficionado, took a long, leisurely whiff of the aroma of the single malt, then took a sip.

"So what happened to this town?" Buzz asked.

"It's a long story," the deacon replied.

"It's a long night."

The deacon proceeded to tell Buzz the amazing story. Father Mark and his religious sister, long since retired from her congregation, had been preparing the Catholics in his parish for years for the "coming tribulations." He established Eucharistic adoration, prayer cenacles, an active youth group. He had even cultivated a relationship—along with Deacon Samuels—with Pastor Ellison down the street.

Ellison was not open to Father Gobbi or Our Lady of Fatima, but like many devout Protestants, had been anticipating the Rapture and the return of Jesus. (Of course, Samuels, as a Catholic, knew little about the Rapture, a more recent Protestant invention.) Some in town had stored up food in anticipation of the crash.

When the lights went out, Sister Emmanuel, allowed to preach after services in both churches, had urged the Christians in town to share their food, just like in the Acts of the Apostles. She told them that no one in the town would perish if they shared everything they possessed in a spirit of faith.

At first, there were skeptics, of course, but her prophecy came true: no one in Blackstone died, not even from the killer pneumonia which had ravaged other towns.

Blackstone's citizens had not set up roadblocks, and shared their meager rations with the dozens of refugees who had come down the hill.

By the end of February, the food had pretty much run out because only a small percentage of folks had stored in. A hundred or so lived in the town, including its few farmers.

For the past three decades, Blackstone's main source of income was summer tourism. They came for hiking and camping, or stopped at the one motel and the three restaurants in town on their way to somewhere else.

At about the same time as the food ran out, the old nun had promised that those who partook of the Eucharist would be nourished. She herself had not consumed anything but the Eucharist and water since January 1st. This was the "miracle" which Pastor Ellison had referred to when Buzz was in the church.

Catholics returned to Mass to receive communion, and despite their physical hunger and shrinking waists, everyone had survived; none had gotten sick.

"If you ask me, the real miracle," Deacon Samuels suggested, "is that Pastor Ellison became a Catholic, along with most of his congregation, and half the Presbyterians. Their pastor had been transferred out last year due to a lack of vocations, and had not been replaced. There were only fourteen people left in the congregation. They became Catholics to receive the Eucharist. Because Sister was holy. The handful who did not convert attend the interdenominational prayer meetings.

"Although I struggled for years to get Ellison to see the Eucharistic truth in John, it was Sister's life which opened his eyes."

Samuels was referring to the passage in John's Gospel where Jesus had said: *Amen, amen, I say unto you, unless you eat of my flesh and drink of my blood, you shall not have life within you.*

"Wow," Buzz said. "No one has died?"

"Not yet, though we're all weak, and we survive on wild onions—which are out of season, by the way, but seem to be under the dirt in everyone's garden—plus there's the occasional deer or rabbit the boys in town hunt for us. There's a pond about three miles from here, but it seems like we've fished it all out.

"By the time we divide up what comes in, it barely amounts to more than a morsel or two per family. Yet the ten mothers in town are breastfeeding their babies just fine. It boggles the mind.

"What little wheat we have left, we've saved for baking unleavened bread for the Mass. When Father Mark had his stroke, and Sister Emmanuel fell, it really discouraged us. We have one consecrated host left—the one we use for adoration. It doesn't decay. That's a miracle in and of itself. Jesus is holding this town together now, and sometimes I wonder if He took Sister and Father away so we would have nothing left but Him.

"I was ordained five years ago. We came here to retire; Dolores and I had come to Blackstone for our summers since we were married. We have no children. When I was newly married, before I returned to the faith, I had a vasectomy—" he saw Buzz's eyebrows rise.

"She had a bad pregnancy, and lost the baby. I was in the Navy, gone half the time, and thought I was doing her a favor. Either way, it's the biggest regret of my life. After I heard the call, my becoming a deacon became our way of making amends, of trying to bring some spiritual fertility to our marriage. Father Mark, who, more than anyone else, was responsible for bringing me back to the faith—he needed help with the parish.

"Dolores is a saint. I admit that there are probably many deacons in the church more dedicated than me; how can I step into the shoes of saints? I don't know what I'll do if Father Mark and Sister don't pull out of it."

The deacon's long confession was over. When Buzz heard him wonder how he could step into the shoes of saints, he thought immediately of his friends—Donna, the Man, Sam. How he missed them!

Buzz sipped his water, thinking.

"Maybe we need to redefine what miracles are," Buzz said. "I guess you could say it's a miracle I'm alive. I've lost weight, and have had to scrounge for food, but somehow, I'm alive and I'm strong. It seems like every time I need something, it's in the next town, or over the next hill."

Buzz was speaking as much to himself as to the deacon.

The deacon nodded.

Buzz wondered if the confession with Father Mark had opened within himself a new window of understanding regarding his journey.

The Man's words came back to him: *You're gonna make it to Bagpipe.*

He decided to tell Samuels about the unusual confession with Father Mark...

"Maybe you were the one who was supposed to receive healing," he told Buzz after. "She did say you would come."

"But barring a miracle, she won't recover."

"We've seen miracles. Amazing conversions. Souls subsisting on the Eucharist."

"Did she make any other prophecies—I mean, besides that I would show up?"

The deacon's eyes darkened. He lifted his glass and, against the etiquette of Scotch drinkers, finished the Mariner with one quick throw. He cleared his throat with an exhale.

"She said war is coming," he began, his voice low, trembling. "She said the antichrist is coming, but not when, only that he would use the shortage of food to get people to give themselves to him. That's why we need to rely on the Eucharist, she said."

There was something extremely persuasive in the deacon's voice. Buzz realized what it was.

He believes.

"I don't know what to say," Buzz responded.

"Me either," Samuels said cheerfully, his demeanor changing quickly. "Maybe she's right. Maybe not. Prophecy is not an exact kind of thing."

"Let's hope she's wrong about the antichrist. That gives me the creeps. Look at me, I didn't heal anyone," Buzz said. "At least not in a supernatural sense."

"But you're here. She said you would come."

"Maybe I should stay here for a while? No, I have to move on. I'll stay for a day or two, until everyone who wants has been adjusted."

"We'd appreciate that."

✛ ✛ ✛

That night, unable to fall asleep in the soft, cushy bed the Samuels had provided for him, Buzz threw his pillow on the carpeted floor and tried to sleep there. Still, he tossed and turned. Finally, he fell asleep, only to wake up in a cold sweat when the recurring nightmare of the burning house with the screaming woman and baby came back.

The events since Sam Fisk had first called him about the computer problem played out before his imagination like a movie in fast-forward. The research on the Internet, when worldwide communication was a click away for anyone with a computer. The psychological burden of fighting the rejection from his friends who had been in denial. The unfortunate croquet game that had totally alienated Mel's parents— Buzz truly regretted punching out poor Howie now. The trip to Montana to see Our Lady. The shouting matches with Mel over what to do next, even after they had decided to get out of Dodge—selling the house, denying the boys time in order to make preparations. And then, finding that most of what they had planned for Bagpipe had been too little, too late.

The numerous trips back and forth to Bagpipe. Painting and digging and dry-walling and wiring and wood-splitting and trying vainly to plant a garden, and on and on.

Then the fall from the scaffold at the convent. Waking up to chaos in Cleveland. The quiet boat ride on Lake Erie with the Man. Waking up to a shotgun barrel near Gerry early on. Adjusting backs—big ones, weak ones, strong ones, little ones, old ones—across Pennsylvania.

The Man. The farmhouse. The flight. The rest of that—

The hunger. Oh, the hunger which never left him. Watching with alarm as his gut shrank and his trousers got baggier and raggier as he and the Man had trudged from town to town. Wiping himself with leaves on those few occasions when he was able to pass stool. And some of the things he had eaten with relish during this walk which he would have passed over in disgust if found in a grocery store before the collapse. How soft and comfortable he had been, fancying himself a poor man because milk was three dollars a gallon.

He had been rich, rich!

If he regretted anything now, it had been letting himself get caught up in worldly preparations, and not spending more time just enjoying Mel, Mark, and Pascal while he had the chance. Yes, he had gone to daily Mass with Markie plenty of times in Bagpipe, and he was thankful for that, but his mind had been on water wells, greenhouses, and stone fences half the time.

A conversation with the Man came back to him. Buzz had been in a confessing mood one day on the road, and for a change, the Man had been talkative.

The conversation had taken place as they walked on another stretch of empty road on Route 6. A particularly cold day. The grandeur of the mountains all around them had become banal. The dull scratch of their soles on the stones on the shoulder of the road their only background music. This was the only distinct detail he remembered now, besides their words—the sound of their soles on the stones. Buzz had been holding the Ruger at the time to give the Man a respite.

"For years, I've known about Our Lady asking people to pray and fast because the tribulations were coming," Buzz had said. "Now we're in the thick of them. You and Sam fasted two or three days a week. You went to daily Mass. Me? I tried fasting a few times, but I usually broke down before lunch. I even ate meat on Fridays.

"I went to daily Mass once, maybe twice a week. Eucharistic adoration twice a month at best. Despite my spiritual director's recommendation, I never really developed a prayer life. I read Dubay's book once, but didn't put it into practice. I noticed that your copy was dog-eared two months after I gave it to you. Yeah, Mel and I prayed the Rosary, but with the boys jumping around, and because I'm basically pretty lazy, I never concentrated all that hard. I was a pretty slothful Catholic. Now I regret it."

"You're right. You were lazy," the Man replied.

He had expected silence from the Man, but this response surprised him, just as the last thing a woman expects from another after complaining that she is overweight is confirmation.

"That's my whole point," Buzz replied. "Do you think God will hold it against me? I feel like, well, that if I had actually been more serious about going the extra spiritual mile before things broke down, no pun intended, that this little joywalk we're taking would have a lot more chance of success.

"I let Mel and the boys down. I've got no excuse. I knew the faith inside out. God even gave me a second chance I didn't deserve when I tried to commit suicide and He saved me. When Sam and Mark saved me on the jetty. I've squandered my second chance."

The Man cleared his throat.

"I don't know what God will do with you at your judgment, Buzz, I really don't. And maybe you don't know either. I think Christians sometimes forget that not only can't we judge others, but that we also aren't even capable of judging ourselves."

"No offense, Hal, but now you're sounding like a Calvinist. Is Original Sin so blinding that we can't know ourselves?"

"I'm not saying that," the Man had grunted. "I'm just saying that God will always know us a million times better than we know ourselves.

"You look at yourself and see a lazy Catholic who should have known better. After all, you even tried to kill yourself once, and by your own lights, blew your second chance after your suicide attempt, and after God sent you the perfect wife and two perfect children—probably three by now in Bagpipe. All your friends are good Catholics, so you *should* have known better. You have no excuses.

"You had fifty daily Masses within a ten minute drive of your home in Lakewood, but you couldn't find the time to attend on most days. You look at me and see a person who prayed two or three hours per day before the crash, and loved every minute of it.

"But for me, it's all a matter of perspective. When I look at you, I don't see a lazy Catholic. I see the man who God used as an instrument of Divine Mercy in my life. While other Catholics were off praying their Rosaries and jumping on planes to go to apparition sites all over the world, you were on my front porch reading the Sports Section.

"When I look into the mirror I see a sinner who squandered forty years of his life in a selfish cocoon. A bitter old man who God probably wanted to be a Trappist or a Carmelite. What a waste."

Like many thoughtful, silent types, the Man was fully capable of expressing himself succinctly. Buzz realized now that Hal's rehash of Buzz's own self-evaluation had cut pretty hard, even though Buzz had said exactly the same thing a moment earlier.

One of the nice things about the long walk, compared to before the lights went out, Buzz reflected now as he rested on the floor of the deacon's house, was that there was never a need to rush a conversation. He and the Man had taken an hour at that point to pray and ponder in silence before reeling in the fish on the verbal hook.

"So you're saying that we aren't capable of judging ourselves?" Buzz asked.

"Not exactly. I'm saying that every person is a mystery to himself. Our judgments are imperfect because we're imperfect. Just because we're Christians doesn't give us a corner on the truth about ourselves.

"I didn't think I needed God or you or anybody else before you brought me to the sacraments. That was an error in judgment. I'm sure I still misjudge myself. One of the reasons why I loved fasting was because it seemed to shine an internal light on my soul. It showed me how weak I really was. And how easy it is to fall into pride. I think I wasted much of my fasting just by being proud that it came so easily to me."

"Did you look down at me?" Buzz asked.

"Never."

That answer came quickly, and like most one-word replies from the Man, seemed to end the conversation. But it was the Man who started up again, after they had conquered another hill in central Pennsylvania.

"Did I ever tell you that I knew Tom Monaghan?" the Man asked.

"The Dominos Pizza guy?"

"Yeah, that guy. You'd be surprised the kinds of people I met when I worked at the hotel. Presidents. Big businessmen. Athletes and actresses. I once drove Bridget Fonda around Cleveland for a whole day. She insisted on me, despite my protests that I could get her the best chauffeur in town.

"Anyway, Tom and I kind of hit it off. We shared an interest in architecture."

"That's right," Buzz said. "He was a Frank Lloyd Wright junkie, wasn't he? You never told me you have an interest in architecture."

It had not struck Buzz that he and the Man often referred to people they had known from the old world in the past tense.

"There are a lot of things about me you don't know," the Man said. "You can't understand history unless you understand architecture."

"So tell me, Hal, what does the pizza guy have to do with anything, except that he was a good Catholic? I used to deliver for Dominos, you know."

The Man made a face.

You're like everybody else. You're so quick to think of him as just the pizza guy.

The Man sighed.

"Mr. Monaghan is a devout Catholic, if he's still alive. I sure hope so," the Man continued. "He's not a big guy—about as tall as me. Looked just like any handsome Irish kid who grows up to be fifty. He wasn't the kind of guy who strikes you as a genius, which I believe he is. He's a regular guy.

"We had a few drinks, was all. He didn't put on any airs like some men with lots of money or power, and he wasn't filled with the kind of phony humility you sometimes run into. I think he had a billion dollars when he finally sold his company. In our few conversations, I felt like I was talking with the real man.

"My point is that it's very hard to judge a man like that. He had hundreds of millions of dollars, and he supported Catholic charities all over the world. He helped build churches in impoverished countries. He started schools. Before you and I were done eating breakfast, he probably had finished his holy hour and a full Rosary in his private chapel.

"Yet, from his point of view, I'm sure he thought all his charitable works were no different than the ten percent you were tithing last year, except as a matter of scale. I'm sure of it. He never said so. But I'm a good judge of character. He never talked about his charities, for one thing. Plus, he had to put up with all these people fawning over him, sucking up to him, asking him for money, looking at him like he was a paycheck—the rich *pizza guy.*"

Buzz felt the sting from the Man's last two words.

The Man continued: "I read once that he stopped building his dream house—an architectural wonder—which he had already poured millions of dollars into, because he read a book by Saint John of the Cross—The Dark Night of the Soul—and realized that he had been living a self-indulgent life, even though by this time he had already donated millions to charity, and was a very public Catholic.

"Does God judge a man like Monaghan and say: You haven't given enough to charity? Your Rosaries and prayers aren't enough for me? If Monaghan had sold his company and given away everything he had, in, say, 1980, he wouldn't have given away nearly as much as he was able to later on by growing his company into the 1990s. Think of the implication for souls this one fact illustrates.

"And I'm sure it must have crossed his mind, or at least that some well-meaning Catholics must have tried to lay a guilt trip on him for not liquidating early. Now, with the crash, most of what he had is probably gone—completely gone.

"Are you going to judge him? How will God judge him for how he handled the tremendous responsibility for all that wealth? How could Mr. Monaghan judge himself?"

"I don't know," Buzz responded after a moment.

"Well, Buzz, you don't realize it, but you have a gift that is worth more money than a hundred pizza fortunes. You have something in you that…"

The Man paused, and Buzz could have sworn his friend had wiped a piece of dust—or perhaps a tear—from his eye with his pinky.

"…something in you that God used to give me Life. And helped Donna become a nun. And helped Sam find the faith. Something big like the stars.

"I don't really care if you're a lazy Catholic or a Mother Teresa or a Tom Monaghan. And maybe God doesn't care either. Do you know who the Bible says is the first person to get into heaven on Easter?"

Buzz didn't try to answer. He didn't know.

"A common thief. The Good Thief on the cross next to Jesus. 'I tell you the truth, today you will be with me in paradise.' Christ came for the sinners, Buzz. Remember that.

"And remember that the Good Thief merited this great promise by a simple act of humility. 'We deserve our punishments, for we are getting what our deeds merit. But this man has done nothing wrong.'"

Buzz pondered these nuggets of wisdom, but they did not compute—not as an integrated whole.

He couldn't help himself when he asked the Man: "So what is the big lesson? Humility? Don't judge yourself? I know you just gave me this great speech about Monaghan and the Good Thief, but I still don't get it."

There was real exasperation in Buzz's voice. He truly did not get it. He didn't get it now.

Maybe this is what it's like for every sinner in the presence of a saint?

The Man, rather than becoming impatient, had not replied.

Buzz, reflecting on this conversation, and all the events which had led up to his coming to the town of Blackstone, felt some unarticulated consolation, a peace in his heart.

Barely two weeks after his death, the Man was still ministering to Buzz.

I'll go with Buzz to Bagpipe! the Man's final words.

Buzz folded his hands.

Dear Hal, Buzz prayed now, *if you can hear me, and if you're in purgatory or in heaven, stay with me. Tell Jesus to keep me safe, and to keep Mel and my boys safe. I miss you, brother.*

Buzz spent the next two days adjusting the backs of the residents of Blackstone, taking his time, not putting on an act, but really doing his best to use his personality and his hands to bring some measure of healing and consolation to these courageous people.

The old nun, despite his predictions, had not died. She was still hanging on, though she had gone deeper into her coma, and her heartbeat was becoming thinner. He even gave her and Father Mark massages, as best he could, under the circumstances. On his recommendation, they had carefully, lovingly moved the nun to a bed. Buzz was glad during the procedure that she was out of it—for moving her surely would have caused a conscious person incredible pain. Perhaps, in her state, she didn't register it.

On the morning he left town, he opened his eyes and saw next to his pillow a newly sewn, heavy-duty pair of khaki pants, along with a neatly folded wool shirt with a grey and green checkered pattern.

"God bless you. Love, Dolores," said the note pinned to the shirt.

He was not without renewed mental and spiritual energy, even though he was hungry. More than half the townspeople came to see him off, many of them shedding tears and hugging him, promising that they would pray for his family and for his safe journey. It was a windy day.

There was an awkward moment, as he mounted his bicycle (which had been given a complete tune-up by Pastor Ellison's oldest son), when he felt obliged to make a speech to them all. It was obvious they expected him to say something hopeful, perhaps something profound.

He prayed to the Holy Spirit for inspiration, and to the Man, and remembered a story that Sister Regina had told him once, before she had entered the convent.

"In the 1500s, Saint Francis Xavier, the great Jesuit missionary, converted many Japanese to the Catholic faith," he had to shout over the wind. "The emperor then kicked Christians and all Westerners out of Japan for three hundred years.

"In the 1850s, when the West was allowed back in, despite brutal persecutions and Christianity being outlawed, it was discovered that there were still fervent, devout Catholics in Japan. They had been given nothing to sustain them: no books, no Eucharist, no priests, no schools, no religious freedom. Yet they had each other, and they had the True Faith. As Saint Teresa of Avila told us, 'God alone suffices.'

"I believe that is what Sister Emmanuel and Father Mark were trying to teach you, teach this whole town—the exact same lesson those brave Catholics in Japan were taught by Saint Francis Xavier. God alone suffices.

"I have been healed during my stay here. You have healed me, and in my humble way, I have tried to heal you. I believe that no matter what happens, even if some of you should die, remember that no matter how bad it gets, that God alone suffices. Pray God I remember the same."

They had hung on every word. Buzz had seen old and young, man and woman, nodding, as he spoke.

Wow, did I say that? he wondered.

He then shook Deacon Samuel's hand; the deacon then helped Buzz put his backpack on.

"We've added a few extra items to your bag. Kinda like good-bye presents—"

"You didn't have to—" Buzz protested, but the deacon waved him off.

"You come back and visit someday, you hear?" the deacon said, Dolores at his side, smiling a real smile.

Buzz nodded. *Sure thing.*

Dolores stepped up and gave him a kiss on the cheek. She fixed her hair in the wind, and wiped away a tear.

"That's right, you come back and visit. Bring your family," Pastor Ellison piped in, hopeful tears in his eyes. Buzz hugged him last, unable to hold back his own tears.

"I have suffered much," the pastor whispered softly into Buzz's ear, quoting a psalm. "Preserve my life, O Lord, according to your word."

Buzz straightened on the bike, balancing, his legs feeling oddly weak yet somehow strong at the same time, and renewed his journey.

Sure are lots of tears in this new world, he thought after he turned from them, and began pushing on the pedals.

Behind him, someone—a tenor—started to sing a hymn. Others joined in.

Several little boys and girls, defying the lack of calories in their diet, ran after him, waving and calling out with the kind of joy only small children know, as he strained to climb to the main road, strands of *Faith of Our Fathers* fading behind him.

Chapter Thirteen

The Guns of Brixton

Buzz Woodward had everything and he had nothing. And he would need both.

His days after leaving Blackstone were the most peaceful of his journey since losing the Man. He had no definite plan except to make a wide southeastern arc around Albany, crossing the Hudson by night at the bridge in Shuylerville. By the fifth day, Buzz was coming out of the mountains and was finding fertile valleys. And more refugees on the roads. Some eyed his bicycle, rifle, and backpack with envy, but he greeted or did not greet them according to the Spirit, prayed his prayers, and shared his food according to the Man's Policy, as he now thought of it.

If he was thirsty, he found a brook around the next bend. If he was hungry, he found a rabbit in his snare when he awoke. If cold, he would find an outcropping facing away from the wind to sleep beneath. If he was lonely, he had the memories of the Man to sustain him. His nasty nightmares abated.

The saints of Blackstone had filled him with faith, and with the Vermont border a day's ride away to the east, Buzz allowed a small ember to glow in his soul that he would be able to reach Bagpipe in one piece. With this hope came images of Mel, holding their new baby; Markie and Packy (who was now over two years old) were running up the driveway next to her at the homestead to greet him.

You're gonna make it to Bagpipe!

With these prophetic words, the grisly cloth of the Man's death-face was never packed far under the cleaner clothes in Buzz's mental suitcase.

I see Mel with Him! the Man had said.

So he tried not to dwell too often on the hopeful images of Mel and the boys (*and girl?* He was ardently curious to know). This kind of thought was dangerous. Too much to hope for…there had been the nightmares, possibly prophetic preparations from God. Buzz knew he shouldn't presume on God and His unfathomable plan, but still…

Why has He allowed me to make it this far?

He finally reached a town called Argyle on Route 40 in New York, east of the Hudson River. Argyle was overflowing with food (relatively speaking). It had many survivors with back problems, most of them having never worked a true day of manual labor in their lives. Here they were now, undernourished or ill, bending over, trying to plant crops and vegetable gardens with tools no more sophisticated than shovels and pitchforks. He had also started to carry the mail again. Argyle welcomed him.

A few forward-thinking farmers in Argyle had put in some extra diesel last year. The town fathers had decided to preserve it for the planting, rather than seize it for winter fuel.

It was late spring.

The exact day didn't seem to matter much to Buzz anymore, except if it was a Sunday and there was an opportunity to reach a Catholic church—something he could never really know in advance. What mattered was that it was warm most days and nights, and it was late enough into the summer for food to grow.

The meek have inherited the earth, Buzz thought, *whether they like it or not.*

Buzz met Johnny Bryant and Tom Kasovich in Argyle. They had waited outside the fire station with their bicycles while Buzz adjusted backs, and when he came out, they asked him if they could accompany him north into Vermont. Johnny Bryant had an uncle with a small church and farm near Holland Pond on the northern border of the state. The three counties comprising the northeast section of the state were called the Northeast Kingdom.

Buzz looked them over. Both were in their early twenties, thin as rails, with long beards and hair. Tom had thin blond hair and refined features, while Johnny had deep, sunken dark eyes, dark hair, and a nervous habit of biting his fingernails in public. They had been roommates at a small Bible college in Albany before taking off on their bikes for Argyle three months earlier. They had survived by doing odd jobs for the local farmers, fishing with homemade poles (which they planned to bring with them on the journey), and on the charity of local Christians.

"Why with me?" Buzz asked.

"Because you're a Christian. We're Christians. We've been waiting for a reason to take off. We need help; you've been on the road and you know what you're doing."

This made Buzz laugh inside. *I have no idea what I'm doing!*

But that wasn't true, was it? Hadn't the long walk hardened his body? Hadn't the Man trained him to live on rabbits and squirrels, to survive by his wits and his prayers?

Upon further conversation, he discovered that they were Assembly of God. Their pastor here in Argyle had been taken by the pneumonia two weeks earlier.

"I'm a Catholic," Buzz cautioned. "I like to pray the Rosary—out loud. I often decide to take detours to go to Mass, to find priests. Will that bother you?"

Johnny and Tom looked at each other.

Johnny, the more talkative one, replied, "We've prayed about it. The Lord told us to go with you. To put aside our differences."

"How does the Lord tell you such things?"

"We received a passage."

Buzz knew this meant that they had prayed for inspiration from the Holy Spirit, then let the Bible fall open and looked at the first passage on the page to strike their eyes. Supposedly, this passage would be a directive from God.

"What was it?" Buzz asked.

"First Peter, five-five," Tom said softly, "'Young men, in the same way be submissive to those who are older.'"

Both men nodded and smiled, squinting at Buzz, who was standing with the setting sun behind him.

That seems pretty thin, Buzz thought skeptically. *But then again, it would be a nice change to have company, and there's safety in numbers.*

He decided to take them on, with the understanding that their group would not be a democracy—Buzz would have the final say on when and where they would go.

Even so, they discussed possible routes, and convinced Buzz to head north on Route 22 into Vermont, and attempt to cross the Green Mountains just south of Burlington, perhaps at the Appalachian Gap, rather than head east sooner toward Rutland to cross the mountains. Their logic was firm—there were smaller population densities on the northern route, and the terrain was less hilly on the western side of the Green Mountains. They would make better time.

Buzz realized that they were hoping his snare, his Ruger, and his chiropractic skills would be a source of food for them along the way, and that they would slow him down during the first week or so while they built up their skinny legs—and that their stamina would depend on finding enough food to sustain the physical challenge of the ride. Then again, gardens were being planted, vegetables harvested, and out-of-the-way Vermonters had always been known for their self-sufficiency, even before the Troubles.

Buzz was also leery of their personalities. What if they didn't gel with him? What if they weren't able to keep up with his pace? There was only one way to find out.

✛ ✛ ✛

And after the first few days on the road, Buzz did not
regret bringing them along. They were sore and tired, but
were obviously determined to keep up with him. They didn't
realize that Buzz was moderating his pace. The Lord blessed
the travelers with a rich harvest of fish. It seemed as if every
pond or stream that crossed their path was teeming with fish.
It was touching how the two men prayed before baiting their
sharpened paper-clip hooks. The rigors of cycling prevented
them from talking much during the day rides. During the evenings, it became clear that they were sincere Christians—or
at least were capable of putting on a superb act.

Tom remained reticent, but Johnny was perfectly willing
to allow Buzz to explain the passages in the Bible that supported Catholic teachings on the pope, the Eucharist, the role
of Mary, confession, and other topics. To make them feel
comfortable, Buzz held his hands in the air and listened silently when they began their extemporaneous prayers and
prayed in tongues.

Buzz, perhaps for their sakes, made a point of praying his
Rosary out loud, with a low voice, after the cooking fire was
out, right before they fell asleep. The nights were warmer
now, which was a good thing because Johnny and Tom's sleeping bags were nothing more than ordinary blankets sewn into
large pouches. Buzz did not ask them to join in his Rosaries.

When they came to towns, Buzz healed with his hands,
and Johnny and Tom offered to teach Bible lessons at the
local churches. Tom was more a private tutor, but Johnny
preached to entire groups. His practice of ending his sermons
by passing a hat for food made Buzz uncomfortable, but his
audiences did not seem to mind. He caught Johnny expound-
ing carefully veiled Catholic concepts during his sermons
every so often.

That had been their dream in the old world—to be preachers. As was his practice during his time with the Man, Buzz

soon began allowing Johnny to do the talking when they came
to roadblocks and town halls. Catholic churches were fewer
and farther between as they made their way north, and these
two sincere Protestant ministers were readily accepted by the
predominantly Protestant town officials.

The men entered into the Northeast Kingdom through the
Appalachian Gap, after some excruciating climbs, where they
often had to stop and rest almost by the mile. Soon they were
past Waitsfield, where Tom was able to trade one of Buzz's
gold coins for a much-needed new front tire for his mountain
bike.

They were making their way up Route 100 now, which
was lovely and scenic. Pennsylvania had been a cold, wintry
grey. Vermont, true to the translation of its name—*green
mountain*—was an explosion of green flora in every direction.

Johnny and Tom were becoming more optimistic. They
were days, perhaps a week, away from their uncle. The two
men talked about God's providence and showed Buzz passages in the Bible about His promises to keep His people
safe from enemies.

It was a rainy, overcast day when they came to Brixton, a
full day's ride north of Eden Mills. Like a few other towns
Buzz had seen along the journey, Brixton was apparently a
ghost-town. Not all Vermont towns had fully developed town
centers. They were points on a map, with a town hall and a
fire station located off the main road or crossroad. Brixton
was just such a town. Besides the telltale green road sign
announcing they were entering Brixton (Population 73), the
only indicator that they were actually near the town center
was the empty, fully-looted, general store/Mobil station a
quarter mile down from the sign.

The terrain consisted of long, rolling hills, with trees coming right to the shoulder of the two-lane roadway. On the
pavement, there were plenty of sticks and effluvia left from
the winter, which slowed their progress.

They continued to ride past the abandoned store, sometimes walking up the steeper hills, looking for a place to camp in the twilight. Buzz got a stitch in his side near the top of a crest and decided to rest for a bit. Johnny and Tom waited with him for a few moments, then remounted their bikes and began gliding down the long hill beyond the crest. A roadblock gradually became more visible to them in the fading light.

There were two men with guns at the roadblock. Neither minister was familiar with the seemingly infinite varieties and brands of weapons. Men with weapons at roadblocks were not at all uncommon in the new world.

This particular roadblock was constructed from a combination of trees and a huge fire truck. One guard, a thin man—weren't they all nowadays—stood up on the roof of the cab of the truck as they approached. The other was napping, sitting on the ground with his green military cap over his eyes, resting his back against a log.

"Halt! Identify yourselves," the man on the cab called out, waking the other guard, who scrambled to his feet, grabbed his shotgun, then ran up to Johnny and Tom. Tom looked at Johnny.

"I'm Johnny Bryant and this is Tom Kasovich. We're preachers, and we're just passing through."

"Are you alone?" the guard on the cab asked. He was clean-shaven, and quite handsome in a rakish kind of way.

It was difficult for Johnny to see the expression on the guard's face in the thickening darkness. The rain had become a light mist, but the clouds were killing whatever was left of the sunlight.

"No, there's another man named Buzz behind us. He should be coming right along."

The guard and the two Christians turned to look up the long, low hill, but there was no Buzz Woodward in sight.

"Preachers, eh?" the guard on the ground, a ruddy-faced man with dull eyes, sneered.

"Yes, brother, do you love the Lord?" Johnny asked.

The two guards laughed.

"Nope," said the guard on the ground, pointing his shotgun at Tom's face. "Do you?"

A moment of truth.

Tom said, "Yes."

The guard pulled the trigger, and Tom's head exploded into a mash of bloody bits. His body folded to the ground.

Johnny screamed, and fell to Tom's side.

The guard on the truck called down: "Dammit, Lloyd! Rheumy's gonna get pissed again. You can't just keep shooting every friggin' idiot who comes down the road like that. Now we're gonna have to bury 'im."

"You killed him!" Johnny shouted.

Lloyd, apparently unmiffed by the other guard's rebuke, swung his barrel around, and placed the muzzle inches from Johnny's face.

"And I'll kill you, too, if you don't shut your goddamned trap."

✛ ✛ ✛

Buzz, sitting next to his bike on the other side of the hill, straightened up with a start when he heard the report of the shotgun.

He quickly scrambled over to the crest of the hill, crawling forward on his stomach, and raised his head to investigate. In the waning light he spied the guard standing over Tom's body, pointing his gun at Johnny.

Oh God!

Conflicting thoughts began to war in his head. Run down there? Get on his bike and take off? Do nothing?

Can't do nothing!

Then what?

He calmed himself. This was not like him. He could deal with this. He would have to deal with this. Violence had always been lurking off-stage during the drama of the long walk. Buzz accepted this so he could pray efficiently: *Mary!*

What would the Man do? she answered.

Now it was obvious. The Man would *follow a plan.*

Yes, a plan, he calculated.

Buzz inched backwards, staying low, conjuring a plan, until he was sure he could dart back to his bike.

Is this why he had suddenly gotten the cramps as his friends glided before him down the hill?

He would never know.

He lifted his bike into the air, then took it into the woods beside the road.

Hurry!

He covered it with leaves and pine needles as best he could. He pulled the backpack off, ripped it open, and rummaged through it. What to keep?

Need a plan. Like the Man.

His hand came to the bottle. The little something Deacon Samuels had stowed away as a gift before he left Blackstone.

Bowmore Mariner. The Scotch. "Buzz, I know you don't drink, but I thought that you could use this for trading—Bob," the note, in careful script, had said.

Trading. A plan. The Man.

He zipped open the side pocket and grabbed his reference letters, then ran further into the woods and hid his pack beneath a log, along with the Ruger, which he wrapped in his winter jacket. He took his Zippo, hesitated, then left it in an open knot on a nearby oak tree.

Run away! Take the bike. Remember Mel. Ride away! the coward in him, the part that valued life over duty, urged.

He batted it away. Johnny was down there, alone, a babe in the woods. Alone.

You can take the boy out of New Jersey, but you can't take the New Jersey out of the boy. He had his bottle of Scotch. But Buzz felt he needed more than a plan, he needed—a conceit. An organizing theme. He prayed.

It came to him. He would...

Tell lies based on truth.

As he hurried back to the road, then over the crest, mumbling the Saint Michael prayer, he found it.

✝ ✝ ✝

"Here comes your friend," Ralph, the one who had been on the cab of the truck, told Johnny. "We were just about to go after him."

Ralph was standing next to Lloyd now.

Johnny, face down on the ground, his hands on his neck, with Lloyd's gun pointed to his head, turned to see a shoe-eyed view of Buzz casually walking toward the roadblock, a happy grin on his face, hands in the air.

Where's his bike? Johnny thought.

"Buzz—" Johnny croaked.

"Shut up," Lloyd growled, poking his muzzle into Johnny's shoulder blade.

Ralph flicked on a large flashlight.

Light, Buzz thought. That was all he needed to know. Electric light. It gave him just enough to make a guess. A Buzz guess.

"Halt," Ralph ordered. "Identify yourself."

"I'm Buzz."

"Buzz who?"

"Buzz nobody. Who are you?" His tone remained casual. Almost jovial.

"I'm asking the questions here," Ralph barked tersely.

"Yeah," Lloyd said.

"Would you just shut the hell up, Lloyd?"

It was dark, but Buzz could tell—just tell—that Lloyd had bristled at that.

The killer is named Lloyd, Buzz filed away. *This other guy is in charge.*

"Are you armed?" Ralph asked.

"No," Buzz replied. "Can I put my hands down?" he added.

"No."

Buzz kept his eyes off Johnny, and what was left of Tom, and concentrated on the bad guys.

He squinted into the flashlight. How he wished he could see their faces.

"What are we gonna do next?" Lloyd asked.

"For the last time, shut up, wouldya, Lloyd. Go search him. I'll cover this other one."

Lloyd stepped over Tom Kasovich's corpse, then walked to Buzz. He searched him with one hand. Buzz's arms, still in the air, were beginning to ache. Lloyd found the fifth of Bowmore tucked into the back of Buzz's pants.

"He's clean. Nothin' but this bottle, Ralph. Shine the light here…"

The leader's name is Ralph, he repeated mentally, trying to ignore the shotgun barrel inches from his face.

Ralph shone the light.

"Bowmore Marine-er," Lloyd spelled out. He had mispronounced *Mariner* the way one would say *Marine* as in Marine Corps.

"You some kind of Marine?" Ralph asked.

"Me a Marine? Hell no," Buzz replied, inserting down-home charm. "It's Scotch. Lloyd sure is a dumb sonufabitch."

"Hey!" Lloyd said.

"You heard me," Buzz told him.

"You got that right," Ralph said, laughing.

"I just wanted to thank you, and thank old Lloyd, too, of course," Buzz pressed on, trying desperately to keep the tension out of his voice, trying not to look at Johnny.

Johnny, please play along, Buzz beseeched.

"Thank me? Thank me for what?"

"For shutting that preacher up. God, he was driving me up the frickin' wall. Jesus this, Jesus that. If I did have a gun, I might have popped him myself."

Ralph walked up to him. They could see each other now. He looked carefully at Buzz, who put his hands down. Ralph, still holding his own rifle on Buzz, put his hand on the barrel of Lloyd's shotgun and pushed it down. "Go watch the other one," he ordered.

"Thanks," Buzz said. "My arms were killing me."

"You're just trying to save your skin," Ralph stated uncertainly.

"Of course I am. The world is a dangerous place, Ralph," Buzz said, nodding sagely.

Buzz spun the words gently, like silk streaming from a spider's abdomen. He was gaining confidence by the second.

"But I really do want to thank you for taking that preacher out. Always running his mouth. This other one ain't so bad."

Buzz spit in Johnny's direction, and stifled an urge to wink. *You'll get a chance to let Johnny know later,* he advised himself. *If there is a later.*

"Lloyd!" Buzz called over with a command voice, surprising Ralph. "You best take care not to drop that god-damned bottle! I just carried it all the way here from—" Buzz almost hesitated "—New York."

"Hey," Lloyd said, startled.

"Shut the hell up, Lloyd," Ralph repeated wearily, then to Buzz, "Rheumy's gonna love you. But I still think you're full of it. I could shoot you right here."

"Sure you could, but you won't," Buzz bluffed coolly, then paused.

He could tell in the ensuing pause that Ralph had taken the bait, and was waiting for an explanation, and after a lifetime of saying whatever popped into his head, he found that the words came smoothly—almost gracefully—

"Because you're going to bring me to see Roomy, because you don't like Scotch, but Roomy does. He loves Scotch. And he's going to like me a lot. "

"How do you know Rheumy loves Scotch?" Ralph asked, true curiosity in his voice.

Buzz's gift of guessing never failed to impress.

"I just know. Just like I know that you and me, we're the same. We let the other guy do the killing."

Boom, take that, Buzz thought, knowing that taking charge when one was not in charge was the only way out of this mess—for him and for Johnny.

Ralph bought it. He bought it all.

A few minutes later, as Johnny dug Tom Kasovich's grave, Ralph offered Buzz a cigarette.

Buzz turned it down. He knew he was in.

✣ ✣ ✣

There was a dirt road adjoining Route 100 directly behind the roadblock. It wound through the woods for two miles before opening into a clearing. A cluster of buildings stood before them. It was not easy to see details in the darkness.

The group of men followed a stone path around the first building to a courtyard in front of a main building—a fairly ordinary-looking, modern split-level with vinyl siding. Buzz was only mildly surprised to see that it had electric lights. He listened, and heard the soft *whop-whop-whop* of a wind turbine in the distance. Wind power. Buzz was certain that there was an array of batteries somewhere in the compound, and filed this information.

"Take the preacher to the work house, Lloyd, and have the boys fit him with cuffs if they've still got the blacksmith shop up and running," Ralph ordered mildly. "I'll take Buzz here up to see Rheumy. And hand me that bottle."

"Hey, okay," Lloyd muttered before giving the Bowmore to Ralph.

Buzz took this chance to wink at Johnny, who was surprisingly calm. Johnny winked back.

Kid's not so dumb after all, Buzz thought, relieved. *I bet he's prayin' up a storm.*

Buzz decided to count on it. *Johnny's praying for me, Lord. Answer his prayers. Give us all the grace You've got.*

Lloyd departed, his gun at his side, leading Johnny toward the dark form of a building to the left of the main building.

"Let's go to the bighouse," Ralph told Buzz. He no longer held the rifle on his captive. Buzz briefly considered jumping him, but rejected the idea. That wouldn't do Johnny any good.

Ralph led Buzz into the house up a flight of stairs. They stopped before a closed door. Ralph nodded at the armed guard—an older gentleman sitting in a chair beside the door.

"Rheumy up?"

The guard shrugged his shoulders.

Buzz took a careful look around. There was clean blue carpeting on the floor—*I guess they vacuum the place.* Power. All the old luxuries were here, obviously. The walls were painted a light beige, and there were cheesy paintings—the kind found in mid-priced hotel rooms—hanging here and there in the hallways. No pictures of people.

Roomy has no taste, Buzz filed.

Ralph reached toward the doorknob—

"Hold on," Buzz said. "What's his last name?"

Ralph stopped, not even aware that he was taking orders from Buzz now.

"Same as mine," Ralph replied. "Marks. He's my older brother. Rheumy Marks. His real name is Ben. But don't call him that."

Buzz nodded. In the lights of the house, he realized that Ralph was young—perhaps in his late twenties. He had brown, well-cut hair, and his features were handsome in that rounded kind of way. He didn't look evil. He didn't look like a murderer.

"Where does the nickname come from?"

"It's short for rheumatoid arthritis, same as our dad. My brother is in a lot of pain most of the time. You better be what you said you are—"

"Relax. You want to give him the bottle?"

Ralph nodded. Buzz smiled.

He had kept his words and his tone conspiratorially friendly and intimate since the roadblock, but now found it difficult to force from his mind the image of Tom's corpse being lowered into the shallow grave—next to three other graves.

Ralph opened the door without knocking as Buzz prepared for the performance of his life...

Forget that they're murderers, he told himself. *Or it will come out in your voice. We're all friends here, we're all friends here...*

And there was Rheumy, sitting in a cushy leather chair, a beer in his hand, facing away from them. Buzz couldn't see his face—only the small bald spot in his crewcut, and beyond it, a television and VCR.

A television! Even in these circumstances, Buzz couldn't help but get excited. It had been so long!

And a movie! Buzz recognized it immediately.

As Good as It Gets, featuring Jack Nicholson giving his Oscar-winning performance.

"Hi Rheumy," Ralph said to his brother's scalp. "I've brought somebody to meet you."

"Shsssh," Rheumy hissed without turning around. "I love this scene. Sit down, sit down."

Buzz and Ralph walked around the chair and sat on the matching couch. Buzz smiled at Rheumy, who was even more good-looking than his brother, but got no verbal response. Rheumy waved but kept his eyes on the screen, smiling, taking Buzz in from the corner of his eye.

Buzz watched the movie, which was about halfway finished, and despite himself, got caught up in the story. He figured this was a better strategy than taking careful glances at his host.

"Get our guest a beer," Rheumy said a few minutes later, eyes on the screen.

Ralph went to the bar on the far side of the room, ducked under the back, and returned with two bottles of beer. He handed one to Buzz. Bud Light.

A moment of decision.

Take the beer? Set a precedent?

"Thanks, man," Buzz said.

He twisted the top, and took a small gulp, trying to make it look natural. Like he had just downed a few beers with the boys at the pub before dropping into this nightmare for a nightcap. On top of it all, he was truly thirsty.

A thirsty alcoholic. This sucks. This is an act.

It was his first beer of the millennium.

Dear Lord, forgive me. Dear Lord, don't let me get drunk. For Mel! For Johnny!

In times of war, no matter the battlefield, good men are forced to do bad things.

The beer went right to his head. Or maybe he just imagined it. Ten years since his last drink. It brought back memories—of the storm, the dark jetty. The attempt.

He shoved them aside.

He had a job to do. He concentrated on Jack Nicholson and Helen Hunt. God, she was awful plain-looking for a movie star. Nothing like Grace Kelly.

He immediately thought of Ellie, and felt a vague longing. Buzz had forgotten how easily movies could rev up his emotions. Or maybe it was the beer.

Saint Michael the Archangel... he prayed twenty or thirty times, the whole prayer, as the movie dragged on.

Suddenly, it was over. Rheumy reached up with the remote control, and clicked it off.

"What's your name?" he asked Buzz, looking at him for the first time, a charming smile on his clean-shaven face. It was a damned winning smile.

Buzz was ready with his cover story...

"Buzz Woodward. I'm just passing through on my way to Maine. Caribou."

"What's in Caribou?"

"Nothing much. A few New Jersey buddies with a place. A place they got ready—just like you did here. Shoulda listened to 'em. I waited too long to take off. I figured it would take several months for the bug to turn off the lights. I was wrong."

"So you were, Mr. Woodward, so you were. A lot of people underestimated the problem."

A sympathetic expression came to his face. "This is the long way around to Caribou, isn't it?"

"Not really. Too many crazies on the roads up the coast. Safer this way. And call me Buzz."

Rheumy was maybe ten years older than Ralph. Perhaps Buzz's exact age. Buzz's gift for guessing now deserted him. The clean room. The TV. The lights. The civilized treatment. The grist for the guessmill was receiving mixed ingredients. But there was one thing.

The way Rheumy sat in that chair. His butt was too far forward.

There must be a pillow behind there, Buzz surmised.

Rheumy turned to his brother. "So, besides meeting Buzz, did anything interesting happen down by the road?"

"Lloyd popped another one today. A preacher."

Rheumy closed his brown eyes, and shook his head slowly.

"That boy is dumber than snot, Ralph. It's so hard to find good help nowadays. What did you do with the body?"

It's all an act, Buzz thought.

"We buried it. Next to the others."

"I suppose you didn't want to drag it back up here," Rheumy mused with understated sympathy. "We'll have to get back down there and dig them up soon. Move them to a more appropriate resting place. So little time. So much to do."

Buzz nodded with empathy, and again, stifled an urge to jump the bastard.

"So how bad is the back?" Buzz asked.

"Buzz is a chiropractor, Rheum," Ralph inserted quickly.

"Excellent. My back has been bad lately. Makes a hard life harder. I miss my chiropractor in the city. Old Jack had the gift. I just couldn't convince him to join us up here."

The city, Buzz noted. A New Yorker expression. Rheumy must have come up from New York.

Buzz gave a knowing nod. He suppressed an urge to brag about his own skills. Buzz knew in his guts—from some instinct without a name—that Rheumy Marks was the kind of tyrant who liked to say all the important things.

Rheumy noticed the bottle by Ralph's side for the first time.

"Mariner!" He turned to Buzz. "How did you know?"

"Tell you the truth, I didn't. I don't drink Scotch. I appreciate the beer, too, but I'm not much of a drinker. I traded an adjustment for the bottle in a little town called Argyle, New York, where I hooked up with the two Jesus freaks. A real nice fella named Bob Samuels gave me that bottle—a real Scotch-lover."

Buzz was concentrating hard on giving his lies a tangential basis in truth.

"So you bring me fine single malt, and you adjust backs," Rheumy said, a note of admiration in his voice. "My ship has come in."

Buzz decided to let loose some of his own charm, his own joy-of-life. It was time.

"You bet, Rheumy. I've got a good feeling—a real good feeling—about this place. I mean, who-da thunk it? A set up like this—the electricity. The workers. You liking single malt, me liking Nicholson. As Good as It Gets just happens to be my favorite movie of the Nineties. Pun intended—your place here is as good as it gets. I've seen a lot of garbage on the road, ever since I left Montclair. A lot of garbage."

"Are you making me an offer?" Rheumy offered.

Buzz waited.

"You bet your life," he said soberly. Finally, finally, he was sure the beer had worn off.

Rheumy stared at him. Buzz stared back. Ralph watched the silent interplay closely, his eyes darting back and forth between his brother and this strange man.

"There's a place for intelligent men here at the Marks Farm, Mr. Buzz Woodward."

"It's so hard to find good help nowadays," Buzz agreed, smiling. "So let's quit screwing around. Let's get you to a bed or a couch and I'll fix up that back of yours."

Chapter Fourteen

Judge Jury Executioner

Over the next ten days, Buzz scoped out the lay of the land at the Marks Farm. As Rheumy's resident chiropractor, he was given a free run of the compound. He spent most of his days playing cards with Ralph or Rheumy or both of them, watching movies, hanging out on the deck, reading Rheumy's huge library of pulp fiction, even going out to hunt with his host—pretending that he loved every minute.

There were four buildings besides Rheumy's house (where Ralph also lived). One house for the eight henchmen, as Buzz came to think of them—including Lloyd, whose last name turned out to be Beaumont. There was one house—a jail, really—for the fourteen "workers," now including Johnny, who were basically well-fed slaves. Two were older women, twelve were men, most of them refugees "recruited" at the roadblock. None were related to each other. Their master had been careful not to recruit any locals; they were all from out of state.

The workers toiled under the watchful eye of Lloyd or another overseer, planting crops, grinding wheat, cleaning, and caring for the horses and livestock.

Everyone was well-fed. There were dairy cows and thousands of pounds of grains, rice, and beans that Rheumy had purchased before the millennium. These were stored in the third building and in two gigantic silos. Buzz guessed that there were other stashes, probably buried underground, on the expansive, four-thousand acre property.

The compound had three propane generators and thousands of gallons of liquid propane in buried tanks. In addition to the wind turbine, there were four large solar panel arrays. Rheumy, during his conversations while Buzz treated his back, or during the meals which Buzz was invited to join occasionally (Buzz usually ate with the henchmen), bragged about his "back-up" back-up systems, and the two million dollars he had invested making preparations.

His proudest possessions were stored in the fourth building—the Hothouse. The prostitutes. Four women who were not slaves, but rather, high-class escorts (no cheap whores for Rheumy—"Nothing but the best," he told Buzz). Rheumy had paid top dollar to rent them for a two week spree just before the turn of the century, knowing they would never be able to return to the city.

There was a short blonde, a buxom brunette, a redhead (tall and slightly chunky), and finally, a musky one named Crystal, with a dark butch haircut. She was reserved for the times when Rheumy or Ralph felt like "mixing it up," and was sometimes loaned out as a reward to a henchman who did a particularly good job.

"Rheumy has foresight," Ralph told Buzz once with nary a hint of irony. "He's stockpiled thirty-five thousand condoms. And if we don't use all of them, Rheumy says they'll make great trade items."

Buzz turned down Rheumy's frequent offers to join in the fun. Feeling nervous, he confided to Ralph that he was dysfunctional in that department. Like his other falsehoods, this had a basis in truth.

The workers were guarded during the day. At night they were herded into a specially-designed building, which sported two floors and a few small windows high on the walls. They were also fed in their mundane jail.

Rheumy took a special satisfaction in his generous treatment of them: they were given home-made beer, dim electric lights, and decent beds with clean sheets in small private rooms. After hours, he let them watch as many movies as they pleased. One day per week, according to a schedule, each man was given use of the frumpy redhead.

"By and large," Rheumy once told Buzz during a late-night massage, "they like it here. Where else are they going to be so well-fed? They're safe. They're protected."

"Then why do you guard them?" Buzz felt bold enough to ask. *Because they know where the bodies are buried?* he didn't ask.

"Just playing it safe. They could become violent. People are unstable in these trying times. You never know when one might turn on you. It's a different world now, Buzz, a different world. We didn't use guards back when I had my own law firm—to keep the clerks, the receptionists. Even the younger lawyers trying to make partner. We worked them the hardest.

"The weapon we used back then was the salary we paid. Plenty enough so they could get by—but never more. That way they had to stay with you. They liked it, too. But they always had a choice. It would have been easy for any of our workers to run off if they really wanted to back in the old days."

Buzz knew this was pure rationalization, but then again, Rheumy had been a lawyer. He could twist ideas with words.

At night, there was a sentry at the door of the slave house, a second sentry at the front entrance to the compound, and another one or two sentries at the roadblock. It was Ralph's job to manage them, and he often complained to Buzz that he needed at least three more men.

Despite Rheumy's outward friendliness to him, Buzz suspected that he was in a probationary period. He was not trusted with a gun, nor asked to help with sentry duty, despite the obvious scarcity of manpower.

It would have been easy for Buzz, who was staying in the henchmen's house, to slip away at night and return to his bicycle and backpack. But there was Johnny. He couldn't leave Johnny behind. Not after what they had done to Tom.

And Buzz was smart enough to know that there were probably more dead bodies in addition to the ones buried down by the roadblock. Johnny was a material witness to a murder. It was perfectly conceivable that if Johnny tried to escape, he would be hunted down.

Rheumy was proud of his three bloodhounds.

Except for one occasion, Buzz was unable to talk to Johnny. The preacher had been off by himself in the fields, planting potatoes by hand. Ralph, who was supposed to come by shortly to take Buzz hunting, was running late. Lloyd was on a horse, on the far side of the field, oblivious. There was a pecking order on the Marks Farm, and Lloyd Beaumont was already below Buzz Woodward.

Buzz was standing on the dirt path next to the field, facing away from Johnny, looking at Lloyd.

"Don't look at me," Buzz began, trying not to move his lips. "Just keep looking at your spuds while we talk. How you doing, brother? Hangin' in there?"

"I'm doing okay, I guess. I miss Tom. I really miss him—it's hard. We were together for three years.

"And these people are depraved. I'm trying to bring them to Jesus, but they just make fun of me. They actually like it here. They're whoremongers. I miss my Bible."

"I know, I know," Buzz said. *They're murderers.*

"Have you got a plan, Brother Buzz?"

"Yes, I do. It's not a pretty one. Expect me to come by at night, very late—I can't tell you which day. Soon. They're beginning to trust me."

"But the guards…" Johnny almost spoke out loud.

"I'll take care of the guards."

"You won't have to kill anybody, will you?" Johnny asked.

"I'll do what I have to do," Buzz replied.

"I'll pray for you," Johnny promised.

"Thanks."

Lloyd brought his horse around to face them, and Buzz, fearful of being suspected of having a friendly relationship with Johnny, walked into stride without another word.

✝ ✝ ✝

Buzz grit his teeth, standing over Rheumy's small but sinewy back, and began to use his hands to heal this…charming, despicable creature. The smaller man's arms hung over the side of the bench.

At Rheumy's insistence, the boys in the shop had fashioned a treatment bench, about knee-high, to Buzz's specifications. It even had leather-covered cushions.

Buzz now knew much of Rheumy's background: childhood in the ritzy Scarsdale, a suburb of New York. Getting beat up by the bullies on the playground during grade school; unable to play sports because of his bad back. High school valedictorian. His numerous sexual escapades at Manhattan College. The abusive alcoholic father he strangely admired; law school at Pace. The millions he made as a trial lawyer.

"Remember that billion-dollar tobacco settlement? That was me. That was partly Marks, Marks, and Spittledorf in New York State."

Rheumy told Buzz how the president of a large computer company with government contracts had tipped him off to the computer bug in late 1997.

The weird fact that some of Rheumy's background, in a sideways-sort-of-fashion, paralleled Buzz's, made it all the more creepy.

Given a different decision here or there, I could have been a Rheumy, he once realized with a chill.

It was more than that. Rheumy Marks had a friendly, clever knack for manipulating others. Buzz realized that he was dealing with an equal. He suspected that Rheumy realized that Buzz was putting on an act—but couldn't know for sure.

He did know for sure if Rheumy would eventually discover inconsistencies in his story, or feel in his gut, in that way that only a lawyer could—especially ones who were as guilty as their guilty clients—that Buzz was playing a role.

Maybe Rheumy knew but just liked having his back feel good. Or maybe Rheumy knew Buzz was acting, but didn't yet know why.

Healing Rheumy, whose back truly was a mess, gave Buzz an extremely ambivalent feeling. Rheumy raved about Buzz's abilities, even claiming he was better than Old Jack.

His healing skill enabled Rheumy to whore all the more, Buzz noted glumly. He was keeping a tyrant in tip-top condition. Was that okay? Was that right?

But it wasn't only that—it was that Rheumy was such a pleasant fellow. Despite himself, Buzz had grown to like him in an odd kind of way. He was a good conversationalist, and Buzz knew that Rheumy enjoyed talking to him. His brother Ralph was bright, but not as interesting or smart as Buzz, who always made a point of challenging Rheumy during their conversations. Buzz was like the vice-president of a corporation who allows the president to win at golf—the key was making the challenge appear real; make the competition feel acute. But in the end, the boss would always win.

This gave Rheumy a chance to debate, and finally, to prove his new friend wrong about whatever was being discussed, whether the topic was a movie, or the ethics of the new paradigm.

It wasn't that Buzz thought that he was immoral—it was that Rheumy was amoral. He showed no signs of guilt about his treatment of his so-called workers, or his sexual indulgences. The prostitutes seemed to genuinely admire him, and to be thankful for having work and good food in a world of scarcity.

Rheumy would take a massage twice a day, sometimes having Buzz awakened in the middle of the night. There was always a guard. During the first week, the guard sat in the room with Buzz and his patient. Now the guard usually sat outside. Buzz suspected this was because the little man enjoyed discussing "management decisions," as he called them, with his private chiropractor.

"You ever think about getting married?" Buzz asked him this evening after dinner, after he began the massage. Rheumy was on his stomach, his chin on a down pillow.

"What for?"

"You know, to have a couple kids. Keep the family name going. The whole white picket fence thing."

"I hate kids. Ralph can pass on the family name if he feels like it. Were you ever married?"

"I told you I was divorced, remember?"

"And?" Rheumy asked.

"And what?"

"And did you have any kids?"

"Yeah, I have a daughter. Or had a daughter. Jenny. She was attending college at Gonzaga in Washington State before the trouble started."

"And?" Rheumy asked pleasantly, almost kindly.

"And she hated me," Buzz confessed.

"She hated you. I rest my case. Love is overrated. Family relationships are cultural constructs, nothing more. Take it from an expert. My old man was a real bastard. Treated me like dirt. But I rose above it. I made something of myself. I ran rings around those prep boys from Yale and Harvard with their skinny, perfect wives and doting, lovey-dovey parents.

"If I'm a happy person today, I believe it's because I rejected the fiction of love when I was a young man, before it ruined me.

"Love makes people soft. Everybody wanted soft before the crash. Not Rheumy Marks. I was hard then, and I'm hard now. That's why I not only survived the collapse, but prospered. That's why I was able to save Ralph. Ralph was too soft and I had to look after him. All these people here, they owe me their lives because I was cold and calculating about the implications of the computer bug.

"And another thing, there were too many lawyers back in the old days," Rheumy added with no hint of irony, now warming to his subject, just as Buzz had hoped.

Rheumy loved to pontificate when he was warmed up, and Buzz was gathering intelligence, and, perhaps, in the back of his mind, holding court.

"Practicing law was becoming a grind toward the end," he continued. "This may sound strange, but I didn't mind when the bug bit. It has given me a great chance to take time off, to relax, become rejuvenated. I like it better this way. Less competition."

When Rheumy had mentioned that love was over-rated, Buzz had immediately thought of Mel: her face, for the first time in months, became a perfectly clear picture in his mind, and he wondered why God had brought him this far, to this place, at this time.

Rheumy had gotten under his skin. On purpose? Buzz couldn't know. But he felt an overwhelming urge to run from the room, to get out of here, to run toward Mel, and the hell with Johnny.

"And what about the future?" Buzz asked sincerely, preparing to bring up a topic which he knew no one else here would dare mention to Rheumy.

"What do you mean?"

"We both know that your little paradise here can't last forever. It might take a few years, maybe longer, but law and order will be restored eventually. There are the bodies."

He felt the muscles in Rheumy's back tense up, ever so slightly. Buzz was careful not to change the rhythm of his massage.

"What about them?"

"Let's not kid ourselves, Rheum. Guys like you and me, we've done...things. We've—uh—taken advantage of the situation; at least that's what the small-minded people will say. And they'll remember."

Rheumy met this observation with silence. Buzz continued his ministrations.

"Dead people don't remember things," Rheumy said after a couple minutes. For once, there was a coldness in his voice.

"And the living don't always know where the bodies are buried—hypothetically speaking, of course. No evidence, no trial.

"I am the law in Brixton for the time being. It sure beats mob rule. When things change again—when law and order, as you call it, makes a comeback—I'll go with the flow. I'll shuck and I'll jive. I'm a lawyer, after all. Law and order always needs a lawyer."

"And the world always needs a chiropractor," Buzz joked casually, drawing a chuckle from Rheumy. "Um, move your arm up, yeah, like that."

But one thing Rheumy had said had given Buzz chills: *Dead people don't remember things.*

Was he threatening me? It was hard to tell.

After a few minutes, Buzz started the conversation again.

"There are other, how shall we say, assets, buried around here."

"I have no idea what you're talking about," Rheumy replied.

"Come on. You had millions Rheumy, you couldn't have spent it all on the farm. You're too smart. I know you didn't let all your wealth disappear into the computers. I'm talking about—" Buzz leaped at just the right word "—coins."

"Ahh! You mean the shiny stuff. Well, if I *had* buried that kind of thing, and I'm not admitting that I did, I sure wouldn't tell you about it. I wouldn't even tell Ralph."

The shiny stuff—gold. Buzz had guessed right. Rheumy probably had hundreds of thousands of dollars—perhaps millions—buried on his property. That was too bad.

Buzz looked down at Rheumy's pallid skin, his excellent crewcut, then closed his eyes. (Lloyd had been a barber before the Troubles, and his ability to keep Rheumy looking sharp probably made up for a few dead bodies.)

"Tell me, Buzz," Rheumy began again, turning his head slightly. "How come you know so much about me?"

"Every doctor should try to understand his patients. You yourself tell me more than you know—"

—as soon as Buzz uttered these words, he knew he had made a mistake. He desperately tried to recover—

"Uh, and I just know things. Maybe I know about you because we're so alike. We think alike."

"Maybe too much alike," Rheumy replied.

You have no idea, Buzz thought. *Stop talking so much.*

He was pressing Rheumy too hard tonight. Pushing too much. Looking for what? For…guilt?

Rheumy's shoulders tensed again, less than before. Buzz almost missed it this time. No matter what Rheumy said, Buzz believed that his muscles could not lie, though Rheumy was getting better at masking himself.

Buzz was running out of time. He had been well-fed for the first time since leaving Cleveland, and had actually managed to gain a little weight. His days here were comfortable, despite the tension of playing a role. Buzz's mandate to get to Bagpipe was still intact, of course, but the daily imperative to keep moving, which had punctuated every minute of the trip before coming here, was no longer in force.

"So tell me, how long do you plan to stay at the farm?" Rheumy asked suddenly, his voice natural, as if reading his mind.

The length of Buzz's stay had not come up before. He hesitated before answering, and unfortunately, allowed his hands to pause in their duties. He tried to cover by cracking his knuckles.

"Uh, I haven't really given it much thought," he lied. Another mistake—a lie not based on a truth.

Is Rheumy cross-examining me?

"I'm pretty happy here. You know that."

"But you never take advantage of everything we have to offer," Rheumy observed.

Both men knew he was talking about the free sex.

"You're not gay, are you?"

"Hell no," Buzz replied honestly.

Rheumy's next question came quickly.

"You're not hiding anything from me, are you?"

"Hiding what? And what's with all the questions—are you cross-examining me? If so, then I confess. Guilty as charged," Buzz scrambled, trying to sound breezy, but failing.

Sometimes the best defense was a good offense.

At least what I said was confusing.

It struck Buzz for the first time that this entire conversation, because Rheumy was lying flat on his stomach, had taken place with neither man looking each other in the eye.

Has he been reading my hands as I've been reading his shoulders?

"Guilty as charged? Of what?" Rheumy asked a bit forcefully.

Maybe Rheumy was thrown off by the strange response. There was no way for Buzz to know.

"Uh, I don't know," Buzz responded. *Boy, that sounds stupid.* And so it was.

Rheumy grunted, then turned over abruptly, then sat up, placing a towel around his neck.

"We're done for the day," he told Buzz.

✝ ✝ ✝

Buzz was not able to fall asleep that night. He steeled himself to carry out his plan—for Johnny. He tried to think of another way, a better way—but could not. Instead, images came to his head.

Tom Kasovich, raising his hands to heaven, praying before dropping his make-shift fishing line into a stream.

Mel running up to him at Bagpipe, Markie and Packy at her side.

Donna, her arms resting on the ledge, just before he fell…

The Man, in his kitchen, before the Troubles began, carefully raising a spoonful of Cream of Wheat to his lips, his eyes concentrating on the newspaper…

…his first view of the majestic Lady of the Rockies, on the mountain with Sam and Lee Royalle.

Throwing a full-court pass to Sam, who catches it and makes the lay-up.

The floor of the living room with Packy in the old house in Lakewood, peaceful, on their backs, listening to *John Barleycorn Must Die* by Traffic.

An older memory of waltzing with Ellie on her wedding day, along with the sense-memory of the feel of his hand on the back of her taut, silken wedding dress...

Markie's innocent voice; screwing his eyebrows together with grave sincerity, saying, "I love you, Daddy," then smiling a boy-smile, showing his perfect first teeth.

Mel's hair, sitting on the bed facing away from him, the gown falling from her shoulders, her skin glistening, on their first night as man and wife...

...the night in New Jersey, on the jetty, with the lightning flashing and the surf pounding. The mirage-boy on the beach, brandishing a sword, crying out "Buzz Buzz Buzz!"

*The Lord gave **you** a second chance.*

He rolled over onto his stomach, and stretched his neck, his back, his arms. He flexed and unflexed the muscles in his thighs. He was in the best condition of his life.

I'm thirty-seven, still at my peak.

And he felt the mastery there, the hardness—the gift of strength which the Almighty had knitted into his frame. Buzz Woodward also possessed the head-and-hand knowledge required for his profession. He understood the human body the way a mechanic—though perhaps not an engineer—understands the innards of a car. The places and connections where the body is robust—and where it is susceptible...

The dialogue with himself began again, as it did every night when he went over his plan. The knock would surely come to the door; if not tonight, then tomorrow night, or the next, because Rheumy kept all hours, and Buzz was at his beck and call.

At the beck and call of a monster.

Buzz didn't normally like monsters. But he liked this one. This monster was charming, and sincere (even if sincerely amoral), and generous in his own way.

I can't do it, his conscience—or his inner coward—protested.

What about Johnny?

What would the Man do?

The Man would never do what I have planned. Or would he?

But it would be self-defense.

Self-defense? You can slip away whenever you please. Nobody's holding a gun to your head.

But what about Johnny? They're holding a gun to his head. They'll kill him.

God can do anything. God can perform miracles. Johnny has faith.

God didn't save Tommy.

But Tommy was a martyr—a saint in heaven now.

A song came to him: *Lord, what is man that You look at him, the son of man that You think of him? A shadow, he passes away...*

Buzz, confused about some things, certain about others, prayed. The words that came to him were the same that had come to him at the O'Mearas during the croquet game:

Yahweh, make strong the hands of your chosen one. Lay mine enemies down before me.

Isn't this what Yahweh has done? Hasn't He laid Rheumy down before you? Put him within the grasp of your strong hands.

But you could stay here, continue building your friendship with Rheumy. Influence him. Convert him—like you converted Sam and the Man. Johnny Bryant is praying for you...

Rheumy is no Sam. Rheumy uses people. He is not your friend. He is not like Mark. He has no friends. He wants no friends.

If you stay longer, you'll get soft, just like Rheumy wants, and you'll grow to need him, and he'll discover the truth about you. And it is pride to think that you can continue to resist the lures of his movies, his food, his alcohol, his whores...

Oh crap. This is going nowhere.

He dove into his own mind, searching for a pearl of wisdom, a clue for action, an imperative for moral decision and found...

Reality.

What was the reality of the situation?

If I don't do it, what will happen to Johnny?

Can you live with yourself if you do it?

Can you live with yourself if you don't?

Buzz realized that the reality of the situation would never be clear-cut. A gray area.

Buzz had read Saint Thomas Aquinas. He knew the queen of virtues, prudence, as the Angelic Doctor had taught, was the application of absolute moral principles, informed by grace, to decide to do the right thing in a given situation.

Until I'm in the room, with my knee in his back, I won't know what to do.

This was the reality of the situation.

Perhaps, he thought now, he shouldn't be asking himself what was right or wrong. He already knew right from wrong.

It was written in his heart.

Sure knowledge of right and wrong, in the abstract and absolute principle, was perhaps the greatest perk of being a Catholic.

Maybe he needed to ask: What is prudent?

He turned on his back and looked at the ceiling of his sparse, comfortable room. His eyes had adjusted to the darkness. Unlike the night at Deacon Samuel's house, Buzz had grown accustomed to a real bed here at the Marks Farm. He longed for a statue or a holy picture. He reached down to his pants, which he had left on the floor, and found his relic of the Little Flower in the pocket.

Little Flower, help me! What is prudent?

He waited.

What is simple? she asked in reply.

I don't know.

Just then, the knock he had been dreading came on the door. Lloyd Beaumont, Tom's murderer, stood in the hallway, flashlight in hand.

"Rheumy needs you again."

Game time, Buzz thought soberly. But he knew this was not a game.

✝ ✝ ✝

Lloyd, shotgun in hand, closed the door behind them and sat on the chair outside Rheumy's door. Buzz knew that Ralph was probably sleeping in his room down the hall.

Rheumy Marks was already on the treatment couch, on his stomach, dressed in a pair of boxer shorts, his chin resting on the down pillow, his right hand comfortably hidden beneath the same pillow.

His shooting hand, Buzz thought suddenly. *Is he hiding a gun?*

Rheumy owned several handguns—Glocks, Rugers, a Colt. He had proudly shown them to Buzz on several occasions. Buzz knew he kept at least one in this room.

"Sorry to wake you," Rheumy greeted him with a wince. He kept his eyes on the wall, away from Buzz. "It's really bad tonight. I couldn't sleep."

Neither could I, thought Buzz.

"That's okay. I'll have you feeling better in a jiffy. Let's begin with the massage, loosen you up, then do the adjustments."

"Sure."

Buzz walked to Rheumy and stood over the man. He seemed so small. Buzz knew he was actually quite strong for his size. He was also coordinated—a seasoned hunter before the collapse. Buzz placed his hands on Rheumy's back, and began the massage.

"I've been wondering…" Buzz began his patter in the usual fashion, pausing to let Rheumy signal for him to go on.

Rheumy did this with a grunt.

Buzz could not see Rheumy's face—only the bald spot in Rheumy's crewcut. Buzz knew Rheumy's back the way a motorhead knows his hot-rod. He eyed Rheumy's forearm, and how it disappeared beneath the pillow.

I could die tonight, Buzz thought. Even though he wanted to live, the prospect of dying did not bother him in the least.

I have a job to do.

He prayed the Act of Contrition just in case: *O my God, I am heartily sorry, for having offended Thee…*

Rheumy was not in a talkative mood tonight. By the painful knots in the man's muscles, Buzz could understand why not. He had the kind of back that always reverted to form, no matter how many times Buzz realigned it.

Why not just get down to brass tacks?

Buzz had a purpose on earth. He was here to cut things down, one way or the other.

"I've been wondering about…God."

"You? God?" Rheumy asked.

"Yeah, God. I mean, what if He really exists? What if He really is the final judge of what is right and what is wrong?"

Like all Buzz's forays into conversation with Rheumy, he was basing his misdirections on truth.

"But God doesn't exist."

"But what if He does?"

"Then he doesn't care about the likes of you and me."

"Maybe not here on earth. But what if there is life after death, and a final judgment? Maybe He cares about how we treated each other. Thou shalt not kill, remember?"

"Buzz, you sound like you're getting a conscience. Have you ever killed anybody?"

"No," Buzz said. "But I've done a lot of bad things in my life. I've lied. I beat my ex-wife. I was… an alcoholic. I tried to kill myself once. What if God holds that against me when I die?"

Buzz let that sink in.

He felt for a sign in Rheumy's muscles, but found none. Nevertheless, he could practically see the wheels churning beneath Rheumy's scalp.

"Buzz drank a beer," he must be thinking...

"If there is a God, Buzz, and I'm not saying there is, then you and me are in deep trouble. And if there is a hell, then you'll go to it. And you'll meet me there."

Rheumy paused, thinking.

"No regrets, Buzz," Rheumy continued. "That's my motto. Rheumy Marks, for good or for bad, is the owner of his own decisions. All the liberal hand-wringing over right and wrong from the old world was a sign of weakness. Morality is for the weak. A real man makes his choices and moves on. No regrets.

"But the afterlife is a hypothetical. The only reality is the here and now. I seriously doubt there's a God. The final judgment is moot court."

"I guess you're right," Buzz agreed weakly, lying.

Buzz was losing his determination. His heretofore bold, heroic plan was fading into a moral cloud of unknowing. Talking too much with Rheumy was all wrong—a big mistake. For all Rheumy's macho Nietzschean hyperbole, his honesty, along with the ordinary sound of his voice, were humanizing.

Buzz had his hands on his flesh.

This is not going to be easy...

"Can I ask you another question, a more personal question?" Buzz began again.

"Sure. Oh, that feels good, by the way."

Buzz paused to work the muscle to which Rheumy was referring.

Give him one more chance, Buzz thought, feeling weak. Procrastinating.

Buzz was concentrating on keeping the movements of his hands light, natural, soothing. Having finished the lower back, he had slowly worked his way up to Rheumy's neck and shoulder area.

"So what's your question?"

"After dinner, you asked me if I had thought about leaving the farm—"

"I knew you were hiding something from me," Rheumy said happily, as if he was pleased to discover that he had been right...

Buzz leaned forward, but Rheumy didn't see this...

"You're right. I've been having...doubts. I guess I'm weak. And I was wondering, like we were talking about, what if I did have a family? Not that I do. But what if I did? What if I was on my way to go see my wife and kids before I ran into you? And what if I wanted to move on...would you let me take off?"

It was a small thing.

A tiny thing, but in the tips of his fingers, he felt Rheumy's shoulders tense up ever so slightly. And he thought he saw the muscles in Rheumy's forearm—the one with the hand beneath the pillow—flex a bit.

Rheumy laughed a small laugh.

He's stalling, Buzz thought.

"Of course I would let you go. You're free to go anytime," Rheumy said breezily. "But it would be too bad for me. I'd have to find another chiropractor. We'd all miss you."

You're lying, Buzz concluded wearily. Buzz himself had been lying to Rheumy for what seemed like forever. One liar knows another.

What happened next, happened quickly.

A unique melancholy flowed into Buzz's heart. A sadness of the ages. A blue melody every untried soldier sings in the trench, in the waning moments before the bullets fly...

Buzz deftly lifted his knee, and brought it down on the center of Rheumy's back...

"Hey—" Rheumy called out, raising his voice, struggling to raise himself up, not yet realizing that even if he possessed three times the strength, he would still be pinned beneath a foe with overwhelmingly superior force.

Yahweh, make strong the hands of your chosen one. Lay mine enemies down before me.

...and in a flick of an eye, Buzz clamped a powerful forearm around Rheumy's skinny, crooked neck; then closed thick, strong fingers on Rheumy's jaw. Buzz's other hand had already darted down onto Rheumy's right forearm, his hand still beneath the pillow...

Rheumy made a fruitless effort to speak.

"Do not attempt to call out," Buzz whispered into his ear.

Rheumy struggled anyway, but could not budge.

"Listen to me," Buzz continued softly, "Listen to me because I'm only going to tell you this once. I do have a wife and three children. They're waiting for me. And Lloyd murdered a friend of mine, a young Christian, Tom Kasovich.

"In a matter of seconds, you will be dead, Benjamin Marks. I will give you this time to ask God for His mercy—"

Buzz, who now felt the adrenaline streaming into his own shoulders, and arms, and legs, and back, watched with detachment from above as Rheumy's eyes bugged out, as understanding dawned, and prepared for the small man to struggle.

Rheumy did not. Instead, he allowed all his muscles to go slack. Anticipating this feint, Buzz clamped down all the more.

Do it now, he told himself. *Or you'll never do it.*

Still, Buzz had to say something more...

"I beg you, Rheumy, I beg you. I beg you to ask for God's mercy. He'll give it to you, He will. He's a merciful God. Maybe then, after I die, we can have another conversation..."

Buzz closed his eyes. He took a breath. One last pang of conscience.

What is prudent?

Johnny. For Johnny.

That was simple.

God have mercy on us both.

After a pause, relying on his certain knowledge of the human body, Buzz pressed down hard on the man's back with his knee, quickly pulled his right hand from Rheumy's forearm, wrapped it around his neck—and snapped the life from him with a quick jerk and crack.

Rheumy Marks went limp.

Buzz reached over and lifted the pillow.

There was no gun in the dead man's hand. It was empty.

In a hard world, there was no time to dwell on details.

Buzz turned the head of the corpse away from the door.

He walked quietly to the bar and tried to open the drawer where he had seen Rheumy stash a gun. It was locked.

No gun, no time, Buzz thought. *Plan B.*

He grabbed a clear bottle on the glass shelf behind the bar—Chivas Regal.

He padded over to the door, then, after a pause to run through the plan in his mind, he opened it, holding the bottle to the side, out of sight.

"Lloyd!" he whispered with concern. "Something's wrong with Rheumy!"

"Hey?"

Lloyd jumped to his feet, and dumbly, left his shotgun leaning against the wall. He walked in, and Buzz calmly stepped aside, letting him go past.

Buzz raised the bottle and brought it down squarely on the base of Lloyd's neck. Lloyd crumpled to the carpet with a dull thump.

Buzz paused, listening for a sound from Ralph's room down the hall. Nothing.

Buzz crouched down, then lifted Lloyd's right hand—his trigger hand—and broke his meaty thumb and index finger with two muted cracks.

He walked out of the room, picked up the shotgun by the barrel, then noiselessly closed the door behind him. Carefully placing one foot before the other, he left the house in silence.

He did not look back.

✠ ✠ ✠

Buzz went to the slave house. The guard had been sleeping. He awoke to a shotgun. Buzz ordered him to turn around, then knocked him out.

He broke bones in this guard's fingers, too, before entering the house. Not only was Buzz sure that the guard would not be able to fire a gun, but also that he was truly out cold—not playing possum.

He padded along the hallway upstairs to Johnny's room, which, fortunately, was marked with a nametag.

Johnny was awake—and packed.

"How did you know I was coming tonight?" Buzz whispered.

"I woke up ten minutes ago from a sound sleep. The Lord told me to get ready."

Buzz wondered, but did not ask Johnny, how the Lord spoke so clearly to him. No time.

They walked out the rear of the compound, on the far side of the dog kennel, and taking an escape route which Buzz had planned from the start, doubled back to the dirt road, well beyond the remaining sentry.

"What happened?" Johnny asked after a while.

"Shush," Buzz cautioned. "No talking."

When they emerged onto Route 100, behind the roadblock, he ordered Johnny to wait in the shadows. He darted out to the cab of the fire truck (he knew, he just knew, that the sentry would be in the cab, facing the other way on Route 100).

He quietly jumped up on the running board, tapped the window with his knuckle, holding his shotgun out of view.

"Buzz, is that you?" the startled sentry, a man named Rory Parker, asked. "Something wrong?"

Rory did not have his rifle in his hands.

Poor training, Buzz thought absently.

"No, everything's great," Buzz said in a clear voice, raising his shotgun. "Now get out of the cab."

Buzz knocked Rory out, too, but decided against breaking his fingers. He was sick of the sound. He found a cord in the cab, and did tie the guard's hands and feet.

"Okay," Buzz called over to Johnny in a normal tone of voice. "We're okay. Come out."

"What next?"

"We're free to go. Let's get my backpack. We can share the bike. We've got about four hours until daybreak, and we've got to put some distance between us and this hellhole."

"Okay," was all Johnny said.

Then they climbed over the roadblock, and started jogging up to the crest. An hour later, they were four miles north of Brixton. Buzz was jogging alongside Johnny, who was riding the bike. Buzz was thankful for the cloud cover. It made the darkness darker.

It made it easier to imagine that the Man was with them, jogging on the other side of the bike.

"Aren't we forgetting something?" Johnny asked.

"What's that?" Buzz replied.

"To pray?"

"Johnny, I've been praying ever since we came to Brixton."

Even so, they stopped, and each man, raising one hand to heaven, and holding hands with the other, prayed a silent prayer of thanks.

"Do you have a scripture?" Buzz asked.

Johnny's eyes were closed. "The Kingdom of God is near you. But when you enter a town and are not welcomed, go into its streets and say, 'Even the dust of your town that sticks to our feet, we wipe off against you. Yet be sure of this: the Kingdom of God is near.' I tell you, it will be more bearable on that day for Sodom than for that town."

When they had gone far enough, Buzz Woodward lowered his danger-antenna, and allowed himself, finally, to think about what he had done.

I killed a man.

It was that simple, and it was that complicated.

He was not happy. He was not sad.

He remembered when it had all started, when he heard the gunshot that ended Tom Kasovich's earthly life. When he had decided to walk down the hill for Johnny, instead of jumping on his bike and taking off south.

It had been the sound. The sound of the gunshot.

That gunshot meant others had declared war in a hard cold world.

Live by the sword. Die by the sword.

War is for men who cut things down.

I knew then. I knew then.

For all the anxiety, moral ambiguity, and second-guessing between that gunshot and the final crack of Rheumy's neck, he had known his purpose. The reality of the situation. That whatever the name, there would be a compound, and in that compound there would be a Rheumy.

He had known all this, because he was Buzz, and because he just knew things.

There are on this earth hard men like Buzz—warriors. Guys who know how things work. Men who cut things down for the sake of other men who raise things up—men like Johnny Bryant.

So when Buzz Woodward had taken the long walk down the hill toward the enemy line, he was prepared to kill.

Chapter Fifteen

The Last Leg

They reached Holland Pond after four days of hard walking and riding. Johnny Bryant was thrilled and relieved when he discovered that his Uncle Reginald, a bachelor, had survived, and was only a little worse for the wear.

Unfortunately, the killer flu had taken its toll in the town. In fact, in the northern part of Vermont, perhaps because the winters were long and harsh, the influenzas and pneumonias had done almost as much damage as in the big cities.

Reginald Bryant's congregation had been cut in half as a result, but the townspeople, by and large, had planted as soon as the weather broke. A hand-tilled harvest was finally coming in. Also, there were still fish in the lake—traditionally called *ponds* in the north country.

Perhaps as disturbing to Buzz as the killer flus were the rumors of bands of roving marauders—some from Quebec—who would appear unexpectedly and plunder farms or towns, stealing food. Some of these gangs were heavily armed, with Hummers or jerry-rigged armoured vehicles. Sometimes, according to the rumors (for Holland Pond itself had never been directly attacked), the invaders more than met their match from resistance put up by the better-organized towns and well-armed farmers.

Buzz, itching to move on to Bagpipe, decided to leave the next morning; he stayed for the night with Johnny in his uncle's modest cabin on the pond.

Because they were both talkers, during the journey to Holland Pond they had talked and talked—about the Bible, about how pathetic Jimmy Swaggart was, about the old world—those toasted almond ice cream bars Good Humor used to make, Mel and the boys, and Johnny's parents and brothers and sisters, last seen in Rochester during Thanksgiving of 1999, and major league baseball and pizza delivered to your door with any kind of topping you wanted—about lots of things, but not about—the killing.

On the day of parting, Johnny, who had spent his summers here since he was a child, walked a few miles to guide Buzz to a dirt trail south of the pond that led east, past Halfway Pond, toward Route 114. Today they walked in silence, praying, taking turns holding the bike, enjoying the sounds of the woods—birds, leaves in the breeze, or, no sound at all.

Finally, they came to the fork.

It was early June. The weather, perfect.

"This is it," Johnny said.

Buzz remembered the first time he had seen the young man standing with Tom Kasovich outside the fire station in Argyle. He noticed that there was a new maturity in his eyes—a hardness, perhaps. But not a world-weariness.

The altruistic, almost childlike, love still shone.

What do you see in my eyes?

Buzz knew they were both thinking about Tom.

"Please, brother, ask Our Lord to forgive me," Buzz asked Johnny.

For killing Rheumy.

"I will do no such thing," Johnny replied tersely, reminding Buzz of the Man more than ever before.

"But I killed him."

"You did what you had to do. You saved my life."

"I didn't *have* to do anything," Buzz replied, a tint of pleading in his voice.

"Right. Exactly. You could have run away when they shot Tom."

Buzz looked up toward the heavens, but the pines and maples had formed a canopy above the trail. There was nothing more to say.

They embraced, then Buzz rode off.

Johnny prayed silently behind him. He had not seen peace in the big Catholic's eyes. The energy that had pulsed out of Buzz before the guns of Brixton was different now—forced, not natural.

There was life in Buzz Woodward's eyes, but there was also something missing that had been there in Argyle.

Forty days in the desert, Johnny Bryant mused sadly, reminded of the half-crazed prophets, the loud-mouth dreamwalkers from the Old Testament.

Did they look like Buzz when they came back from the desert?

He didn't know. Johnny did know that he was alive, and that Tom was dead, and that Buzz was now alone, still a long way from home. Buzz put himself into mortal danger to save Johnny; but Buzz had also sacrificed something else, had killed something inside himself, when he took the life of Rheumy Marks.

Childhood? Innocence? Joy?

Johnny couldn't find the right word. And he was sure Buzz couldn't either.

Bring him peace, Lord. Bring him peace.

✝ ✝ ✝

Buzz Woodward found the going difficult on the dirt road to Route 114. The path was rough, uneven, filled with rocks caked into the ground, steep hills, and washouts.

Gliding down the backside of one of the hills, he reached to clamp on the brakes, as he had done a thousand times before. Technology failed him. The brake cable snapped, the bike gained speed, and he rolled into a huge trough caused by a washout. The front tire of the bike jammed and he went flying head-first off the bike. The accident was silent except for the muted harrumph that came from his lungs as he landed, and the clicking sound of the back wheel of the bicycle.

He felt pain in his bad ankle.

326   Bud Macfarlane Jr.

Oh no, it's broken, he thought. *Maybe it's just a bad sprain.*

He could not tell. He limped up, dusted himself off, tightened the laces of the worn-out boot on his bad ankle, and waited for the first wave of pain to subside.

It's only pain, he told himself, well aware that the pain in his heart, duller, was worse.

He hopped over to the bike and inspected it. The front wheel was mangled and bent.

Totaled.

He would have to abandon it. He would have to start walking again.

So be it.

He waited for a few minutes, gathered up his back-pack, checked his compass, and limped down the rest of the hill.

Mel, Markie, Packy, he repeated his mantra, but there was something missing. He knew this in his heart.

But he kept putting one good foot in front of a painful other. He did not hear the songs of the blue jays. Despite himself, he was listening for a particular kind of sound. There it was. He heard a twig snap somewhere in the woods, and he thought of the bones in Rheumy's neck.

✝ ✝ ✝

The ankle slowed him. Buzz guessed it was not broken. He found a loose branch and, using his hunting knife, fashioned a rough crutch. This helped. It took him the entire day to reach the Coaticook River (which was not really more than a stream).

He found a railroad track just west of Route 114, and decided to hike north alongside it rather than take the road. He camped just south of the town of Norton that night. Reginald had given him a road map. He knew 114 bent east toward Canaan at Norton.

Unlike all the other towns during his journey, he recognized the name of Canaan. He had been there. It was on the border of Vermont and New Hampshire. He knew there was

a faithful little Catholic church called Saint Albert the Great
in Canaan's sister town, West Stewartstown. He knew he could
cross the Connecticut River there into New Hampshire.

✝ ✝ ✝

Big Steve (*Grand Stephan* in French) was a collie with a
bloodline that stretched all the way back to the hillsides and
heather of Scotland. A working sheep dog, he was born and
lived his entire dog life on a farm on the outskirts of a hamlet
called Saint-Pascal in the Province of Quebec, Canada. He
spoke only French.

Big Steve was in a quandary.

His master was dead.

Centuries earlier, the Indians who originally lived in what
is now known as Quebec told their children a story about the
original tribe. The Story of the Dog.

As it was told, the Great Spirit had provided a perfect
paradise for the first people, where the deer ran in huge herds,
and the wheat grew wild without tilling or labor. Man and
the animals lived in harmony.

But then a giant earthquake had erupted violently from
the bowels of the earth. This earthquake trapped the original
tribe outside of paradise. As the world heaved, an enormous
gap opened up in the land, and, as it was told, man faced
eternal separation from all the animals on the other side. And
then, a lone dog, seeing a man across the huge divide, had
leaped across the gap to be with his master.

This is why, the Indian parents told their young maidens
and fledgling braves, all the other animals are wild, and why
they fear and hate man, while the dog alone remains his loyal
friend.

Poor Yves Charbonneau. He had been Big Steve's master.
The gnarled, devout, eighty-nine-year-old widower did not
die because of the computer collapse. He had died from old
age. But Yves was now across a chasm over which Big Steve
could not leap.

A week earlier, Big Steve had trotted in from the fields and found the body. He had mewled and whimpered, barked and licked, but the old Catholic had not woken up. He had fallen from his prie-dieu, rosary in hand, before the ancient statue of Saint Joseph on the little altar in his living room.

The collie could smell that the old man's spirit was gone. Just a carcass. It was difficult for Big Steve to stay in the house. The smell. So he stayed outside on the worn, unpainted boards of the porch.

The dog wondered—in the way that dogs wonder, that is, without words but with smells and sounds and images—why no people came to the Charbonneau farm anymore. Surely a human would come and put the spirit back into his master?

Yes, this would happen. Another human person would come. And Big Steve would wait while his heart ached. The collie was not accustomed to going without the affections of his master.

There was plenty of food lying around, and rabbits in the stand of trees beyond the glen. Though his appetite had diminished in the first two days after Yves fell, Big Steve had forced himself to eat; he continued to fulfill his duties, watching the sheep, guarding the body. Keeping his ears and eyes open toward the dirt road for the sounds or sights of a man who would most certainly come and end his quandary.

✛ ✛ ✛

Well over two hundred miles south of Saint-Pascal, Gwynne "Buzz" Woodward, born and raised as a boy in New Jersey (and later on, in Ohio), a graduate with a degree in English from Notre Dame, divorced and annulled and remarried, a recovering alcoholic, the killer of Rheumy Marks—was almost to Bagpipe. He adjusted backs and received food in Norton, Vermont, and limped his way to Canaan, where he delivered the mail, then made a beeline for Saint Albert's across the river in West Stewartstown. He did not even see the *Welcome to New Hampshire* sign when he limped across the bridge.

"Bless me, Father, for I have sinned. It seems like weeks since I've been to confession," he told the priest. "I killed a man in Vermont."

"Was it self-defense?"

"No."

"Then tell me the circumstances," the priest, a young man behind a screen, requested gently.

Buzz complied.

"I am not sure if you are culpable," said the priest finally. "But you have done a good thing to come to the sacrament. I will grant you absolution because I can hear the sorrow in your voice. For your penance, say one Our Father—"

"Only one Our Father, Father?" Buzz interrupted.

"Yes, and when you pray it, concentrate on the words: 'deliver us from evil.'"

✝ ✝ ✝

Buzz was pleasantly surprised to find that public transportation was making a comeback in New Hampshire. A horse-drawn wagon was making a twice-daily trip to Pittsburg, which was about twelve miles north of West Stewartstown on Route 3. Pittsburg, despite being hit hard by the flus early in the year, was prospering, he was told.

At a general store in West Stewartstown, Buzz traded his fourth-to-last gold coin for a small plastic bag filled with dried corn, a tomato, a packet of beef jerky, a new pair of pants, and a bag of ten silver coins—two of which he used to pay his fare to Pittsburg. During the bumpy trip, he could not help but notice that all three of the other men in the wagon (two of whom were travelling with their wives) were carrying rifles.

Then again, so was he.

It's a new world, Buzz thought. *Live free or die.*

Pittsburg had indeed survived the Troubles with remarkable vigor. Apparently, the locals had not only prepared, but had worked together after the lights had gone out and the diesel had run dry.

No, they told him, they had not heard word from Bagpipe across the mountains.

There were no direct roads from here. If he wanted to take roads, Buzz would be required to double back south all the way down to Colebrook, then east on Route 26 past Dixville Notch to Errol, then north again to Bagpipe—well over sixty miles. Three to five days of walking, maybe longer if his ankle got worse. His ankle was tender and swollen, but was carrying his weight again.

"As the crow flies," an old hunter next to him at a counter in Pittsburg told him, "I'd reckon Bagpipe is less than thirteen miles away."

Buzz would have to walk through the mountains to get there, hugging the trails south of the First Connecticut Lake, then north to Magalloway Road (not much more than a summer trail, really), around Magalloway Mountain, finding his way east by compass until he reached the Dead Diamond River.

Noting Buzz's rugged appearance, and hearing his clipped version of how he had boated and walked and biked all the way from Cleveland, they advised him that it should take less than two days.

Had he not walked through the mountains of Pennsylvania in the winter? It was summertime now, and no weather was more perfect than summertime in the North Country.

He rented a room in the small hotel in town (one silver coin), ready to set off in the morning on the final leg of the long journey to his wife. The long walk was almost over.

For the first time, he consciously allowed himself to miss her. As he fell asleep, despite his efforts to concentrate on the Glorious Mysteries of the Rosary, one word welled up from his heart to his mind:

Mel.

✠ ✠ ✠

He opened his eyes with the sun. It was a beautiful day. June 11th, in the two-thousandth year of Our Lord. He knelt by the bed and prayed his morning offering. He packed carefully and methodically. There was no Catholic Church in Pittsburg, so he set off directly up Route 3. He passed several travelers—not refugees—and exchanged hellos and smiles.

He felt beautiful. The same as the views from this lazy, winding road. Strong like these mountains. His soul sacramentally purified, like the bubbling water in the wide river which paralleled the road.

There was civil peace here. The locals were making a go of it, taking the worst and spitting it right back. The rest of the world, the world he had walked through, and the world to the south, where there were wars and rumors of wars, seemed like a universe away.

He remembered the car ride back from the airport after he and Sam had returned from Montana. The U-Haul and the Durango with New Hampshire license plates.

They had chosen well.

The Lord has chosen, he reminded himself.

He tried to pace himself, but found it difficult to avoid hurrying. He reached the dam on the western side of the First Connecticut Lake and abandoned Route 3 by early afternoon, heading east into the wilderness, which quickly closed in around him like a living green blanket.

The dirt road became a trail. A few miles into the woods, the trail slipped through a boggy marshland as it curved around the southern end of the large lake (which he was careful to keep in sight). Buzz hiked north for another mile before making camp off the road.

It was a warm evening. He decided to forego starting a fire. He ate his last slice of jerky and the remainder of his corn, except for a mouthful, which he set in his trap.

He checked the load in his Ruger (this was bear country), then climbed into his well-worn sleeping bag.

One more day.

✝ ✝ ✝

There was no game in his trap when he awoke. He stretched, rolled his sleeping bag, then set off. When he reached what he guessed was Magalloway Road (there were no street signs this far into the bush), he pulled off his backpack. He reached to the bottom to get the Man's compass.

It was not there.

He always kept the compass on the bottom of the pack to make double sure it would not accidentally fall out.

Probably in a side pocket.

He checked the three side pockets. Nothing.

He staved off a temptation to panic.

Saint Anthony, Saint Anthony, please come around, the Man's compass is lost, and cannot be found.

He checked his pants pockets. No luck. He emptied the backpack completely onto the trail, then searched through the contents. No compass.

He tried to remember where he had seen it last. Yes, at the hotel in Pittsburg. He had held it in his hand before packing it into the bag, all the other items laid out on the bed. He had held it in his hand.

But he could not remember packing it into his bag. He had not needed to take it out yesterday.

He searched through everything again. It was gone.

Had he left it in the hotel?

Dropped it on the trail?

If on the trail, should he go back and look for it?

It would be a great waste of time to double back to look for it *(It's in the hotel!)*. He could lose a whole day, maybe two. Probably not even find it.

Mel.

He looked up.

The sun rises in the east and sets in the west. If I use the sun, I'm sure to run into the Dead Diamond River eventually, probably before nightfall, he reasoned.

He was standing on a crest. The trail was open here, with a natural field leading almost all the way to the lake, which he could clearly see to the west.

The lake is west, isn't it? Sure it is. It has to be.

He checked for the sun overhead. It was still rising, opposite to the lake.

East. Mel is east.

I'll go with Buzz to Bagpipe, the Man had said.

He didn't need the compass. He had the Man.

Buzz started walking again, following a trail he thought was Magalloway Road, but in reality, was not.

✝ ✝ ✝

By nightfall, he accepted the fact that he was lost. After an hour, the trail he mistook for Magalloway Road had narrowed into a path, and then, later, into a deer path. Moving away from the setting sun, now at his back, he plowed forward, thinking he would eventually run into the river. Then he tried to double back in the dusk, but lost the trail, or perhaps the little deer path had divided, and he had taken the wrong turn without realizing it.

Getting lost did not come as a surprise. Twice last year, he and Sam became disoriented and had gotten lost on the homestead simply trying to find the river on their property. It had been an occasion for laughter or mild aggravation.

A lost hour.

But they both learned a lesson as men which little boys who grow up in rural areas learn early on—it's easy to get lost in the bush. The trees all look the same. The bends and the hills and the swells become indistinguishable. Without a compass, navigation is difficult, sometimes impossible, as the leaves in the trees overhead hide the sun. Or the sun itself, never truly west or east, shifting in the sky depending on the season, plays its tricks on the inexperienced hiker.

He decided to make camp and wait for morning. He would follow the sun east again in the morning.

He was thirsty. His canteen was empty. He had not run into a creek or stream since morning.

He prayed a very, very heartfelt Rosary, but had trouble falling asleep. He tried not to listen to the sounds of the night-forest, but heard them anyway. Instead of bogie monsters, he looked into the shadows and saw phantom bears.

He would follow the sun tomorrow. Yes, that was what he would do.

One more day to Bagpipe, he told himself. *And Mel.*

✛ ✛ ✛

He dreamed one of those dreams without things. He was floating, floating in a mist that was watery and cool, but it was not a pool or real water, or an ocean, or a lake or a pond. It was a mist.

Where am I? he asked.

He did not know. He tried to cry out, to call for help, but could not find his voice. He tried to swim in the mist, to find its borders, but did not know if he was moving forward or moving further into the cloud.

He felt…others.

Angels, souls. Others. Millions of them. Souls and angels. People, living and dead. They were there—beyond the mist. The elect. Just beyond his reach.

My God! he bellowed in his dream-mind. *Rescue me!*

Buzz listened for the Lord's reply. And the Lord replied. Familiar-sounding words in an authoritative voice:

"Look and you shall see a white cloud, and seated on the cloud is one like the son of man, with a crown of gold on His head, and a sharp sickle in His hand."

Buzz knew it was something from the Bible.

"A sharp sickle, Lord? What does this mean?"

"I shall test them in the furnace, like gold, as I tested Maximilian. By their sufferings you shall know them."

Gold? Furnace?

"Lord, I do not understand," he cried aloud.

But the Lord did not explain, and Buzz did not reach the others, the elect, or understand anything before falling into another dream—

✟ ✟ ✟

Buzz woke hungry, as he had woken up many times during the long walk. Again, there was no rabbit or squirrel in his trap. He used a rag from his pack to wipe the dew off the stock and barrel of the Ruger. He checked the load, and held it as he began to head east—or what he thought was east.

Maybe I can bag a rabbit?

Every so often, remembering a trick he had read in *Last of the Mohicans,* he marked his trail by scraping bark off trees with his hunting knife.

He was starting to worry. Praying in that way a worker prays—short prayers. Aspirations.

Oh Mary, help me find a road.

At this point, he was in the thick of the pines. Any road would do. If he found a road he could follow it until he found—somebody.

A local.

A local could give him directions.

Wilderness everywhere.

He hiked all day, up hills and down hills. Along little glens. He found a stream once, drank deeply, filling his canteen. In his haste, he was making too much noise, and knew that any game was fleeing before him, long before he came near, sending out unseen signals to the other animals. Perhaps the smell of fear emanating from his pores was warning them away.

He could not accept the fact that was closing in all around him. That he was lost in a different kind of way, in a different kind of world. There would be no search parties sent to look for him. No one really knew he was here.

And he barely knew where *here* was. He could be north, east, west, or south of Magalloway Mountain. He could hike west for days, searching for one of the big lakes.

Or he could continue east, mistaking the Dead Diamond River for just another stream *(Is it running dry this year?)*, cross it and shoot north past Bagpipe altogether, going east into the vast, empty wilderness of central Maine.

He could starve to death.

He was already hungry.

Lord, no, not that. Not after coming this far.

Who are you to question me? the Almighty, or his own conscience, or perhaps just a voice in his head rebuked.

You who took the life of Benjamin Marks? Who are you to judge My ways?

As the dusk came, he spotted a tree with his own marking on it, and realized that he had gone nowhere.

Mel! his soul cried, as he crawled into his sleeping bag, his ankle sore, his stomach empty, to begin another Rosary.

✝ ✝ ✝

He came to a steep hill the next morning, saw the sun to the east, and started to climb down backwards on all fours to keep his balance. Weakened from lack of sustenance, a bit nervous about being lost, mentally fatigued, not *making sure* to be careful for a split second, he reached for a branch, failed to test it—it came loose, and he lost his balance…

…and fell, rolling down the hill, the Ruger flying out of his hand, over pine needles and small brush, tumbling thirty or forty yards before a large oak tree broke his fall with a dull thud and a waffling of leaves.

Pain, shot like a bullet from his ankle, streaked up his leg to his brain. He wanted to reach for the ankle, but it was even more steep here, and he was afraid he might roll or slide down the rest of the hill, which cut downward beyond his sight…

..the pain. The hunger. Being lost. Having come so far since riding the Waverunner across Lake Erie…being so close to Bagpipe…and Mel…

Mel. Markie. Packy.

Buzz broke. He began to cry—tears of frustration, not despair.

"No!" he hollered at the top of his lungs, revealing his anger to the forest. "I will not give up. I will not give *up!*"

His voice did not echo, it sponged up into the pines and the leaves and the soft bed of brown needles all around him.

Lord, help me!

Buzz flopped back, resting for a long time, simply enduring the pain in his ankle until it subsided. He remembered the game of dirty croquet, and how he had realized that he could not win. The deck was stacked against him.

I'll go with Buzz to Bagpipe, the Man's dying words. A promise.

God alone suffices, he had told the people of Blackstone.

In a matter of seconds, you will be dead, Buzz had told Rheumy.

Utter regret welled up in Buzz's soul.

He was confused.

But he did not despair.

I'm still strong. He encouraged himself.

I still have God. I'll crawl out of these damned mountains if I have to.

Overwhelmed, he waited for the pain in his ankle to shift down to a throb. He dropped the back of his head onto the pine needles, and the world spun. His brain did him a favor, and crashed. Blacking out allowed him to sleep for a time he could not measure.

When he woke up, the light was fading. He climbed and crawled and clawed back up to the Ruger, shouldered it, and took another hour to continue on, resting often, until he reached the top of the ridge.

He had not eaten in over two days. Before he fell asleep that night, he accepted the reality of the situation.

No food. No Mel.

✛ ✛ ✛

He woke up before sunrise. He had a bit of water in his canteen. With much effort, he pulled himself up and leaned back on a pine tree. He drank the water, trying not to spill a drop.

He knew his body was growing weaker. There was no fat left on his frame to burn for fuel. His system would soon start breaking down muscle as a last resort.

✝ ✝ ✝

Morning came. Little Miss Hunger was a much more insistent companion today, sharper now, a carrion bird picking at the walls of his stomach. He ignored this; he crawled until he found a branch of fallen maple, and made himself a crude crutch.

Find water.

He climbed to his feet. He willed himself forward, dragging his foot, time passing, the skin under his arm rubbing raw from the makeshift crutch, unshaved, smelly, and…tired, oh so tired, of the long walk.

Voices started chattering in his head, offering advice. Telling him what to do. He recognized the voices, the demons. Buzz had gone insane before—the jetty on the beach—and he knew how to deal with them.

Ignore the bastards. Pray Hail Marys.

His energy was waning.

He needed to find water.

The town of Bagpipe might just as well be as far away as Cleveland…

You'll never find water, a voice teased.

That wasn't the issue. *Mel.*

So he ignored the voice, summoning from his soul all he had left: his will.

Each limping step required the full act of his will now. Instead of this draining his will, he discovered that his will grew stronger, even as his body grew weaker, even as each

righteous forward movement of muscle screamed for mercy
against his goal to…

…reach Mel.

…until he collapsed on the floor of the empty forest, and
felt his head spinning, beginning to black out again, even as
his will raged against the…*the reality of the situation…*

He willed…

What now?

to pray. He willed to pray.

No longer able to walk, he shifted his will toward prayer,
and his last prayer against the blackness took more effort than
any previous footstep…

Hail…

Full black came. He didn't finish his night prayer, but not
for lack of will.

Four days without food. Two days without water. He was
no longer starving. He was dying.

Mel. Mel. Mel. Mel. Mel.

He pulled himself up.

He tried to open his backpack, having imagined there was
a Twinkie there, or a cheese dog, or one of those great-smell-
ing salty street pretzels his father had bought for him that
time he had seen the Statue of Liberty when he was eight…

In a lucid moment, on his back on the bed of needles, the
sun setting *(to the west? or was it east?)*, he could no longer
move, no matter how much he willed.

It was chilly today.

Or was the air warm and his skin was cold?

No matter.
I don't want to die.
It was the truth.
What you want doesn't matter, Gwynny. A gentle, familiar voice—a trustworthy voice—whispered to him. *You must, you must…it's time to…examine your conscience.*

God, that voice inside his head sounded just like his dad. He missed his dad, the old lush.

Forget the friggin' voice, he told himself. *Examine that conscience. Get ready for…the day of glory.*

And so he did.

What have I done wrong since my last confession?
Nothing.
Good. Then I'm ready.
He had kept his hand to the plow.
He slept, peace of mind his pillow.

Time passed. He woke.

Despite the pain, and the scorching thirst, and the hunger—merely a distant throb now—he felt good.

I kept my hand to the plow.

"I see Mel," the Man had said, and said again, now, here, in the pines.

Mel has died, he finally admitted.
She's in heaven. I'm gonna see her soon.
He felt good. Good for her.
It was okay.

Buzz's dream was a song sung by a woman…
Back when my hair was short,
I met some friends in court,
for stealing hubcaps from cars…
Where had he heard this song?

Then he remembered. One of those K-Tel albums from the Seventies. A one-hit wonder. What was the name of that group again? He could not remember. He had only heard the song a few times—during high school, at a party at the house of a friend lost in the mists of memory. But the lyrics were not lost. The lyrics were right here, right now, in the dream...

Chain-smoking under the stars,
played all-night pinball in bars,

He loved this song. Then he remembered replaying it on the phonograph several times, trying to memorize all the words. What was the refrain? So lovely. The dream lady was still singing. Ah, yes...

I'll tell you of love,
more than ever it's love.
No lack of faith undermines it,
'cause it's the hope that we'll find it,
that makes us go on.

But hadn't that song been sung by a dude, not a babe? He wasn't sure. Who was this woman singing?

The dream-answer came.

Donna. Donna Beck was singing to him.

That's lovely. Donna had such a nice voice.

Hey, didn't she go into the convent?

At first far away, then closer, like recovering a sense of touch when shaking off pins and needles, Buzz felt a warm, damp cloth on his cheeks as his dream morphed from musical to material, in that strange way of dreams.

The consolations of affection. A warm hand on his face. Donna's hand. Then, a gentle tamping of a warm, damp cloth again. He tried to open his dream-eyes to see her. He had to see her!

A damp cloth. A gentle hand.

Then a word, his name, "Buzz."

He recognized her voice. So it *was* Donna! He was sure of it.

"Wake up," she urged, her voice low and soft. Soft like a mist. "It's time to wake up, Buzz. One last chance. A third chance. It's up to you."

He tried to open his eyes, but couldn't. He felt a panic coming on.

"Use your will—choose love," she confided to him, letting him in on the secret. He felt the damp cloth again, on his forehead. "Your will is strong."

"Time to wake up," she repeated.

Okay, he replied, and he *moved* his will. Nothing. It was no use.

"Buzz…" her voice was fading, singing again, "more than ever it's love…"

No! Don't go! he cried.

He moved his will again (for love this time, for love of Donna) and a strength came—a strength from the Other, a strength of purity, and majesty, and glory. His will was filled with this Other's strength, and he was…shocked!

Shocked by the *endlessness* of the Other. The love. More than ever it's love.

Why was this happening again? What was he moving his will toward?

"Wake up," Donna had said.

That's right.

He willed to wake up, his will super-charged by the Other, infused with—pure grace…toward…waking up…waking up…

✝ ✝ ✝

…waking up in the pine forests of New Hamsphire, somewhere near Mount Magalloway, on a bed of needles.

What was that on his face?

It was wet and slobbery—and moving around. Almost yucky. But also, warm, and wet, and Buzz was oh so thirsty.

Curious and thirsty, with great effort, he opened his eyes, and though they burned, when he focused, he saw the dog.

A dog had been licking his face!

Here, in the middle of nowhere.

Hi, big fella, Buzz thought, directing the thought toward the dog.

As if reading his mind, the dog barked back a greeting. He recognized that it was a collie.

Lassie. Is this heaven? Buzz asked himself, still disoriented. *Are there collies in heaven?*

No. No way. It all came back to him. The pain in his ankle. The hunger peck-peck-pecking away. The utter lack of energy. These were all here and now. Not heaven.

This sucks. Buzz was genuinely disappointed—and also angry.

Obviously, this dog was a hallucination.

Go away! Buzz shouted inside. *Let me die in peace.*

The dog, real, licked his lips. Buzz coughed.

It barked twice. Simple.

Buzz accepted the reality of the situation.

He looked at the dog, if only to distract himself from the pain and hunger. If a dog could smile, Buzz swore, this one was grinning ear-to-ear.

The dog suddenly trotted off; Buzz was alarmed—quickly disappointed—and he tried to arch his neck to follow the dog's path, but pain and lack of energy defeated his effort.

The collie returned in a flash and came and stood with its head over Buzz's face, his front paws practically on Buzz's right arm.

There was something in the collie's mouth.

A rabbit.

When the smell of the rabbit wafted into Buzz's nostrils, and his brain processed the message, the jitter-pangs in Buzz's belly cranked up all the way, like an instinctual gong sounding: *Food! Food! Food!*

"Good boy," Buzz rasped to the dog.

The dog barked.

"Now go get me a Pepsi."

✝ ✝ ✝

It took him almost an hour, but Buzz willed himself to sit up. He willed himself to open his backpack. He willed himself to take out his knife and gut the rabbit. This was all very difficult, but the golden brown dog was pacing around him all the while, licking his face, barking; basically goading him with a happy kind of dog-joy.

Eating the rabbit, raw, bony and bloody, however, was not difficult. Buzz chewed on the tiny pieces of flesh slowly and methodically, pausing often, wishing he had more saliva.

The best meal of his life. He savored it.

When he was finished, the dog darted off.

And came back twenty minutes later with a squirrel.

Dessert!

✝ ✝ ✝

After the squirrel, Buzz took a closer look at the dog, which had layed down beside him, resting his muzzle on his thigh. It was big for a collie. Extra-large-jumbo. Its hair was matted and dirty, filled with pine needles and the flotsam and jetsam of the forest. There was plenty of fine, dark black hair around its face, and a giant plume of white on its wide chest. It had no dog collar. Buzz felt plenty of muscle on its bones.

It was a beautiful, lovely animal. In a way that he couldn't quite put his finger on, its mane reminded him of… a nun's habit. It reminded him of Donna.

Come a long way, too, eh?

He scratched its snout; the dog let out a long groaning belly rumble of pleasure.

"We'll have to give you a name, pupster," Buzz told him, patting him affectionately on the head, which obviously pleased the collie.

Buzz's voice was still raspy; his mouth was dry, parched. He was barely able to lift his arms. The pain in his ankle was an excruciating clamor, yet, as he waited for the rabbit and squirrel to digest, he felt the old energy—that special brand of Buzz energy—coming back. Coming back for a...

A third chance, he thought.

He looked at the sky. There was still plenty of sun left in the day.

"Help me get to my feet, pupster, and lead me to some water—so we can get moving. You're coming with me on the long walk."

The dog lifted its head from Buzz's leg and barked loudly.

"That's right, pupster. We're going to Bagpipe."

PART FOUR

On the Jetty

I know what you're doing, I see it all too clear.
I only taste the saline when I kiss away your tears.
You really had me going, wishing on a star…
Duncan Sheik, ***Barely Breathing***

Know how sublime a thing it is
to suffer and be strong.
Henry Wadsworth Longfellow

In the bar we sit like blackbirds
With our broken wings
Like clocks without their springs
Just like time doesn't mean anything
Fastball, ***Which Way to the Top?***

A trifle is often pregnant with high importance.
Sophocles

Against all hope, Abraham in hope believed and so became
the father of many nations…without weakening in faith,
he faced the fact that his body was as good as dead…
and that Sarah's womb was also dead.
Saint Paul, Romans 4:18-19

I am his Highness's dog at Kew;
Pray tell me, sir, whose dog are you?
Alexander Pope, ***The Dunciad***

Chapter Sixteen

Grace in Her Arms

Big Steve was glad Buzz's spirit was alive. He didn't understand this new man's words, but this did not matter. Like all dogs, all he really cared about was the tone of voice, and his new master's tone was easy to understand. With a few sniffs, even a dog as dumb as a cat could tell the master needed food and water.

Strangely, the new man also smelled like roses.

As the big collie trotted alongside the limping man, he was happy. Completely happy. Dog emotions don't come mixed and cut and conflicted. Simple. Big Steve was *simply* happy. Big Steve could tell that Buzz was happy, too, even though he was weak and slow.

The world was all right.

But the world had not been all right two months ago, with his master's corpse rotting away in Saint-Pascal, eighty-five kilometers north of the City of Quebec, draining the soul-life from Big Steve. The dog had eventually stopped eating. He had allowed the sheep to wander. The other night, when the bear had come near the porch, Big Steve had growled him away with a sickly desperate rage. Even a bear knew better than to mess with a love-sick dog.

Still, Big Steve continued to hold out hope that a human would come and put the spirit back into Yves Charbonneau.

Then, one day, just like that, a man had come. (For dogs, time is often *just like that*. For dogs, there are three basic kinds of time: *now*, *back-then*, and *back-then a-lot*.)

The collie heard him first, singing a song, the soles of his shoes lightly scuffing the road. The melody was familiar—one of Yves's favorite hymns—although the words were not in French:

"O sacred head, now wounded,
With grief and shame weighed down,
Now scornfully surrounded,
With thorns, thine only crown..."

Dogs don't care about words anyway. It was the tune that mattered. Most certainly, this approaching person—the wind was going the right direction, and Big Steve suddenly smelled *male/not/female*—this man coming must be a friend of his master!

Wary of leaving the porch, Big Steve jumped up, suddenly filled with energy, and waited for the man to appear over the crest of the road. His ears perked up in that special way that only collies can manage.

Then Big Steve saw *him*.

He was not a tall man. He was thin, with a silky, smooth gait, and sported a bald head with gray, frizzy hair cropped close to his ears.

And he was black. Singing and smiling, the black man reached up and waved, and *conveyed* to Big Steve that everything was going to be okay, by saying silently (in French):

Hey there, Grand Stephan! Sorry I'm late. I was waylaid in purgatory. The Master sent me.

Big Steve had no idea what *purgatory* was, but this black man knew his *name,* and sang the master's song—and now that he was closer, almost to the porch, the collie could tell this man smelled just like his favorite smell in the whole wide world.

He smelled like roses.

Just like the master! The master always had roses in the house. Always always always. Always long-stem roses, always next to the statue of the blue woman on the stand beside his bed.

Big Steve barked as loud as he could, conveying: *Come on come on come on, hurry!*

The man skipped up the porch steps, and reached down to pet Big Steve's excited head.

Attaboy, Grand Stephan, good-dog. Good-dog.

He sounded just like Yves Charbonneau.

Big Steve did not register the dark, wrinkled hand on his head the way a dog normally registers a real hand, but the dog did *feel* the sensation of being petted—in his heart. It was as if Yves himself was petting him.

This all registered as my-master/this-black-man, if one could put words to dog thoughts. Big Steve was confused, but being a particularly smart dog, only for a second.

After all, what did it matter? The new man was here, and the new man felt and smelled and sang and gave affection in precisely the same way as the master, and used Big Steve's *name* just like the master.

You can't serve *two* masters.

Every dog knows that.

The master had once been lost, and now he was found. It was quite simple, really.

That's right, Grand Stephan. I'm here now. Good-dog. Attaboy. That's right.

Big Steve looked up at the black man and *accepted the reality of the situation,* in that way of dogs.

That body rotting in the house was not his master. That corpse was…just nothing.

His master was here. It was as if he had never left.

Big Steve was happy.

Let's go, boy, said the Man cheerfully. *Got a lot of work to catch up on. Lots of stuff to do, you and me. Got promises to keep. So let's get some food in your belly. We're going on a long walk.*

Big Steve was five years old—thirty-seven in dog years—the prime of his life. With a little food and exercise, he would quickly return to his normally fabulous condition.

The collie's father, and his grandfather, and great grandfather had also been strong, intelligent, energetic extra-large-jumbo-size collies. They had to be to work the farm, all right. In fact, Big Steve was the fifteenth *Grand Stephan* in the Charbonneau of Saint-Pascal line, all of them named after the first Christian martyr, Saint Stephen.

Big Steve leaped off the porch and followed the Man to the barn, where the chow was kept. He quickly caught up and started barking and bounding around the thin black holy ghost who smelled like roses. He loved to bark for joy, and was almost always frisky—even for a collie. Big, strong, smart, faithful, stubborn, and frisky.

Kinda like our friend Buzz, thought Hal Smith from his lofty perch in the Beatific Vision, as he turned to the soul of the woman who had been stout, and had worn a brown habit on earth.

Hal was with Big Steve, and at the same time, not really in Saint-Pascal, Quebec, just as he was with Buzz, yet no longer on the long walk.

I wonder what Buzz will name the collie?

✛ ✛ ✛

Buzz wanted to run, to finish strong, but his ankle slowed him, and so it looked rather strange—a big man with a crewcut and a crutch, lope-limping on a dusty, hilly road in Bagpipe, New Hampshire, led by a barking, golden-brown collie struggling not to get too far ahead of his master.

After two days of rest and recuperation, the dog had led Buzz—first to water, bringing him more food, then south to a path that traced around the southern end of Magalloway Mountain, and finally to the river.

They emerged from the bush then crossed over the Dead Diamond River south of the town, and though he was discouraged when he discovered that the town was completely empty—abandoned—Buzz knew the way by heart now.

The ensuing six miles, from the center of town to the homestead, were the longest of the long walk. For the first time since Buzz left Donna at the Poor Clares, he was certain he would make it. And now, there it was, coming into sight, at the top of the swell, the long driveway.

Long? Buzz laughed to himself. *I can tell you about long.* He stepped up his pace.

It was just over the swell. The homestead.

Mel, the boys. The new baby. Ellie and Sam and Chris.

Buzz Woodward stopped abruptly at the beginning of the driveway, his ankle pounding with pain; he could not bring himself to feel happy.

He could not smile.

Mel; the boys. Mel.

He rubbed his crewcut in the sun, and for the first time, noticed how dry and tan his forearms were. The rest of him was all sweat and dirt. There was no time to shave.

"I see Mel!" the Man had said.

He could tell the dog wanted to run ahead, but he dropped his hands onto his knees—screw the ankle—and caught his breath.

Thank you, Jesus. Thank you, Hal.

Maybe he should say a better prayer?

He remembered the reality of the situation. This wasn't a movie. This was the new millennium.

The town had been empty. There might be *nobody* down there, beyond the stand of trees, where the houses had been built.

Our Lady had never left the side of her consecrated son— her little man of sorrows—during his long walk. Hers had been the unseen hand which had lifted him after his many falls on the road of suffering. The kind of road which tested gold in the fiery furnace.

She herself was a woman of sorrow. She procured from her Son the graces needed here, and thereby prompted Buzz to pray, though, in his blindness, he did not know it.

He closed his eyes. He stood up straight, like a man, and clasped his dirty, sweaty hands together. He prayed.

"I am an unworthy servant of the Lord," he said aloud, feeling a bit numb. "Let it be done unto me according to Thy word."

He opened his eyes. He threw away his crutch. He pulled the pack off his back, and held it in his hand.

Mel.

He walked down the hill, slowly.

Weeds. Ellie Fisk was concentrating on the weeds.

In the old world, she had spurned the joys and frustrations of gardening. What had been the point? What with the bounty of perfect, fat, waxed vegetables from all over the world crowding each other in open, refrigerated stalls down at the supermarket.

Now she was on her knees, her blond hair tied back tight on her scalp with a clean rag, the skin on her hands etched with the kind of dirt that permanently lodges in the creases and calluses.

Weeds were the enemy—just one enemy among many in a world filled with adversaries. Weeds suffocated the fruit-bearing plants. She needed these tomatoes, these beets, these cucumbers.

She was bent in warfare, her back like a board on a hinge, folded on her haunches, her thoughts on the words she had read in the Bible this morning…

…unless a seed falls to the ground and dies…

Get these weeds. Or a little baby would die. It was that simple, really.

And besides the baby, what else was there?

A new thing—a nuzzle. It almost startled her. But the dog had so gently tucked his long nose under-between her arm and ribs…

"Ellie?" A voice.

She turned and looked up, then brought her hand up to her brow to shield her eyes from the glare of the sun. She saw a vision of a man framed by a middling sunset. She squinted. A stranger? A beggar? Another violent lunatic... a *stranger* who knew her *name?*

She remembered her rifle. She had left it on the deck.

"I—" he began. *I—made it, Ellie.*

The collie barked, shaking her out of her daze.

Ellie Fisk did not recognize him, but she was not alarmed. She watched the figure drop the backpack, take a rifle off his shoulder, then lean it on the stump next to him. Her eyes adjusted to the sun behind him, and she saw, all at once...

...the word *Tabasco* on his ratty shirt. And then his sleepy eyes, the crewcut, and the rounded shoulders...

"Buzz!!" she cried out, and now she was running the last five steps toward him as he opened his arms.

She practically rammed into him, and unlike the old Buzz, it was like slamming into a solid wall, not a thick couch, and his arms closed around her.

You're a reed, Buzz thought.

You're a rock, she thought.

Somehow, they fell to their knees, the barking dog bounding around them like a wacky circling golden tumbleweed.

They sobbed, kneeling on the dry dirt path; the kind of weeping that wells up from the soul. The cry of the weak, the alone, the lost, the empty. Tears they knew not in their old world, but which now defined their new one.

"Buzz, Buzz, Buzz," she blurted sadly, over and over, her chin on his shoulder.

He said nothing.

Mel.

A time passed, and they were empty, dry. Tears a luxury, they pulled it together, and pulled away. They were not married, but friends. There was no urge to kiss, and when she looked at him, she saw that their tears had mingled to carve tan clean channels on his cheeks before disappearing into the sweat of his stubble.

He saw the damp grey bags beneath her eyes.

"Mel said you would come," she whispered.

"Mel?" he asked, courage hidden in his serene question. He knew the answer, but still...

Unable to stop herself, she looked toward the house, beyond the garden, to the mounds of stone, with the make-shift, wooden...

...he followed her gaze and saw the five crosses.

He stood up, and she remained folded at his feet.

"Buzz..." she said. "They—"

She couldn't finish.

Where were the tears when you really needed them? They both had spent them so frivolously just moments earlier. Words, words from a mystic—one of Mel's favorite books— sprouted from between the weeds in Ellie's soul into her mind:

Tears are the only river on which fire can burn.

She looked up, and he was still looking at the five graves. Keeping his eyes on the bitter reality, he reached down and opened his hand, and she rested her cheek into it.

Hard, she thought. But warm, too.

"I knew all the time, even though I didn't admit it to myself," he told her calmly, his voice above her, toward the graves. "During every step on the long walk. That was the worst part, Ellie, knowing all the time that they were gone. The Lord told me."

"Buzz," she said, closing her eyes. "I'm sorry."

"The Lord told me. Prepared me."

Where was the sorrow in his voice? She could not hear it.

He pulled his hand from her cheek, reached down, then lifted her up as if she weighed nothing.

"It's okay," he told her, concern in his voice.

"I miss them. I really miss Sam and Chris, Mel, Markie, Packy. Every day."

Saying their names, out loud, was good.

He knew. He held her again, this time in perfect silence, the birds and the dog and the winds a world away.

Let the dead bury the dead, he thought, for the first time understanding the hardest saying of Christ.

After a time, she took his hand—"Follow me. Her name is Grace."—and led him into his house to see his daughter for the first time.

✛ ✛ ✛

He wanted to know it all. Not out of curiosity. Out of want. After a Rosary, on the deck of the bigger house, the one that Sam had built, Buzz sipping warm water, Grace in her arms, she told him. She was not much of a storyteller, which was a blessing. She did not embellish. No need.

✛ ✛ ✛

The killer flu had hit the town of Bagpipe like a steel pipe swinging into a boy's temple. In December, there were a few dozen souls living within her borders. By March, less than a dozen. The priest had died. Except for the Fisks and a few others, the remaining survivors had gone to Colebrook or Pittsburg in the spring, where things were supposed to be better.

Perhaps, if the flu had visited the homestead in early January, while there were still medical supplies in Colebrook or Berlin...

But in late February, when Sam came down with it, there was no penicillin left. No antibiotics. Sam pulled through, but not before Markie and Packy—

—she couldn't finish.

"Did they fight? Did they go quickly?" he asked.

For some reason, it was important for him to know, though it tore him to tear it from her, knowing she was reliving it all in the telling...

"They...they went quickly."

He nodded. "Just kids. Just little kids. That's good. If they don't go to heaven, nobody does."

His lack of sorrow continued to shock her. Mel had been the same way when the boys went. Almost flippant, making Ellie wonder about her sanity.

"I have a baby to deliver," Mel had told her calmly, standing by the graves. "I will mourn the boys after. Buzz would have it so."

At the time, Ellie couldn't help herself, because she herself had not prepared correctly for the Troubles, and so she asked the little red saint named Mel: "But you almost sound happy. Shouldn't you cry?"

"Can't afford tears. It's a long winter. The boys are in heaven," with a note of finality, the hardness already there, like a switch clicked on.

"And Mel?" Buzz asked now, on the porch.

"She was—inspiring. She delivered the baby. There was a lot of blood. Sam and I, and Tommy Sample from down the road, because he stayed in Bagpipe, too—we had no idea what we were doing, with the medical books open on the utility table Sam had brought into the room, by the bed…"

She was going into way too much detail, and stopped herself. *Tell him about Mel, not the blood.* There had been so much blood.

She could not bring herself to say *bled to death* to Buzz.

"She said many things, before and after. And I tried to remember them, for you, for when you came home. She kept saying you would come home."

That's right, Ellie told herself now. *Tell him the good things. Like Sam—oh Sam!—always used to tell me: take the good and throw out the bad.*

So she threw out the bad, and continued.

"Mel saw the Blessed Mother at the end, Buzz, right before she…went…she saw Our Lady. She told me so."

Just like the Man, Buzz thought, and this gave him consolation—

"I forget a lot," Ellie continued. "But I remember her last words. She was so peaceful, almost happy. I know that sounds crazy—"

"No, it sounds like Mel," he consoled, proud. This was what he needed, to hear about the saint he had been married to…

"She was so happy the day she died, and she asked me to baptize the baby, and promise to be her mom. She named her Grace. Said you would like it."

He nodded. He liked it.

Continue, his silence said. *Tell me Mel's last words.*

"Her last words got me through everything, Buzz, even when Sam and Chris…" she wouldn't finish that line, but continued, "It wasn't the words, but the way she said them. She said: 'Today is the day of glory.'"

And then Buzz did feel like crying, on the porch, with Grace in the arms of his only friend left, but not tears of sadness—tears of joy.

Today is the day of glory, the Man had said.

Buzz was empty, so he didn't cry.

Ellie slowly absorbed his latent serenity.

"Now is the day of glory. What does it mean?" she asked. "I still don't know. I've had time to ponder it. I believe it has everything to do with the cross and the resurrection, and how we always try to separate the two, when they're really the same thing, just like the Holy Trinity is three-in-one. Oh, I don't know what I'm saying."

She was gaining momentum, retelling a saint story, drawing lessons, as Christians always had, since the first martyr.

"But I do know that for Mel, in the last days, after the baby came, there was no separation between the cross and resurrection. It was like she was saying to all of us: Bring it on. Bring it on. She was running—sprinting—up Calvary."

For the first time since coming over the hill, Buzz heard some of the old Ellie in her voice, the Ellie he had loved since the waltz, on the night before she married Sam.

She waited.

"I'm proud of Mel. She's my girl. She's my girl," he told her. "Good for her."

A silence ensued.

He had not told her any details about the long walk yet. Ellie felt the need to ask him. But she waited.

There was no light but moonlight, and their rockers were slightly angled toward each other, facing out toward the majestic purple hills. She looked at him, still not used to the thinness of his face, the way his cheekbones and jaw were now so prominent.

She dove for his eyes. His eyes were the same.

Two friends, with nothing between them but a baby, they held each other's gaze.

"How did the Lord tell you?" she asked, needing to know, not looking away. "You said He told you."

Buzz thought of the Man. And Buzz smiled, but he was more concerned about Ellie. There was something so melancholy in her voice he felt he could reach over and pull it off her shoulders like a veil.

She hasn't gone on the long walk, he thought, but not with any sense of superiority. But he was wrong about Ellie in this regard.

He pulled a small consolation out of his pocket.

"Funny," he observed. "I used to badger the Man with the same question. He could never give an answer that I could understand.

"But I'm not the Man, so I'll explain it my way. Just the facts, El, just the facts. First, God told me when the Man died—when Hal said to me, 'I see Jesus, I see Mel with Him.'

"But you know me. I wouldn't listen. I needed to walk more miles. I needed a nun in a town called Blackstone. Then I killed a man in Vermont."

He waited for her to digest this.

It's the old Buzz, she thought, *talking in riddles.*

This *was* a comfort to her, a familiar exasperation, something he might have done at the kitchen table in Bay Village. Talking in riddles, as if it made all the sense in the world.

And who cared if he killed someone? Not her. If she knew Buzz, he had a good reason. It was a different world now.

Maybe a better world, too, Ellie thought disjointedly, strangely.

In the old world, they killed in secret, in the womb, or by pressing a button from a plane three miles high in the sky.

Despite themselves, the words and thoughts, at first so halting, were pouring out now, naturally; they were like best friends from college having coffee after a chance meeting at an airport.

"God told me Mel was dead when I was starving, dying," he began again, his voice with the lilt of a storyteller, "in the pines near Magalloway Mountain. But not in words. I had walked so far, and for whatever reason, God withdrew His Providence, and I was starving. I had tried my best to get here—"

Now his voice cracked.

"—and my best wasn't good enough. So when I was dying, with nothing left, I made an examination of conscience, and since I had just gone to confession, that was cool, and then I accepted that Mel was dead.

"After all, Hal had told me. It makes me wonder how many other clear, clean messages from God I've missed over the years. Missed because I hadn't taken the long walk."

She reached over and took his hand, chastely. He gripped it tight. A clear, clean message.

It didn't matter if what they were saying made sense. What mattered is that what had *happened* made sense.

"Ellie?"

"Buzz."

"There has to be a reason why God gave me a third chance. We don't need to know it, just that there is one. I know it must seem strange to you that I'm not sad about Mel and the boys. Maybe I should be. Maybe God just designed me for these times: without feelings.

"I refuse to be sad about Mel and Mark and Pascal going to heaven. That's just not right. It's selfish. That was my only responsibility when I got married: to make sure that Mel and my children went to heaven. I *should* be happy. At least, not sad."

Who am I to question God?

"They are gone," he reiterated. "You and Grace are here. That's what is. I have to deal with that first. Lots of things are gone—electric lights, cars—and I don't miss them. But as far as the faith goes, nothing has changed. I might break down and cry about Mel later, like some repressed macho guy in a bad movie. But probably not."

She waited. He was not just preaching. She knew he was working toward something—for her. Just like the old Buzz.

"I'm moving on, Ellie. And I want you to move on with me."

"Buzz, it's okay," she replied. "I've already done that. I'm moving on, too."

The wisdom of the age was in her voice, with a power that almost rocked him back in the chair, even though her voice had not changed cadence.

"Good. May I hold the baby now?"

She got up to give him a turn with Grace, and he wondered again where her strength came from. Surely not from her body—*Must be faith*—she was as thin as a sapling.

He wanted to ask her about Sam and Christopher. But he couldn't. She had revealed enough for one night.

Brave Ellie, he thought.

They spent the rest of the evening making silence. Then they left the deck and returned to Buzz's house, where she had moved after—the killing. Her old house was as empty as Bagpipe. She took the baby to the master bedroom, and Buzz tried to sleep on the floor in the kids' room, the dog by his side, next to Markie's bed, but could not.

Chapter Seventeen

Protesting Her Peace

Perhaps it was because Buzz had returned to Bagpipe, but it came back to her in the night. It played before her as she lay awake on the bed, Grace at her breast.

The killing.

It always came to her in three parts, like those essays she had written in grade school: Introduction, Body, Conclusion.

The introduction was the day before, when they had gone to confession.

The body—falling. Sam falling. This was the body, and it was the worst part, the part she could never skip no matter how hard she tried.

Conclusion: a running stream.

She kissed the child on the forehead, and tried again to stop the memory. Sometimes she could stop it with a kiss. Simple. Sometimes with a single Hail Mary.

She prayed a Hail Mary. Started a whole Rosary.

Not this time.

Introduction, falling-body, conclusion.

Please, God no—not again.

This is what Buzz didn't know, and she doubted she would ever tell him—*keep the good and throw out the bad*—what had happened to Sam, and to Chris. The day after the confession. Her mind had latched onto the confession in those horrible days after the Frenchmen came down the hill. It had all happened on a cold, damp morning in April, the day after she, Sam, and Chris had gone to confession.

Sometimes, it just came, and lashed her like the tide rising in a storm, and the best she could do was simply endure it, until it was over, until it got to the part with the water flowing in a stream.

It—what happened to Sam and Chris—always started with the confession, and always ended with the water by the stream. With the falling-body in between.

No, unlike Buzz, Ellie had not gone on the long walk, but she had been dragged, helpless, up a shorter, more brutal path, to watch the innocent slaughtered, right here...

✝ ✝ ✝

...on the homestead. Spring was coming early to Bagpipe. Almost two months after Mel had died, and Ellie was finally growing accustomed to...being a mother again.

She had a baby!

On loan.

On some days, Ellie half-expected Mel to walk through the door of the kitchen and ask for the baby back. Mostly, though, Ellie had accepted the reality of the situation. Grace Woodward was her baby, and Sam was probably going to be the baby's foster-father, and Christopher was going to be Grace's older brother.

In fact, Christopher was adjusting better than his parents to the loss of the baby's family, to the hard work, to the harsh diet—perhaps because he was so young. Or so it seemed on the surface.

Chris, with his keen smiles, adult-like wisdom, I'll-do-it attitude, and serene recollection during family prayer, was a constant source of daily consolation for his mother. A tall, gangly ten-year-old with silk hair like his mom.

Mel had insisted that Buzz would show up. Sam said nothing about this, as was his way. Ellie had her doubts. It just didn't seem—*likely,* even for a tough guy like Buzz. The last Ellie had known, he had been in a coma. Perhaps God had taken Buzz early to spare him what would happen to Mel and his boys?

Until the unlikely event of Buzz coming over the hill, it became a small, private indulgence, and a reasonable one, for Ellie to believe that Grace would one day be adopted by the Fisks.

Not that she didn't want Buzz to come back. She often told Sam how she pictured him returning—big, round Buzz, loping down the hill, arms flying every which way—

"You'll have to tell him about Mel," Ellie had practically ordered Sam.

"Okay." Sam had not hesitated in this reply.

She loved him so.

Grace was gaining weight now, too, taking a bottle. Sam had donated most of their supply to the food bank in Errol. They had sent a nice man up to ask, and Sam had not hesitated to pitch in. Sam and Ellie had been giving most of their wealth away for years, and so it wasn't hard; it was habit.

Nevertheless, there was still plenty of dried milk, and a year's worth of grains on the homestead, and plenty of seed for the garden in spring. (*And fewer mouths to feed,* Ellie had thought sadly.) More than a few gold coins in a secret place that Sam refused to divulge to her. These were for trade when things came back around.

It was April, and the flus had taken their toll, but the hardy people of the North Country were already fighting back.

Things were going well in Pittsburg, a few of the other parishioners had told them, after Father LeClaire was taken by the flu, before they said their good-byes, carrying everything they owned on their backs and hand-drawn wagons.

"Why don't we move to Pittsburg?" Ellie had asked Sam, the day before the last confession.

"God brought us to Bagpipe. There's no Catholic Church in Pittsburg. We'll get another priest for Saint Francis Xavier eventually. We need to trust in God."

"We could start a Catholic Church in Pittsburg," she had suggested right back, never one to just accept Sam's gentle dictums—a far-off fear rising in her heart, like a distant ship horn.

A premonition.

"Maybe. But I think we would be better to consider going to Colebrook first. There's the shrine there. But I like it here. I like Bagpipe. That reminds me: let's walk into town tomorrow. Tommy Sample says one of the priests from the shrine is coming to Xavier to say Mass and hear confessions. Tommy's bringing him in by wagon."

There was a wonderful Shrine, Our Lady of Grace, just south of town in Colebrook.

In the new paradigm, as Sam still called it, Tommy Sample was materially rich. He was just over forty, handsome in that farmer kind of way, and he owned several horses and had a wagon and hitch. He had good land. He had four milk cows, and was only a three-mile walk down the road.

He had lost his wife of one year to the flu in late January. Dede (pronounced *dee-dee*) had been a slight, sweet, young lady with lustrous, dark—almost rusty—red hair. She had been twelve years younger than her husband. No kids.

Tommy's gentle faith and anticipatory charity, Ellie believed, was one of the reasons why Sam was so adamant about staying in Bagpipe.

Despite what happened to Mel and the boys, Ellie had thought after the faithful Dede passed away.

Then there was their last conversation, just before sleep the night before they had gone to confession, the same as every night. He had eased into bed, the baby between them. He pushed himself up on one long arm, and leaned over to kiss her on the forehead. It was dark—he had blown out the candle (the generator had long since broken down, and what little power they got from the solar panels, they used almost solely for refrigeration).

"I love you, Ellie, and I always will."

"I love you, Sam."

During the ten years of their marriage, Sam had told her this every night, using the same eight words, and never once without his gentle sincerity, like a priest who never loses his zeal for praying the awesome words of the consecration at Mass.

It always reminded Ellie that marriage, like Mass, was also a sacramental miracle.

The next morning, Tommy Sample had come by with his wagon, saving them the walk, and took them down to the church in Bagpipe. Before Mass, they all went to the sublime sacrament, including Christopher.

As it replayed, Ellie remembered how she had felt particularly unemotional during her confession, like most times. She confessed her usual sins, the kind of sins strong-willed wives confess. Ellie remembered asking Sam how his confession had gone.

"The same as always—excellent," Sam told her as they bounced in the back of Tommy's wagon on the hilly road back to the homestead.

Then, that night, he had told her he loved her, as always, and she was happy enough. She had a baby. Mel was gone. Buzz was gone. Those beautiful little miniature Buzz-Mel boys were gone. But there was still the Catholic Faith. There was confession.

The world was not all right, but it was okay.

The introduction was over...

..then came dawn, with Sam shaking her awake. He was already dressed.

"Get the baby," he ordered.

She saw he had the shotgun in his hands. Sam was terrible with guns. He had barely practiced shooting it last year after Buzz showed him how to use it.

When Sam woke Ellie, she sat up in the bed, still groggy. She flashed back to something Buzz had once told them all, during the planning stages, back in Ohio, when the decision was made to get the shotguns: "If it comes down to us actually using these guns to defend ourselves, then the situation is already pretty ugly."

"But why the gun—" she started to say.

"No time!" he practically shouted, fumbling to insert the round, red cartridges into the gun. "Get the baby into the holder. Out the back door. Now!"

The alarm in his voice had bolted her out of her daze.

Grace!

Trying to avoid waking Grace, she reached down and picked up the child—her baby. She was so tiny.

Ellie struggled to throw on her robe and her sneakers— no socks, the details came back like little knives pricking her—and put Grace into the cloth holder that kept the baby tight next to her ribs and breasts. Her hands were free.

Live free or die, she thought.

As she dressed, Sam breathlessly explained to her how he had been pounded awake by an unseen force—by "my guardian angel," he had said—from a sound sleep, just before the sun had risen. There he was, in bed, listening. He listened until he heard it...

"The sound of an engine, don't you hear it?"

No, she didn't.

"Why are you so afraid, Sam?"

"El. You have to trust me; trust my instincts. I'm always right." —*Sam, you're always right,* she had thought, truly afraid now— "Something bad is going to happen. Now get out of here. Go to the woods. Now! I'll get Chris."

He came over and gave her a peck on the cheek, and ran out of the room, to the front door, and out onto the deck, holding the shotgun, waiting, facing the driveway. Waiting.

"What about Chris?" she called to him when she came out the back door, walking back over to the side of the deck.

She could hear the rumble now as whatever-it-was turned into the driveway.

"He's not with you?!" Sam asked, panic in his voice. "I woke him! He's still getting dressed. He'll be right behind you. Now go! I love you!"

She stood on her tip toes, arching her chin, and saw them— *the bad guys*—now, through the stand of trees. A Hummer, painted black, machine gun up top, with five men walking next to it, each man carrying a rifle. There was a box truck with huge tires—chains on the tires—trailing behind.

Marauders. Bad guys.

They had heard the stories. Tommy had told them about the rogue gangs which were supposedly raiding farms and towns across the North Country, taking advantage of the chaos. The received wisdom was that the locals were getting organized, setting up roadblocks and patrols to deal with the threat. Bagpipe, a ghost town, seemed too far off the beaten path. There was nothing left there to raid.

Except for our farm, Ellie thought, as she saw them, feeling like a scared little girl from the suburbs.

"Run!" Sam urged in a whisper, breaking her reverie.

She didn't want to run. She wanted to stay with her husband.

But there was Grace in her arms, and she had promised Mel, and she was not in the habit of defying Sam's direct orders, rare as they were.

She was a woman, and she had intuition.

It said: *Run!*

She listened to it.

She ran. *Saint Michael! Saint Michael!*—

There were clouds overhead, a morning sun behind a mountain, and it was cold, and her sneakers were getting soaked, squishing in the tall dewy grass as she ran the fifty yards down to the thicket of pines, toward the unseen river far below.

Despite her frantic rush, she was careful about baby Grace, hugging her thin arms around the holder, hoping the little one would continue to sleep.

Ellie slipped into the trees, found a big rock for refuge, then stopped, gasping for breath, and turned back, peering up as she dared.

What if the baby starts crying?

She felt instant regret over leaving Grace's pacifier in the crib (attached to the bed the same as Mel had done in her house—another cutting detail).

She wondered if she should pray, and decided not to. Not because she didn't want God's help, but because she assumed God would help—

Angels won't come to save you, a dark little voice taunted her.

—and because she calculated that she could help Sam and Chris most by *paying attention.*

She watched the two vehicles churn slowly up to the porch and…

…the rest was a bleary, streaking contrail. Yet each time it came back, she saw every detail, replayed from her viewpoint behind the rock.

They had held Sam at gunpoint. She saw them forcibly push Chris out of the house. She always remembered exactly what he was wearing: his favorite outfit, which she had given him for Christmas, before they moved to Bagpipe, and before all this horror—his red-checkered shirt, and his heavy cotton, khaki pants. He had even put on his boots.

It was like he was getting ready for what was about to happen, and didn't want to die like a kid in his jammies, but rather, as a man in his work clothes.

Even now, despite the mourning, Ellie felt proud of him. He was a smart kid.

Of course he knew.

Then they had Sam on his knees on the porch, his hands tied behind his back, Christopher was next to Sam the same way, with a short skinny man standing behind them, a stubby cigar jammed in his mouth, holding a rifle to the back of their heads.

Sam and Chris did not look over at her—and she knew why. They did not want to give these thieves a clue where she was.

Chris is smart, she kept thinking. *My Chris is smart. Only ten. But just like his father.*

She could not make out what they were saying, only that they were not speaking English. They were speaking French.

Down from Quebec? Through the wilderness.

They had turned onto the driveway from the north. She knew that there were rough roads through the forest—mostly snowmobile trails—

She heard their laughter. The minutes dragged on. She saw there were eight men in the gang. Wearing a hob-gobble of para-military attire, or baggy black pants. She tried to memorize what they looked like, their faces—*For what? The trial? Are you kidding, Ellie?*—but she was too far away. It was clear that Sam was not allowed to speak unless they asked him a question.

The seven who weren't guarding Sam worked quickly to take the booty from the house, which they loaded into the box truck, and onto a small, open trailer hitched to the back of the Hummer.

There was no way for the adrenaline rush that had been a part of her run to the rock to remain at peak, and during the loading of the trucks, she felt an awful, pithy feeling of dread breeding in her gut. She started to think. She could not care less about losing the food and clothes and tools. There was one big question:

What will they do to my men?

She was not a sentimental woman. She guessed the *likely* answer to that question.

What can I do to help them?

She rejected the option of going to them.

There was Grace.

It was not fair to bring the baby into this—scenario. And that was that.

Yet here it was, plain as paste. This was her worst-case scenario. The scenario which had obscurely taken up lodging in the limbo of her heart when she first saw the New Hampshire license plate in Ohio: *Live free or die.*

Everybody was so quick to accept the first part of that maxim. Now, with one of her soft white hands on a damp baby, and the other on a gritty rock as real as real could be, Ellie Fisk was literally watching *the business end* of that phrase unfold before her eyes.

She could not look away. The options in her head were simple: stay here; go there.

Now she started to pray.

Mary, please, Mary. I never ask for miracles. But I need one now. Let them live. Let them live…

Then, after the loading was done, two of the thugs went to the hand-pump at the well, just on the other side of the deck, holding big wrenches. They were going to take the hand-pump.

She saw Sam try to stand up. The man behind Sam rammed the butt of his rifle into Sam's shoulders. She heard Chris yell something.

She still couldn't make out the words!

She saw Sam talking. He was now on his side on the deck, his hands still behind his back.

Another man—*the leader?*—came to stand in front of the deck, and he spoke with Sam.

Sam is bargaining.

She just knew it. She knew him. He had waited to bargain for the pump. Sam had always told her it was their most important tool—even more important than the woodstove.

The discussion ended abruptly, and the leader, waving, directed two men into the house. They came out a few minutes later. One was carrying a black metal box…

The gold, Ellie thought. *He's trying to bargain the gold for the water-pump.*

She felt, for the first time, a tiny human glimmer of hope. Sam was intelligent. His bullets were ideas. Sam would make a deal. First for the pump, then for their lives.

Sam was Sam.

Everyone always underestimated him. Things always came to him.

Then, to her dismay, they continued to work on taking out the hand-pump.

Liars. Cheats. Thieves…

…Murderers.

She tried to un-think it, but couldn't. It was blur time…

…as she saw Sam struggle to rise to his feet—and next to him, just barely visible, she saw Christopher's hands—his wrists were so, so very thin—come loose from the ropes…

…and she saw the leader pull the gun from his holster, shouting at Sam, who was trying to leave the deck—*to go to the hand-pump?!*—taking blows on his back from the little man behind…

…she saw/heard the gunshot…

…Chris rolled off the porch under his own speed, under the railing, out of her sight…

…and Sam's body, his body, his body…

fell.

And she screamed—she couldn't help it, though she tried to muffle it.

And the rest she missed, because she didn't see it, because she ducked under the rock, because she had seen the head of the leader—the killer—turn toward the woods where she was. Because she was a smart girl, and from one minute to the next she became…

…a wife without a husband in a hard cold world, but still smart and practical and she hated herself for it, even as she took the first step to do it, but she had Grace to consider—*Bring it on!* that was Mel—and so she slipped down the hill, into the dense, wet woods.

And heard the second gunshot. Then a third. Then none. The image of Sam's falling body etched forever into her mind, like like like—like hell on earth.

Hell on earth.

Christopher is dead.

She was in hell on earth, moving, crying, but not screaming—*they would follow*—stumbling down the hill, toward the water, afraid and already mourning, toward the river, oblivious to her wet, cold feet in her wet, cold sneakers, and not even feeling on her skin the sharp, dead pine branches slicing and dicing at her forearms—*Grace, cover up Grace!*—until she came to the river, and went north, hopping over stones, splashing right in the middle of the Dead Diamond—

How appropriate!—Ellie's cynical side, groping for sanity, joked darkly, referring to the little ring on her finger—up to her slender calves in the roiling freezing water—"You might want to run in the river," Buzz had advised, not kidding, serious, "because they can't track you"—just like Buzz had told her to do, last year, when Plan C seemed like such an absurdity, and now that she—she was a practical girl—now that she was *implementing* god-damned Plan C—but Sam is dead! Sam Fisk is dead, and, and, Ellie Fisk—new widow!—Ellie needed to just …what? —she needed to just finish this run, this run from hell, in hell, towards hell, and she needed to go-go-go because she had promised Mel, and because Grace had no part in this, or because Grace had every part in this, oh-what-did-it-matter, because it was Good Old Plan C, and if she was going to keep the meaning behind that ring—*marriage is a sacrament just like confession*—that better-or-for-worse vow, worse-right-now-vow, right now was the exact right time to keep it, and so she needed to…

…continue running.

Until she found, a half-mile north, just where Buzz had said it would be, the little stream pouring down into the river from the direction of Magalloway Mountain.

The baby was crying now, she realized. Ellie's lungs were screaming for air. She stopped and climbed out of the riverbed, knowing—just knowing—they would never find her now. She began to try to regulate her breathing, sifting oxygen from nitrogen over the tiny screams of the little one.

She prayed one Hail Mary, then resumed thinking about—what to do next in a valley of tears.

For the first time for what turned into thousands of times, Ellie forced the image of *Sam-falling* out of her mind. She had a baby next to her ribs.

She listened for sounds. Nothing. No one following her. Yet.

I could turn around. Go back to the house.

No, she couldn't.

That would be suicide.

It made her think of Buzz.

She wasn't the suicidal type, so it didn't seem like she had much choice.

For Ellie, her walk was right here in front of her, up a scrubby little hill on a day in April. It was drying out now, getting warmer, although she could not see the sun through the trees from the valley.

It did not seem like a choice—because she was Ellie, because she had a helpless baby, because she had a diamond ring on her hand, because she was a smart, practical girl. She had been doing the right damned thing for so long that it was a habit.

Turn around?

No way. Bring it on. There was a house of gold up there; hewn from wood, ironically, just like a cross.

She looked up the hill, straining her eyes, but did not see the place. It would be several hundred feet up, waiting for her.

"Hidden but with a good view," Buzz had said. He had searched for days to find the perfect location; then he spent almost three weeks hiking here to set it up. The brush and trees were thick.

It had been chosen.

She was breathing lightly now. She listened. No sounds of the...murderers.

And so Ellie chose, and Ellie began. She climbed the crags and crevices, one hand on the baby, using the other to steady herself.

She climbed right alongside the stream—up the steep hill for almost forty minutes until she came to the place, about twenty yards shy of the crest.

The Plan C Place.

She was thirsty, so she sat down on her bum next to the little gurgling bit of moving water (for the stream was quite narrow here). Her body felt bony and skinny, and she regretted this for the first time in her life. Thin would not be "in" for a long, long time.

She cupped her hand and drank. She drank for the baby.

Behind her there was a tiny cabin hidden by hastily trans-planted shrubs and low pine trees. It was made of rough-cut logs, literally built into the side of the earth. Buzz had then camouflaged its roof with tarpaper covered with moss and earth.

Tiny. Barely big enough for a tall woman like Ellie, who was exactly as tall as Buzz, and six inches shorter than Sam. Funny how these stupid details came to you at the weirdest times. Just big enough for an iron-post bunkbed like the ones they made you sleep in at summer camp, and an extra-small woodstove—and a little wooden table.

Ellie would take an inventory first thing, but only after she spent time thinking. She knew there wouldn't be much food—a week's worth, at most. This was a hiding place, not a living place.

Think, Ellie.

That's what Sam would do. He would think things through. And so would she, because she was his wife, even if he was dead.

Emotionlessly, she thought of the two men in her life—Sam and Buzz. The unique combination had saved her life.

Thank you, Sam and Buzz.

Sam had thought up the idea of this place, then Buzz had built it.

Thank you, Jesus. Thank you for Sam and Buzz.

The prayer was just words, like all her prayers. Yet she surprised herself with her own serenity—with her resigna-tion. Sitting by the stream, not thirsty, with Grace in the little cloth sack on her ribs.

Is this God in my heart?

Not the mystical type, Ellie did not know. But yes, it was God in her heart.

God alone suffices, the words came to her. Where had she read or heard that? Had Buzz said it?

She blew a blond lock off her brow. She brushed the bro-ken leaves and pine needles off the denim baby-sack, then opened it. The baby, red hair protesting her peace, was sleeping again.

Chris! Sam! her old-world-self cried out in agony.

Later, she told herself soberly, buoyed by Mel's example, suddenly understanding everything Mel had meant about Packy and Markie. It all came down to time. Mel just didn't have the time to bury the dead with Grace due a week later.

Mel delivered Grace, on time.

No time. Though the electricity was gone and the clocks had all stopped, there was still no time. There never had been any real time; time was a resplendent illusion, a luxury for pampered moderns with plastic digital toys.

There was only *now.* Sam and Chris were in a better place, outside of time, outside of *now.* Ellie was not there...with them.

She was here. Now. With a baby.

She kissed Grace again, loving the child.

The whole thing was so incredibly screwed up; that was just the way it was. Ellie was smart enough to recognize that she could not change one thing about it. And it was already time to move on, whether she liked it or not. She resigned herself to the weight of this cross, her faith and sanity intact.

She looked down and noticed that Grace had opened her eyes. She had a face like Mel—*and that hair!*—but eyes like Buzz. Ellie began to hum to her, trying to get her to smile. Grace had just started smiling a few days ago.

Ellen Fisk began to hum a nothing-tune. It was just a little-something she made up as it came to her. Because that's what babies like, and that's what this baby needed.

Buzz's long walk had lasted for months, for more than seven hundred miles, and each step had seemed a choice to him.

Ellie Fisk, feeling she had little choice, widowed and barren, but definitely not alone, had finished her own long walk, up a steep hill, in less than an hour.

Chapter Eighteen

Rocks in a Bucket

Five days later, she went back to the clearing where the houses were—*where the bodies are*—and after ascertaining from the woods that all was clear, she buried her dead.

They had left the bodies where they had shot them. Chris's body was not far from Sam's. Near the deck, where Ellie had last seen the leader-killer standing.

She pieced together the story (and because she was a smart girl, she was correct). Sam had risen to protest the leader going back on his deal to leave the pump, or to try to negotiate another deal (knowing her Sam, this was the most likely case). Chris had planned to roll off the porch from the start, and chose the time of confusion to follow through with his plan.

When the boy saw his father shot, and heard his mother's far-away scream, Chris had seen the leader-killer turn his head toward the woods. To prevent or distract the leader-killer from investigating his mother's whereabouts, the boy had made a dash toward the leader. (Knowing her Chris was a smart, practical—and now, brave—boy, she felt it more likely that he was trying more to distract than to attack.)

The evidence was in front of her. At her feet, his thin little body was face down, arms forward, bullet holes in the back of his red-checkered shirt. He had been running, perhaps diving toward the leader-killer, when he was shot twice in the chest.

My brave little hero.

Cowards? Not Fisk men.

It's too bad there won't be any more Brave Fisk Men, she thought joylessly.

The old yearning, overshadowed by the deaths, and superficially relieved by her responsibilities for Grace, was still there.

Brave. But was he prepared? a cold, knife-edged voice evaluated, against her will. *He should have run with you.*

She tried to force this out of her mind.

Even so, the image of her husband fumbling with the shotgun came to her. She willed it away.

She focused on the task at hand.

Inspecting the grounds, it was easy for her to deduce that the evil men had come back again, perhaps on the day after the shootings, dismantled the solar panels, and stolen the batteries and inverters. This didn't bother her. These were only things. She doubted they would return: the houses were pretty much cleaned out, except for some furniture, a few tools, a few meaningless items.

There is a special grace; it does not have a name. Ellie needed it for the task she now faced. She received this nameless grace in buckets, without even asking, because she was a good girl, and smart enough to know that God can give and do whatever He wanted, and that He still loved her.

She found water in the tank in Buzz's basement, which she hauled to her own house in buckets. With great effort, she carried the bodies into her kitchen, and undressed them, first Chris, then Sam, on the big kitchen table. Then she bathed them, pausing time and again to care for the baby.

Then she dressed them in the finest suits—the thieves had no desire for such odd-shaped, extra-long clothes. She rejected the idea of building caskets. She was not a carpenter. She found a large roll of thick, dark green plastic sheeting. She used this, along with two tablecloths, to fashion burial shrouds.

The smell? Yes, there was a smell. Ellie imagined the scent to be the scent of frankincense and myrrh, and she imagined herself Our Lady, preparing the broken body of her only Son,

Who had also been an innocent victim. She found a bottle of perfume under the bed upstairs, and used it to anoint the bodies. It was all quite difficult.

She allowed herself to cry as often as she pleased, but did not turn from her task.

Once the bodies were in the shrouds, it was not so difficult. It took her the remainder of the day to dig the graves. By the end, her hands were covered with blisters.

She did not mind these.

"It's only pain, darlin'," Mark Johnson had once told her, but she could not remember when or where.

That's right, it was only pain, physical pain. She wished it could cloak the numb ache in her heart right now.

Ellie's back was becoming sore—*it's only pain*—but she managed to put the bodies into the graves, next to the grave sites of Melanie Anne Woodward, Mark Aquinas Woodward, and Blaise Pascal Woodward.

She methodically filled the graves, shovelful by shovelful, the sound of the metal blade scraping into the dirt providing an almost hypnotic cadence.

She was tired. The sun was setting. She could not bring herself to fall asleep in her own house, so she went over to the Woodwards'. She stripped off her filthy clothes, gave herself a sponge-bath, then slipped into Melanie's bed with the baby. She was fatigued, but she was grateful that the worst was over, and thankful that (because of the special nameless grace) she was still sane.

Unlike Buzz, she had never gone insane, and had no plans to give insanity a whirl. There was Grace to care for. She fell asleep meditating on the fourth sorrowful mystery of the Holy Rosary—Jesus carrying the cross.

The next morning, Ellie ate a breakfast of boiled rice (taken from the supplies at the hiding place, already running low). She stretched for ten minutes, then performed her back exercises (she had no plans to ruin her back). She hauled stones for almost four hours, using the wheelbarrow to bring them from across the field. There were plenty of loose, white, moss-flecked stones—the same kind they had used for the Woodward family—in a low, ancient wall at the far end of the clearing.

She got a saw, found cedar planks in Buzz's basement, then made the crosses. These she pounded into the ground, using a mallet, next to the graves. She did not mark the crosses. The crosses were *temporary,* even if it meant waiting years to find a stone-cutter to give her men proper monuments.

She was almost done.

She went inside her own house and retrieved her favorite jeans, a clean blue polo shirt, white socks, her favorite leather belt, a brand-new scapular, and her penny-loafers (which she would shine after bathing, then dressing, at Buzz's house). In Mel's bedroom, looking at herself in the big mirror above the dresser, Ellie brushed her hair, then she put on her favorite diamond earrings, the ones she had been wearing the day Sam won the basketball championship with Buzz.

Over the graves of her husband and son, she said short prayers, out loud, holding the baby. She was careful to say separate prayers for each soul.

Never together.

She would never, *ever* insult their distinct, separate acts of valor by letting *Sam and Christopher* degenerate into a nebulous, impersonal *them* or *they*.

The *theys* had murdered Sam and Chris.

A Sam and a Christopher had saved her.

Her Sam.

Her Christopher.

Now she was done. She asked Saint Anthony to help find her a priest—any priest—from no matter where, from no matter how far, to give Sam and Christopher a proper funeral Mass.

Like all prayers, this prayer changed the world.

The task was complete.

That wasn't so bad, she told herself, not quite sure why it mattered whether it was bad or good. The duty had just been there, needing to get done, so she could move on, move on and take care of Grace.

Now, for the hard part.

Getting food. Walk to Errol—go begging? No way. Not Ellie. The world was filled with beggars. She knew that the dark times could take away everything she loved in the world, but she was also the kind of woman who buried her dead, and she would never allow it to take away her dignity.

There were hundreds of acres here, and she owned most of them (except for the few owned by Grace Woodward). Plenty of fertile, tillable soil and old-growth timber. Spring-time was bursting out of the brown and grays all around her, flowing down the hill…

…*like a man walking with a dog…*

…flowing down the hill was Spring. This was her land, and she was a smart, practical girl, and realized that she was rich, *new-paradigm-wise,* as her beloved might have said.

All she needed to do was avoid starving over the next two or three weeks. She had to find some food, some way, some-how.

She figured her odds were fifty-fifty. And she liked her odds. She took them.

She didn't feel good. In fact, she felt rotten. The worst pain of her life.

It's only pain.

✛ ✛ ✛

Five days later, the sun was setting, and she and Grace were beginning to starve. Although she couldn't bear to go into her old house—*the House that Sam Built*—unless it was absolutely necessary to retrieve something worthwhile for Grace, she did not feel this way about the deck facing the mountains. She liked to sit on the deck.

The deck was the place where Sam and Chris lived their…

…*day of glory,* her friend in heaven whispered.

She was very hungry.

She sat on the deck now, trying to ignore the little moans from the baby so she could think, concerned that when the crying did cease, it would indicate that the baby was out of time.

Hunting had failed; she had carried the rifle (which Buzz, the dear, had hidden in the safe place) into the woods, baby on her hip, but had seen nothing. Nothing. She suspected that the animals knew she was coming, their survival instincts honed more sharply than her own. And being a smart girl, she was right.

Reading Buzz's how-to books about how to find things to eat in the woods failed. She had considered eating a beetle, but she wasn't that desperate yet, and maybe never would be. Eating insects seemed to her like eating poison, and Ellie doubted she could hold down this kind of food for long, much less find the hundreds of grubs it would take to supply enough calories.

She had wasted a day walking down to Tommy Sample's place. It was burned out—*marauders*—and cleaned out. There was no sign of the quiet farmer. His livestock was all gone. His mutt was by the barn, shot dead.

She came home and planted tomatoes and cucumbers and whatever else she got from the little seed packets she found in Buzz's basement.

Let's face it, she told herself. *I'm not much of a gardener, and those tiny sprouts popping their heads from the earth don't look too filling.*

Too bad Buzz wasn't here. Or the Man, or Mark Johnson. They were the kind of guys who would just go out and kill something. Hunting food was a man's job. They had a knack for disgusting, difficult activities such as hunting and fishing, even going as far as glorifying them into *sports.*

Boys will be boys, she said to herself, rocking back, chuckling over the irony of it all.

Yes, Buzz had practically enjoyed building that little safe place by the stream. That had not been the kind of thing a woman would do for fun. It had almost been like a game,

Buzz coming back every day last summer, giving her and Mel daily reports.

He was hiding this here, and that there. And so on and so forth. Just as Sam had hidden that gold. Men, with their guns and tree-forts and hidden-caches.

Boys will be boys, she thought, sadly, wishing for the first time in her life that she was a boy, and not a suburban chick doing such a lousy job of play-acting at Little House on the Prairie, starving this poor little baby.

Boys will be boys. Always hiding things...

It made her think.

Has Buzz hidden something in his house?

Food maybe?

Something clever hidden cleverly? And then, not telling a soul, not even Mel, because that's the way boys are. So his Mel wouldn't have to worry about *deceiving* bad guys. So Mel could say honestly, with a gun to her head, that there was no more food in the house.

That's the way boys think; they take the worst and best about human nature for granted, and plan accordingly.

The Other affirmed all these things in her heart, because He didn't want her to die.

She rose from the rocker, then walked slowly to Buzz's house. She walked into the cluttered basement.

Guardian Angel, guide me, she prayed gravely.

She stood in the center of the big room, the family room, next to the large, masonry fireplace.

Okay, I'm Buzz. Where would I hide something?

In the storage room? No way, too obvious. No fun, either. In the ceiling, next to a joist?

But the joists were all open, empty.

Knowing Buzz, he would hide something in a—she reached for a clue—*a Catholic place.*

Just then, her eyes came to rest on a little photograph on the wall. The Little Flower, Saint Thérèse, grinning one of her trademark Mona-Lisa smiles.

There you are. Buzz's favorite saint.

Something simple. She walked over to the wall, and pulled the painting down. It was…

…attached by velcro, not hanging on a nail. And behind it, drilled through the sheet-rock, was a dime-sized hole.

But how fun! Just big enough to look into!

She peered in. In the dusk, however, it was too dark to see into the hole. Her heart sank. Still, there might be something there. *Boys will be boys.*

She scrambled over to the masonry fireplace, where she found a box of Ohio Blue-Tip matches. She ran back over to the little hole, her stomach growling, the strap of the baby's holder stabbing a little pain in her shoulder blade, her fingers trembling.

She struck the match and held it to the hole. She looked in, then read:

Parmalat.

Milk! Long-life milk.

✝ ✝ ✝

Ellie Fisk got a hammer, and, as the storytellers some-times say, the rest was history. There was plenty of space in the pre-fabricated walls of Buzz's house. The wide gaps were designed to be filled with fiberglass insulation. In the entire wall with the picture of the Little Flower, Ellie found lots and lots of milk—*Buzz had boys and boys drink milk!* she sang in her soul—cereals, cans of corn, salt, honey—enough to feed a family for three months—and Ellie and Grace for at least five. Enough time to learn how to plant a garden.

A couple days after she found the milk, Ellie wondered if Providence was sending her some sort of message beyond the obvious. She was again rocking on the porch, watching the sunset, enjoying the sensation of not being hungry. She made a mental note to never take the comfortable feeling of a full belly for granted.

She was making a lot of mental notes lately. She made a mental note to start taking real notes on paper instead, or to at least find a blackboard and chalk.

What had she been thinking about?

Oh yeah, the milk.

The kind of milk Buzz had stored was quite popular in Europe. It was long-lasting, liquid whole milk in super-sealed, quart-sized cartons. It could store for up to a year. It tasted delicious, unlike the powdered milk she had been drinking until the safe-place supplies ran out.

Too bad I can't breastfeed this stuff to Grace.

What a weird thought. It was so weird it seemed almost— Buzzian. Or Mel-like. Like a thought that was not her own.

Ellie could give the milk to Grace whenever she pleased, using the bottle—there was no need to breastfeed Parmalat. But...

Maybe I can?

There was something Ellie had heard one time, during a La Leche League meeting, back when she was learning how to breastfeed Christopher—*Oh my little Chris!*

Move on, she rebuked herself. *Back to work.*

Yes, that was it. Something very interesting about wet-nursing. Something about how any woman could start her milk flowing using the right technique. Women who adopted babies did this. She did not remember the technique.

What was it?

It's not hidden, she told herself, prompted by another. By a saint named Melanie.

Ellie went back to Buzz's house and found it. It was a book on breastfeeding. Sitting alone on the top of Mel's desk. Ellie had even read parts of the same book when Chris was a baby. Breastfeeding was something she had learned to forget about—because of the yearning.

She opened the book and it fell open to the right page.

During the following days, she taught Mel's baby to take her breast as a pacifier. The baby began to suckle. She hunted around the supply room in the basement until she found a slender, clear plastic tube designed for something else—for funneling water into the batteries for the solar panels. She jerry-rigged the tube to a carton of Parmalat, and began feeding the milk into Grace's mouth as she suckled on her breast.

The baby—instinct being the most powerful force in nature—began to pull on Ellie's nipple as she drank the Parmalat. This tugging sent hormonal signals to Ellie's breasts. She who was barren began to produce real breastmilk—motherly, perfectly-designed breastmilk.

On the best day of her life since—*the killing*—Ellie pulled the tube from Grace's mouth…and it worked. Mother's milk flowed directly from Ellie's body into Grace.

Ellie was elated. Happy.

This was exactly what Grace needed.

This was what Ellie needed, too. She was proud of herself. She felt like a mother again. She *was* a mother again, not just a dedicated caretaker. She began to think of Grace as…

…her baby.

On the warm summer nights, rocking on her deck, Grace suckling peacefully at her full breast, Ellie found some warmth in a hard cold world.

May became June. Ellie became a mom.

A real homesteader in Bagpipe. Down, but definitely not out. Bent, but not broken.

Mourning? Yes.

Soul-sick? No.

Boys will be boys, the mom mused serenely, watching the sun inch down over her mountains, just plain thankful. *And girls will be girls.*

✝ ✝ ✝

In the days that followed his return, Buzz and Ellie had little time for conversation. They rose with the sun, then worked.

On the morning after he arrived, Buzz found two five-gallon containers, then hiked down to the river where he filled them. Ellie was standing in front of the deck when she spotted him coming back up the hill, his forearms bulging, sweat on his brow.

She waited, hands on her hips.

He smiled.

"Gonna dump these in the toilets, so you can flush," he told her. "We can purify the rest with bleach for the drinking water."

"We also need water for the garden. Too bad you can't use the well," she told him.

Her beast of burden smiled at her.

"Yeah, too bad."

After three days of killing three hours of sunlight per day hauling water, he went over to the well, and peered down. Ellie was not far away, in the garden. Grace was sleeping in a portable baby-hammock he had cobbled together.

"El, how far down is the water?"

"Uh, I think the driller said something about the static water level being forty feet."

"Wish I had a flashlight," he replied.

He jogged into the house, and came back with a rope. He lowered it into the wellhead, which was ten inches wide. When he pulled the rope out, he discovered the static water level was around thirty feet.

Twenty minutes later, he lowered a small bucket tied to the rope. Buzz was having a hard time getting the water to flow over the rim into the bucket.

She came over.

"Put some rocks into the bucket. Then it will sink into the water easily. You'll get less water, but you'll save time."

"The bucket will be heavier."

"You're a strong man," she told him frankly, giving him a little smile, then turned and walked back to her garden.

He did this. It worked. They had more water in less time.

The next day, he called her over to the potato patch he was planting. Buzz showed her what he was doing—how he was digging the mounds, hoeing them, inserting the potatoes.

"Well?" he asked.

"Well what?" she replied.

"Do that rock-in-the-bucket thing," he told her.

Three minutes later, he was holding the hoe differently, building the mounds wider, plus a few other minor changes. She had taken the time a few weeks earlier to read up on the process.

Buzz decided to time himself using Sam's Rolex (she had given it to him). He found he was almost twenty-five percent more efficient.

It was a dynamic, a pattern. Buzz was a good observer. It took only one time to recognize the pattern. He was humble enough to accept that Ellie was more intelligent than he was. And he was shrewd enough to realize that her perspicacity was a scarce resource.

After all, Sam had done the same thing.

✛ ✛ ✛

Tommy Sample showed up two weeks after Buzz arrived.

He claimed that his guardian angel woke him up an hour before the thugs arrived; he too had heard the phantom sound of a diesel engine.

He abandoned his home, driving most of his cattle and horses into the bush with him, through the forest, to the abandoned ranch of a friend who had migrated to Pittsburg. Tommy decided to stay there for several weeks.

His mutt, Casey, had stayed behind to guard the house, and paid with his life. Tommy was now living in his barn. On Saturdays and Tuesdays, through July, Ellie and Buzz walked to his ranch to help him build a new log home.

✛ ✛ ✛

Working in the potato patch, Buzz had time to reflect. His ankle was healing now that he wasn't walking ten or twenty miles per day.

He recalled how out-of-shape he had been the time he climbed the mountain to see Our Lady with Lee Royalle. He realized that he could now hike up and down that mountain two times a day without missing stride or losing his breath.

A third chance in Bagpipe.

Is this a hard life?

No. Not compared to the long walk.

Is this a full life?

No.

Mornings.

Buzz rose from the couch (just as Ellie could not bring herself to enter her old house, Buzz found it difficult to walk into the bedrooms of his home, much less sleep in one). He walked across the kitchen and knocked on Ellie's door.

"Angels are singing!" he called through the door.

He didn't know why he said this. But it became a ritual.

When she came out several minutes later (no showering, except for the occasional sponge-bath, in the new paradigm), she found cereal and Parmalat ready. Often they were able to share a tomato or a cucumber from the garden.When the Parmalat finally ran out, they would switch to real milk from Tommy's place. Might as well use up the Parmalat before it went bad.

They bowed their heads, Buzz intoned his morning prayer, then asked their guardian angels for guidance. He sometimes asked for help from the guardian angels of Mel and Sam. This was usually the only time he said their names during the day. He and Ellie reconsecrated their hearts and their labors to Immaculate Mary.

Then he and she began working, using the simplest of divisions of labor which lasted, with a break at noon for lunch and the Angelus, until the sun was just above the mountain. The day ended with a Holy Rosary on the covered deck, rain or shine.

There was no Mass to attend on Sundays, so they read the readings from the Lectionary which Mel had bought last year, followed by a spiritual communion. They tried singing hymns a few times, but it just didn't feel right, so they stopped. She trimmed his crewcut on Sundays. He liked this; she was a good barber.

"You're going gray," she told him every week.

They mourned in silence.

Sometimes, when she looked at him bent over the potato mounds, the muscles in his back flexing, she thought of Sam, and turned her eyes.

Sam was much taller.

Sometimes, when they were walking to Tommy's, he looked at her from the corner of his eye, and was jolted to catch the side of her face at eye-level.

Mel is much shorter.

Had been, he corrected himself.

But they were both smart, practical types, and they were also thinking about—things.

After four summer weeks of mourning, Buzz and Ellie had veiled conversations about their futures. More often than not, they talked on the deck, worn out, as the sun went down. Sometimes they stole a few lines during breaks from their labors. They never talked about serious stuff in front of Tommy. Not that they didn't like him or trust him. It was too early to get too close to somebody in a hard, cold world.

Sometimes, when Tommy visited their homestead, Buzz left her and hunted with the dog. He trapped. They ate rabbits. One time, he bagged a deer, his first. Tommy showed him how to gut, skin, and dress it. No squirrels, though. Squirrels were emergency rations, not daily diet.

"Rats with tails," Buzz told the woman.

They were working in the garden. Today the baby was in the sack around her ribs. He was about ten feet away, and he stopped. He stood. He sat on the big rock next to the garden, and watched her, the graves many yards beyond her shoulders.

She looked up after a few minutes.

"What are you looking at?" she asked.

"You."

She returned her gaze to the weeds.

On the deck. After the nightly Rosary.

"We've got to start thinking about Grace," he began simply. "About her future."

She looked at him.

Ellie Fisk was the most beautiful sight in his world, but when her eyes glared like this, and that hard line came to her forehead, it was not easy to hold her gaze. But he managed. In some ways, he was much stronger than she was.

It's time, she told herself. Hating herself.

But she was a smart, practical woman. She remembered her fiat, the day they saw the license plates.

Let it be done unto me according to Thy word.

"Yes," she said.

That was enough for one night.

Two days passed. They were walking back from Tommy's place. They were both tired, but not aching.

Their constitutions were growing accustomed to the life.

"Okay, out with it!" she accused him all of the sudden.

Perhaps she spoke because she was tired. She kept her cold, leather-brown gaze on the road, toward the homestead.

"It's scandalous," he said.

Living together, they both thought.

They were still Catholics to the core.

"No, it's practical. Nobody sees it. It's safer if we're in the same house. I'm the aunt."

"You're the mother," he stated.

No reply.

He spied a stick, walked off the road, then tossed it. The dog took off after it.

"You're gonna have to give that dog a name."

"Yeah," he replied. "I can't call him pupster forever."

✝ ✝ ✝

A hundred yards from the house, near the top of the hill. She was on a ladder. He had climbed the apple tree, above her. It was a large tree, bearing sour green apples, but unfortunately, the only fruit tree on the property, though they had been able to pick plenty of raspberries growing wild beside the pond in the grazing fields down the road. The Sample place had lots of blueberries, and they traded.

"I thought of a name for the dog," he told her. "At first, in the woods, for some reason, I wanted to name him something practical, like Hacksaw or Slide-rule. Black Axe. But the pupster needs a real name."

She waited.

"Chesterton," he revealed.

She didn't look up.

"It fits," she said.

"So you get it?" he asked.

"Chesterton was big and smart," she huffed, blowing a golden lock off her brow, inspecting an apple. "And Catholic. Just like the pupster."

Her tone was plain. Fake, bored. As if he had been badgering her about it for weeks.

She can't help it, he told himself.

If she had been Mel, this kind of tone might have started an argument. But that was another Buzz. And Mel was gone. And Ellie wasn't Mel.

They both looked down at the collie; he was napping at the base of the tree, next to the baby, who was toddling next to him. His ears had perked up when Ellie said *pupster,* but his eyes remained shut.

"And Chesterton loved smoking. I swear, this dog would drink Scotch and smoke cigars if dogs could. But what about you, El? Do you like it?" he asked.

She didn't smile at all. He had hoped—

"What does it matter if I like it?" she snapped.

She could be cold sometimes. Most times, lately, in fact.

"I'm giving you veto power, El."

"Why?" she said, reaching for an apple.

She plucked it and put it into the bucket hanging from the ladder.

She wiped her brow, and looked toward the houses.

"Because Grace loves the dog."

She didn't answer him for a long time. To him, it seemed like an hour.

"I like the name," she said, finally looking up at him, her eyes watery.

Good girl, he thought.

She tried not to resent his little ways, but this was taking a lot out of her. His simple, relentless ways.

Yes, they were simple, but she knew he was doing that— *that thing*—he could do, old world or new.

Taking a big axe and chopping things down.

Unless a seed falls to the ground and dies, she thought, relaxing her jaw.

She had watched Buzz do the same thing to Sam, bringing him slowly to the faith with his videos, his riddles, and his basketball games. She had heard the stories about the Man; how Buzz went to Hal Smith's porch time and again, like a stray mutt, tongue hanging out.

The big lumberjack had walked across the whole damned country, killed a man on the way, buried his dead. Buzz Woodward was a persistent bastard, and in her way, she did not mind.

And deep inside her, in a place she did not wish to explore in the daylight of consciousness, she knew that Buzz was a hard man. And that Sam—had not been Buzz.

And they both knew he was right. But he was still waiting on her. That was the part of it, the waiting for her, that kept her from resenting him. Buzz had loved Sam, too. She had loved Mel.

Simple.

"Chesterton it is," he said finally, sadly.

At least he's not rubbing it in, acting happy, she told herself.

✝ ✝ ✝

Sunday. Sponge-bath day. They still had soap, which was nice. Tommy said somebody was making soap in Pittsburg, and that he was going to take the wagon up there soon. Chesterton was with Tommy today, helping him herd some sheep Tommy had found wandering on the other side of Bagpipe. The farmer had promised to keep an eye out for an abandoned water pump.

After breakfast, the prayers, and the haircut, Buzz Woodward asked Ellie Fisk to walk with him. It was August. The days were perfect, but the early mornings were sometimes chilly already. Not today, though. The morning was warm.

He led her into the woods. She was holding Grace, even though he had offered to carry her. It was a path she did not recognize, because she had taken a different route the other time. They came to the river, and there it was, the stream. The rocky hill.

You're a cold bastard, Ellie thought, not really angry at Buzz. She willed the body-falling image out of her mind.

They carefully hiked up to the safe-place, Buzz leading, turning frequently to take her free hand to help her keep her balance.

They reached the little cabin on a small, natural plateau by the stream. He went into the cabin to retrieve the stool for her. Then he pulled a large, flat rock from the stream for his chair, and sat down next to her. Ellie lowered Grace to the ground.

It was a spectacular view—but weren't they all in the North Country?—to the southeast; they could see part of the road near the topside of the homestead (but not the houses). Mostly, they saw wilderness.

"I haven't been here since last summer," he began.

"I have," she replied, but immediately regretted her words. Sam had been his friend, too.

He let it bounce off him, and showed her this with a smile.

She decided to start.

"You've got to start paying attention to Grace," she told him.

It wasn't an accusation. It was true.

He seldom held the baby unless Ellie needed him to do so for a practical reason. He did not play with her. Grace was almost crawling now. Ellie knew how he had been with his boys. Always wrestling and jumbling around on the floor. She had seen him administer Startle Training many times in the old days.

In fact, his playfulness, which seemed almost completely purged out of him now, was something about his fathering she had admired. She remembered how she had wished for Sam to be more playful with Christopher when the boy was younger.

"But Grace reminds me of Mel," he admitted.

So it's truth-speak time, she thought, looking at Grace, who was backing into the little stream now, smiling brightly, daring them to stop her.

Another Mel, Buzz thought.

The water was no more than a trickle at this height, so they decided to let the baby have her fun.

"That's not fair to Grace," she told him.

Buzz turned, and he leaned in on one arm, placing his hand on a wooden brace under the stool. She knew he never did anything arbitrarily. He had gotten the stool just so he could lean next to her like this, with his face close to hers. He had chosen this very place last summer, and he was choosing it now. He was choosing everything.

But he's waiting for me, she thought, looking him in the eye.

He kept his face close to hers. He searched her eyes. She felt his physical presence, maybe for the first time since he had come down the hill. She was so used to Grace, the sprite. So tiny. He was so—large.

She was not afraid; she knew that he could crush her, but this made her feel safe. He had not told her the details about Rheumy Marks.

She did not look away.

He wasn't going to do this with words, she realized. But he was forcing the issue, because winter was coming.

"Okay, you win. I guess we have to," she conceded.

Have to what? his eyes asked.

She wanted to look down. But she was Ellie Fisk, and she buried her dead, and supposed that she was still doing so.

"Get married," she said. "Get married for Grace."

His eyes watered up.

Mel, forgive me, he thought, the melancholy of the whole damned thing, the long walk, the Man, the ugly sound of necks and fingers snapping, the dog saving him in Magalloway Mountain, the five graves—*two big/three small*—the graves he avoided looking at.

All of it welled up.

The worst part now, he realized, was that time was passing, healing all wounds, and his memories of Mel were fading. It had been ten months since he had seen her last. He definitely did not want time to heal this wound. He wanted to mourn her forever.

But he was still holding onto the boys—in a secret place. He had stowed Packy and Markie in the secret cache inside— a safe place—and he would continue to do so, even if this meant bearing incredible pain.

Somehow this kept them alive, kept them from—fading into the past. And he was used to pain.

That's not fair to Grace, Ellie had just said.

He knew this, of course, but he couldn't help it. Not yet.

She saw the sadness. She knew he wasn't looking for sympathy. Just that he was hurting bad.

Paper, rock, scissors, she thought, giving in to his simple way.

Still sitting, she forced herself forward. Feeling like a puppet on her own string, she reached up carefully and placed her forearms around his neck—and pulled.

When she came to him like this, he forced himself to put his free arm around her thin ribs; and a word entered his mind: *cling.*

They clung to each other like this, awkwardly, to the music of flowing water. She gave her weight to him, and he held her up, taking care to balance for them both. She was beautiful, and he was strong, but their bodies did not react. The embrace remained chaste.

Still friends, they were consciously placing their friendship on an altar of their hearts, pulling out the blue-tipped match, striking the friendship aflame, making it an oblation in exchange for another's life.

For Grace.

She allowed herself to cry small tears, for a time, until the baby, noticing that something had changed, crawled over, and climbed on her knee.

The moment ended. The decision was made, and agreed upon. They pulled away, which was easy.

He drew off the rock, and flopped onto his back in front of her.

Ellie looked at her wedding diamond, his face below it, and like the climbing of this very hill, accepted the situation for what it was.

She screwed it off, along with her engagement ring, and focused on the tender-white shadows left behind on her finger. Then she held the diamond up to the sun, and he saw this—and the sparkle.

"You don't have to take them off," he told her, looking up.

"Sorry, Buzz. Don't go soft on me now. You know I have to do this. You know I can't wear these."

He sat back up, in front of her, and held out his right hand, palm open. She dropped her rings into it; he took her wedding ring and put it into his shirt pocket. He closed his hand on her diamond, and held out his left hand.

She looked at him. He nodded.

His ring. She pulled it off; it was quite loose. He had lost so much weight. The baby reached up for it.

"Let her have it," he said.

Ellie let the baby take it. Grace dropped it into the dark soil. She looked down to the child, away from him.

He took her left hand, and held it, then, tenderly brushed the back of it with his fingertips. He brought his lips to Ellie's hand, and kissed her.

His simple way, she thought.

He followed her gaze to the child. He saw Mel; he couldn't help it.

We can't waste anything in the new paradigm, he thought, Sam-like, knowing what he had to do next.

Buzz gently placed the engagement ring back onto Ellie's finger.

It was Buzz's ring now. And hers again.

Her face remained turned; he watched her set her jaw. He was a witness to her successful effort to not cry again.

"For better or for worse. For Grace," he whispered hoarsely.
Oh Mel!
"Til death do us part," she replied.
Good-bye, Sam.
He put a thumb to her hair, and brought it up over her ear.
He wanted to see her.
"I know it's not the same—as Sam," he said.
Now you're gonna start talking again, she thought. *Now that it's decided. Now that you've cut it down.*
But she did want to hear what he would say. She didn't hate him. She loved him.
She remembered the first time she had ever really understood him—had accepted him as her friend, during the first waltz. The night he had saved her marriage before it began, when Sam had gotten the fool idea that he couldn't go through with the wedding.
Buzz had—intervened—like a white knight from days of old, swooping in, sword flashing. Yes, he had intervened for Sam. But mostly, Buzz had done it for her, because he loved her, all because of a single waltz. She knew it then, the night before the wedding. She knew it now. His chivalrous love for her had cemented into a deep friendship over the years.
This love between them had never been discussed. Not with Sam. Not between Ellie and Buzz.
She could not recall Buzz Woodward allowing his eyes to rest upon her with even the slightest hint of desire during the past decade.
"I know it's not going to be the same as Mel," Ellie told him.
He reached down and lifted the baby. He jumble-kissed Grace on the stomach, bringing a smile.
He was already moving on.
"Thinking about our first waltz?" he guessed, looking at the baby, making a funny face.
He could still guess well. She was not surprised.
She nodded.

"And I know it's not the same as Sam," he repeated. "But I've loved you since that first waltz. I didn't know it would come to this. Something so bitter."

Baby in his hands, bile in his belly.

On the day of her wedding, at the reception, she had waltzed and waltzed with Buzz. She had been so happy, so thankful to Buzz, so in love with Sam.

She remembered throwing her head back, as Buzz spun her 'round and 'round, the music in her ears, her dress pure white.

"You're a good waltzer, kiddo," she said as cheerfully as she could, finally looking at him again. "The best ever, Buzz. Perfect for me."

She smiled, making the best of things. Taking the good and throwing out the bad.

"Rocks in a bucket," Ellie's fiancé added, resuming his riddles. "But what choice do you have when you need water?"

He kept the baby, and they began down the hill. At the bottom, when they came to the path, before they reached the clearing, she took his hand.

Chapter Nineteen

Five Plus One

They announced the engagement to Tommy Sample that afternoon when he stopped by, as he did on most Sundays. Ellie saw a brief flicker of disappointment in his eyes.

"When is the wedding?" Tommy asked innocently.

Buzz and Ellie looked at each other. Buzz decided to let her do the talking.

"Uh, we haven't set a date. We need to find a priest, I suppose," she said.

"Maybe next summer," Buzz suggested. "We've got a lot of work to do before winter."

✛ ✛ ✛

Two nights later, Buzz was asleep on the couch. He felt her hand on his shoulder.

"Buzz, wake up," she told him.

"Huh?"

Then he bolted upright, and before she could blink, he had the Ruger in his hands, and was over to the window, peering out.

Chesterton was up and at his side, nuzzling his arm, seeking affection.

She shook her head with a quick little jerk. Buzz was not Sam. Buzz was—*lightning*.

She remembered how they had been on the courts. Sam: smooth, but slow. Buzz: as powerful as a bear, as quick as a cat.

"Shouldn't the dog be more agitated?" he whispered back to her, keeping his eyes out the window, scanning for danger.

She giggled, still kneeling by the couch.

"Oh, Buzz," she called over in a low voice. "I just wanted to talk."

"About what?" he asked in a normal voice, feeling foolish.

She held a finger to her lips, then whispered: "Keep your voice down. Don't wake Grace."

He padded back and sat down on the center of the couch. Chesterton jumped up next to him.

Buzz patted on the cushion on the side opposite the dog; Ellie pulled herself up next to him.

"It's too silent in this house at night," he told her in a lowered voice. "When I was on the road, there was always some kind of low-level noise in the forest. Too much silence is a bad sign. I get jumpy. I'm sorry if I frightened you."

"Don't be sorry. You keep your danger cap on."

Her voice was soft—but her tone was hard.

They were both thinking about the same thing. The shooting; their lack of security.

"So what's eating you?" he asked.

She took his hand.

"I had a nightmare. About your boys. Only it was—it was more like reliving what happened."

There was moonlight. Her eyes were growing accustomed to the ambient light. She could tell he was looking forward. He did not want to talk about the boys. Neither did she.

"And?" he asked gruffly.

Sam had never been gruff.

And Sam never bolted to a window like that, her practical side reminded her.

"And I know you don't want to hear this Buzz, but the winter is coming. The flu will come back."

She knew how quick his mind made connections. She didn't have to spell it out. She was trying to learn how to communicate with him—more intimately.

There it was. The flu. No medicine. No hospitals.

Grace. The flu.

"We'll stay away from people until the winter ends. Quarantine ourselves," he suggested.

"That's what I was thinking," she agreed, lightly squeezing his hand.

"But what about Tommy? He goes into the towns. He might pick something up."

She was glad he was talking. Being practical.

"We can't ban Tommy from the homestead," she replied. "He's our friend. He's the only person we know up here. He wouldn't understand."

Maybe he would, he thought.

"Are we being paranoid?" she added.

Not if you saw what the flu did to the towns I saw during the long walk, he thought.

"Grace won't get sick," he stated, but with none of his usual confidence. "We'll just have to trust God."

She couldn't help it, but she had grown to resent that phrase. Not the concept. Just the phrase.

It reminded her of—all the bad things.

"We can't ban Tommy," he said.

"No, we can't. He's our friend. He's our link to the outside world."

So they were back to square one.

"What if—" she couldn't finish.

"What if she dies?" Buzz finished.

Ellie and Buzz had been thinking about this dark possibility. Now that they were engaged, they could talk about it. It was one of the grisly bonuses of their pending marriage of convenience. Their engagement allowed them to talk to each other more openly, even if the subject was death or danger; ultimately, this was best for Grace. It could save her life.

"I don't know what to say," he said.

Her grip on his hand tightened.

The Lord's got a big plow ready for you, the Man had said.

"Say anything," she suggested.

There was a long pause.

He allowed something to flow from nowhere—he had no idea what it would be…

"Did you know the Little Flower's parents were married as brother-and-sister for the first ten years of their marriage?"

"Brother and sister?"

"Yeah. Saint Thérèse's parents didn't, uh, sleep as man-and-wife. Maybe it was less than ten years. But it was several years. I don't have the book anymore. It was called a brother-and-sister marriage—that is, a marriage directed toward a spiritual, as opposed to worldly, good. It was pretty rare, even back then, but it happened."

"Is it still allowed?" she asked.

"I don't know. I read that her parents had the same spiritual director. Her father was older, a clock maker. The priest suggested the marriage, along with the brother-sister arrangement. Then, later, after they were married, he suggested they change over to, uh, man-and-wife. And thank God they did, or else we wouldn't have gotten Saint Thérèse, or her wonderful sisters.

"But I think you and me would need special permission, you know—to get married and live as brother and sister like that."

He had changed the conversation. But she was intrigued by this new twist. She had simply put the idea of—what to do on the honeymoon—out of her mind. She was almost pleasantly surprised that Buzz was indicating that he was not looking for a physical relationship. Flattered, even, in a weird kind of way.

"Are you saying we won't have to—"

"Yes. I'm saying we won't have to. That is, if we can get permission."

Her grip on his hand loosened, and he felt it, and he interpreted it as a good sign. He relaxed.

"I read once that the Catholic philosopher, Jacques Maritain, was married to Raïssa as brother-and-sister," he added. "Maritain was much older, dedicated to his work. She helped him with his work, and they shared a higher love. Their passion for Thomism joined them together, made them one."

Buzz and Ellie had both heard audio tape lectures by Ralph McInerny explaining the brilliant insights of Maritain. There had been few references to Maritain's marriage; Ellie had just assumed that the Maritains had been married in the usual fashion.

Directed toward a spiritual good, she thought. *Let it be done unto me...*

Ellie shifted her weight slightly toward Buzz.

"And Grace is our shared passion?" she asked.

He nodded in the darkness.

"We're already living as brother-and-sister," Ellie mused, feeling a certain elation. A light, distant knowledge that divine destiny was in this conversation overcame her, but in a hidden, sublime way—the way the tide comes in—slowly, surely, inexorably.

Buzz Woodward, the man, felt nothing, except her hand in his own. Like the natural unity they found waltzing, her hand *fit there*.

Serendipity? Perhaps.

It made him nervous.

"Ellie. I do love you. I really do. And you're the most beautiful girl in the world—"

"Sounds like we're breaking up," she interrupted gently, not concerned. Not ready to let go of his hand, or the feeling that there was a design in this midnight meeting.

"Huh?"

"Like two kids in high school. 'I really like you, but.'"

"You know what I mean."

She reached over with her free hand and slapped him lightly on the shoulder.

"Buzz, I feel the same way about you."

They pondered this. Their hands tightened, then loosened. She rubbed her thumb on the crest of his rough hand. This was going well.

Buzz knew that there was something else. Something practical to tell her. Never the mystic, yet always a quick-prayer bandit, Buzz prayed: *Saint Anthony.*

It came to him.

"In the old days, farm widows and farm widowers often married for—convenience. But that's a bad description. They really married out of necessity. It takes two to run a farm the right way. A man and a woman."

"And to raise a child," she said.

She leaned over suddenly and kissed him on the cheek, but instead of pulling away, kept her lips near his ear.

"I love you, Buzz Woodward," Ellie whispered sweetly. "I love how you ran to the window. You're my knight in shining armor."

Now she pulled away, slowly, watching him.

He was a little boy, blushing.

He turned and kissed her back—on the cheekbone, missing his target—her cheek—just a bit. This was the way he had always kissed her, when she was married to Sam. Like a sister.

He liked being her knight.

"And you're Grace's mom. Kind of like Saint Joseph with Jesus, but just reversed. Or side-ways."

That did it for her. Like the Holy Family. The bolt of destiny locked into the latch of reality.

This was meant to be, she thought.

It truly *felt* like Providence. It was gritty enough. The missing piece. Brother and sister. It made sense for the baby. For the commission Mel had given her, long before there had been any hope that Buzz would show up here. (Though, Ellie admitted, Mel had always insisted he would.) She would marry Buzz as his sister, and then, finally, together, they could buy some time; buy some time to—

Recover, she thought.

She felt his presence in the darkness, and it comforted her. Made her feel safe, sitting next to a white knight, and his dog, Chesterton. A girl could do worse in this kind of world.

Oh, she missed Sam. He was always there, behind the curtain or in the cupboard of her imagination.

But she didn't think that Sam would mind that she was moving on—especially in the direction Buzz was taking her. She still had her edge; a sort of self-aware calculation which many children from divorced backgrounds have.

They listened to the dog breathe.

Despite the hand-holding, there had been no sexual attraction between them since his return. She had no inkling that this part of him wasn't working.

As for Buzz, he was thankful that this part of himself had gone away, even if temporarily. Hot-blooded, he had always struggled with sexual temptation. The outlet for his drive afforded by marriage had been a blessing to him, as it is for most men.

Being shut down in this area was one less cross to carry. His condition had already become just one more item on Buzz's litany of his broken life: drunkard, divorced, suicidal, killer, widower—impotent.

Maybe something broke in my brain when I hit my head, during the coma? he asked himself now.

It made the idea of marrying Ellie for Grace's sake easier to accept. He believed his motives were pure, untainted with chemical influences.

What if your sex drive comes back? a trendy little voice asked.

He didn't have the answer to that one. Then it came:

My word is my bond. I will make a promise to Ellie and that will be that.

He was a man, not a schoolboy. He was not a pig rutting around in the mud. Enough said.

Ellie will find the right priest, then she'll convince him to give us permission.

He knew what she was like when she really wanted something. That priest, whoever he was, even in this world, was as good as found.

"Brother-and-sister, eh?" she asked again, bringing him out of his thoughts.

Buzz and Ellie, alone in a house on a swell in the shadow of Magalloway Mountain. A tiny redhead on a big bed. They were only vaguely cognizant that there was no longer an anti-Catholic culture around to mock their pure desire for a simpler union of souls for the sake of a helpless baby.

Not that Buzz had ever cared what people thought of him. "One of the great perks of being a sociopath," he had once joked to her, back in the old world.

"You got it. Brother-and-sister, sister," he agreed, smiling in the dark in the new world.

"Amen, brother."

He rose, then walked her over to the door of her bedroom, the dog's claws clicking on the formica floor beneath them; he was still holding her hand. They embraced briefly, then she retreated to her sanctuary behind a closed door.

"Well, there you go, Chetmeister," he told the dog. "That takes care of that."

He knew that Ellie was barren. Because of his gift, he had also known all along, during her married years, that she had yearned for more children. He realized that Grace was a fulfillment of a soul-deep desire in her. He was happy for her, and for Grace. It did not strike him as ironic that he was impotent and she was barren; it lined up. It was—poetic.

It was okay.

✝ ✝ ✝

Buzz and Ellie returned to separate cells that night excited by their first whiff of the sweet perfume of a new destiny breezing in from the heavens. In each of their minds, it fell together simply—

He thought: Mel had already died by the time I left Ohio. Grace is why He inspired the Man to store that gasoline in the boathouse; this is why God helped me cross the Badlands. So Grace could have a father. So Ellie could have a brother.

Ellie felt: If Sam and Chris had to die, then at least God has given me a reason to live. Mel's baby needs a mother. Buzz needs a sister.

And who could blame them? If God had not arranged this unfathomable marriage of necessity from before the beginnings of time, then He had sure shimmied and shaked to reset the table to help Buzz and Ellie force down the realities of their post-modern world.

Brother-and-sister? Surely the idea had come from *outside* themselves. For Catholics accustomed to the ways of Providence, their new arrangement was just too strange, too absurd, and too wonderful to have come from anywhere—or anyone—else. The evil one frightens; only the Almighty surprises.

And so it was.

Yet they fell into their dreams having completely forgotten the germ of this conversation which had ended so well.

The flu. A killer flu way too small, even for a man like Buzz Woodward to wrap his arms around. Too tiny for him to administer a lethal jerk.

✠ ✠ ✠

Tommy Sample grabbed two udders and milked, with hands so knowing of their task that he could pray or daydream or probably even sleep during the chore.

It was an especially pleasing task in the summertime, before the sun came up, when it was warm in the barn, and he beat the birds to their songs. Today, he banged out his Rosary in no time at all, then gathered wool about his little Grace; Grace Woodward up on the Henderson Swell.

Grace's little life meant almost as much to Tommy Sample as it did to Buzz and Ellie. She was his hope, too, for the future. The little red bean represented for him the children he would never have.

Tommy had been forty-two when he finally found the right woman, and the flu had taken Dede away so quickly. One miscarriage—their only child. Tommy was forty-four now, and accustomed to living alone, if only because he had lived that way for so many years before meeting Dede.

Finding another Catholic woman like her would be a miracle. ("Not with all the widows around," his practical side piped in sometimes.)

Before Buzz came over the hill, Tommy had hoped for such a thing with Ellie, but only dimly—because she was close in age; because she was so achingly pretty and so staunchly Catholic. But he accepted in his heart of hearts (in that unabashed way a man who grows up tending animals) that he could never tame an intrepid filly like Ellen Fisk.

As his wife, she would no doubt end up dominating him, and he cherished his independence. But she sure had pluck, and he liked that in a gal.

Besides, she was two inches taller. And it was so obvious (at least to Tommy) that she was meant for Buzz now that Sam was gone. She and Buzz had a history. Buzz was rugged, too—tough as tarpaper after that long jaunt. This was not a world for a woman to go it alone. He was glad Buzz had convinced her to get married again. Good for her.

Good for us all. (Tommy had a big heart.)

Little Grace again. Even if Buzz and Ellie weren't meant for each other, it was clear to Tommy that a marriage of convenience would be necessary for the sake of the child. The myth of the gentleman farmer was no more. *Real* farms and ranches were back, and were back to stay, and would once again return to the most exalted status in a new economy which catered to no luxury, now that those fool computers had made everything local again, like it had been when Tommy's parents were just starting out here in Bagpipe.

A real farm took two—a man and a woman—to run it right proper, and them two up on the swell had plenty to learn. (Although Tommy thought of himself more as a rancher-trader than as a farmer.)

Tommy believed his own role in the passion play unfolding in Bagpipe was clear; he would be the one to teach 'em what they didn't know how. He was the dutch-uncle, stage left. A johnny-on-the-spot in a jam, ever ready to jump over the candlestick. Wasn't there a guy like Tommy all in the best westerns, the kind John Ford used to make which had flickered across the silver-screen when he was a boy?

You're darn tootin'—and Tommy was the guy with the wagon. The guy who spotting the bad guy hiding in the barn, early in the movie, tipping off the hero, and thereby saving the good guy's life. Helping the hero win the pretty girl's heart. It was much more rewarding to be an active member of the cast than to sit in the theater munching popcorn, Tommy reckoned.

Did or didn't that angel wake him up an hour early with the rumbling sound of the engine that wouldn't leave his head? Merely to save the lives of a few cows and mangy old plow horses?

And what were cows for anyhow?

Milk for human babies, that's what.

God Himself designed the dumb-animal for that specific purpose. You didn't need a fancy college degree to put two-and-two together about cows.

The blessed animals provided twice as much milk as they needed to feed their young. What was all that extra milk for?

It was a wonder there was one atheist in the world, but Thomas P. Sample was damned sure that if there were any, they didn't know nothing 'bout cows.

Nature is lots of things, after all, but there was one thing for certain about her: she was not *generous*. The double-extra milk from cows was a complete anomaly. Every farmer knows that cows get sick if they aren't milked, if the extra milk isn't taken. It took a human being to keep a cow alive. In all of history ain't nobody ever see no *monkey* milk a cow.

Now why was that?

The milk was for babies like his Grace.

The double-extra-milk coming out of the udders in his hands proved there was a loving God who cared for mankind. A God who loved Grace Woodward.

Squirt-squirt. Squirt-squirt.

The distinct melody zipping into the steel bucket helped him think.

During this chore, even though the bulk of the milk would be sold in Errol or Colebrook, he indulged himself with the fiction that he was milking these cows exclusively for the little red wonder up on the swell, his godchild—or at least, that he was providing the nourishment needed to keep the lovely, round breasts of Grace's mother brimming.

Sure, he traded with Buzz and Ellie because that's what farmers do—"you scrub my back/I'll scrub yours"—and because those poor folks up there kept taking it on the chin, yet always managed to pull themselves up from the canvas to keep on punching back. Some locals here had run off, and maybe there was no blame there, because Bagpipe had practically been a ghost town even before the Troubles, but by staying on the land, the Fisks and Woodwards had made their bones as true Bagpipers by Tommy's reckoning.

Old-time tough, that's what they were up on the swell. Just like the Samples, God rest the souls of his dear parents.

Tommy, in perfect rhythm, reached up from an udder and made the sign of the cross.

Yet Tommy always insisted on giving them the milk free-and-clear. For Grace. Just a few weeks ago, while chopping wood, Buzz had even asked Tommy to be the "stand-in" godfather now that Sam was gone. Tommy's heart had swelled, and he had accepted with understated farmer-relish.

He had loved that, loved being asked by Buzz; he loved being the godfather. And he loved Bagpipe. Let them kill his dog and burn down his house. Like Buzz and Ellie, Tommy Sample wasn't going *anywhere*.

His frequent trading quests to Colebrook and Errol and Berlin were not optional. He needed tools. He lived on the margin. He needed to stay alive until the people came back here so he could sell them the raw materials they needed for butter and cheese. And he was always coming back with something necessary for the Woodward/Fisk homestead, not just notions.

Buzz and Ellie were his best friends, and he loved that baby, so Tommy had understood perfectly well when they discussed the semi-quarantine with him. Come winter, he would hole up for two or three days after coming back from a town, unless it was a dire emergency. (Tommy had a sleigh-wagon, too, for winter travel. He had been waxing and buffing it all summer.) If he had a sniffle or even the slightest cough, he would stay off the swell.

Tommy Sample did catch the bug, in Errol, on the twenty-eighth day of September, from a ten-year-old kid just up from Berlin. Only Tommy had no way of knowing that he was carrying. He was immune. He lugged the virus back to Bagpipe in his lungs, though the deadly germ revealed no symptoms in his body.

He sneezed on a peppercorn while having a hot cider with Buzz when the big man came down to the cabin to pick up the hand-drill for the new woodshed he was trying to build before the snows came.

Neither man noticed that one little sneeze, laughing as they were at one of Buzz's patented, corny observations about farm living.

Buzz was also immune to this strain of flu—a hardy little mutant that had marched on its own ugly path to Bagpipe all the way from Asia, leaving women keening over graves in its brutal wake.

He did not know he was carrying when he took it back to the swell, where he passed it on to his daughter while playing with her on the deck of Sam's old house.

✝ ✝ ✝

"There he is, do you see him?" Buzz asked Ellie after he plopped a chunk of wood down on the kitchen table, at the end of a long day in early October.

"See who? I see a piece of oak," she told him.

He had that impish smile.

"Found him in the woodpile, looking up at me."

"Stop with the riddles. Is this one of your man-in-the-electric-socket things?"

She touched her hand to it. A chill wind had trotted down from Canada last week, and Buzz had been keeping the woodstove burning at night.

It was a friendly, solid piece of wood.

"Exactly. You got it. It's Saint Joseph. I saw him in there."

He pulled out his blade.

"You're going to carve a statue?"

He nodded.

"You bet, sister. For the altar. It's going to be a long, long winter—with no videos to watch. I have read every book in this house. I have got to keep myself busy while you knit me sweaters."

She looked across the kitchen to their altar. A small table with a lace cloth. Mel's picture of the Shroud of Turin. Buzz's porcelain statue of Our Lady of Grace. Two candles. Four wooden rosaries. One leatherbound Douay-Rheims Bible opened to the Gospel of John. When it was too cold outside, they prayed their nightly Rosary before this jiffy-chapel.

"Sweaters? I don't know how to knit."

"Mel stocked in plenty of yarn, El. Plenty of yarn sitting in the roof rafters in plastic bags, behind the toilet paper. I'll show you how."

"You know how to knit?" She raised her eyebrows and smiled in that bright, silly way he loved.

"No, El. But three months ago, I didn't know how to hoe potatoes or use a root cellar, either."

She rolled her eyes. No way, José.

But it would be nice to have something for Grace for the winter, she thought.

She did not give him the satisfaction of knowing he had guessed-her again. That's how Ellie thought of it now: *Buzz guessed-me.*

His gift could be quite annoying. Now she understood some of Mel's hints of frustration, though she had not told Ellie about his preference for laying on the floor after dinner with his thick calves on the chair. Ellie just did not like that. It was too weird.

But what could she do? She tried to tell him once, last month, while looking down at him on the floor, potatoes steaming on her plate. He got that hurt-little-boy expression on his face. Then, for three straight meals, he sat in his chair, fidgeting after his food—

"Ellie, may I please have your permission to sit on the floor tonight?" His voice had been so sincere.

That's what he called it. Buzz wasn't *lying* on the floor. He was *sitting* on the floor. Bizarre.

So she blew a lock of hair from her brow, nodded slowly, then finished her potatoes, chatting with him *down there* as if he were in the cockpit of Apollo 13, ready for blast-off.

Chesterton had better manners.

By the end of October, his block of wood was taking on a likeness, and Ellie had two-thirds of her first sweater knitted, although little Grace would need to grow her right arm two inches longer than her left to fit into it.

✥ ✥ ✥

Buzz was outside, getting wood for the stove.

She knew he would stack, dither, and daydream. With the harvest in, there was less to do. It had been a week since Buzz had returned from helping Tommy Sample bring in the hay using nothing more sophisticated than two scythes.

It had warmed up, and it was a pleasant, almost summery day, as sometimes happened in the North Country in the fall.

Ellie was in the bedroom, hovering with the child in her arms. Pacing, back and forth, between the bed and the changing table. Waiting for the thermometer again.

The second reading.

She took it out; looked at it.

"One hundred and one," she mouthed.

How many times had she taken Christopher's temperature over the years? Had a temperature this high caused her the least bit of worry with him?

Take another one.

And so she did. No need to alarm Buzz.

Same temperature.

Maybe the thermometer was screwed up. She put her hand on her own forehead, then on Gracie's.

Ellie took her own temperature.

Ninety-eight point-six, she read.

She took Grace's temperature again, but found it difficult to get a reading because the little dear—and who could blame her—was not cooperating with the procedure.

One hundred and one...point-four.

Point-four!? How long since the last reading?

Ellie looked at the brass, wind-up alarm clock next to the bed.

Five minutes.

She scrambled into the living room to Mel's desk, and put the child, who was already becoming a bit listless, on the floor. Gracie cried and pulled herself up on her mother's leg, holding her dress. The baby could not walk yet, but she could stand and balance like this. Her red hair was growing now, too, starting to curl.

Ellie ignored her little sobs.

Where is that stupid book!

There it was, a thick, intimidating medical home-reference. There were two yellow post-it notes sticking out of its pages, marked in Ellie's indeciferable hand: *Flu. Colds.*

She had practically memorized these two sections. Nothing in them about her clue, the rate of a temperature rising.

She quickly thumbed it open to the index, running her finger down the page, eyes searching, leaning over the desk—

Temperature. Temperature...

She heard the door in the kitchen close behind her. Buzz. Holding an armful of logs.

He saw the thermometer in Ellie's free hand, and the baby standing at her feet, clinging to the dress, crying. The tear streaming down the sweet, beautiful cheek of his future wife.

He guessed-them.

"Ellie, what's happening?"

She straightened up, then bent to pick up the child. As she wrapped Grace tight in her arms, Ellie had a nanosecond flash-back to the run from hell, down to the river.

He already knows, she thought.

Buzz faked a convincing smile. He walked over to the middle of the kitchen and began stacking the wood next to the stove. Way too casually.

"Gracie's got a temperature," she told him.

His hand stopped in mid-air, holding the stick of maple in stasis, then he placed it gently on the stack.

Buzz straightened, clip-clapped the wood dust from his hands, then walked over to her. He put a hand on the back of the child, patting gently.

He looked into her eyes for a long time.

"Oh Buzz," Ellie whispered.

The baby had stopped crying as soon as she was lifted. In that smooth feline way of his, his arms were suddenly around both of them. His cheek was on the baby's cheek.

He felt the heat. But he had already known, as soon as he walked through the door, and saw Ellie hunched over like that.

He thought of the Man's face, in the last moments, on the road in the Badlands. *Lord's gotta big plow for a big guy like you, all ready to go.*

It took a lot out of Buzz, for he was only flesh and blood, but he pulled his hand up and grasped the plow, once again.

"What was it—the temperature?" he asked Ellie softly, still holding the both of them, going by the numbers, following the script.

"Over one-oh-one, and rising," she said.

"I'll get some aspirin, we'll knock it down."

He pulled away and went to the kitchen.

She walked over to the couch and sat down. She looked out the window and watched Chesterton, full of life and health, bounding around the now-empty garden, chasing an unseen critter, as Buzz went to the cabinet to get the Saint Joseph's aspirin. Mel had stocked in twenty bottles.

Near the graves. The dog was near the five graves.

Five plus one equals six, Ellie thought woodenly.

Chapter Twenty

The Jetty Redux

Buzz and Ellie were faithful. Each had been weathered by—
the reality of the situations, even as those situations piled up
like stones on damp, broken earth. These parents did not give
in during the next five days.

Screw the guess, thought Buzz, ignoring the knowing,
donning his courage like a breastplate.

Ellie did not allow the baby to leave her arms—or the
prayers to leave her lips, except to kiss the little one, even as
the aspirin knocked down the first fever, which came back,
stronger.

And the father ran—ran, full speed, till his lungs screamed,
then ran some more—past the pond, under the stars, until he
found himself, chest heaving, at the Sample place.

Tommy took off on the wagon for Errol, and if need be,
for Colebrook, hoping against hope to track down penicillin
or some antibiotics. Before Tommy left, he hitched his spare
buckboard to the old mare for Buzz, then loaded it with fresh
milk, along with a satchel filled with dried herbs for making
teas from his mother's cabinet. A bottle of menthol.

✝ ✝ ✝

When Buzz returned home, he threw his ghosts into the
wind, and allowed himself to go into the bedroom—Mel's
room—to assist Ellie and the child, with the vapor rubs, with
whatever Ellie wanted. He even tried massaging the child,

adjusting her tiny spine, knowing, like he had known with
the ancient nun in Blackstone, that this thing eating up his
daughter's insides was beyond the reach of his fingers, his
courage, his pleas to heaven. Grace needed—

—*a miracle.*

Instead of sleeping normal hours, Buzz stayed up around
the clock, taking nodding naps on the couch, Rosary in hand,
facing the altar. He tended the fire. He cleaned the kitchen
table with a damp cloth. He boiled potatoes, then cajoled Ellie
to eat.

Chesterton paced with Buzz, never leaving his side. The
collie had smelled this same scent before in Saint-Pascal.

Ellie, poor Ellie; she stayed always with her baby. The
whole time, until Grace's little lungs, filled with fluid, keeping tortured-time, forced the mother's burning eyes to close
for a minute, or fifteen.

Grace Woodward was merely a tiny child, a baby. A little
one. A soul like all unrepeatable souls, with her own destiny,
a destiny as bitter for her parents as the roots in the teas they
brewed, then spoon-fed onto her blue lips.

✠ ✠ ✠

The end came in the living room, on the couch, in front of
the altar. Grace was in Ellie's arms. The heavy stovepipe
breathing had disappeared from the child's fragile torso, replaced by strained wisps of breath.

Ellie held the Man's relic of the Little Flower on the baby's
chest. Ellie was no longer praying; she was simply enduring.

Buzz was on his knees before his unfinished Saint Joseph, his prayers wordless, soul-begging for a medical Egypt
to which to flee, listening for the sound of Tommy's wagon
cracking down the hill with a vial or a needle or a pill from
the old world.

But Buzz knew, within his inmost self, in the place where
Packy and Markie were hiding—*boys will be boys*—in his
heart, what would happen next. Tommy would not come with
medicine. It didn't exist.

Buzz had been certain of the brutal truth from the very moment he stepped through the door with the wood; since he imagined Ellie's thin ribs beneath her blouse, bent over in that first-time way, with the tear leaving a salty trail on her fine cheek.

Grace Woodward was going away. Pascal and Mark Woodward were coming to visit—coming for a visit real soon, and when they came, Ellen Fisk would see what he, Gwynne Woodward, really was—nothing.

Nothing. A sepulcher. An empty shell of faithless bones encased by muscle and flesh.

"Buzz," Ellie whispered.

He turned and opened his eyes. Ellie was tearless, having depleted that watery remedy days ago.

Weary.

The little body in Ellie's arms—*red hair*—the last of Mel, lifeless, small. Not Grace anymore.

Gone away.

He stood, and took a long walk to the two forms.

"Do you know what to do?" she asked.

He nodded.

He knew, even now, numb, he knew.

Tenderly, slowly, he took Ellie's wrists, and helped her lift her arms off the baby. He took the blanket off the child, then the sweater. The final layers.

He lifted the naked body from her arms. He held his Grace in two hands, before him, like a velveteen pillow for a wedding ring. Limp.

"Now, take my arm," he told Ellie gently.

Ellie was so beautiful, so sad, her eyes closed. She reached up and took his forearm, then rose to her feet on his strength.

Together, as a family, they took the journey to the altar; Ellie moved the Bible, making a place.

Buzz placed his daughter's body on the altar.

The dog, outside now, keened bluely.

The two friends fell to their knees. He took her hand. They were—alone.

Buzz will know what to do, Ellie told herself. *Buzz will know what to say.*

Packy and Markie came to their daddy then. They crawled right out of his heart and into his *there,* his *now,* and the sorrow, oh the sorrow, the wordless, awful, terrible-hard-packed grief unfolded with their arrival.

Five-plus-one, Ellie counted souls, still waiting for Buzz. *Thy will be done...*

...and Buzz received the purest of graces, because he was the only Saint Joseph in Bagpipe, as words, which all his life came to him, came now...

An oblation. A bloodless oblation. Jesus is on the Altar. Markie and Packy are here. Don't be selfish.

"Jesus God Father," he began, and Ellie squeezed his hand tighter, almost hurting him.

Packy and Markie charged up the ramparts now, then pounded down the gates, like true Woodwards, like he had taught them, cutting down their big daddy with their little broadswords, and despite the soul-pain they bore with the crosses on their tiny shields, he was grateful they had finally come, finishing their own long walks to their daddy—"I love you, Daddy!" so cheerful they were—

I love you, too, my sons, oh my sons!

And the words came to Buzz for his sons. He greeted them thus:

I have a gift for you, Peanut. Your sister! Do you see her, Packy? She's so beautiful, isn't she?

Like Mommy...

"We offer this beautiful little baby to you, Lord, your little light in the darkness. Our little Gracie. We offer her because she is yours, and because this world hates the light. Thank you—"

Ellie was sobbing now, unable to balance, so he reached over, took her. He supported her frame. The mother was a shadow of light; Ellie turned and clung to him, her arms around his shoulders, her tears on his cheeks.

…and Packy and Markie ran off with their sister, laughing and calling out, like children running up a grassy hill to meet their mother—no longer babes—but rather, white-robed warriors alongside a silken-robed, crimson-topped princess; they ran toward the Court of the Two Queens; toward Mother Melanie and Mary Immaculate—

And Buzz was sucked back into Bagpipe, again alone with his best friend, the blond girl.

"Gracie," Ellie sobbed. "No, not my Gracie. I loved her, Buzz. I loved her all the way, 'cause I promised Mel, and if I hadn't loved her so much, I wouldn't feel so bad—"

"Then feel bad, my love," the only Saint John left in Bagpipe told the beautiful woman, his words coming like water down a stream in a safe-place.

"Feel as bad as you want. As much as you loved. Today— today is the day of glory, and little Grace only gets one."

She lifted her face and pressed a soft, chaste kiss on his lips.

"It's so bad, Buzz. So bad."

He pulled her close.

"I love you, Ellie," he whispered into her ear, pulling her so tight that he felt her ribs straining.

She clung all the tighter.

The pain equals the love.

Buzz had cut it down for her, as she knew he would. So she must have loved the child perfectly, because she ached perfectly. That was real. Fire burning on a river of tears.

Here was the reality of the situation, dark though it be. The reality: love and pain.

Beauty and sorrow.

A man and a woman on a rocky hill, after a long walk, with an innocent on a cross, gone.

Bring it on! Ellie imitated Mel, though in her own way. *You want pain, Lord? Here it is! I've got pain in buckets, so take it. Are You happy now?*

She screamed inside, cursing God, getting angry now, being Ellie.

Which was okay.

Anger, pain? Cursing God. Her words didn't matter. The pain equaled the love, and this was how Ellie was living her fiat, carrying her cross. Ellie was a Catholic all the way, and she wasn't going anywhere, except up a hill, the rocks on the path stained with blood.

At least Yahweh gave Abraham a ram as a substitute for Isaac. Gracie was up there on the altar. Gone. A bloodless oblation.

"Gracie saved our lives," he told her, still holding her, still keeping his cheek to her temple.

She nodded, dry.

Your sons shall number as the stars in the sky, the Other whispered to Buzz, who was open to anything.

Even nonsense about the stars.

A silence ensued.

"What do we do next?" she finally whispered to him.

She was shutting down quickly, he could tell. She was relying on him completely.

He put his hand to the plow. Or maybe it had been there all the time, since the first waltz, when he took her up in friendship.

Buzz was still breathing, and there was still blood in his veins, and Markie and Packy had finally come at last to their *da-da,* and though their father had been dreading—

This oblation—for days, ever since he had known for sure in the kitchen, with the firewood in his arms, with Ellie bent over the book, a child clinging to her dress—

It was okay.

Ellie needed him now. In ways, he was stronger, according to a divine design. His arms orbited around her. Brother moon, sister earth.

The day of glory, so dark.

A cross on a hill.

Alive, watching: a man, a woman.

He stood, then let her rest the side of her face in his palm, as she had the day he came over the hill to this burning house, until she looked up, her hair unkempt, her eyes weakened embers, spent.

Simple.

Two little children, looking for all the world like adults, standing in a little house on a hill, next to an altar of sacrifice.

No music for the waltz, he thought, words still his friend. But he began the dance anyway. Who needed music? They were perfect for each other.

Ellie had said so.

She was idling on fumes now, just enough left for a slow dance.

He reached down and carefully helped his fiancée to her feet—she was a feather—and then he took her slender arm and pulled it around his own neck, her eyes on his eyes. He bent his back and nested his free arm beneath the crook of her knees, then lifted her up. She closed her eyes, sleepy, and nestled her forehead into his neck. A perfect fit.

He carried Ellie, asleep, into their bedroom.

Years later, he would remember her hair on his own cheek, and the sound of her breathing.

On this night, the little candle on the altar without a flame, they tumbled into a dark sleep in each other's arms, fully dressed, until the sun came up, and the dog came in to wake them.

✝ ✝ ✝

Because Ellie was who she was, she prepared and dressed the body, then made the shroud while he dug the little grave. Then, together, as a family, they buried the body of their only daughter, in the rain, as the sun slowly followed its track across the sky, hidden by the clouds. The dog followed Buzz back and forth across the field as he carried the stones.

Ellie made the cross.

Buzz and Ellie prayed in the silence, simple Catholic prayers remembered from childhood.

After, they went to the deck, and watched the rain, until it became dark.

Later, he slept on the couch. Finding her bed too big without Grace, she came in later, and found her place next to him. They did this for weeks, as brother and sister, because it had been decided—he let her decide—and it did not seem like God minded.

✝ ✝ ✝

Tommy picked up a wrinkled, wiry old priest from the shrine in Colebrook; the priest prayed a funeral Mass over a make-shift altar next to the graves.

November was coming, and with it, winter.

Thomas Sample cried over the grave with them.

After the sacrament, Buzz, Tommy, and Ellie talked with the priest over tea in their kitchen, and being an old Frenchman, he knew exactly what they needed when they told him about Saint Thérèse's parents.

Buzz and Ellie set a date—weather pending. December the eighth, Feast of the Immaculate Conception. It fell on a Friday, and even though it was a holy day of obligation, the priest allowed the wedding because travel was so difficult.

"I'll get you there in a blizzard," Tommy Sample promised.

✝ ✝ ✝

November. White snow on cold fields. The pines, painted flecks of green on the hillsides. A conversation on the deck. Warm cider. Ellie on the rocking chair, snuggling in a blanket. Buzz was wearing the jacket the Man had bought for him in Cleveland.

"You've got to start eating," he told her.

She snorted.

"You've got to start eating," she replied.

She waited.

"Will it ever end?" she asked, feeling as if she was reading from a script.

He guessed-her, as she knew he would. She wasn't talking about death. Not Mel's or Sam's or Grace's, or even their own deaths. She was talking about the suffering. The numb ache within the living.

"No," he told her.

Why beat around the bush?

"Then why?"

"I don't know. I've started to pray again. I've been trying to find God. I believe He's there, inside my soul. Saint Teresa of Avila says the whole entire Holy Trinity is supposed to be in there. Big as He is, you'd think I could find Him."

He had been reading the Man's favorite book, *Fire Within*. To pass the time, he finished the statue of Saint Joseph. He sat before the altar, on a stool, wordless, listening, at times searching, for hours each day, between his chores.

"Have you found anything?" she asked. Ellie was not really curious—just going through the motions.

"Not yet."

A time passed.

"You've been cleaning my old house," she stated. There was a slight hint of accusation in her voice.

"Just killing some time."

He instantly regreted his phrasing.

These words ushered in a prolonged, destructive silence. Within it, he could practically hear the sound of her heart breaking.

"How you holding up, El?"

"I need to eat more. I'm sick of potatoes."

"You know what I meant."

She shook her head, looked at the snow. A clear, clean message she was sending:

No, I am not holding up.

This was the worst, when the crying time was over.

"Me neither," he agreed, partaking her grief. "I'm dying."

He did not mean to sound melodramatic.

"Don't you dare, Buzz Woodward."

"Or what, you'll kill me?"

A miserable joke.

No laugh.

✛ ✛ ✛

They were walking to Tommy's house, holding hands, even though it was cold.

It's only pain, they thought. Automatic. Corporal pain was pepper sauce for their souls.

Chesterton, still subdued, was way ahead. The dog knew there was but one place to go on this road. The Sample place.

The wedding was next week.

"We need to plan it," Tommy had told them two days ago. "Come to my house."

Plan it? Ellie had thought. Because poor Tommy was in mourning, too, she held her tongue.

Okay, Tommy; you, me, and Buzz show up. Done.

Buzz decided to say something—anything—when he noticed that he no longer cared about mountains, except that he was tired of them.

"Ellie, do you ever, you know, wonder—wonder why we don't go over the usual stuff?"

"What usual stuff?" she asked.

She waited for him to talk. At times, Buzz's chatter—his stupid riddles—could even make a second tick by less slowly.

"The Book of Job stuff."

"Not really."

"Why not?" he asked.

They were coming up on the pond now, perhaps a half mile ahead of them. It was not frozen. Probably would be in a couple weeks.

"Because I've lived it," she explained. "There is no answer. There is no answer to the problem of evil. Little babies die. We live. Sam and Chris get shot. It's not our fault, and it's not God's fault. What does that leave?"

"Nothing," Buzz said.

She was smart, dammit.

"Faith," she finished.

Simple.

"But there has to be a reason why all this has happened."

He was still clinging to it.

His grand, Unknown-Reason-Behind-It-All theory.

This made her angry for some reason, though she cared not to investigate why.

Oh yeah, she remembered tersely. *Grace had been the latest big reason-for-it-all to go awry.*

"I thought you just said you read the Book of Job?" she snapped at him.

She felt this slap him. She couldn't help it. He was the one bringing up Job.

"Where were you when I created the foundations of the earth?" she quoted God. "In other words, Buzz, piss off—"

—she slipped on the snow-pack.

Without thinking, he instantly reached and grabbed her arm, holding her up, preventing her from falling.

Like a cougar with vice-grips, she thought.

She still liked this about him, and instead of saying thank you, she gave him a smile.

A little rose-in-a-snow-covered-field smile.

Simple.

He lapped it up, and gave her a big one right back—one of those good-old-Buzz smiles from the halcyon days of spring, when life was good.

And something stirred inside her.

A simple thing. Too small to notice.

Ellie remained the most beautiful—and only—woman in Bagpipe, and she was going to marry him. And she had given her beauty to Sam—as man-and-wife.

Why not to Buzz as brother-and-sister?

Can't waste these little gifts while the malls are closed, she thought, wondering, not for the first time, just how much of him was rubbing off on her.

"Where were we?" she asked, her voice suddenly lighter. Had she been angry just a second ago?

"A reason for all the crap," he explained.

"Well, if you read the Book of Job—" she began, but lost her train of thought.

"Let me start over, El. Before the millennium, I had dreams for Markie and Packy—"

—funny how he could talk about his boys with such ease since their visit the night Gracie died—

"—you know, ordinary father-type dreams. That they would grow up, get married, have families, love Our Lady. Change the world; win it for Christ. Cut things down in the Woodward family traditon."

"Nothing wrong with that," she observed. "Me and Sam had the same kind of dreams for Christopher. Even more so. Because he was the only child…"

…the only child you could have, he finished.

"…I could have," she finished.

And it came. The old yearning, as always, even after all this crap, as Buzz just put it.

He waited. Because he had his gift, and because he knew her better now, he also knew it was back—the old yearning—like she had just stepped on an itsy-bitsy land mine.

He allowed time to pass, and for the wound to seal back up. He didn't always cut things down.

She appreciated this about him. She had been able to hide the yearning from Sam for ten years. Buzz had known all the time, she realized, even in Cleveland, even before all this crap. At least she could share it now. She was Just-Ellie to him.

Always had been. Since the first waltz. And lately, there had been a plenty of practice for waltzing with each other's pain.

"So, you were saying," she started again, surprising herself with her desire to talk.

We should get out walking more often, she made a mental note.

"I was thinking about that man, or the angel, or that vision on the jetty. The words that were said to me on the jetty."

During the suicide attempt, she thought.

She knew the details. He had told her way back when, in Cleveland, and she had a good memory.

"What were his exact words again?" she asked.

Ellie was curious. The sensation of curiosity felt—novel.

"Do not lay a hand on the boy," Buzz recited. "Do not do anything to him."

"I remember now," she said. "Odd words."

"Well, I read them yesterday, when I was praying. Before yesterday, I never knew where the words came from—"

"So don't keep me in suspense, Buzz."

"They're in the Old Testament. Word-for-word what the angel told Abraham just as he was about to slit Isaac's throat."

She pondered this. Buzz was leading up to something. But he was not leading her. He was...

...*searching,* she realized.

You sly dog, she thought. She was fully capable of guessing-him when she put her mind to it.

You're still taking the long walk, aren't you? Even though the boys are dead, and Mel's gone, and Grace is dead. Why are you still searching?

She felt betrayed. As if he had been doing something sinister behind her back. Which is exactly what he had been doing—continuing the long walk—while she had been standing still in that damned house, not knitting, forcing down potatoes.

You've been praying, you bastard—

"Ellie, I need your help with this. Those words mean a lot to me. They represented my dreams, my dreams for my children, at least until they died."

You need my help, do you?

Her fury was returning. The anger felt good. Much more comforting than mere curiosity. A better fit.

"You see, with those words, Yahweh made the covenant," he continued. "He cut the deal. A deal we're still right smack in the middle of here in Bagpipe. God spared Isaac, and substituted Jesus down the road. With a lot of crap in between, but that pretty much sums it up.

"And God made His promise to make Abraham's children like the stars in the sky. That was the prize behind Door Number One. I'm not a scripture scholar, but I do know that 'stars in the sky' means the biggest friggin' number possible. It means infinity."

"What are you driving at?" she tried to keep the resentment out of her voice.

He took a deep breath. They were almost to the pond now. He needed her help on this one. She was the smarter one, a girl with rocks in her bucket.

"Well, Ellie, I always dreamed that my boys were a legacy of those stars promised to Abraham and Isaac, and that after me, Markie and Packy would have more stars of their own. *Stars* equals my kid's kids. And their kids.

"My fatherhood dream for the boys was that hundreds of years from now, with me and Mel as a starting point, there would be millions of us; that is, if the world could last that long before Christ came back."

His tone ended plainly with: *Do you follow me?*

"I understand," she said. She sure did.

She might as well give it to him straight. Right on the chin. He was the one bringing up Job and stars in the sky.

"And so, Buzz, when your boys died, their stars died with them. And so did the legacy going all the way back to Abraham, then all the way forward to those words you heard on the jetty, which ended with Markie, Packy, and Grace in their graves, up by the house. Your second chance was a dead end."

She got it!

Buzz was overjoyed well beyond the congruity of this conversation, completely missing her clear, clean message of despair. Perhaps this was because Buzz was pondering stars while she was concentrating on the little bodies in the graves, and both of them were in between the two, near a pond, on a road in a little ghost town called Bagpipe.

It's okay. She got it, he thought.

"You understand," he whispered with awe.

Ellie Fisk understood all too well. Perhaps better than he did. With their wedding a week away.

The old yearning came back. Worse than ever. She looked at the pond, trying not to cry.

He stopped in his tracks and pulled her to himself.

"Sorry, El, I didn't mean to bring it up—"

"Yes, you did!"

She was in an awful state.

"But I didn't bring it up to hurt you—I only brought it up because I needed your help figuring it out, to figure out why God would make a promise and then not keep it—"

"But what could I possibly give to help you with all your stars in the heavens?" she spit, her voice pitching low, her eyes catching fire.

Her tone was unhinged. He was frightened by it, and by the look in her eyes.

"I'm barren. Don't you understand?" she continued, almost wailing.

"I can't have children—you bastard. All your stars are dead! Dead. They're all dead. And then you made me love you, you manipulative sonufabitch, and now we're going to get married."

He wanted to console her, but he could not think of a way on this cold, cloudy afternoon.

She was distraught; he had gone too far. He had set off the biggest land mine, blown out her legs from under her, crippling her.

He tried to pull her closer, but she clenched her fists and began to pelt him with blows—

"Shriveled up! Do you hear me? Barren, I'm as barren as a blade, you bastard."

—her little blows fell on his face, on his chest, but he didn't feel these; his heart breaking for her—

"I'm all shriveled up. Let go of me! Shriveled up. Let go of...*me!*"

She wrenched away from him, and though he could have easily kept her in his grasp, he let her go, and she fell to the snow, weeping bitterly.

"Ellie, I'm sorry—"

She continued to sob, no longer talking to him—

"Don't you get it yet, you stupid, stupid glutton? You glutton for punishment. Both of us. Gluttons for punishment. Death-death-death. Everywhere. The rocks and stones themselves are singing it!

"We sleep in coffins. We garden next to graves. We're getting married because of an ugly, meaningless death."

She buried her head in her arms, her dress falling around her like—like a mist.

She was lost, adrift in a fiery ocean of tears.

"Poor Buzz, you just don't get it," she continued, her voice muffled now, by the snow, by her closing in on herself.

She appeared to him just as she was, a fallen princess.

She was so beautiful; her entire body shaking with abject sorrow.

He felt utterly powerless. Completely at her loss. No more consolations in his pocket.

I just wanted to know the reason, he thought, dazed, trailing off, into a mist, unable to save her or himself, the despair creeping over him like a cloak, like a shadow emanating from the lifeless dirt beneath the snow.

He fell to her, her sorrow his.

He reached for her with his hands, but Ellie Fisk violently shook him away. She did not wish to be consoled. She did not want his hands.

She did not want him.

In some ways, Buzz was stronger than she was, and this weeping star was the sole light remaining in his sky. Already her brother, for better or for worse; he was going to be her husband, because God had taken everything away from him but his faith.

So he placed his hands on her shoulders—in that way of strength that could not be unclasped—and lifted her face to his, and he began to kiss her...

...and she began to kiss him back, repeating, over and over, between kisses: "Don't you see, Buzz. I'm barren. I'm shriveled up. Angels won't come to save us. There's no Mark Johnson racing to the jetty to save us this time. There's no angels. Don't you see?"

...and she continued to kiss him, her lamentations yoking her lips to his; her supple lips. A fresh yearning was here—the stirring that had begun earlier, when she had smiled...

"—there is no—"

she brought her lips to his, opening them, so soft,

"—no Mark Johnson—"

and Buzz wanted to keep kissing Ellie forever,

"—at the end of our jetty—"

tears, salt water, pliant lips joining—

Chesterton heard it first.

A sound.

The sound of something in a dull grey sky.

A sound coming out of the mist, like a son of man on a cloud.

The dog bolted back up the hill toward the master, barking wildly, leaping, bounding—

Buzz and Ellie, still embracing on the barren snow, sharing their suffering with their love, waiting on the death-edge of a jetty after taking a walk that had been so long, oh so very long—

—while the big collie kept barking, now right next to them, circling them, all three of them one hundred feet from the pond.

Chesterton's labors were not bearing fruit.

Buzz and Ellie were in their own world, on a jetty, finding the Holy One in the soul of the other…

So Chesterton jumped them.

"Hey?!" Ellie came out of it first. She did not want to stop; she wanted to keep *having Buzz,* but this damned dog—

"Chesterton!" she shouted.

She looked at her man.

Buzz was looking up at the sky.

"What is it, boy? What is it?" he asked the dog.

Chesterton barked again; the dog's voice was becoming hoarse.

Buzz sprung to his feet, and now she was looking into the sky, too, because she also heard the sound. Buzz pulled her up, and she returned to his arms, and together, they saw it.

✛ ✛ ✛

It had been so long since they had seen an airplane. But there it was, a twin engine, coming toward them, as if bursting forth from a rip-tear in the overcoat of time.

It was closer now, almost on top of them, just beyond the pond.

"Look! Ellie!" Buzz pointed.

"What?" she demanded.

"Somebody's gonna jump, see?"

And she saw it. A man poised in the doorway, holding something in his arms, something golden, fluffy…

Chesterton stopped barking; he catapulted toward the pond. It wasn't much more than a puddle.

Puddle jumper, Buzz thought disjointedly as what they were about to witness unfolded to him. He turned to Ellie to tell her—

But before he could, the plane was practically upon them, on the tops of the trees, maybe fifty feet above the ground…

…and the man jumped out, holding his golden pillow, and…

Swooosh!

The plane streaked fifteen feet above their heads…

…and the puddle-jumper landed feet-first into the pond with a splash—but Buzz and Ellie didn't see his landing because they could not pull their eyes from the airplane…

…which Buzz now noticed didn't have…

"Buzz, there's no landing wheel," Ellie told him, but he was already running away from her…

…toward the plane as it bounced on the gentle slope over the crest, the one good wheel snapping off, flipping into the air behind the aircraft.

Buzz braced for the explosion. None came. The plane touched down again—

—a wing-tip caught in the snow; the entire wing sheered off with a metallic screech, and the fuselage began a long, slow spin, and came to a halt, tipping to a rest on the remaining wing.

Buzz was loping full-speed, almost there.

Ellie spun around, and saw the man in the pond; he was swimming to shore. His ball of fluff was doing something just plain queer: it was motoring away from the man, toward Chesterton. The big collie was now in the water, too, swimming toward the puddle-jumper and his bizarre toy pillow—

She pirouetted, her long skirt whirling in the air, the now-ancient tears drying on her cheeks—

—and saw a vision.

…of man jumping out of the plane, his face covered with blood. He was huge. Bigger than Buzz.

It can't be, she thought, in the netherworld between terror and joy.

Her legs began to move, toward the plane, toward Buzz, toward…

✝ ✝ ✝

"Give me a hand!" the big man shouted at Buzz.

The giant had the doors open now. He reached into the back of the cabin, unbuckled the other passenger, who was

out cold—Buzz saw this—the passenger was facing the opposite way of the cockpit seats.

Dead, Buzz thought.

But the giant grappled the body out of the cabin anyway,
and delivered the corpse to Buzz, just as the pungent odor of
aviation fuel reached Buzz's nostrils—

"Get him clear!" the bigger man ordered.

Buzz took the command; he hefted the corpse onto his
shoulders, arms and head dangling over his back, and began
laboring back up the slope toward Ellie.

When he reached her, he carefully, but quickly, laid the
body down at her feet.

"Ellie, see what you can do with him," he instructed breathlessly.

He wheeled then charged back toward the plane.

The bloody-faced pilot had four huge duffel bags out of
the cabin—plus two rifles. He tossed a bag to Buzz, who
caught it—it must have weighed sixty pounds—and kept his
balance. Buzz immediately reversed field and ran toward Ellie.

The bigger man, three bags around his body, caught up to
Buzz in an instant, and they matched strides until they were
within a few yards of the woman, who was down with the
corpse now. She looked up as they reached her—

—and the plane blew. And Buzz dove toward Ellie, in an
effort to cover her, even as she fell onto the dead man to
cover him.

And the giant landed on Buzz.

The ground shook.

Bet Tommy Sample heard that, a thought blew into Buzz's
head...

...as little pieces of junk and shrapnel landed all around
them...

...and Buzz unsqueezed his eyes and realized that they
were plenty far enough away from the plane.

The wind was eastward, kicking up, and the black smoke
and roiling fire immediately turned away from their little pile
of humanity...

Along with Buzz, Ellie lifted her head, and together they looked back toward the pond to recognize—

—Chesterton and—*a golden puppy!*—which was no longer fluffy; it was dripping wet.

Not a pillow, Ellie thought, dreamlike. *A puppy.*

The puddle-jumper was right behind the dogs.

"Dad!" the puddle-jumper shouted, water sopping off his black pants and shirt. "You okay Dad?!"

"I'm fine, Shay," the giant said, getting to his feet, lifting his arms and legs, inspecting for injuries.

"At least I think so."

Buzz climbed to his feet.

Ellie snapped her head from the puddle-jumper to see her Buzz standing beside—

—this living mirage. An Olympian monster with blood pouring out of his temple onto his face and beard.

A booming laugh spurted from the beautiful ogre's face. He slapped Buzz on the back.

"It's great to see you, buddy," it said.

There was a sudden silence, except for the panting of the two dogs, and the crackling sounds from the burning plane.

This outlandish crew paused, looking at each other, mentally processing the impossible.

The man from the pond was not a man.

He was a tall boy. Almost as tall as Christopher had been, but with more bulk, like his ogre-father. When the boy's gaze came to rest on Buzz, recognition dawned on the boy's face. He wiped himself on his soaked pants, and thrust out his right hand.

"Hi, Uncle Buzz," Shay greeted him.

Buzz, mouth hanging open, shook the boy's hand. A strong grip.

He looked to Ellie, who was staring, blank-faced, at the bloody giant who had just dropped down from the clouds.

Fee fi fo fum, she thought oddly.

"Mark?" she asked, her voice shaky.

"Hello, Mrs. Fisk," the giant replied, leaning back, his hands on his hips, still standing next to Buzz. "If you aren't the prettiest damned thing I've seen in ages. A sight for sore eyes."

The giant looked at her hand, then spied her lonely diamond; he remembered how she had been in Buzz's arms when he first saw them from the clouds.

He turned to Buzz.

"Sam's gone. Christopher too," Buzz told him.

Buzz and the other father watched a dream die in Seamus's eyes; the boy fell to his knees and put his hands over his face.

But he did not cry because he was his father's son.

"Maggie. The girls?" Buzz asked the bigger man, foreknowing the answer.

But he had to ask; one must honor the dead.

The giant shook his head slowly.

"Mel? Your sons?" he asked.

Buzz shook his eyes.

"And a little one," Buzz stated somberly. "A girl named Grace."

The giant, smaller now, put a steady hand on his friend's shoulder. Another long walk had ended.

"Mark," Ellie breathed to herself, eyes stilled, no longer on the jetty. "Mark Johnson."

Chapter Twenty-One

A Breed Apart

They turned to the corpse.

"Sorry about your friend," Buzz told Mark, looking at the body next to Ellie.

Mark crouched down next to the body, and then grabbed the hem of Ellie's cotton dress.

"Mind?" he asked her.

She shook her head.

Mark Johnson wiped his hands and face on her skirt, then lowered his ear to the man's nose. Still looking at the man's face, Mark extended his arm to grab a canvas bag, zipped it open, and pulled out a bottle of Tabasco sauce. He spun off the top, opened the corpse's mouth with his free thumb and index finger, then shook four or five squirts onto the tongue.

The corpse coughed.

"Fadder Tony? Wake up!" he commanded.

The corpse opened his eyes. "Aacch. Hey?!"

"He's a priest," Ellie stated.

Seamus crawled over, the shivering puppy under one arm.

"Is Father gonna be okay, Dad?" he asked.

"Sure, he's okay. See that welt on his forehead? Something in the cabin must have hit him in the head during the touchdown."

"That was no *touchdown,* Dad. That was a *crash.*"

Mark fixed a look on his son. The boy sure was getting a mouth on him. The elder Johnson, deciding this wasn't such a bad thing, harrumphed in agreement.

The priest's head remained on Ellie's lap; his eyes were scrunched closed, but he was coming out of it, wincing as he reached for the bump on his forehead. He felt her warm hand on his cheek, then looked up into her almond-colored eyes.

"Ah. I am in heaven. Is Mark here?"

Ellie nodded slowly.

"Right here, Fadder," Mark said, still crouching, taking the man's wrist. "We made it."

"You're in Bagpipe, Father. I'm Buzz Woodward, and the heavenly vision is, uh, my fiancée, Ellen Fisk."

Father Anthony McAndrew's gaze darted from Buzz to Mark and then back to Ellie.

"And they got a collie, Father," Seamus added happily. "Another collie."

"His name is Chesterton," Buzz added.

"Rest your head back," Ellie offered gently.

Buzz Woodward was scrutinizing Father McAndrew, making his guesses. The priest was young—no older than thirty. His accent was pure Cleveland-native, with a twist of the east side. (Buzz correctly guessed that he grew up in Euclid.) He had a premature, receding hairline, with thin black hair, navy-cut. His face was open, but there were worry-lines etched into the outer cracks of his unfocused eyes. A goatee was making a half-hearted attempt to escape from his chin.

Probably wears glasses, Buzz thought.

"Collie? Bagpipe. Mark—did you get my glasses from the plane? And where is the plane?"

"I got the glasses," Mark said.

Buzz stepped aside to give McAndrew a view, and the priest, turning his head, squinting, followed their gazes to the smoldering wreckage down the hill. He turned to look back at Ellie for a lingering moment.

Buzz could have sworn he saw the brief flash of a chaste blush come to the priest's cheeks.

"Crashed it, eh? Help me to my feet," Father Anthony commanded.

Mark and Buzz complied.

The priest took a measured look at Buzz.

"Did you say your dog's name is Chesterton?"

Buzz nodded.

"Good name," the priest said with a squint, adding a closed-mouthed nod of approval.

Buzz felt as if he had passed a test of some sort.

"Well then, Mr. Woodward, perhaps you can name this puppy for us?"

Buzz nodded.

As if he were watching a high-speed film of the sunrise, it dawned on Buzz that perhaps Mark was not the one in charge here.

"Are you in contact with your bishop?"

The priest directed this question toward Ellie, and Buzz, honing in on the essence of the priest, noticed that the young man diverted his eyes from a direct view of her face.

"No, Father," she demurred, looking down.

McAndrew was wearing khaki pants rolled up at the cuffs, and a red-checkered, wool shirt which obviously did not suit his accountant's build. Buzz noted the black shirt beneath. The neckband was the distinctive kind needed for donning a Roman collar.

Seamus's pants? Buzz thought.

The priest was thin, perhaps three inches shorter than Seamus. The shortest soul in the group.

McAndrew stretched his shoulders as he surveyed the landscape.

As smart as the day is long, Buzz surmised. *You're the kind of guy the bishop sends to Rome to get your doctorate.*

Buzz, as usual, was correct.

"All in one piece, Fadder?" Mark asked.

"Oh, I'll be okay in a minute, Mr. Lindbergh. But my back is out again," he replied brightly, reaching behind with his hand, a pained expression on his face.

Ellie looked at Buzz. Buzz nodded.

"We can take care of that, Father," she said, breaking out into a smile, her world all right.

Father Anthony, she thought, remembering her stern entreaty to the miracle worker of Padua, Saint Anthony, on another cloudy day, over the graves of Sam and Christopher.

For once, a reminder of her two brave-hearts did not cause her stomach to constrict.

Sam and Chris would get their Requiem Mass.

Chesterton barked.

They all heard the whinny of a horse, then looked down the road. It was Tommy Sample on his sleigh-wagon, slip-sliding along the snow-pack, the concern on his face transforming into a wide smile when his eyes found Buzz's happy wave.

"Here comes Our Man Friday," Buzz observed.

"Alas, poor Yorick, I knew him well. A fellow of infinite jest," the priest quoted.

Only Buzz got the reference (Buzz briefly wished the Man were here, because he would have gotten it, too). Shakespeare. Out of context, but it fit.

Everything seemed to fit today.

This sent Buzz back in time, nine whole minutes, to the *only-you* feel of Ellie's lips on his own, the rising rouge in her cheeks, the warmth of her breath—

Buzz needed a distraction.

So he continued his guessing-game regarding the priest. An image sprung to his mind of the abandoned white-clap-board church down the road, in the center of Bagpipe, past Tommy's place, Saint Francis Xavier; and of the little house of gold within her wooden frame, begging for a wafered I-Am-Who-Am to once again take up residence therein.

Buzz saw the future. He saw the little church being torn down. He saw a stone basilica rising in its place.

It was a plain fact.

Hamlet, eh? I was wrong, Father. You're the kind of guy who becomes the bishop someday.

✝ ✝ ✝

Buzz and Ellie, Tommy, along with Mark Johnson, his son Seamus, and Father Anthony (only Mark had the authority to call him "Fadder Tony"), with no other direction to take except toward that church in Bagpipe, continued the long walk, that glorious long walk, like children on the beach hopping from stone to stone atop a jetty under a sun-drenched sky, the ocean waves a chorus to their laughter, in a universe of infinite potentials, plans, and possibilities, a universe designed by their unfathomable Creator, Who loved them.

Over hard cider with a soft kick, a bottle of Maker's Mark (from Mark's cornucopia of contraband), homemade cigars Tommy had picked up down in Errol, pure well-water for Buzz, carrot cake (for Tommy knew how to bake), and potato-pancakes smothered in butter and maple syrup (Tommy was emptying his ice-box), Mark Johnson told, with precise (often humorous) asides from the good father McAndrew, for the first time, the story of the flight from Oberlin.

The story as told at Tommy's table in his brand-new log cabin, would, of course, be retold many times in the coming years, by grandchildren and others. Future renderings would certainly be embellished as hagiography, which is the destiny of all xeroxed tales which strive to convey the tender infinitude of the Divine.

But this first telling, as with stories of the arrival of a child, had the authentic ring of pride, even bravado, which comes when recounted by the father who witnessed the inevitable suffering that precedes the baby's first breath…

Mark Johnson decided to play the cards he had been dealt. The father and son had buried the littlest sister, Megan, and mourned, joining hundreds of millions of fathers and sons (and mothers, daughters) across a darkened world of grief.

Mark reluctantly decided, despite long weeks of pondering alternatives, to make his stand in Oberlin. Following a similar line of reason as had Mrs. Ellen Fisk in Bagpipe, he realized that he had good land. Ten acres, most of it tillable with some clearing and effort.

Compared to most, he was rich.

Then Mark cast about for allies, and over the summer months, as his supplies dwindled, he went into the security business while tending his "farm," trading for seed, fashioning his own tools. Starting with his neighbors, he recruited, organized, and trained a local security detail, which grew quickly, until he was made the unofficial commander-in-chief of the surrounding towns.

The division of labor slowly returned to the local economy. One made bullets, one fashioned hoes, another churned butter from the cow of another. It fell upon Mark Johnson to be the local Charlemagne: to provide for the defense of the borders, organize the care of the widows and orphans, to give the hard orders.

Leadership is always a vital business. And it was in short supply. There were plenty of random, roving Rheumys to crush. There were only a few knowledge specialties remaining in the post-modern economy, but Mark found his niche. He knew how to use a gun, but he didn't always need bullets. His powerful voice could convince a man to lower his gun and raise his arms. That was a service much needed by the folks in the area.

As for Seamus, when he wasn't cleaning guns, he was reading books and writing stories, which he never allowed his father to read, but Mark guessed they were about Maggie and his sisters in one form or another. A way of dealing with his loss in his own way.

So he allowed the boy his writing and reading, and traded soybeans for pens, books, and paper scavenged by the cityfolk who came to town to seek profit from the remains of the old things.

A harvest came, and though there was little surplus, all surplus was used for trade. Trade begot trade, which begets additional surplus. This dynamic was being reenacted by mankind the world over; with the imperative to consume daily bread, survivors did not need to learn how to barter. It just happened, because it cannot be forgotten.

So Mark was moving on by staying put.

Until a day in November, when he heard a knock on his cabin door, which he opened to find a skinny priest holding a fuzz-puppy. The stranger introduced himself as Anthony McAndrew. He was wearing a Roman collar.

"Are you Mark Johnson?"

"Yes, and sorry, Father, we don't need a dog. Can't afford to feed it," Mark told him, not unkindly.

"I am not here to peddle this dog," the priest replied brusquely, giving Mark a familiar look.

Mark thought of it as the *You're a Dumb Jock* look.

"I am here to ask you a favor," he continued. "But first, take this animal from me; a gentleman in North Royalton tithed it to me after I said Mass for him this morning. He made the suggestion that I eat it."

Mark leaned a hand on the door frame, and investigated the young priest's emotionless face for clues and found none.

"Do you want me to, uh, cook it for you, Fadder?" he asked, feigning sincerity, playing the dumb jock.

"Do I look like a cretin?" the priest asked, dripping with sarcasm.

Mark laughed, and in the laugh, fell into that unique brand of love for which only men have a faculty; a love reserved exclusively for first encounters with other male friends.

The priest smiled wanly, then thrust the dog to Mark, who had no choice but to take it.

The stranger-friend was a priest, after all.

"Shay!" Mark called back into the cabin, turning his head. "Take this dog."

Mark turned back to look the priest in the eye, but continued to speak to his son. "You can't keep it."

Shay came running over.

The visitor took this respite to polish his wire-rimmed glasses with a handkerchief which appeared from nowhere.

"A puppie! Excellent," the boy said with the same excitement he showed whenever Mark handed him a new mystery novel.

Mark rolled his eyes.

"You'll have to give that dog a name," Father McAndrew prophesied.

"Okay. You win. Come on in. Tell your story."

Father Anthony McAndrew filled Mark in over scotch and apples. He grew up in Euclid, Ohio, and moved to Nashua, New Hampshire when he was twelve. He was ordained in Manchester and was still attached to that diocese. He was studying for his doctorate in biochemistry at Case Western University in Cleveland when the collapse stranded him. (His first doctorate, which he received in Rome, was in sacred theology.)

Biochemistry? Mark wanted to know. McAndrew was being groomed by his bishop for pastoral work in medical ethics. A law degree would follow, or that had been the plan before the Troubles.

Facing the extinction of the inner city, McAndrew became an itinerant minister of the sacraments, wandering from one neighborhood to another, eventually heading south of Cleveland, then west, before coming north again to Oberlin, at which time the surviving priest in the parish on the west side of town had directed him to Mark's little cabin.

During his travels, he had been welcomed at some places, not welcomed at others. He celebrated hundreds of funeral Masses, often two or three a day.

"The collapse is divine alchemy; it sifts gold from souls," he explained in his terse, confusing (at least to Mark), almost lyrical manner.

"So what is the favor?" Mark asked.

"Assist my return to New Hampshire."

"But Father, how—"

"The world is changing quickly, Mr. Johnson. My heart discerns the call of my bishop. Your reputation precedes you; I'm confident you will find the means."

Mark glanced over the priest's shoulder and observed his son with his newly adopted puppy. A former officer in the Navy, Mark knew when an order was being couched in terms of a request.

Yes, sir.

"Father Anthony, I have two friends who tried to walk to New Hampshire. They left in March."

God rest their souls, the big man thought.

Mark noted the quick hint of admiration—or was it fear?— that flickered across the man's eyes.

"You were in the military, no?" the priest asked.

"The Navy."

"Aviator, line officer, or submariner?"

Father McAndrew pronounced *submariner* in the British fashion.

"Aviator, Father."

This guy knows the lingo, Mark thought.

"Then procure for us an aircraft."

Mark tapped his fingers on the table.

He looked at the boy and his dog again. Mark recalled his Bagpipe pipe-dream on the day he buried his Maggie. And his phone call to Sam at the butt-end of preparing his place here. And how, when Sam gave him the cash to bribe the guy at the hospital for the nutrient bags, Sam had promised to drive Mel back to Bagpipe in a rental car.

"I don't need to look," Mark said. "We've already got one."

✠ ✠ ✠

When they arrived at the little country airport in Elyria, Mark was disappointed when he spotted Sam's plane. It was amidst a jumble of other abandoned planes, missing a wheel, bullet holes in the fuselage.

He checked both fuel tanks in the wings—empty.

Siphoned dry, no doubt, months ago.

He searched the cabin and found this note under the front seat, sealed in a ziplocked bag, in Sam's neat, cursive handwriting:

> M,
>
> Sorry about the wheel and the bullet holes.
> Remember, the worst place to hide something
> is within plain sight. No pun intended.
> Fly like a demon.
>
> S

He showed the note to the priest, who had been chatty during the hike, but had carried the heavy bag containing ammunition and Seamus's books without complaint.

Here, Mark thought, handing it over, *you're the friggin' genius.*

"You told me that Sam Fisk predicted computer malfunctions would cause the Troubles. He is a devout Catholic."

The big man nodded.

Mark imagined little flywheels turning—rapidly—inside McAndrew's head.

"The cypher is revealed in the last line," McAndrew announced after a pensive minute.

"A reference to the demonic is not Catholic in this context. Therefore every sentence in this note is a falsehood. It is obvious that your friend is playing on the pun—that is, his pun *was* intended, and what you need is within sight of the plane. Including this plane itself, which he camouflaged by making it appear worthless to ruffians by removing the wheel, discharging a firearm at an inconsequential section of the fuselage, and locating it next to these junkers."

"I need some fuel, two starter batteries, and a wheel," Mark explained, pleased.

Mark sent Seamus (rifle in hand) to the hangar to search for a battery and the wheel.

The priest looked around, slowly, carefully, standing in each of four directions for over three minutes, praying to his patron, Saint Anthony.

Mark Johnson searched with his eyes, but was also waiting for the supercomputer standing next to him.

"I expect we will find the fuel over there," the priest announced, pointing to a large pile of empty drums dumped behind the hangar. "Near the bottom of the pile."

"And the batteries?"

"I do not know."

So he's human, Mark thought, not disappointed.

It took three hours. Seamus found two serviceable car batteries beneath a stack of dead batteries in a storage room in the hangar. The Beachcraft needed two batteries, and these would do in a pinch. Mark found two full drums in the dump— just enough aviation fuel to reach Bagpipe against the wind, though the prevailing tailwinds would give them a reserve.

They never did find a wheel. Mark figured that the wheel may have been scavenged. None of the rusty wheels on the junkers fit the bill.

"So we can't take off?" the priest asked, becoming more human all the time.

"Hell yes, Fadder."

"But how?"

"I'll improvise. We're still Americans, you know."

Mark ad-libbed by attaching a heavy-duty loading cart to the plane, using a hobgobble of rope, wire, and metal strapping. He then had the good father bless the plane with holy water; each engine fired up on the first crank.

Betcha Sam had it tuned up, Mark thought.

It was a rough go on the runway; the rickety cart squealed like a pig, but they made it into the air.

When they climbed to five hundred feet, the cart fell off the plane. Mark said nothing about this, even though he spied the priest's nervous gaze following its descent. Mark returned his attention to the charts, which featured two routes to Bagpipe marked neatly by Sam's yellow highlighter.

I'm the captain of this ship, Mark laughed, wondering if he liked this priest or not.

Then he decided that it didn't matter. Buzz, if he was still alive, would like this guy, he realized.

Buzz knew all sorts of useless things.

Mark had decided early on to avoid blurring his memories of his friends with inaccuracies.

The priest was in the back seat with the boy and the puppy. After turning his gaze from the fallen cart, he pulled out his beads and asked Seamus to join him in a Rosary.

For four hours, Mark flew as low as he dared to avoid unforeseen security problems (as he still thought of them). To the unmusical hum of the two engines, Sam's plane danced over the Green Mountains after a relatively peaceful flight. The priest poked his head up into the cockpit just as Mark visually confirmed that they were passing over Colebrook—using notes describing landmarks carefully prepared for him by a man who was now dead, but was anxiously monitoring their flight from his air traffic control headquarters in the sky.

Thanks, Sam, Mark prayed, turning the airplane a few degrees northward.

Next stop, Magalloway Mountain.

"What about the missing wheel?" the priest called to Mark over the engines.

"What about it?"

"Improvise?" the priest offered with a noticeable lack of confidence.

"Roger that." Mark then called back, "Shay!"

"Yes sir?"

"Get ready to jump, son. Take the puppy. I'll find you some water."

The next thing the priest heard gave him his biggest jolt since the collapse itself, if only for reflexive ease and casualness in Seamus's voice.

"Sure thing, Dad."

A true Johnson.

A breed apart, the priest thought.

Then, directed to Mark, *You knew precisely what that note meant before you handed it to me.*

"Strap yourself in, Fadder," Mark ordered. "Time for the fun stuff."

Fun stuff?

The tables had turned, and now it was Fadder Tony who had no idea if Mark was kidding or not.

Mark checked his charts for the last time. He saw the top of Magalloway frowning at them from above the clouds.

Father Anthony McAndrew scrambled to attach his safety-belt.

The boy, armed with only a pupster, unlatched the door of the cabin, which promptly banged open as his father shaved the airspeed, letting in the frigid, screaming wind.

That there was a body of water below came as no surprise to Seamus. Then he saw a collie running away from a woman in the arms of a man.

Excellent!

Mark eased his baby out of the clouds. The two fathers looked through their respective windows and saw their first glimpse of Bagpipe.

And it grew on them.

✠ ✠ ✠

Buzz named the puppy (a pure-breed of the female persuasion from a long line of sturdy Ohio farm dogs) the day before the wedding.

He named her Lady.

Chapter Twenty-Two

Hidden Tabernacle

Nothing had changed, except the whole world.

That night, after the stories had been told about kings and days-not-old, Tommy Sample gave them a ride back to the homestead. Mark and Seamus retired immediately to Markie and Packy's room.

Boom, snoring.

The priest prayed the Divine Office in silence before the altar in the living room while Buzz and Ellie whispered their Rosary on the couch behind him.

Buzz had set up a cot in the basement office for the priest. Before retiring, Father Anthony solemnly placed his hands on their heads, invoked a blessing (in Latin), then bade them good-night.

Buzz jumped from the couch, ran to the stairway, then called down a promise to adjust the good father's back the following morning.

Buzz walked back toward Ellie, following her gaze to her hands. She was standing in front of the altar, still in her simple cotton dress, Mark's blood on the hem. She was looking down, at the ring, appearing for him and all the world like a little girl.

A candle on the altar, burning wax; throwing light.

He lifted a hand to her face, but did not touch her, wondering. She kept her gaze on the diamond. He lowered his hand.

Buzz was seeing *her*.

He was waiting for profound words to come. Words failed him, perhaps because they no longer mattered.

He was not thinking of Mel because he was a man; he was a man who lived in the present.

Because, wordless, since Grace had gone, he had accepted that Melanie would have it so for Ellie's sake. One cannot serve two masters. He needed simplicity. So he opened his mouth and let the words come out.

"Good night, sister Ellie."

She looked up now, directly into his eyes, and held him again; she had been waiting for this moment since the party at Tommy's; all during the sleigh ride, then here, during the Rosary.

Because she was a woman who falls, then rises, she fell into remembering; remembering their jetty in the ocean of snow. Remembering the stirring in her belly when this man had kissed her. Remembering when the angels came to save them.

She had loved Sam with all her heart and soul. All the way. Til death did he part. No problem there. Yet with Buzz, with Buzz on the jetty—

To have and to hold, she remembered.

Buzz was a new *having.* A different holding. Buzz gave something that Sam had not given her. Perhaps because Buzz had given her Buzz. Having carried other crosses, she accepted this one. A new fiat.

After all, she was an intelligent, practical girl.

"Can I ask you something?" she said.

"Anything."

"In all this time, why did you never offer to adjust my back? My back is not strong."

She retained his gaze. Buzz smiled as he stepped forward, closer.

"Because we're not married," he said.

"But you worked on married women during your long walk to Bagpipe," she countered deftly.

"That was different."

"But you'll give me one now, if I ask, won't you?"

"Sure, anytime," he replied.

"Why?"

They were inches apart, not touching, enjoying the ocean crashing inside. This tide was coming in fast.

"You know why," he said, waiting for the wedding.

"But I want to hear you say it. I want to hear the way you will say it. No pressure, Buzz, but I want to be surprised."

"You're starting to figure me out," he observed, seeing her, seeing her eyes, ready for anything.

"You're stalling."

"Not at all."

"Then tell me, brother Buzz, why would you give me therapy now if I asked?"

She was truly, sincerely curious.

"Because El, one day, after Grace died," he began, "I started to pray, and I couldn't find God inside me, like I told you, and I realized there was no Jesus-Eucharist on that altar right there behind you.

"So I decided to keep taking the long walk to find Him. How hard could that be? I walked to New Hampshire to find Mel. That wasn't so hard. So I kept walking, kept walking to find Him."

Buzz was a big wave, she realized, knowing—just knowing—what would come next, even though she still did not know how he would tell her.

"I got up from the altar, Ellen, and I walked into your bedroom, even though I never go into your bedroom," he began again, his words deliberate, just above a whisper, his brown eyes shining.

He was charming her, being Buzz, doing that thing he could do. For her.

"It is a sanctuary, your room, and I'm not a priest. And I saw you sleeping there. You're so pretty with your eyes closed. And I heard your heart breaking—that sound never goes away, not until Mark came today. And I felt like an idiot just looking at you sleeping in the bed. Maybe it was the beauty. Beauty can save the world.

"Then pure grace came. Then I knew. I knew where God was. He was in you, my Ellie. Right there all the time. So simple. I'm such a moron.

"Then, at that moment, I made you my tabernacle, Ellie, and I found the Holy Trinity inside you. And I worshiped Him there, and—"

He paused.

"And?" she asked.

"And I love you now. And I couldn't stop even if I wanted to. So you can have a backrub whenever you want."

She closed her eyes, and let the wave flow through her, and unaware, allowed a healing to begin—

—as Buzz reached for her hand, no longer able to keep himself from touching her.

Oh Buzz, you're my knight in shining armor.

✚ ✚ ✚

He did not give her a massage that evening; instead, a simple, chaste kiss on the hand, as he had at the safe-place on the day they were engaged. She found this courtly and chivalrous, and it made her feel like a princess.

She slept alone, for the first time in years, in their bedroom, while he slept on the couch, with the dog and his Ruger. They kept this arrangement because they were still faithful Catholics, and because it was the right thing to do. And because, wisely, he no longer trusted himself.

Also, though Ellie did not know it, Buzz had been cured on their jetty in Bagpipe, just as he had been cured of alcoholism on his jetty in New Jersey so many years ago. The particular condition that had beset him since his fall from the scaffold a year earlier had disappeared.

Miraculously cured, as a believer might diagnose. Buzz thought of it as a matter of grace. A surprise gift with the added benefit of good timing.

God is never late, he thought, echoing Mother Teresa, as he fell off into his sleep, waiting for the wedding night. *But rarely early.*

✝ ✝ ✝

It was December the fourth, a Monday in the two thousandth year of Our Lord. Just four days left until the wedding. Mark, Seamus, and Father Anthony moved into Ellie's old house, which Buzz immediately dubbed the Monastery.

The next day, Mark had Buzz give him a thorough inventory of the physical plant. He told Mark about what happened to Sam and Chris, successful in his effort to remain clinical. They hiked down to the river, and Buzz showed him the boundaries of the property. It took several hours.

"Well?" Buzz asked.

"Looks like you need better security and a hand-pump for your well."

"No shit."

"Sorry," the Naval Academy graduate said.

Mark reminded himself that Buzz was a Notre Dame man, and therefore, was practical, quick-minded, and caustic.

One hour later, Mark Johnson disappeared over the hill with Seamus, who had started Latin classes with the priest that morning. (Johnsons, ideally suited in many ways to the new realities, don't waste time.) They left with a canvas strap, two rifles, a backpack, and a bag of potatoes.

They returned with a deer, no potatoes, the rifles, the pack, and strapped to Mark's back, an enormous, heavy-duty hand-pump, including piping. Together, the load must have weighed over three hundred pounds.

"You carried that all the way?" Buzz asked.

"Of course not. Shay helped me."

Shay gave Buzz an open smile.

"Where'd you get it?"

"I didn't steal it."

"That's not what I asked," Buzz replied.

"Look Buzz, if I didn't steal it, then does it really matter?" Mark rejoined.

Buzz thought about this.

"No."

Mark was glad that Buzz was not the type to sweat the details. Mark's kind of guy.

Mark unloaded it next to the well, and wiped his brow with a sweaty hand in the chill air.

"Mark," Buzz asked. "Can I ask you for a favor?"

"Yeah, sure."

"Don't move away from here."

"Okay."

Buzz, wasting no time, walked into his house, then talked to Ellie for two minutes. He strolled out of the house twelve minutes later with two copies of a contract (post-dated five days), pen on paper, which read thus:

> I, Ellen Woodward, resident of Bagpipe, New
> Hampshire, as testified by my signature below,
> agree to give forty-five acres of land on my property,
> no less than ten of which shall include cleared,
> tillable farmland, ten acres of timberland, and a right
> of passage to Dead Diamond River Road, to Mark
> Joseph Johnson, in exchange for the delivery and
> installation of one hand-pump. Said property shall
> include the post-and-beam structure, referred to
> locally as "the Monastery." The exact dimensions
> of said property shall be determined by mutual
> agreement of both parties to this contract before
> 8 December 2001. And screw all the lawyers.

This was followed by Ellie's signature, and the signature of one witness, the Reverend Anthony T. McAndrew, IV.

"That last line was my idea," Buzz said proudly.

"Why forty-five acres?"

"Isn't that how old you are?"

"I'm forty-six now."

Buzz shrugged his shoulders, then turned around and bent his back.

"Shay-Shay, give me a hand here," Buzz asked the boy.

The boy came and placed one of the contracts on Buzz's back, holding it in place for his father.

Mark, never one to sweat the small stuff, took a deep breath, prayed one Our Father, then signed the documents, handing his copy to Shay.

"Go ahead and put this in our new house, son—in with the birth certificates."

"Yes sir."

The kid ran off.

✚ ✚ ✚

It did not snow on December the eighth. They were able to take Tommy's sleigh all the way to Colebrook.

Ten minutes before the Nuptial Mass, Buzz Woodward approached the wrinkled, wiry French priest in the sacristy of the plain, large, wood-hewn church at the Shrine of Our Lady of Grace. Father Anthony was already robed, ready to concelebrate, and preparing for his duties by praying on a kneeler before a crucifix off to the right of Buzz and the Frenchman.

"Ellen Fisk and I have decided we want to drop the whole, uh, brother-sister thing," he stated baldly, though in a whisper.

The old Frenchman, familiar with the second part of the story of the parents of Saint Thérèse of Lisieux, nodded politely.

"Are you both certain?" he asked the groom.

"Yes."

"You have my blessing."

This development gave the priest a spiritual boost.

It is always uplifting to have one of your prayers answered.

✧ ✧ ✧

Ellie wore the same wedding dress she had worn for Sam, along with her favorite diamond earrings. Seamus had brushed her hair in the morning as she sat before the mirror in the bedroom. She did not have the veil from her first wedding, so she put her hair into an elegant pony tail (or at least, as Seamus thought, it looked pretty classy).

Finding Buzz a suit of clothes proved troublesome. Nothing they owned fit, including his one cruddy suit from before the Troubles. In true North Country style, not sweating the details, he wore a carefully pressed pair of khakis and a woolen, red-checkered shirt over a white T-shirt (they had used precious bleach to make it bright), his shoes, cordovan wingtips, shined to perfection by one Mark Johnson, the newest homeowner in the town of Bagpipe, New Hampshire.

Tommy Sample was the best man. Shay, passing the ultimate test of filial obedience, stood in as the maid of honor.

Before the sacrament:

"Good luck, Uncle Buzz."

"This is one of the happiest days of my life," said Tommy.

"Hey buddy," Mark said. "You look like crap. Good strategy. Make the bride look better."

"Thanks, Mark. I knew you would understand."

Both men had grown up in New Jersey.

✧ ✧ ✧

To begin the Nuptial Mass, Mark gave the bride away. Buzz and Ellie looked directly into each other's eyes as often as possible, nailed their vows like two marksmen shooting skeet, then received Holy Communion with understated reverence.

Aiming to finish strong, in accord with his unique vitality, the groom kissed his bride for a prolonged period of time, while achieving his secondary objective of turning the Right Reverend Anthony T. McAndrew three shades of red.

Grace Kelly, eat your heart out, thought Ellie, on the arm of her king, when they threw the rice.

By the new standards, it was an expensive wedding—six gold coins, including the cost of the rental hall. It was not attended by many, though Tommy did his best to invite some of his trading partners from Errol, the Notch, Colebrook, and Pittsburg. Tommy's cousins from West Stewartstown, Harris and Cordelia Maye Sample, attended. The main course consisted of roast beef sandwiches because Ellie had decided at the last minute to go all out.

"Kill the fatted calf. Bring it on," she had ordered.

Tommy Sample, who *had* definitely planned for this wedding, unveiled his most ingenious wedding gift (in addition to the one milk cow) during the reception. A wind-up Victrola he found, along with some old 78s, in the attic of the abandoned ranch he fled to when the bad guys had come.

As Tommy watched Buzz and Ellie Woodward waltz, he judged their sublime perfection worth the cost of his parent's rickety old house.

Except for Father McAndrew (who, an excellent waltzer, having been forced to take years of dance lessons by his parents, was offering it up), the men and the boy took numerous turns dancing with the ravishing Mrs. Woodward, including the old priest, who was almost as good a waltzer as her husband, by her reckoning, and much better at the jitterbug.

Mark allowed Seamus to drink homemade beer, but only after testing six large steins to ascertain the purity of the local brew, a robust little barley number called Bear Rock Wolfbrau. Its bouquet contained a slight hint of potato.

The newlyweds' song was O Danny Boy—because it was the only song Mark Johnson knew by heart—and he rendered it sweetly in his halting tenor, accompanied by Seamus James Johnson.

Buzz began to cry, his dulcet bride in his arms, as they swayed to the Irish standard.

"What is it, Buzz?" Ellie asked, lifting a hand to his face, wiping a tear with her thumb.

"Reminds me of Tim Penny, that's all. The parties. Opus Dei Bill. Hal, all of them. All our friends from the old life. I still miss them. Mel, too. Mel most of all. I fell in love with Mel on Tim and Marie's porch."

They stopped moving, and she hugged her husband, whispering into his ear like a good wife.

Ellie remembered her best friend, Mel, and how Buzz was all she had left of the red elfin terror, and she was glad he wasn't letting the cross become too far removed from the day's resurrection.

✝ ✝ ✝

Like all good weddings, the hour grew nigh, and the Woodwards retreated to the honeymoon suite below the crest of the Henderson Swell, on Dead Diamond River Road, in the town of Bagpipe, New Hampshire.

✝ ✝ ✝

Buzz carefully unbuttoned his red shirt, then placed it on the virgin sheets of the bed, all the while looking at her across the room. He was still wearing his khakis and the white undershirt.

Every day is a long walk, he thought, his mellowness mixing with a warm kindling.

He was seeing her, facing away from him, standing on the other side of the room, by the dresser, still wearing her wedding gown, her blond hair glistening in the candlelight as she lowered her neck, then reached up fluently to pull her locks free from their bonds. The earrings sparkled, then disappeared beneath her golden tress. She left one hand on her shoulder, waiting.

He cleared his mind.

He prayed one Hail Mary.

He knew Ellen was waiting for him.

She was waiting for him to take the first step.

He was waiting for himself, too, partly because he had a habit of not hurrying, a habit beaten into him during the long walk to Bagpipe. In a world without time, there was no need to rush—at least not after the potatoes were in the root cellar.

He was nervous, too, and she was the most beautiful girl ever, newborn, as all brides are.

He thanked God for this perfect diamond.

The feel of his hand on the back of her satin dress during the waltzes had been different today than at Sam's wedding. The dress had been looser this time, not as tight on his fingertips. This detail didn't really matter, except that he was Buzz, and he could not help knowing these details.

He took the first step; then another.

Then he was there, and she turned her head, her shoulders, but did not turn around, and he moved closer, enveloping her with his arms, and they kissed each other the way a brother and sister never kiss, lingering.

Not hurrying.

The new stirring was here to consume them. They could tell, and it was a relief—a gift. Mark had pulled them off the jetty and carried them to this warm sand.

However, the old yearning was there, too.

She pulled her sweet head away, her eyes closed, but still wrapping tight her arms over his arms, as he stood behind her.

Knowing, he moved an open hand onto her womb, and his other onto her ribs.

"I'm barren," was all she whispered.

He knew exactly what to say, trusting the flush on her face more than her words.

As she knew he would.

"Not to me," he replied, oh so gently, in a whisper from his soul. "You are my house of gold. A Trinity within. So take the walk with me. Be mine, Ellie."

A practiced husband, he waited.

An experienced, practical woman, she took the yearning from her shoulders, and placed it upon his. He was a big, strong man, tough as they come, she knew, in love with heavy plows.

It was okay.

Eyes still closed, Ellie drew her lips to her lover's, and allowed a warm wave to wash into shore.

After a time, still standing, to complete the sacrament, she allowed him to unbutton the satin pearls on the back of her gown.

Hands shaking, he drew her golden mane to one shoulder, then lightly, gently kissed her neck three times in a melody of silence, then pulled the white curtain from her; he beheld the cream-colored skin of her shoulders, her back, then washed his fingertips upon this warm coast with a tender, refreshing wave, until she shuddered, eyes closed.

Anticipating tidal flows.

She turned completely, a word, wordless. No longer waiting, prepared for the consummation of grace.

She received the totality of his hands next, then more of him, as he discovered the rest of her, according to the perfection of a divine plan.

✝ ✝ ✝

The two-thousandth and first year of Our Lord came, but the lights stayed on this time. It's mighty difficult to blow out lanterns and candles all at once, much less the sun—that great-big-clock—which still burned beyond the blow of men.

Apparently, some never learned, for in the south, where there were still wars and rumors of wars, even after the fall of the Tower of Silicon-Babylon, men were attempting to bring back the electricity.

Not in Bagpipe.

✝ ✝ ✝

In January, a hand-carried letter arrived from the new bishop of Manchester (his predecessor, who had stayed in the city with his flock, did not survive the Troubles).

Father Anthony McAndrew's humble request to be assigned to Saint Francis Xavier parish was officially approved, under the conditions that he also serve the mission church in Errol, and the old Frenchman in Colebrook, if asked.

✝ ✝ ✝

In February, while his wife was at the Monastery teaching Seamus math, Buzz descended into their basement with a hammer and a drywall knife.

Behind a picture of Saint Anthony in his office, after a little pounding and sawing, he took out a box and a container.

He got the eggs from Tommy, and the milk from Old Bessy (he just couldn't help himself when it came to naming that blessed cow). He baked it at the Monastery after she came back to the house.

Later that evening, he presented her with a Duncan Hines chocolate cake covered with premium honest-to-goodness double-chocolate frosting from the best source for frosting in the history of mankind—some long-since-defunct factory back in the butt-end of the twentieth century.

"Happy Birthday!" he shouted.

Mark, Shay, Tommy, and the priest busted up from the basement, hollering manly, gleeful shouts. That stupid song began, all tenors and bass.

She broke down and cried, right there at the table.

"Buzz, you bastard," she moaned, hiding her face in her forearms.

Frowns all-around.

"Men—everywhere!" she cried. "We need more women on the swell or I'm going to lose my mind."

She lifted her head from her arms, eyes burning, daring them to look her in the eye.

No takers. They were all getting to know her well. Her three wise guys and a boy.

"But Honey, I don't understand—"

"Buzz, I'm forty, you idiot!"

Women, each man thought in unison.

✤ ✤ ✤

Buzz and Tommy started to go down to Errol once a week to begin establishing a center for chiropractic medicine. Mark built him his first treatment table. Doctor Woodward took chickens, Zippos, venison, silver, candles, sewing needles, rock'n roll albums, paper, gold fillings—all sorts of valuable things, as payment.

He will be a healer, the old nun had prophesied about him in Blackstone, in a much darker world, a world where lights like Sister Emmanuel had shone brightest. These healings he gave, like the one the nun had given him, filled Buzz with hope.

Ellie and his friends got freebies, of course. Buzz adjusted her back in the mornings, and then gave her a massage every evening, after praying the Rosary or after the marital sacrament (whichever came first), except on Sundays, when she gave him a massage.

She was a quick study. Her fingers were not strong enough yet, but when it came time to pound with her fists, she was first rate. First rate.

He treated her in silence, as was her preference. As he placed his hands on her shoulders, then her back, he prayed. She was a house of gold, and he adored the Trinity within.

✝ ✝ ✝

During the winter, at daily Mass, they prayed for God's protection against the killer flus, which were still taking their deadly tolls in the towns, although not as severely. Perhaps those with natural immunities were now in the majority; the local economies were coming back, so there was food again (and fewer mouths to feed, Ellie often thought sadly).

One afternoon, on the Ides of March, before spring came, Tommy Sample picked up his cousin from West Stewartstown, Harris Sample, and brought him up to the swell. Seems Harris's lower back was in an awful mess—he could barely walk—and Buzz was happy to give him an adjustment. Three days later, Tommy received word that all three Sample boys had come down with the flu the day after Harris's treatment.

Two days later, Ellie Woodward began to vomit in the mornings. She sustained a mild temperature.

They prepared for the worst, and took her west to Colebrook to see the doctor there. Now a few crude medicinal powders and herbal medicines were being used, with middling success, and there was a pocketful of ordinary hope for a recovery.

Ellie and Buzz had thought themselves immune. Perhaps this was a new strain, and she could fight it off. She knew how to fight.

Buzz and Mark went to the shrine to pray before the life-size, lovely white statue of Our Lady of Grace while Tommy walked Ellie to the former motel across the way, where a medical center on State Route 3 had been founded by a husband-and-wife doctor team—an excellent location for serving the constant stream of wayfarers coming into Colebrook for trade and to make pilgrimage to the shrine.

Mark and Buzz knelt down before the statue.

It was a bright, chilly day with no wind. Buzz saw no flowers growing on the grounds of the shrine. But they would be poking out soon.

"You okay, buddy?" Mark asked, taking out his beads.

"I'm fine," said Buzz.

"You sure?" Mark asked, skeptical.

His friend with the crewcut was a facile actor—like all New Jersey boys. Mark remembered losing his Maggie; he made the sign of the cross as his own, old wound opened up a little.

Probably eating him up inside, Mark thought, looking to Mary Immaculate. *They've been through hell, Mary. Let's give Buzz and Ellie a pass on this one—*

"Mark, just cut the crap and pray your Rosary," Buzz interrupted. "There's a reason for everything. We just don't know it. You're the one who's always telling me not to sweat the small stuff. Well I'm telling you right now: don't sweat the big stuff, either."

Talking in riddles, Mark thought.

But then, Buzz was a riddle, so Mark took him at his word—or they would never get this Rosary started.

Mark's skepticism was baseless. For Buzz, it was okay, it truly was.

If Buzz could find the Holy Trinity in Ellie, then he could find the Trinity everywhere, even at death's door, alone in the pines in the shadow of Magalloway Mountain, or in the face of a dying saint named Hal. In the lifeless body of a baby named Grace. Even there. God was in there somewhere; even in Buzz's scarred soul. In every body's soul.

Simple.

It was time for Buzz to cut it down, this death-threat to his Ellie. Because he was who he was, and had been where he had been, hand to the plow, and had swung a bad axe his whole life.

If Ellie dies, Lord, that's okay. Thy will be done.

Buzz Woodward prayed in his usual way, without much feeling, but with boatloads of faith, like a little kid with a broadsword on a beach, cutting down sand-dragons next to a jetty in the summer rain.

*It's okay. It's okay if Ellie dies. I have no claim on her. I
wasn't at the foundations of the world. I was in New Jersey.
I'll offer Ellie back to you, Mary.*

*So bring it on. Thanks for letting me have her for such a
long walk. Amen.*

Like a little boy, he added a few things.

*Oh yeah, Ellie's the best. I love her. Just give me a chance,
and I'll walk around the world for her. Twice. For as many
miles as the stars in the heavens I'll walk for my Ellie. Just
for one smile, for just one look in her eyes, 'cause she's my
house of—*

"Buzz."

"Yeah Mark."

"Let's start the Rosary."

"Sorry, man. Yeah right. Let's go. I'm ready."

And he was ready. Ready for anything.

Even nonsense like stars in the heavens.

The two Catholics began praying the Rosary out loud.
Before they reached the second decade, they heard her shouts.

The two big men turned, jumped up.

There she was, racing across the roadway, shouting wildly,
her sweet golden hair aglimmer in the sun.

She was smiling hugely, calling his name.

"Buzz! My Buzz!"

Full of grace. Full of life.

"You see," Buzz said, elbowing his friend. "I told you we
had nothing to worry about."

"She sure seems happy—" Mark observed.

—but Buzz Woodward didn't hear him, because Buzz had
guessed-her, and now Buzz knew the truth, the reason, and
the reality, and was loping away from Mark, sprinting into
another long journey—

Buzz knew the beautiful, lovely, warm, sweet, happy, wonderful truth about her, so he ran and shouted inside, losing
track of everything else around them—

My Ellie! My beautiful Ellie!

Buzz and Ellie collided right in front of the Little Flower's statue, and joined in a long, luxurious kiss, then kissed each other all over their cheeks, their eyes, their joyful tears, his hand cupping her face, her arms around his thick neck.

He lifted her like she was a little girl, and spun her around time and again, as Mark walked toward them, completely baffled.

"So you know!" she shouted, laughing between kisses, waltzing with his lips.

"You're my house of gold!" he cried out, tears streaming down his cheeks. "The old nun told me! She told me!"

These lovers, still in each other's arms, fell to the ground, next to an early rose sprouting from fertile earth, a rose delivered by the littlest saint in heaven—the Man's saint—and both saints were smiling upon their two friends in the embrace, still kissing, still bubbling meaningless words of joy, intoxicated with the glory of it all.

"Oh thank you, Lord," Ellie shouted to the skies, believing in stars. "Oh, Buzz, you're my knight in shining armor!"

Another long kiss. Like two kids gorging on one luscious piece of chocolate.

"What's all the fuss about?" Mark Johnson asked.

They stopped kissing because Mark had a voice that stopped things.

They didn't mind. His voice couldn't stop this long walk. No way.

She shook the stars from her head, then turned to look up at the one who had come to them on the jetty. A soul who had been part of the reason-for-it-all. Her happiness, bursting with generosity, focused on this wonderful giant above her.

Oh thank you, Mark. Thank you for saving my wonderful Buzz! For saving me!

Ellie caught her breath, then sat up.

Buzz pulled up on one arm, and instantly reached for her hair and pulled the thin strands over her ear, because he had to see his princess's enchanting face; he had to drink in every detail of the miracle.

"You tell him, El," Buzz said softly, unable to take his eyes from his most beautiful wife.

Mark stood above them, waiting, without the gift of guessing.

She sighed, and closed her eyes, smiling perfectly, and carefully formed her words inside, and Buzz saw all of this, and it was good.

Ellie Woodward opened her eyes again.

"I'm pregnant, Mark. Buzz and I are going to have—*a baby!*"

EPILOGUE

A Heavenful of Stars

The cross is the symbol of absolutely endless expansion.
It is never content. It points for ever and ever
to four indefinitely receding points.
Monsignor Robert Hugh Benson

Anyone can see the road that they walk on
is paved with gold;
It's always summer, they'll never get cold.
You can see their shadows wandering off somewhere,
they wanted the highway, they're happier there, today.
Fastball, **The Way**

Love me, love my dog.
Saint Bernard

If I had a thousand lives
I would take a thousand wives
And each my soul to keep
G.K. MacBrien

The Lord appeared to Isaac and said, "Do not go down to
Egypt; live in the land where I tell you to live...
for to you and your descendants I will give all these lands
and will fulfill the oath I swore to your father Abraham:
I will make your descendants as numerous as
the stars in the heavens."
Genesis 26:2-4

Ellie Loves Buzz

Ellie loved Buzz, and she bore him a son.

The story of how this son came to be was just told.

Buzz asked Ellie to choose the child's name. She named him Isaac Samuel. Buzz called him Zack, and so did his wife. He grew strong and true.

Zack Woodward had blond hair like his mother, and round shoulders and sleepy eyes like his father. He became a potato farmer when he inherited his godfather's farm, the Sample place, where he raised four sons and three daughters with his wife, Thérèse (who grew up in Columbia, New Hampshire, just south of Colebrook, and she fell in love with Zack during the Voices of Spring waltz at a wedding).

Zack Woodward was partial to cows and crewcuts, and often gave Thérèse earrings, some with diamonds, and some with pearls, all with gold.

Buzz loved Ellie, and fourteen months after Zack's birth, she bore another child. Another boy.

Zack's brother was named Hal by mutual consent of his parents. During the first week of his life, Hal was nicknamed Mel by his father above the protests of Ellen Woodward, his mother. (The nickname made sense to Buzz, and Buzz alone, and fortunately, it did not stick.)

Hal Woodward became a priest when he grew up, and in fact, was ordained by the bishop of the diocese of Manchester, His Excellency Anthony T. McAndrew. Hal was known as a priest who would play pick-up basketball at the request of any child, young or old, and he was nicknamed the Man on the courts one day.

This nickname stuck.

Hal was the best point guard in the history of the Bagpipe pick-up courts behind Norbert's diner. A man of few words, Hal adopted thousands of souls into the Woodward line through the administration of the sacraments.

After persistent effort in a private sanctuary by mutual consent of both parents, Ellie conceived, and presented a third child to Buzz three years after Hal was born.

The child was named by her mother.

Her parents christened her Rebekah Mary, and her father nicknamed her Becky because he thought it sounded like an excellent name for a farm girl.

Becky married a very tall, handsome widower with bushy auburn hair named Seamus Johnson, although he was fourteen years her senior. Seamus's first wife had been taken by the flu. Shay was a workaday writer, and his novels chronicled the events of the dark years. Becky Johnson bore Seamus twelve children (two of whom died in miscarriages); these twelve joined his two daughters from his first marriage.

All of their children, including the daughters, were excellent hunters.

One daughter became a Poor Clare.

One son became a priest.

The other ten married, and among them, had seventy-two grandchildren, sixty-three of whom managed to get married. These sixty-three souls in the Trinitarian explosion that was the Shay-Becky union, after a lovely multiplication of waltzes on wedding beaches with seventy-one spouses (including second marriages), added a healthy five hundred and seven bright-shining stars to the Woodward/Johnson skies.

Every single star an immortal wonder.

Many souls in the Woodward-Loves-Johnson miracle soup, by this time, had left Bagpipe because of an itch to get walking. Even so, these folks comprised the generation which built the splendid stone church in downtown Bagpipe.

A century after Ellie's soul departed from her body, there were thousands of stars in the Woodward and Fisk heavens, including the first bright novas, Christopher, Markie, Packy, and Grace—just about all of them swinging bad axes, donning Miraculous Medals, praying to Saint Anthony, and, whenever possible, in the great Woodward tradition, getting back up whenever they fell down, because it's only pain, darlin', and there's a lot of walking to do on the road to the day of glory.

And they were smart, dammit—like Ellie.

And things were just getting warmed up.

✢ ✢ ✢

An antichrist came. The details are chronicled in other histories by far more talented storytellers.

This particular tin-pot antichrist overlooked backwaters such as Bagpipe, distracted as he was by his relentless focus on destroying Rome. As foretold, he failed, and his minions were vanquished—because of his pride in thinking that all he needed to do was control the wills of the weak.

Woodwards and Johnsons fell bodily in the wars, but not for lack of effort or willingness to fight. Their souls rose into pure light, which they accepted as the reality of the situation, keeping with the honorable family tradition.

When the histories were written, it became known that the stars from Bagpipe were particularly adept at making a pain in the ass of themselves for the bad guys. There were common threads. Something about being persistent. Spouting riddles. Praying Rosaries all the time. Getting married at the drop of a hat or on the top of a grave, as well as siring well-mannered children willing to jump out of planes while holding puppies.

Eating squirrels if need be. Always buying shoes with thick treads and real, honest-to-goodness stitching because you never knew when the call would come to start walking.

In other words, they were Catholics.

After the worldly empires fell, as they always do, nothing much was left of value except, of course, for the humans themselves, and the body of those who together constituted what has been called the Mystical Body of Christ, rebuilt the Holy Catholic Church on the charred remains, using flesh for brick, and blood for mortar.

✠ ✠ ✠

Rheumy, realizing that his father had been a sadistic drunkard who had distorted his son's sense of reality, figured that Buzz was only giving him what he deserved after a lifetime of shacking up with evil, asked God for mercy while clamped between Buzz's vice-like arms, during his minute of glory.

And, as Rheumy Marks was promised, he received mercy, and was welcomed into the house of gold forever, eventually, after a period of, ahem, *cleansing,* in fire. (Rheumy also chose mercy because, for one thing, he believed Buzz, and, for another, he wanted to continue their interesting conversations.)

✠ ✠ ✠

On a day of his own choosing, Buzz Woodward, feeling strong, with the deviousness only a New Jersey-born Notre Dame man could muster, after lying in wait for over two years, challenged Mark Johnson to a rematch of a wrestling contest that had first taken place in Mark's backyard in the town of Rocky River, Ohio, in the late 1980s. Buzz, a seasoned observer of important detail, had watched Mark's bum knee grow weaker, and the hairs on the older man's head fall to grey.

At stake: one of the female pupsters from the first litter which issued forth from the decidedly Catholic marriage of Chesterton and Lady. All Buzz needed to do was prevent Mark Johnson from pinning him for a duration of three minutes.

Piece of cake, thought Buzz.

Mark decided to pin Buzz at just over one minute (instead of thirty seconds, as he could have easily managed—

but only because he was getting soft in his old age, and, did not want to embarrass Buzz too badly in front of his wife Ellie, whom Mark adored).

A breed apart, Father Anthony concluded as he watched the debacle unfold.

Ellie, a smart and practical girl, bet against her husband, and won back the Saint Joseph statue Buzz had lost a year earlier to Mark when Buzz challenged him to a game of Scrabble.

Mark named the female dog Gwynne.

✚ ✚ ✚

Many in the Woodward line became chiropractors. Others grew potatoes. Some became adept at carving statues of Saint Joseph. Three won Olympic gold medals running the marathon (the last won the gold eight years after winning a bronze).

One, by the name of Patrick, climbed every mountain over an elevation of three thousand feet in the state of New Hampshire (this took an entire decade because he was in a hurry). Some died of the flu. Others fell on the bloody field of warfare. Writers, dancers, horsemen, drivers, accountants—even guys who milked cows and made a few bucks on the margin, just like Tommy Sample.

There were plenty of things to do on the long walk, including answering the supernatural call to religious life.

Two hundred years from the beginning of the Ellie-Loves-Buzz line (which, if one is keeping track, goes back to a guy named Abraham on a mountain in the old country), there were three hundred and fifty-seven women who took final vows, forty-seven of whom became Poor Clares.

There were over two hundred priests, the majority of them diocesan. Ten abbots. Fifteen Trappists. A handful of bishops. Only one cardinal. Lots of workaday parish saints. Some went to hell when they died, because they threw their gift to the three carrion birds of evil: the devil, the world, and the flesh.

Three founded new religious congregations, which still exist. One of the new congregations consisted of pairs of itinerant priests who traveled on assignments for two years to lands with mountains and jungles and deserts and seas while two brother priests spent their off-road rotation in prayer before the monstrance, interceding for the two walkers.

These intrepid priests administered sacraments to wayfarers, and, according to their zeal and God's grace, found the Holy Trinity within souls encountered on the road, even the Rheumys of the world.

The founder, besides being a persistent fellow, had the genius (known to believers as a *charism*) to institutionalize the basic principles of Buzz-Loves-Ellie under the roof of a House designed by a perfect Architect.

There was even one priest in the Woodward line who became—well, let's not get ahead of ourselves. There is no need to rush during the long walk to the house of gold.

✜ ✜ ✜

Twelve years after his historic flight to Bagpipe, when the traveling became safer and more reliable, Mark Johnson went with his son Seamus to Oberlin. Mark then returned to New Hampshire with the remains of his wife and two of his daughters. He did not spit on the ground in Oberlin before he left, but he was tempted; he held his temper because he knew that most of its surviving residents were not witches and warlocks.

He buried his Maggie, Angela, and Megan on the homestead next to Buzz and Ellie's saints.

Mark Johnson learned the fate of his daughter who had lived in California when he received his day of glory, in the state of grace, at the age of eighty-four, on the field of battle, kneeling before the Holy Eucharist, all caught up in a vision which contained three crosses, the Virgin, the Innocent Victim, a son named John, and one Roman centurion who accepted the reality of the situation.

✛ ✛ ✛

During his walk on earth, Buzz never learned the fate of his daughter, Jennifer, who remained a fallen-away Catholic until the second she died. Fortunately, in the infinity of that final second (for there really is no such thing as time), she prayed,

I love you, Daddy.

Her prayer, freely chosen in the mystery of grace, was the fruit of persistence merited by thousands of Rosaries and Holy Communions by Buzz and his friends.

It has not been revealed whether Jennifer Woodward was referring to her father, Buzz, or to God the Father, on her day of glory. It went around heaven, however, in certain tight circles within the Beatific Vision, that a Poor Clare nun by the name of Regina interceded for Jennifer during that pivotal eternal second, and with the help of Immaculate Mary, convinced the Big Guy that Jennifer was not referring to Buzz.

And so Jennifer entered the House of Gold, and was able to greet her dad when he arrived. (Parts of the above story were translated from the language of divine reality into English so people on earth could vaguely comprehend it.)

✛ ✛ ✛

The number-three bestseller on the Free Nation of New Hampshire list, as published by the Manchester Union Leader, May 12th, 2017:

The Man, by Seamus J. Johnson

Shay thanked his Uncle Buzz in the preface for the material. It was a history book, without a whiff of hagiography, in accord with the wishes of its subject.

Late in the year, four rotations of the earth around the sun after he walked to Bagpipe, Buzz went down to the storage room in his basement with a hammer and a drywall saw, and emerged with a small velvet bag he found behind the wall, along with two bottles of Maker's Mark.

He gave the bottles of golden liquid to his neighbor, Mark Joseph Johnson, of the Bagpipe Johnsons, to facilitate the celebration of Mark's fiftieth birthday.

When Mr. Buzz Woodward presented the pearl earrings from the velvet pouch to his wife Ellie for her forty-fifth birthday, she broke into tears, but they were tears of happiness. Ellie was wearing Mel's earrings on the day she died, many years later.

✥ ✥ ✥

Buzz's great-great-great grandson, William "Opus Dei Bill" Woodward, was ordained a priest, but only after he finally grew up (prolonged adolescence being one of the lesser Woodward traditions rarely mentioned, but roundly demonstrated, after O Danny Boy has been sung at parties on the porch during summer evenings).

Fadder Bill was eventually, after many, many years of mortification, work, and prayer, assigned to be the bishop of the Prelature.

✥ ✥ ✥

Many generations after Buzz and Ellie Woodward's long walk began, most of the children born into their line were taught how to waltz at an early age by their parents. Many had a natural gift for this particularly beautiful expression of human love. The art of waltzing was considered a must—

for the weddings.

For the weddings!

Stocked with big, strong, tall players from the Woodward/
Johnson line, a varsity basketball team from the towns of
Pittsburg, Colebrook, Bagpipe, or Errol won the New Hampshire schoolboy championship eight out of ten years during
the decade between 2040 and 2050. During this decade, the
high school football team from Bagpipe won the championship *every* year.

The generations of pup-stars which were born through
the union of Chesterton and Lady rivaled the sands on the
beach. The pedigree of this line of collie was highly valued
by farmers who appreciated big, smart sheepdogs with excellent hearing.

Chesterton's line spread throughout New Hampshire, then
to Maine and Vermont, even back to Scotland, as the years
progressed.

One of Chesterton's pups, by the name of Belloc, at the
age of one, broke his leash and ran off one day, heading north
past Magalloway Mountain, following a black man who was
singing a hymn—until, weeks later, he reached a little town
in Quebec called Saint-Pascal, where Belloc met a lonely little
boy, fishing for trout by a stream, by the name of Yves, who
liked to pray the Rosary.

Yves named him Grand Stephan.

Summer. Ellie was completely gray now, still thin, fighting hard to keep her shoulders back, her chin up, and winning the battle. (It helped if your husband was a chiropractor
and if you enjoyed a good fight.)

She remained the most beautiful woman in Bagpipe to the men and boys who gazed upon her with the eyes of the soul.

She was on her porch, the Sam/Chris altar. Mark had retired for the evening. She was knitting one hell of a sweater.

"El?"

"Yes, Buzz."

"Did you ever wonder about cool?"

"What on earth are you talking about?" she asked.

"Cool. Like those cool kids in high school. Like Snoopy. You know, Joe Cool."

He hummed a bar from the song, then, sang:

"Hangin' by the water fountain…"

She pressed her lips together and rolled her eyes.

"Didn't you tell me about this once before, about twenty years ago?" she asked.

"Maybe. You have a better memory."

He rubbed his crewcut—what was left of it. He jumped up from the rocker, winced, then stretched his arms into the air.

The bad ankle was killing him, she could just tell. Even so, the way he stretched: he still had that Buzz *stuff* that got her going.

If I could only bottle it, she thought. *I could make a fortune.*

"So tell me about cool again," Ellie said, sounding for all the world like a little girl, not yet weary of his surprises.

You already did bottle him, her most-trusted voice told her. *The names on the bottles are Zack, Hal, and Becky.*

"Cool is a great word because it describes an indescribable thing," he began. "I mean, did you ever notice that the truly cool person never talks about being cool. And if he knows he's cool, it's not cool. There's a kind of coolness about that."

"You are baffling me beyond words," she told him.

As usual, they thought together.

"Yeah. I guess so. It's just that I was never cool."

"That's cool," she said with a straight face, hiding a smile.

"Ha ha."

A silence ensued.

Sweaters.

Buzz scratched a few lines on his notepad for the kid. Seamus had been bugging Buzz for notes for another book. (Buzz still thought of Seamus, who was past pushing forty, as a kid.) He put the pad down. Looked at Magalloway.

Buzz and Ellie pondered cool.

All her life, Ellie had been the blonde with a hard edge. Even now, except for this man who had taken her on the marriage bed (melted her with his hands), most found her aloof—cold. A bit bossy at times. Very bossy at other times.

I'm too cold to be cool, she thought happily, without a hint of apology.

It was a given that Buzz was not cool. A plain fact, which he accepted.

Still, there was something…

Then, as often happens with lovers who have paid attention the whole time during the marriage, a gentle image came to Buzz and Ellie at the same time, like a silken breeze.

They knew what cool was.

Cool was how it left the hand—the basketball—left the hand so smoothly…

"The Man was cool," Ellie whispered.

✛ ✛ ✛

Becky was seven, pretty. Her mother came in from the garden, holding a white rose, and saw that Buzz was teaching his daughter how to waltz.

✛ ✛ ✛

He was an old man. This year, as he had done every year, on the anniversary of Mel's death, and on the anniversary of her birth, Buzz hiked up along the stream to the safe place.

He had outlived his friend, the blonde, and was glad of it, for her sake, because he had not wanted Ellie to have to bury him.

It was okay; every spring he saw Ellie in the buds of grass, in the cold snow. He heard her sweet voice in the sound of a stream of water—in any beautiful thing.

The safe place. A band of gold. This is where he kept the wedding ring Mel (and only Mel) had put on his finger. The location of the ring was known only to him (he kept it in a *safe place* in the safe-place).

He placed the golden lasso he had used to snare the tiny sprite onto his gnarled finger.

The old man sat on a stone and waited. He began with the same image. Mel's skin glistening, in the hotel, light streaming in, on the wedding night. Her hair. She was on the bed, turning, turning to look at him…

"Buzz," she whispered.

Eyes closed, he saw Melanie, and he cried softly, his face in his hands, yearning.

The red-elfin wonder always came, always in his tears. Sometimes Packy and Markie came too, with little Grace, brandishing broadswords, slaying him.

This always took a lot out of him, ripped his guts out, because he was man of sorrows, and he stayed up here all day, twice a year, every year, until he was very old, until it was dark, until there were stars in the sky…

…when he saw Grace—her red hair—his yearning grew, despite the happiness he had been given on the swell a world away.

Took a lot out of him. Made him empty. Broke his heart—

But it was worth it. He could take it.

He was a family man.

So it came to be that it was here, in a safe place, reaching up, wearing Mel's ring for a day, longing to take just one more step (still not giving up on getting to her), whilst looking directly at stars, that Buzz's heart began to yank all the way out, toward that bright shining light—

The hour grows nigh.

All the Ellie-Loves-Buzz stories have not been told, and cannot be told, because they are as numerous as the stars in the heavens. But they all really happened—because there is no such thing as time—they really do happen, and they really will happen, for these stories have been seen with the eyes of the soul.

Two more true stories from the long walk which never ends…

They say the mother of all learning is repetition. Perhaps that is why there was that big flood way back when. Or why the barbarians invaded.

Perhaps this is why the computers shut down and the earth darkened. Long after Buzz and Ellie Woodward were buried, this lesson came with fire, for mankind had relearned his fearsomest machines of war, and the cities were burning, the widows were weeping, and orphans again roamed the streets and countrysides in search of food.

Same old, same old.

Was it the final conflict, and were Elijah and Enoch scheduled to return to Jerusalem within the fortnight to begin the crushing of the head of the serpent, with help from the Woman Clothed With the Sun?

As usual, it was hard to tell. Not yet fully revealed, but the situation, for those who accepted the reality, was bleak. The knife was again poised at the tender throat of Isaac.

The blue-tip match which had set the world aflame was another variation of the timeless heresy—that only a raving fool, much less a God, runs up a rocky hill to embrace the cross.

While the nations of the world burned, the cross-haters had the Eternal City surrounded when a little star entered the stage—with a crowd, violence in their hearts, tearing a pope from his open vehicle; a pope who dared to venture beyond the marble walls of Saint Peter's. They tore off his white robes, then ripped the holy man to shreds, spitting and cursing at the helpless Swiss Guards, laughing and challenging God Himself to smite them down.

Two weeks later, the white smoke rose over the Vatican. The red hats had chosen another lamb for the slaughter.

Within five minutes of his pontificate, the new pope lost his temper, even as the cardinals—those who had dared to travel here—filed out of the Sistine Chapel.

A short, wiry black man, a cardinal from South Africa, pulled the new pope aside, grasping him by the wrist.

He wished to speak to the first American pope…

～ • ～

The new pope was the first who was known to have committed murder—during his youth—and the first to have done hard time, in a filthy prison in Texas.

He was the son of an alcoholic father.

His mother, a practical girl from New Jersey (what was left of it), had been teaching him how to waltz the day his father beat her to death. Back in the dog years, in Omaha.

The boy ran away after that, to Houston. Turned to the usual vices, but because he had the spark of leadership—and because the bullets fired at him somehow missed their target—he became the head of a youthful criminal syndicate. He did as he pleased, swinging a bad axe at everything in sight.

Persistent in his sinfulness.

Until the two Wayfarers of Mary Immaculate, the insane Walking Priests, came to the armored den of his headquarters, preaching Christ crucified.

The boy, fifteen years old, had one of the priests beaten to within an inch of his life, then warned the other one off.

The second Wayfarer returned. Again, and again, and again he returned, claiming divine designs on the boy. Claiming to have dreamed about collies, mountains, and this boy standing on a balcony.

The boy also ordered the second priest beaten. The first Wayfarer returned, in bandages, limping. The boy, true to his word, had him killed.

The second priest, covered with bruises, returned on the day of glory of the dead Wayfarer to recover the body, which he buried—and then asked the boy to give the eulogy.

During this dark period of history, the average lifespan of a Walking Priest was thirty-two years.

The boy was finally pulled off his jetty when a lovely woman with blond hair and chocolate-cream eyes appeared to him in a dream, holding a baby with red hair, then dream-kissed him on the forehead, asking him to waltz (just like the boy's mom).

The beautiful woman then showed him a dream-vision of a black man running across a field littered with the martyred bodies of Wayfarer priests.

In the dream, the black man turned to the boy and solemnly intoned:

"Follow me, Eduardo."

Eduardo followed.

Eduardo Ramirez confessed his sins, then turned himself in. He did his time in prison—all the while studying, praying, preparing, learning the languages. After the dogged pleas for leniency from the Walking Priests were answered, he was released early (and because the world was in the first stages of burning and the prisons were once again too crowded for mere murderers).

Eduardo Ramirez joined the Wayfarers when he was re-leased—praying for two years, walking for two years—the finger of God on his head; he was tougher than any cross he found on the road because—

Because it was in his blood.

Bagpipe had flowed in his mother's veins.

Eduardo's mother was a distant great grand-daughter of Ellie Woodward's third child, Rebekah (the one who married Seamus Johnson). Eduardo had Ellie's eyes, in fact. Eduardo's voice was powerful—not unlike that of Mark Johnson. And the young priest had a strong back and rounded shoulders—not unlike those of Buzz Woodward.

But he was not tall, and his skin was brown, because some-body in the Ellie-Loves-Buzz line had walked south, down Mexico way.

Father Ramirez swung that big bad axe in the right direc-tion, and rose in the ranks, and became the Father Director of the Walking Priests.

Then the black cardinal from South Africa pulled some strings when other cardinals were assassinated and forced Eduardo to take the red hat, even though he tried to refuse the honor. But his demurrals were ignored.

As he was taught, a Wayfarer does not choose his plow; the plow chooses him.

In the Sistine Chapel, with the world aflame, his name was still Father Eduardo Ramirez, Wayfayer of Mary Immacu-late, and his dead mother's name was Ellen Johnson. He was a direct descendant...

∽ • ∾

"What name will you choose for your pontificate?" the cardinal from South Africa now asked Eduardo.

"I don't know. I can't believe you did this to me," the new pope whispered bitterly, his Hispanic accent stronger, reveal-ing his frustration.

"What did I do to you?"

"Don't play your mind games with me, Your Eminence. You swung the votes in my favor. I shouldn't even be here. A convicted murderer for a pope. A sick joke."

He watched the cardinal smile.

"Are you second-guessing the Holy Spirit, Your Holiness?"

The American fumed.

Your Holiness! A regular laugh riot.

"They can call me John Paul the Seventh," he spat at the old cardinal, then walked off, angry, looking for a house of gold so he could take out his wrath on God in person.

Eduardo was a part of an unfathomable plan. More than enough cause to send a guy named Hal to a backwater like Saint-Pascal to recruit a collie to help a selfish, strong-willed, persistent man named Buzz get a third chance in the pines of Magalloway Mountain.

The white smoke had risen.

In Saint Peter's Square, the crowd waited for him, terrified of the evil cloaking the earth in flames, casting smoke as black as any during the days of Silicon Babylon so many centuries ago. So the people waited (in the same square where a priest from Ohio named Father Dial had once successfully administered the sacrament of reconciliation to a dead man).

Eduardo stood in the shadows of the balcony. The Walking Priests had told him about this balcony, before his conversion, calling it an altar of sacrifice.

The crowd beheld their brown-skinned pope and they cheered—they always cheer during this moment when the rock brings forth water. But this time it was different. The crowd was small. Their enthusiasm was forced. The cross-haters were here, too, hissing and booing.

The world was in flames.

Eduardo waited, for he was a man who had learned not to rush during his long walks as a Wayfarer. He waited for the silence.

Because Eduardo knew he was a weakling, flesh and blood, an empty sepulchre without enough faith to tell a mountain to move. He was terrified. As had happened during his entire priesthood, he found himself wordless.

The flock gave him silence.

Eduardo accepted the truth. He was the runt of the litter, because all the holy ones, his immediate precursors, had been compromised, corrupted, or killed by the evil one, and the cardinal from South Africa needed cannon fodder so he could buy time to plan for a real pope. Indeed, Eduardo's predecessor had been torn to shreds, with the world watching, just two weeks earlier, in the square below, in just the third year of his reign.

Bring it on, he thought, donning his courage like a breastplate, still wordless, weak, and bitterly intimidated by this plow thrust into his hands.

Bad axe time, he thought.

He took the first step, out of the shadows.

No words came, and so, an accomplished thief, he stole three small words from his new namesake, the one whom they called the great one, the Magnificent Pole.

Little Eduardo raised his arms, his knees shaking, throwing his voice:

"Be not afraid!"

In Latin.

Silence.

He repeated the phrase in Italian.

Some moderate clapping. They wanted real words, not tired maxims from the past.

A bad start to this new walk.

Eduardo prayed to the old reliable, *Saint Anthony!*

He repeated the phrase again, in Italian. Then English, then German. Until he ran out of languages.

He was finally finished with this failure of a first step, but he was on the road now, walking.

It was okay.

With nothing better to do, and despite the snickering from the cross-haters, the American pope pulled out his well-worn beads, then began to lead the crowd in the Most Holy Rosary.

He started with the Sorrowful Mysteries, because these were his favorites, and because all Wayfarers started here. All Wayfarers were taught in the seminary that the cross comes before the resurrection.

During the fourth decade, a shot rang out; a bullet tore into his leg.

Eduardo fell.

The Swiss Guards rushed to his side, along with the seven cardinals who had the courage to join him on the balcony.

His ears burned when he heard laughter below. A fight had broken out in the square.

Ignoring his pain, because it was only pain (and because the pain in his heart was much worse), he barked at the guards and the red hats to leave him be. Eduardo made a tourniquet using a cardinal's sash.

He reached up.

The more sentimental historians, years later, wrote that the image of his bloody hand gripping the balcony, seen by the world, turned the tide.

He rose.

He saw the cause of the commotion. They had captured the boy, the boy with the rifle, the one who had shot him. A cross-hater, who was now amidst a gaggle of Swiss Guards and others beating Eduardo's would-be assassin with their fists.

Discipline has broken down!

This was not okay.

"Do not harm the boy!" Eduardo threw his voice to the square, cutting through the confusion. "Do not lay a hand on him!"

He had a voice which stopped things.

The vigilantes relented.

"Care for his wounds. Then bring him to me."

They obeyed the voice of authority.

Still bleeding, Eduardo finished the Rosary with the crowd, then collapsed.

He was fired at five more times over the next seven weeks, always during the Rosary, and was hit twice.

Once in his good leg. Once in the shoulder.

Three times he fell. Three times he rose.

The theologians, years later, knowing that God repeats lessons, made this Eduardo's epithet.

Eduardo returned to the balcony. Again, and again, and again. Always with the Rosary. He returned because he was a Wayfarer of Mary Immaculate, and a persistent bastard, and the old wrinkled cardinal from South Africa had been right, and Eduardo had been wrong, which was not a big surprise to Eduardo.

The new pope was a stupid fool running toward the cross. He just couldn't stop jumping into puddles of his own blood. Feeling useless, he wept as his fingertips moved methodically across his beads.

The crowds began to grow during the third month.

A romantic, Eduardo told the old South African that he wanted to become the first pope to walk around the world on foot.

But this plan, as with most plans formulated through a lens darkly, was not written in the Book of Life.

Pope John Paul VII, the Walking Priest who had never seen Magalloway Mountain, died in the tenth month of his pontificate from a gunshot wound to the heart—while leading the flock in the Rosary.

He published no encyclicals. He never left the Vatican grounds.

On the day Eduardo Ramirez was martyred, two billion souls across the planet were praying with him.

His death added hundreds of millions more within three weeks—because his successor was also a Wayfarer, and kept up the family tradition, swinging the old axe with abandon.

Turns out the old cardinal from South Africa was also a persistent bastard, and also had Bagpipe in his blood, though he was not from the Woodward line. He was from another Bethlehem, and another soul-line of Man-Loves-Woman overlooked by the evil one.

Bethlehem. Bagpipe. Same thing.

It's always the little ones.

Simple.

Eduardo Ramirez was credited by those who wrote the histories of his time as the one who put out the flames with his blood. It would take three more Wayfarers to finish the job. The last two actually began the long walk around the earth.

The last Wayfarer pope actually made it to London before he was assassinated in a slum called Brixton.

The South African cardinal started bringing in Carmelites and Dominicans to mop up. After all, they were not crazy like the Wayfarers.

Carmelites traveled by jet, like normal popes.

The Dominicans stayed in their studies, composing encyclicals, because it always takes a Dominican to explain what a Wayfarer really meant to say.

It took fifteen years before things returned to a more normal level of suffering. No other Wayfarers were elected pope after this dark period.

Eduardo was just doing his job, and would be embarrassed by his own story because, to him, he was taking the easy way, the long walk that never ends—letting his plow carry him to the day of glory.

Eduardo Ramirez was but one star in the Ellie-Loves-Buzz heavens, and a rather small one (yet the smallest stars are always the ones that burn hottest). He was certainly not the most intelligent pope. But he was in love with plows. Eduardo was mentioned here because he became the first soul in the line to be canonized.

∽ • ∾

✝ ✝ ✝

Buzz and Ellie were sitting in rocking chairs on the deck of the Monastery, the glorious altar of sacrifice where Sam and Christopher had given their lives for holy and unfathomable plans.

It was summer, and the memorial garden Buzz and Mark had planted years ago for their lady Ellie was in full bloom.

Chesterton and his Lady were snuggled together at their mistress's feet, waiting for the Rosary to begin.

Mark had retired for the evening. Zack and Hal were asleep at the house.

There was enough light from the full moon to see the outline of Mount Magalloway to the west. It was the only reality in Buzz's presence which could make the claim to have been at the foundations of the earth. The mountain answered to no one, except to those with faith enough to tell it to move.

Buzz, because he was Buzz, was thinking about this plain fact, and accepted it, recognizing once again that his own faith, however precious, must be quite small.

If the dog hadn't showed up, he told Magalloway, *you would have kicked my ass.*

He rocked, pondering about the mountain, the long walk, the Man, how much he still missed Melanie, and about his seventh child, little Becky, serene at Ellie's breast. He then decided to let the Word all these things represented come forth, not knowing, as usual, what it would be.

"I love you, Ellie."

Simple.

She gave him her beauty with a smile, and, as always, his heart melted. He was still sentimental.

As she knew he would be.

"This is our last child," he told her.

"How can you possibly know that?" she asked, quickened to anger. Being Ellie.

"Just guessing, El."

You're so full of it, she thought.

They listened to the music of silence for a time, rocking gently, counting blessings in a wordless waltz.

Later tonight, they would waltz on the beach in their bedroom, despite his prophecy, because they would always want babies, always want each other.

Sometimes they danced slowly. Sometimes they danced the other way, and that was okay, too.

That's how we got Becky, Buzz mused.

Becky. He looked at his wife, as Ellie looked down at the child. So peaceful. Perfect for each other.

Could any child be loved more than a child born to his Ellie?

Buzz doubted it, and realized that Somebody had moved Magalloway for him during that dark year, little though his faith had been.

All for the baby in his wife's arms.

More silence, more rocking.

"Will it ever end?" she asked.

He knew she was talking about the love.

The fertile love within the hearts of the living.

"Maybe. But it will never end for the stars. There will be stars in our skies forever."

Why beat around the bush?

"Good," she said.

Becky was sleeping now. Ellie rose and put the baby in the little crib which was kept on the deck.

Ellie came back to him, and lowered herself onto his lap, and began to kiss him the way a sister never kisses a brother, blood rushing to her cheeks, one hand around his neck, her fingers into his crewcut.

Buzz placed his hand on her waist, and the other on her ribs, holding her this way, her back and neck arched *just so*.

So that her lips floated on his own, and he closed his mind to everything but the warmth of her mouth, concentrating— on *her*.

They did this until they were done, and she lifted her head, breathing, her eyes closed, praying.

He waited. He could wait forever. Then she began kissing him again, this time with sorrow.

She did not want to stop *having him,* but she was afraid, because she was a practical girl, even at the age of forty-five, that she would forget their first real kiss, on the jetty, before Mark came down from the clouds.

He realized she was crying when he tasted her tears. He stopped, opened his eyes, looking into hers. He moved the strands of hair from her brow.

"Buzz," she whispered.

Their faces, their eyes, their bodies—close.

"Ellie," he breathed.

There was so much more to say, but he remained silent, because she had crushed his defeated heart, a heart for which there was no cure.

Melancholy always came when he heard the mysterious music within Ellie's soul, his soul searching for the Trinity.

Her passion became his, and he offered himself to her, in love with this cross which carried him. This was the way, the way the man of sorrows began again the long walk with the beautiful woman.

Did You Enjoy Reading
House of Gold?

Would you like to introduce Ellie, Buzz, Mark, and Mel to
your…

Parents

Brothers and Sisters

Friends

Relatives

Prayer Group

Church or Parish

Business Associates

Local Bookstore Owner

Neighbors

Local School

Local Library

Pastor or Priest?

Saint Jude Media would like to help you.

We're ready to send you as many copies as you want for a
nominal donation. Use the convenient Request Form on the
next page and write to us today. Available at Catholic
retailers everywhere. May also be ordered through most
bookstores.

DISCOVER THE REST OF THE STORY…

Read the original story of Buzz, Ellie, Sam,
and the Man in Bud Macfarlane Jr.'s
bestselling novel, **Conceived Without Sin.**

REQUEST FORM #1

Dear Saint Jude Media:
Please send me **House of Gold** and/or other novels by Bud Macfarlane Jr. I understand that a donation is **not required** for one copy of each book. I am not asking you to send a book or books to someone other than myself.

Signed: _____

(Please Print)
Name: _____

Address: _____

Town: _____

State: _____ Zip: _____

Suggested **Optional** Donation for one copy of each book: **$1 to $12**
Donation for **more than one** copy of each book, any quantity: **$2 - $8 each**
(For more details about Saint Jude Media, see next page.)

Quantity *House of Gold*	+	Quantity *Conceived Without Sin*	+	Quantity *Pierced by a Sword*	=	Total Number of Books
_____		_____		_____		_____

X Donation Per Book _____

= Donation for Books _____

+ Optional extra gift for shipping _____

+ Optional gift for Saint Jude Media _____

TOTAL DONATION* = $_____

*Your contribution to Saint Jude Media is tax deductible. Sorry, no phone requests for books accepted. We'll ship your book the day we receive your letter. Please make checks payable to "Saint Jude Media" and send to:

Saint Jude Media • PO Box 26120 • Fairview Park, OH 44126

How Saint Jude Media Works

- If you do not have a request form, writing a simple letter to receive our books is okay. You can also make requests online at www.catholicity.com on the Saint Jude Media home page.

- Personal correspondence is encouraged. Tell us what you think of our books. We also welcome typographical, grammatical, and fact-checking suggestions for future printings (please include page and line number). Email us at saint.jude.media@catholicity.com

- We will send one free copy of each of our books to each person who writes to us directly. A donation for one book is not required, but you may send a donation if you wish.

- Using the honor system, we ask that you please refrain from sending us the addresses of people other than yourself. Please ask others to write to us directly. We will only send materials to those who personally ask for them, whether a donation is enclosed or not.

- At the present time, we only accept requests for materials by mail. Sorry, no phone requests. Only requests from the United States and Canada will be honored unless a sufficient donation to cover shipping is enclosed.

- Saint Jude Media will gladly absorb shipping charges on all requests, but feel free to add extra for shipping if you wish.

- Fast Delivery—all requests will be shipped on the day we open your envelope!

- Under normal circumstances, we are not able to "advance" quantities of books before receiving a donation.

- We will periodically write to let you know about new books and developments, but you will never receive a "fund raising letter" from us. We will not sell or lend your name to other groups—ever.

- These details apply to individuals as well as organizations such as bookstores, etc. Individuals, bookstores, gift shops, schools, and other organizations may accept donations for our books no greater than $6 each. A promotional retail display is available upon request.

REQUEST FORM #2

Dear Saint Jude Media:

Please send me **House of Gold** and/or other novels by Bud Macfarlane Jr. I understand that a donation is **not required** for one copy of each book. I am not asking you to send a book or books to someone other than myself.

Signed: _____

(Please Print)
Name: _____

Address: _____

Town: _____

State: _____ Zip: _____

Suggested **Optional** Donation for one copy of each book: **$1 to $12**
Donation for **more than one** copy of each book, any quantity: **$2 - $8 each**
(For more details about Saint Jude Media, see next page.)

Quantity *House of* *Gold*		Quantity *Conceived* *Without Sin*		Quantity *Pierced* *by a Sword*		Total Number of Books
+		+		=		
_____		_____		_____		_____

X Donation Per Book   _____

= Donation for Books   _____

+ Optional extra gift for shipping   _____

+ Optional gift for Saint Jude Media   _____

TOTAL DONATION* = $_____

*Your contribution to Saint Jude Media is tax deductible. Sorry, no phone requests for books accepted. We'll ship your book the day we receive your letter. Please make checks payable to "Saint Jude Media" and send to:

Saint Jude Media • PO Box 26120 • Fairview Park, OH 44126

How Saint Jude Media Works

- If you do not have a request form, writing a simple letter to receive our books is okay. You can also make requests online at www.catholicity.com on the Saint Jude Media home page.

- Personal correspondence is encouraged. Tell us what you think of our books. We also welcome typographical, grammatical, and fact-checking suggestions for future printings (please include page and line number). Email us at saint.jude.media@catholicity.com

- We will send one free copy of each of our books to each person who writes to us directly. A donation for one book is not required, but you may send a donation if you wish.

- Using the honor system, we ask that you please refrain from sending us the addresses of people other than yourself. Please ask others to write to us directly. We will only send materials to those who personally ask for them, whether a donation is enclosed or not.

- At the present time, we only accept requests for materials by mail. Sorry, no phone requests. Only requests from the United States and Canada will be honored unless a sufficient donation to cover shipping is enclosed.

- Saint Jude Media will gladly absorb shipping charges on all requests, but feel free to add extra for shipping if you wish.

- Fast Delivery—all requests will be shipped on the day we open your envelope!

- Under normal circumstances, we are not able to "advance" quantities of books before receiving a donation.

- We will periodically write to let you know about new books and developments, but you will never receive a "fund raising letter" from us. We will not sell or lend your name to other groups—ever.

- These details apply to individuals as well as organizations such as bookstores, etc. Individuals, bookstores, gift shops, schools, and other organizations may accept donations for our books no greater than $6 each. A promotional retail display is available upon request.

REQUEST FORM #3

Dear Saint Jude Media:
Please send me **House of Gold** and/or other novels by Bud Macfarlane Jr. I understand that a donation is **not required** for one copy of each book. I am not asking you to send a book or books to someone other than myself.

Signed: _____

(Please Print)
Name: _____

Address: _____

Town: _____

State: _____ Zip: _____

Suggested **Optional** Donation for one copy of each book: **$1 to $12**
Donation for **more than one** copy of each book, any quantity: **$2 - $8 each**
(For more details about Saint Jude Media, see next page.)

Quantity *House of Gold*	+	Quantity *Conceived Without Sin*	+	Quantity *Pierced by a Sword*	=	Total Number of Books
_____		_____		_____		_____

X Donation Per Book _____

= Donation for Books _____

+ Optional extra gift for shipping _____

+ Optional gift for Saint Jude Media _____

TOTAL DONATION* = $_____

*Your contribution to Saint Jude Media is tax deductible. Sorry, no phone requests for books accepted. We'll ship your book the day we receive your letter. Please make checks payable to "Saint Jude Media" and send to:

Saint Jude Media • PO Box 26120 • Fairview Park, OH 44126

How Saint Jude Media Works

- If you do not have a request form, writing a simple letter to receive our books is okay. You can also make requests online at www.catholicity.com on the Saint Jude Media home page.

- Personal correspondence is encouraged. Tell us what you think of our books. We also welcome typographical, grammatical, and fact-checking suggestions for future printings (please include page and line number). Email us at saint.jude.media@catholicity.com

- We will send one free copy of each of our books to each person who writes to us directly. A donation for one book is not required, but you may send a donation if you wish.

- Using the honor system, we ask that you please refrain from sending us the addresses of people other than yourself. Please ask others to write to us directly. We will only send materials to those who personally ask for them, whether a donation is enclosed or not.

- At the present time, we only accept requests for materials by mail. Sorry, no phone requests. Only requests from the United States and Canada will be honored unless a sufficient donation to cover shipping is enclosed.

- Saint Jude Media will gladly absorb shipping charges on all requests, but feel free to add extra for shipping if you wish.

- Fast Delivery—all requests will be shipped on the day we open your envelope!

- Under normal circumstances, we are not able to "advance" quantities of books before receiving a donation.

- We will periodically write to let you know about new books and developments, but you will never receive a "fund raising letter" from us. We will not sell or lend your name to other groups—ever.

- These details apply to individuals as well as organizations such as bookstores, etc. Individuals, bookstores, gift shops, schools, and other organizations may accept donations for our books no greater than $6 each. A promotional retail display is available upon request.

For more on the Blessed Virgin Mary:

<u>Audio Tapes</u>: **Marian Apparitions Explained, The Truth About Mary,** and other great Catholic audio tapes. No Charge. Optional donation accepted. Contact: Mary Foundation, Box 26101, Fairview Park, OH 44126. www.catholicity.com

<u>Internet</u>: **CatholiCity.** Contains homepages for numerous Marian organizations, national prayer movements, libraries, books, audios, chat rooms, links to other Marian sites. Contact: Box 26101, Fairview Park, OH 44126. www.catholicity.com

<u>Newspapers</u>: **Special Editions** available on Mary, Divine Mercy, Eucharistic Miracles. Summary of Marian apparitions. Contact: Pittsburgh Center for Peace, 6111 Steubenville Pike, McKee's Rocks, PA 15136. (412) 787-9791.

<u>Book</u>: **The Final Hour** by Michael Brown. Historical summary of Marian apparitions. Contact: The Riehle Foundation, Box 7, Milford, OH 45150. (513) 576-0032.

<u>Medal</u>: Handmade **Miraculous Medals** in silver, gold, and brass. Contact: Saint Catherine's Metalworks, 4289 Wooster Road, Fairview Park, OH 44126. (440) 331-1975. www.catholicity.com

<u>Video</u>: **Marian Apparitions of the 20th Century.** Contact: Marian Communications, Box 300, Lincoln University, PA 19352. (800) 448-1192.

<u>Book</u>: **To the Priests, Our Lady's Beloved Sons.** Contact: Marian Movement of Priests, Box 8, Saint Francis, ME 04774-0008.

<u>Information</u>: **The Knights of Immaculata.** World lay association of consecrated souls founded by Saint Maximilian Kolbe. Contact: Militia Immaculatæ National Center, 1600 West Park Avenue, Libertyville, IL 60048. (847) 367-7800. www.marytown.org

<u>Book</u>: **Our Lady Builds a Statue** by LeRoy Lee. The story of the statue of Our Lady in Butte, Montana. $13, including shipping. Contact: Our Lady of the Rockies, 2845 Nettie, Butte, MT 59701. (406) 782-9771.

For more on the Catholic Faith:

<u>Bethlehem Books</u>: Catholic children's fiction. 15605 County Road 15, Minto, ND 58261. (800) 757-6831, Fax (701) 248-3940.

<u>CatholiCity</u>: Internet site with chat rooms, dozens of Catholic organizations, free books and tapes, news, comprehensive links, more. www.catholicity.com

<u>Catholic Answers</u>: Apologetics books, *This Rock* magazine. Box 17490, San Diego, CA 92177. (619) 541-1131, Fax (619) 541-1154. www.catholic.com/~answers

<u>Catholic Marketing Network</u>: Professional association of Catholic suppliers, apostolates, and retailers. 7750 North MacArthur Boulevard, Suite 120-323, Irving, TX 75063. (800) 506-6333, Fax (972) 929-0330. www.catholicmarketing.com

<u>Envoy Magazine</u>: Apologetics and evangelization. Box 1840, West Chester, PA 19380. (800) 553-6869, Fax (610) 696-9977. www.envoymagazine.com

<u>Ignatius Press</u>: Theology, fiction. **Father Elijah** and other great novels by Michael O'Brien. Box 1339, Fort Collins, CO 80522. (800) 537-0390, Fax (970) 221-3964. www.ignatius.com

<u>The Mary Foundation</u>: Free Guide to 100 Catholic Resources, donation optional. Box 26101, Fairview Park, OH 44126. www.catholicity.com

<u>Saint Joseph Communications</u>: Audio tapes by Scott Hahn, others. Box 720, West Covina, CA 91793. (800) 526-2151, Fax (626) 858-9331.

<u>Saint Raphael's Bookstore</u>: Short wave radios, starting at $60, order by phone. (800) 548-8270, Fax (330) 497-8648.

<u>Tan Books</u>: Hundreds of titles, pamphlets, children's books. Catalog. Box 424, Rockford, IL 61105. (800) 437-5876, Fax (815) 226-7770. www.tanbooks.com

<u>WEWN 7.425</u>: Catholic short wave radio, 24 hours/day. Order program guide. 1500 High Road, Vandiver, AL 35176. (800) 585-9396, Fax (205) 672-9988. www.ewtn.com

For more on Catholic Family Issues:

<u>Couple to Couple League</u>: Natural family planning, chastity education program. Box 111184, Cincinnati, OH 45211. (513) 471-2000. ccli.org

<u>The Gift Foundation:</u> Dedicated to exposing the harmful effects of contraception on families, children, the Church, and society. Great audio tape series at cost. Box 95, Carpentersville, IL 60110. (847) 844-1167. giftfoundation.org

<u>Human Life International</u>: Books, newsletters, audios on prolife issues worldwide. 4 Family Life, Front Royal, VA 22630. (540) 635-7884. hli.org

<u>La Leche League</u>: Natural child-spacing through breast feeding. 1400 North Meacham Road, Schaumburg, IL 601731. (847) 519-7730, Hotline (800) 525-3243. lalecheleague.org

<u>National Association of Catholic Home Educators</u>: (NACHE) Network of homeschoolers, annual convention. 6102 Saints Hill Lane, Broad Run, VA 22014. (540) 349-4314. nache.org

<u>One More Soul:</u> Audios, videos, and other materials on the beauty of Catholic teaching on sexuality by Dr. Janet Smith, including the excellent audio tape **Contraception: Why Not?** 616 Five Oaks Avenue, Dayton, OH 45406. omsoul.com

<u>Priests for Life</u>: Supports thousands of priests committed to promoting Catholic teachings on life issues. Books and tapes by Father Frank Pavone. Box 141172, Staten Island, NY 10314. (718) 980-9711. priestsforlife.com

<u>Saint Joseph Covenant Keepers</u>: Resources for Catholic fatherhood. Box 6060, Port Charlotte, FL 33949. (800) 705-6131, (941) 764-8565. dads.org

Come to where the Catholics are...

Come to CatholiCity.

Bud Macfarlane's Weekly Email Message
News & Commentary • Comprehensive Links
Keyword Search • Discussion Groups
Prayer Movements • Free Books and Tapes
Publishers • Book Previews
Online Audio • Homeschool Groups
Gift Manufacturers • Lay Apostolates
and More...

www.catholicity.com

An Internet Service of The Mary Foundation

If the mail-in coupons for requesting copies of
House of Gold and Bud Macfarlane Jr.'s first two
novels are missing, send your requests to:

Saint Jude Media
Gold Offer
PO Box 26120
Fairview Park, OH 44126

An optional donation for the first copy of each novel is
gratefully accepted but is **not** required. The suggested
donation for more than one copy is $2 to $8 each.
Free shipping. Make checks out to: "Saint Jude Media"